Katz Cradle

Bob Henneberger

www. temptpress. com

Books by Bob Henneberger

Crackstone Chronicles – Extinction

Crackstone Chronicles – Connections

Crackstone Chronicles – Extraordinary Solution

Katz Pajamas

Katz Box

Hunting Paradise

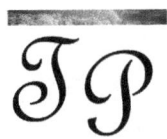

Tempt Press
PO Box 77
Colchester, VT 05446

Published by **Tempt Press**
P.O. Box 77, Colchester, VT 05446

First Print Edition, 2010

Copyright © 2010 Bob Henneberger

ISBN: 978-0-9830118-6-6
Library of Congress Control Number: 2010936747

To Sandy

The object of art is to give life a shape.

Contents

1

So far, and yet so near

Fall was in its full glory in Atlanta, Georgia and the year was 1981. It was mid afternoon and early going home traffic was just a hint of what it would be in mid-town in a few hours. Clouds raced overhead, sometimes hinting that the sun would come out, but it never did.

"Hey Luanne."

An Atlanta policeman called to a middle aged waitress who had stepped out the side door to light a cigarette. Luanne Hollingbeck was dressed in a nondescript mid-calf black skirt with a light pink sweater and a white plastic name tag pinned to it. Like many long term waitresses who walk eight hours a day, Luanne was fairly trim, although she wanted to lose just ten more pounds. She had long since ceased eating snacks on the job, but she still loved fried foods a bit too much.

"Timmy Parish." She recognized him.

Luanne's fifteen year old daughter baby-sat for them from time to time.

"What's going on over there?"

One of the cooks told her that the cops were swarming all over the parking lot, but she had too many customers to sneak a peek up until then. Luanne slowly walked towards the back of the poorly paved parking lot beside the restaurant where she worked. It was a cool overcast Fall day with a strong breeze coming from the north west, which is why she had put on the pink sweater this morning.

The temperature was hovering in the low forties, and that was cold for Atlanta at this time of year. The cloud filtered light pouring through the trees still cast shadows across the parking lot. Even with the strong wind, the smells of deep fat fried chicken and potatoes mixed with burgers being grilled permeated the area. The sound of the wind in the nearly leafless trees wasn't as loud as it might be in Summer, but was still loud enough to mask much of the background noise. Traffic was light on Ponce De Leon; it was the lull between lunch traffic and going home traffic.

Two police cars with their blue lights flashing were parked askew near a large silver Cadillac while a sizable crowd of twenty or so milled about the parking lot, all of them trying to see something towards the rear of the lot. Officer Parish walked towards her as the other three policemen were busy pushing onlookers away from the scene.

"I think one of your customers sort of took a dirt nap out here," Officer Parrish said.

Timmy now stood in front of the waitress.

"Do you mind looking at him and maybe you can confirm who he is."

"Was he shot?" Luanne asked.

"No, I don't think so," Timmy replied. "No one sees any blood; I suppose he might have had a heart attack or something."

"I hope it wasn't the food."

Luanne nervously leaned from one foot to the other, not knowing what else to do, given the situation.

"Come on over there." Timmy pointed to the car at the center of all the attention.

"Sure thing."

Luanne walked slowly, like a rubber-necker at a car accident, towards the car with the dead man in it.

"Yeah, sure." She glanced quickly, then turned to the policeman. "That's Simon Belchamp, he's a regular here."

"So, when was he in there for lunch?" Timmy pulled out a small notebook from his back pocket.

"Oh," Luanne answered. "I'd say it couldn't have been more than an hour or so, maybe a little less."

"Did he seem upset, or sick?" Timmy pulled a pen from his breast pocket and began taking notes.

"No, not at all." Luanne pursed her lips as she remembered. "He seemed to be in a great mood, but he's always a happy man." She stared at the car. "He was a happy man."

. . . .

"Detective Gary Brown, what're you doing here?" Timmy asked.

Officer Parish noticed a tall man in a suite walking slowly towards the scene of Simon Belchamp's death.

Gary Brown stood about five foot ten, weighed about one hundred eighty pounds and dressed in a clean upscale suit. He had been with the Atlanta Police Department for about ten years, before that he had been an MP in the Army, completing one tour in Viet Nam, but spending most of his career at Fort Stewart; he met his wife, Alice, while he lived in Hinesville. Gary made detective two years ago, and was now assigned to the homicide department.

"It's a slow day." Gary grinned at the uniformed police officer. "The lieutenant likes to send me out to view dead bodies to keep me out of trouble, something about it being my job."

"I guess so," Timmy sounded a little flustered as he smiled back at the homicide detective. "But, I'd bet this one was a heart attack."

"Show me the dead man," Gary requested.

"No problem."

Timmy stepped aside, he knew better than to second guess the detective. He had been on the scene of several murder cases with detective Brown and he knew to let the man work.

"So, he's been dead only ninety minutes at best?" Gary asked as he moved the dead man's head from side to side, he then moved his arm slightly. "He seems a little stiff and cold for that, but I guess we'll find out when the coroner's office is through with him."

Gary carefully glanced at the inside of the car, then he walked around that area of the parking lot. Too many people had trampled over the area so not much was left of interest. Detective Brown bent over to inspect the car door which was splotchy and grubby looking from the fingerprint powder spread over it by the forensic team which had arrived ten minutes before. Gary cocked his head to one side as he focused on a small spot of white powder barely visible on the bottom eighth of the driver's side door; the car was silver color, and that spot wasn't that obvious."

"Excuse me." Detective Brown tapped the shoulder of a technician lifting fingerprints from the passenger door.

"Yeah?" The man stood up and faced Gary Brown.

"Could you get a small bag and follow me?"

"Sure thing." The man dug around in a medium sized container that gave the impression of a cross between a suitcase and a fishing tackle box.

"Scrape that off and tell me what the hell it is."

Gary Brown pointed to the white substance on the driver's door.

"Sure."

The technician began doing what he was requested while Gary walked quickly to the photographer who was loading his thirty five millimeter Nikon with another roll of film.

"Did you get shots through both sides of the front window?" The detective asked.

"Yeah." The photographer closed up the camera. "I got shots through the side and rear window too."

"Without being too obvious, I'd like you to take several shots of the gawking crowd on the sidewalk." Gary thought for a second. "You did get the whole parking area, right?"

"I did."

The photographer began changing the lens, putting on a twenty eight millimeter lens.

"It seems like a heart attack, one that the paramedics arrived at too late," the photographer observed.

"Maybe," Gary Brown surmised.

He liked the photographer, he always worked well with him before.

"But, you know, a dead body in a parking lot of a popular restaurant, we sort of have to go through at least the motions."

"I suppose," The photographer muttered.

"When did you get here?"

"Let's see," The photographer thought. "The paramedics got here first, they found him dead and cold. They called the uniforms, and the uniforms called the medical examiner, then they called homicide."

"Just to be sure, I suppose," Gary chuckled, mostly to himself.

"Do you need all of us here?" Officer Parish asked.

He was the ranking uniform officer at the scene, and he thought it was wasteful for so many uniformed patrolmen to be at the scene of a heart attack.

"I guess not, maybe two to keep the curious back."

Detective Brown scanned over the scene at the parking lot. "Sure."

"Say, officer Parrish," Detective Brown spoke up as the policeman started to walk away.

"Yeah?"

"Which EMTs first answered the call?"

"Those two over there." He pointed to two men in white shirts with black pants and black coats on. "The one smoking called us."

Timmy Parrish walked back to his men to assign the two junior officers to the mindless detail.

"Hi, I'm detective Gary Brown," Gary introduced himself. "Which one of you two looked at the body first?"

"That would be me," Charles spoke up. "My name's Charles Bremerton."

"Was he in that position when you found him?"

"No, he was slumped over into the passenger's side." Charles indicated with his right forearm flopping to his right. "I checked for a pulse first and found none. He was cool to the touch, like he'd been dead for a while."

"Yeah," The other EMT spoke up as he put out his cigarette by crushing it under his left heel. "Charlie was pulling him upright when I mentioned that we might ought to call the cops."

"My partner was right," Charles agreed. "Even though I've

11

seen hundreds of heart attacks, and that man sure as hell had one, I guess a body like this needs the cops."

"That was a good idea," Detective Brown spoke to the men. "You guys did give a complete statement to the uniformed officers, right?"

"Sure did." Charles nodded.

"With the times and observations," His partner added. "We even took his temperature."

"Great." The detective nodded.

"Can we go now?" Charles asked. "Our shift is up in an hour or so."

"Sure, you guys can go on now."

The police detective carefully opened the driver's side door and leaned into the car, rummaging around the front seat. The dead man was slumped over the steering wheel; the body seemed grey in color, truly lifeless.

Cautiously, Gary Brown lifted the dead man's arms from the steering wheel. He then slid the body towards the passenger side. In most high end cars, the seats adjusts quite easily, in some it adjusts automatically. This corps seemed to fit quite nicely in the driver's space. The deceased, as most do, had lost sphincter control on dying, but it wasn't that pungent, yet. The interior was extremely clean, there didn't appear to be any loose paper, coins, maps, or food on the floor or seats.

Detective Brown walked to the passenger side, leaning into the door, he opened the glove compartment which was clean and almost empty. Inside, lay only the three booklets that came with the car, a map of downtown Atlanta, a box of automotive fuses and one spare turn signal bulb.

On the floor of the back seat, laid a golf umbrella and an ice scraper; the back seat seemed unused. One of the policemen had already opened the trunk, using the remote latch. Gary marveled at how clean the trunk was, as if it had never been used at all.

Gary Brown walked slowly towards the two attendants standing near the coroner's van who were leaning against the vehicle waiting for the detective to finish.

"I'm through," Detective Brown said to the younger of the

two men from the coroner's office. "You can bag the body now."

"I think the EMTs were right, the guy dropped dead from a heart attack, he's overweight and old, prime target for a heart attack," The young assistant commented.

"Been on the job long?" Gary asked the young man.

"No, sir." He became quieter. "Only a few months."

"When did you say it happened?" Gary turned to the uniformed policeman closest to him.

"Well." The policeman glanced at his watch. "According to the waitresses in there, this man was inside the restaurant eating lunch about two hours ago."

"So, you have a good ID on the man?" Gary looked around the parking lot.

"Yeah." The policeman nodded. "Several of the waitresses recognized him as a regular, and the ID in his wallet matches him to a tee."

"Has anyone called his family?" Gary asked.

"Not yet," The policeman fell silent for a second. "We were waiting until you showed up and gave the scene the once over."

"I guess I'll contact the family," Gary sighed. "Give me the address and their names."

"Right here." The policeman tore a sheet from his small notebook. "He has a wife and one son, they both live in Decatur. The deceased owned a car dealership in Decatur."

"I'll drive out there in a few minutes."

Gary wasn't too happy about this, he never was.

"You think something funny happened here?" The uniformed policeman asked the detective.

"That's why they pay me the big bucks." He smiled back at him. "I guess I'll find out if there was."

2

Now, where did I put that deal?

Cheshire Katz Detective Agency, Los Angeles branch, was about to be sold. My feelings were mixed about that prospect; I think my mind-set had been altered somewhat by my recent wedding, Benjamin and Cassandra Katz still sounded strange.

I run a detective agency out of Atlanta, that's my day job at least. I'm a tad over six feet tall, mostly in shape, with brown hair & eyes and not too ugly; at least my wife tells me so.

Cassandra and I were in the middle of our fabulous honeymoon, we were staying in the magnificent Hotel Pales in beautiful Hunting Beach, somewhere in the suburbs of greater Los Angeles. Okay, enough of the sarcasm, Cassandra and I were living in her old room at her parent's house. That, in itself, is enough to make me have mixed feelings about my career.

My partner and now wife, Cassandra, was busy maneuvering her dissertation through all final obstacles and teaching a second year political science class at UCLA. I didn't have enough time with her. We used to have only one Cheshire Katz Detective Agency office right here in Los Angeles, but a year ago we set up another office in Atlanta. We were now in the process of selling the Los Angeles branch to Peter Schroeder, the office manager here. Cassandra was close to finishing all her school work as we approached the Thanksgiving break; she managed to fix it so the one class she taught would take their final before the coming break so the two of us could have almost the whole month of December alone together. Maybe then Cassandra and I could have more quality time together; I'd settle for more of any kind of time together. At least I could concentrate on selling our Los Angeles branch office while she was otherwise occupied.

Peter Schroeder had put in a bid for the business a few months ago which was only two thousand higher than the next bid, but I was tired of waiting for more buyers. As I told our sales agent, the universe of possible purchasers was quite small.

"So, what's the plan today?"

Cassandra stood by the front door, ready to venture forth for another stint in front of three hundred eager students.

"I'm headed to our agent to go over the paperwork one more time." I smiled at her from the sofa. "We have a preliminary agreement signed, but the final papers have yet to be signed."

I was such a man of leisure these days, no, I didn't like that one bit.

"What's the hold up?" She asked.

"I'm not sure." I shrugged. "Anna wants me to meet with her lawyer, it's got something to do with the books."

"I hope it isn't a problem, the last time I went over the books, everything seemed fine."

Cassandra shot me a concerned expression as she left for school.

. . . .

"I'm your agent, and your friend," Anna began, I knew this had to be a problem. "I asked Tom to come into this meeting because your buyer has rescinded his offer, and countered with another."

"Excuse me?" She got my attention all right.

"It seems that the profit for the past six months has not been properly stated," Tom interrupted as he sat next to me with a stack of papers.

Tom Merchant was a lawyer Anna was comfortable working with on commercial sales.

"Your buyer, Peter, had his accountant go over the books in great detail over the past week and your company, it seems, has actually posted a four hundred thousand dollar loss for the past three quarters," Tom continued

"How?"

I was shocked, I knew that the company had gotten long term contracts to do background checks on new employees for five Los Angeles based top forty corporations; that income alone was staggering, at least to me it was.

"Apparently your rent has quadrupled this past year, and the medical benefits you offer your employees has gone up ten fold. Then, there's that contract for cleaning services," Anna added.

"Excuse me?" I focused on the paperwork. "I didn't know about any of this."

"Peter says you knew, and that you signed off on all this?"

Tom seemed to be waiting for another shoe to fall, perhaps on his ass.

"First of all, as far as I know we never offered medical benefits to our employees beyond Peter Schroeder and the two full-time secretaries. And, secondly, how the hell did my rent go up that much? I had a deal with the owner of that building, the rent couldn't go up more than ten percent a year. And, finally, I thought the building owners paid for cleaning, I've never paid for that in the past."

"That's not what Peter told us," Anna studied me.

I was surrounded by people staring at me as if I were Mr. Potatohead who had lost one eye and both ears and didn't notice a thing.

"Wouldn't one think that Peter might say that since he's the one trying to buy the business?"

I shook my head, I knew I was being screwed; at least the people talking to me weren't at fault.

"How much did he drop his offer?"

"He's now willing to offer fifty thousand in cash," Tom replied.

He was now looking at me as if my head would explode any minute.

"The haggled out amount was two hundred and ninety thousand dollars," I insisted.

I didn't explode, no sense in exploding there, these two were supposed to be on my side. But, Peter Schroeder was the manager of MY business and he was supposed to be on my side too.

16

"He said he cannot be expected to pay that much and assume all that debt," Tom added.

"So." I turned to face Anna. "What do you think?"

"I think he's trying to screw you, but unless you take him to court and prove he fixed the rent, and made up the medical coverage and cleaning costs, your chances of finishing this deal with any profit to you are fifty-fifty at best." Anna shrugged her shoulders.

"You could always fire him, take over the business yourself and fix it," Tom added.

"I don't have a year to do that," I pondered out loud. "I know he's betting on that."

"So?" Anna put her hand on my shoulder. "What are you going to do?"

"Stall him." I began to plot my revenge. "I'm going to do what I do best in the meantime."

"What's that?" Tom asked.

"Make that son of a bitch sorry he ever tried to screw me."

"Now, that's the Katz I know and love," Anna laughed.

. . . .

"He what!" Cassandra took this harder than I did. "I scrutinized the books two weeks ago, and none of those expenses were there."

"Did you keep a copy of the books?" I quizzed.

"No." Cassandra was still angry. "Why the hell would I? Everything seemed fine, the last quarterly payment we both got from the business reflected what the books told me."

"Don't worry about it," I said without expression, at least a visible expression.

"Don't shoot him," Cassandra insisted.

She saw what was bubbling just under my surface.

"We can't afford the legal bills right now."

"I won't," I hesitated, more to cool down than anything else. "I probably won't."

"What do you want me to do?" Cassandra thought for a second. "I can't do that much while I'm still teaching, but I want to do something?"

"Could you do some phone work tomorrow?" I was glad she wanted to help. "The building changed hands six months ago, and the new company that raised our rent without us knowing is Five Star Investment, Incorporated."

"I'll find out tomorrow." She sounded happy to help in this endeavor. "Anything else?"

"Well," I thought. "If you could find out about the Wellness For All medical insurer."

"Is that the company overcharging us for medical insurance?" She asked with a sharpness to her voice. "I've never heard of that company, are you sure that's the insurance company?"

"It is." I nodded. "The last piece of paper I signed was for Blue Cross coverage for Peter and the two full-time secretaries, and that was a huge enough expense."

"Right." Cassandra nodded again. "I remember that, all the detectives and accountants were hired as independent contractors. All we had to cover for them was the social security taxes, part of their bonding, daily expenses and some of their mileage."

"And, I thought that was too generous," I said. "But, I've always been cheap."

"So, when are we supposed to have changed the insurance, and agreed to the higher rent and damned cleaning services?" Cassandra still sounded pissed.

"Anna showed me the three memos I allegedly signed."

"Were they real?" Cassandra asked.

"Not hardly." I shook my head. "He must have taken my signature from another document and put it on those three."

"So, was it your signature?"

"It appears to be, but I didn't sign those documents; I'm headed to Whitney's office tomorrow."

"The handwriting and document expert?" Cassandra followed my logic.

"It'll be worth the two hundred to have her check it. We can use her testimony in the lawsuit too." I then slightly changed thoughts. "Speaking of spending money, I'm seeing our lawyer after I see Whitney."

"What for?"

"We're going to sue Peter for at least a million bucks." I nodded.

"I like that idea, but why?" Cassandra asked.

"I'm going to time the suit to fall on him right after I have a chance to get a few more ducks in the row I'm building." I grinned. "I have a master plan."

"I like the sound of that." Cassandra smiled back at me. "You sound like Fearless Leader when you talk like that."

"He vill be crushed mit a sneak attack unt a lawsuit," I faked a Russian accent.

"That sounds like fun." She shook her head and chuckled. "Let me know what's really going on soon, though."

....

"Hi." I cradled the receiver in my right hand. "What did you find out?"

"Five Star Investment is a holding company, held by Waters Investments, owned by Service Company of the West," Cassandra said, almost out of breath. "And guess who's the primary partner in the company that handles our medical insurance?"

"One of the aforementioned companies?" I guessed, it wasn't a hard question to answer.

"Waters Investment," she answered. "It took a few hours of digging and begging, but all of the money fronts, and dead ends, are owned by Benton Schroeder."

"Funny last name, don't you think?" It was all becoming clearer.

"Where are you, by the way?" Cassandra asked.

"In my old office."

I leaned back in the comfy chair.

"Where's our erstwhile manager?" She was apprehensive.

"I threw him out."

"Literally?" She had to ask.

"He protested a little." I enjoyed reliving it. "But Bennie held the door while I shoved his ugly ass out."

"How's Bennie doing?"

Cassandra liked the picture I had painted.

"He's doing fine," I answered. "He said he was going to

19

quit and take a dozen of our detectives with him if I had sold to Peter Schroeder."

"Why didn't any of them tell us about this?" Cassandra asked.

"He didn't know about the money problems, he didn't like Peter that much."

"Didn't he know he had medical insurance?" Cassandra asked. "He should have loved Peter for that."

"None of the PIs knew they were insured." I settled into the large chair; I kind of liked the chair that weasel had bought with our money. "It sounds like Peter thought we were real idiots."

"We almost were," Cassandra said. "So, I assumed you fired Peter."

"Fired and more." I wickedly grinned. "I took out a restraining order against him; he can't come near this building, and he's lost all access to any part of this company's records."

"What did he say on his way out?" Cassandra asked.

"Something about suing us for firing him, and me for kicking his ass out the door." I slapped another satisfying grin on my face. "Not that I think he will."

"Why not?"

"Do you remember the contract he signed?" I was rechecking it as I spoke to Cassandra. "We can fire him without prior notice for a large list of reasons, one of which is falsifying the financial records."

"Speaking of the books, you have someone we can trust going over the books, right?" Cassandra asked.

"Right."

"When do we sue him?"

"He'll be served tomorrow," I replied. "But, for now, I'm checking out his father, Benton Schroeder."

"Where's the old man?"

"I'll be in Sacramento for the next day," I said. "I've got a few more calls to make from here."

"Who's going to run the place?" Cassandra sounded a little worried.

"I called Janet and she agreed to come back to work until we settle all this."

I knew Janet could pick up all the pieces. I used to work for the Sterling Detective Agency here in Los Angeles before I struck out on my own. The Sterling Agency closed after it's owner died and we took over most of its business. Janet was the office manager with the Sterling Agency for a long time before she retired, as well as being a life long friend of Cassandra's mother.

"Great," Cassandra sounded relieved. "I'm glad she agreed to do it."

"I shouldn't be more that a day in Sacramento." I didn't want to be gone even that long.

"Oh, I almost forgot," Cassandra said hurriedly. "Someone named Katzen called from Atlanta and wants you to do a job back there.

"In Atlanta?"

If I was hesitant to be gone for a day in Sacramento, why would I want a job in Atlanta?

"I told him you couldn't get back with him for a day, and he was okay with that, but, he sounded like he wanted you out there soon," Cassandra said. "You know, we could use some real income now."

"I suppose you're right," I said with a tinge of resignation in my voice. "I'll call him back as soon as I'm through with Benton Schroeder."

. . . .

It's always a good thing to have a friend on a police force and in Los Angeles, my friend is Mark Hatton. The two of us became friends right as I moved to Los Angeles, actually, we met in Hawaii as we both mustered out of the Marines; he was an MP and I was something else. Mark and his wife were right there a little more than two months ago watching Cassandra and I get married. Mark had a good contact on the Sacramento police force.

Benton Schroeder was well known to the Sacramento police, he owned a string of rent to own furniture and appliance stores. Schroeder's establishments charged two hundred percent interest in the guise of rent to people who could least afford it. In addition to the legal usury, he was also suspected in actual loan sharking, drug dealing and a major prostitution ring.

No wonder he was able to loan the money to his weasel son to buy our detective agency, I should have followed my own advice and investigated Schroeder a little better before I hired him, and especially before I signed an intent to sell our business to him. Peter Schroeder had a spotless record, he was an upstanding citizen and was easily licensed and bonded by the state of California, but one cursory check of his father, however, would have shown another side to Peter. The acorn, in this case, didn't fall far from the tree.

. . . .

"Benton Schroeder?" I smiled and extended my hand.
"That's right."
Benton was a tall, fat man, maybe six foot two and three hundred fifty pounds. He was dressed in polyester pants, a narrow red tie and a pale yellow blend shirt. His face was large and sweaty, a short, brushy mustache hung from his upper lip, looking like it didn't belong there; the mustache was sort of like the cheap toupee perched on top of his head.
"Your associate sent me down here to the stock room," I cleared my throat. "I had to talk to you in person."
"And, what do you gotta say?"
Benton stopped what he was doing and stared at me.
"Tiny told me over the phone that you was lookin' for a loan," he added. "Somethin' about one hundred large."
"Actually," I took in a deep breath.
Tiny was about seven feet tall, and I assumed Tiny could be there in a heartbeat if Benton called for him.
"The amount I'm here about is one million dollars."
"I don't loan that much to nobody." Benton glared harder at me. "Who the hell're you?"
"Actually, it's not a loan, it's a lawsuit and consider yourself served."
I plastered a stupid grin on my face, pulled the court papers from my inside pocket and handed the papers to him.
"Get the fuck outta here!" He shouted as he threw the

papers on the floor. "Tiny! Get the hell in here, now!"

"That's not a good career move." I moved back a few steps. "Especially for a two bit mobster like yourself."

"What kind of dumb shit process server are you?" Benton shook his head slowly. "Do you have some sort of death wish?"

"I'm not a process server," I insisted. "I serve my own papers, I'm Katz."

"Oh, I get it," Benton glowered at me. "Maybe my son can now buy the business even cheaper from the grieving widow."

"Is that a death threat?" I asked, as the tape recorder was slowly preserving this conversation for future lawsuits and trials.

"Not a threat." Benton heard the large assistant rushing towards the stockroom. "It's a promise."

"Thanks."

I picked up a four foot long one by six from a half demolished shipping palate I had noticed as I came into the storeroom. Tiny was slowing from a full lumber as he burst through the door of the storeroom.

"Watch out!" Benton shouted, it was too late.

I had enough time for a complete swing; the flat part of the two by six smashed Tiny across his face with enough force to make Tiny's feet fly forward, while his body fell backwards. Crumpling to the floor, the giant henchman didn't even make a sound, other than, thud. A small trickle of blood oozed from his mouth, and a drop slowly fell from his right nostril.

"You killed him!" Benton shouted as he reached his right hand around behind him.

"Don't even think about it."

I pointed the barrel of my Smith and Wesson at his head.

"Tiny's fine, look at him breath in and breath out, if you reach for that gun, you won't be."

"What now?" Benton hissed at me.

"We wait for the cops, they should be here soon, I called them right before I walked in."

I motioned for him to move further away from me.

3

A dead man is hard to find

"Don't give me such a hard time." Gordon Jenkins stared at Detective Brown as if he had been accused of starting the Civil War.

"I don't mean to, but I wish you had kept the body for a little while longer," Gary Brown answered, trying not to show his annoyance. "Maybe you could've done some more tests."

"Why?" Dr. Jenkins sounded confused. "It was obvious from the autopsy that the Belchamp man died from a heart attack."

"Could the attack be induced?"

"Anything is possible, but not likely in this case," Dr. Jenkins insisted. "We did a toxicology screen searching for almost everything, but it came up negative; no drugs and no alcohol were in his system, neither were there any poisons in his blood."

"Did you do a stomach contents?" The detective asked.

"The medical examiner who preformed the autopsy checked the contents, but did not analyze it any further than note it was there and didn't contain any poison."

"Why not?" Gary asked.

"The dead man was identified by his wife, his son, and three of his employees and his face matched his two picture IDs," Dr. Jenkins took in another breath. "According to your notes, the man had just eaten lunch, and the contents of his stomach indicated the dead man had eaten. We did do a tox screen on his stomach contents and there wasn't anything unusual. Other than that, why in the hell would we analyze what he ate for lunch, ask his waitress."

"I know," Gary sighed. "I did."

"His wife insisted the body be released, and since you never said this might be a homicide, I didn't see the harm in letting his wife have the body." Dr. Jenkins was becoming flushed. "I gave you ample time to tell me to keep the body, and I have given you too much time to clear this case. Remember, I already did issue a death certificate."

"You're right, your right." Gary took in a deep breath. "Something doesn't feel right about this."

"What?"

"You said he had cirrhosis of the liver, right?" Gary glanced at the doctor.

"Yes," Dr. Jenkins agreed.

"According to his wife and son, Belchamp didn't drink more than a beer a week." Gary stared at the floor, thinking. "Also, he seemed kind of rough for a man who did nothing more strenuous than sit at a desk and go fishing on weekends."

"Dying can make anybody appear rough." Dr. Jenkins calmed down a little. "As far as the liver problem, well, that could have been caused by something other than drinking. Besides, who knows what he did when he was alone, or what he did in his youth."

"I guess you're right."

Gary reluctantly agreed; he didn't completely buy it, though.

"You know." Dr. Jenkins stared at the papers in front of him. "The pathologist that conducted Mr. Belchamp's autopsy made a note that the liver did appear like that of a heavy drinker."

"Like I said," Detective Brown took a concerned tone. "His family said he didn't drink that much."

"Maybe he was a closet drinker." Dr. Jenkins shrugged. "As I said, maybe he drank a lot when he was younger."

"Maybe."

Gary Brown shook his head slightly; this didn't sound quite right, but what actual evidence was there?

"That white powder wasn't drugs either." Dr. Jenkins calmed

down some more. "It was powdered sugar, like from a doughnut or something like that."

"Yeah," Gary Brown mumbled. "Your assistant told me that."

"Have you been able to check on his fingerprints?" Dr. Jenkins asked.

"The FBI didn't have them on file." Gary shook his head. "He was in the Army back in the early fifties, but Army Records cannot locate his complete file yet."

"Well, when you get a copy of his fingerprints, we'll know for sure it was really him." Dr. Jenkins looked hard at the detective. "You know, if that dead man isn't Simon Belchamp, he'd have to be his twin brother."

"That's not as strange as it sounds, you know." Gary shook his head. "But unfortunately, he only has one sister."

"You checked?"

"Yeah, I did. His wife and son knew of only the one sister, and I called the local police from his home town and they confirmed that for me."

Detective Brown shook his head as he tapped his right foot on the floor. He knew something wasn't right, but couldn't put a finger on what. What was a good reason for someone to kill Simon Belchamp; his wife and son had all the money they needed. The son who would inherit the car business was already almost running the business now. Belchamp didn't have any outstanding large debt, he didn't gamble or drink too much. Gary couldn't find a mistress hiding somewhere in Belchamp's life, so what would the motive for murder be?

"Is there anything else?" Dr. Jenkins asked.

"I guess not." Gary started to turn and leave, then he paused by the door. "Are you one hundred percent sure he had a heart attack?"

"Nothing in this life is one hundred percent sure, but my conclusion about what killed that man is at least ninety nine percent sure," Dr Jenkins answered. "That's what I put on the death certificate."

"Why?" Gary turned to face the doctor.

26

"His heart was enlarged." Dr. Jenkins picked up the report and turned to the proper page. "Extensive damage to the muscles was obvious on the right side of the heart, some of the damage was quite recent. Blood tests showed that he had a heart attack within the last seventy two hours and the man had advanced arteriosclerosis. A ninety percent blockage was found in three arteries feeding the man's heart. We contacted his family doctor about his medical history."

"What did his doc Say?" Gary asked.

"It seems Mr. Belchamp didn't like doctors." Dr. Jenkins shook his head. "He hadn't seen our dead man in over three years. But, the last time he did check him out he had high blood pressure, arteriosclerosis, and was obese, he was a heart attack waiting to happen."

"That sounds like Belchamp probably died from a heart attack." Gary turned again to the office door. "Probably."

4

I'll think about it.

"Dr. Hiller?" Cassandra said tentatively

She leaned into her major professor's office; he had called her, saying that it was urgent so Cassandra was slightly panicked. She thought her dissertation was a done deal, after all, her reading committee had approved it and she had already given it to the typing service to make the final copies. All she was worried about was getting the typing done in time for her defense which was scheduled soon, all too soon.

"Yes, Miss Pales." He blushed a little. "Excuse me, Mrs. Katz."

"You were there, Dr. Hiller." Cassandra smiled at him. "You remember my wedding."

"Yes, I'm not used to your new name yet, my wife says I'm really bad about that sort of thing." Bernard Hiller grinned as he shook his head slowly. "I remember your wedding very well, that was the strangest wedding I have ever seen."

"It sort of reflects my career as a private investigator more than my academic life."

Cassandra was still a bit worried as to why he had called her to his office. She hadn't had a meeting with him in two months, after she got married; what was this all about?

"That's why I called you down here," Bernard said.

"I thought it was something to do with my dissertation," Cassandra let out a gasp of air.

"No, no," Dr. Hiller reassured her. "Your dissertation is perhaps the best one I've read in the past ten years."

"Really?" Cassandra smiled.

This was a relief, that was also nice to hear.

"Yes, really," Bernard Hiller eagerly responded. "You are a

28

very talented young woman."

"And, the reason you need to talk to me is?"

Cassandra began to get worried about the cause of this meeting; she hoped he didn't want to hire her as a detective for some unknown reason, or to hit on her. He hadn't so far, but he was grinning at her a lot more than he ever had before.

"It's about what you'll be doing after you finish the degree," he said.

"We've talked about this before."

Cassandra sounded curious, why this discussion again?

"For the short term, I'm going to stay with the detective agency to help my husband."

"I know you told me that before, but I'd like you to reconsider."

Hiller was now moving to his argumentative stance. Cassandra had learned to recognize his tells; Hiller would hunker down in his chair, his shoulders would slouch, as if to brace for a fight. Any actual fight Dr. Hiller would enter would have to be a verbal one; he was about fifty and way out of shape. Cassandra doubted if the man could run fifty feet without falling over from a stroke.

"I know, but I have to try again." Hiller leaned forward.

Cassandra knew this meant he would begin his verbal attack, Dr. Hiller wanted to help, that's always his motivation, but even if he was wrong, he was self convinced that he was right. He always felt his logic was impeccable, even though in this case it wasn't; Hiller had no idea why, but it wasn't.

"I have to help my husband for the next year or so." Cassandra stopped Hiller before he started. "Maybe two years from now, I can start searching for a job in academia, but not now."

"Do you really think…."

"I could spend the time working my dissertation into a book and look for a publisher in those two years." Cassandra didn't let him finish his statement.

"I suppose you could, but…."

"As a matter of a fact, we have a new case coming up back in Atlanta right now."

29

Cassandra was determined to stall him to see if he would give up.

"Can you let me finish a thought," Hiller loudly insisted.

"I'm sorry."

No, he wasn't going to give up.

"I have someone who wants to meet you."

Dr. Hiller seemed slightly angry, he didn't like being stifled, in particular by a graduate student, especially by a woman.

"Who?"

Cassandra was considering if she had made the correct choice, maybe she should have let him prattle on about how she should jump into an assistant professorship right away, and recommend the right places to start a career in academia.

"She's waiting for us in the conference room down the hall." He got up and motioned for Cassandra to follow him.

"Is it someone from another university?" Cassandra tried to make small talk.

"No." Bernard Hiller had calmed down.

Cassandra was the best graduate student he had mentored in his career at UCLA, he couldn't stay mad at her.

"She was recommended by a friend of mine from Georgetown University, she works in the government and wants to talk to you," he added.

"Oh," she responded.

Cassandra began to sweat and it wasn't that hot in the building; the government, what the hell was this all about? How many people knew about all those papers she had signed a few months ago? She had already signed her life away to the CIA, what the hell else was going on?

"Here we are."

Dr. Hiller pushed the door to conference room 106 open and let Cassandra go in ahead of him.

Sitting at the head of the small rectangular wooden table was a woman about forty years old with short curly blonde hair who appeared five foot six and weighed about one thirty. Cassandra noticed her eyebrows were a light brown, probably her real hair color. The woman had a pleasant expression but she was wearing a little too

30

much makeup in Cassandra's opinion, at least she wasn't wearing too much perfume. Dressed in a dark blue dress, white blouse and a suit coat that matched her dress, the woman appeared quite professional, whatever that profession was.

"Hello, my name is Margaret Stanley." The woman extended her hand to Cassandra.

"Hi, my name's Cassandra Katz.""

Cassandra shook her hand, it was a firm handshake for a woman.

"Please, let's all sit down." Margaret politely said.

Ms. Stanley sat back down at her seat. She had a leather briefcase open to her left side and one closed file folder was positioned on the table in front of her. Cassandra tried to peek inside the open briefcase and recognize anything but all she could see were two brochures about the diplomatic service; that was a good clue.

"Mrs. Stanley is a dear friend of my colleague at Georgetown," Dr. Hiller broke in.

He seemed as if he didn't know what to say right then.; that was unusual and Cassandra felt something didn't seem right.

"I couldn't help but notice the brochures in your briefcase." Cassandra leaned towards Mrs. Stanley. "Are you here to try to recruit me into the diplomatic corps?"

"You are perceptive, Mrs. Katz, I'm here to do just that."

Margaret smiled at Cassandra as she passed her one of the brochures.

"I've spent the last several years or so being a private investigator as well as a graduate student." Cassandra considered her next sentence. "Perception is my stock and trade by now."

"Precisely why I'm here." Margaret began to gear up her sales pitch. "My department would like to offer you an exciting career in the State Department."

She passed Cassandra a business card.

"As what, an analyst?"

Cassandra took Margaret's card.

"Yes." Margaret nodded. "Your expertise in Arab speaking countries is needed right now, it's much needed right now."

31

"Although this job isn't an academic job, it is a respectable job in your field and it pays better than a university could pay a first year assistant professor," Dr. Hiller added.

Cassandra felt like she was between two nagging bookends; never make Cassandra feel like she's in a trap, that's when she gets testy.

"What do you think about the situation in Iran right now?" Margaret quickly changed the subject.

"That whole debacle defeated the last president's re-election bid," Cassandra quickly replied. "But, I think this country should be more weary of is Saudi Arabia."

"Anything else?" Margaret shrugged. "What do you think the root causes are?"

"The root causes of what?" Cassandra asked.

"Of the conflict there." Margaret faced Cassandra.

"Lots of conflicts exist there; conflicts between local factions, tribes, and expressions of Islam."

Cassandra was wondering what this was all about, but for the sake of her major professor, she continued.

"As well as the conflict between the middle east countries and the west," Margaret added. "That's the conflict I'm interested in."

"Israel."

Cassandra kept staring at Margaret, without changing her expression.

"Anything else?" Margaret Stanley pressed.

"Besides it being another battlefield of the Cold War, oil, ignorance, and history have to be some of the top reasons."

Cassandra looked at the table, then back up at Margaret.

"I'm sorry, I'm really not interested in interviewing for this job."

"History?"

Margaret ignored Cassandra's last statement.

"White western Christians equal the crusades," Cassandra replied. "The educated Arab dictators and radical Muslim leaders know better, but that's the hook that keeps the Islamic masses in an uproar. We have to worry about the militant fundamentalist factions more than anything going into the future."

"Mrs. Katz does have an enormous grasp of the economic and political forces in that region," Dr. Hiller said.

He seemed compelled to tell Margaret Stanley that Cassandra did know more than her cryptic answers indicated.

"I know she does," Margaret agreed

"She will make an outstanding addition to your team, a fine job is waiting for her in your division."

Dr. Hiller made his point to Margaret, then turned to Cassandra. His expression made Cassandra that much more pissed off about the whole railroading act going on in the closed room.

"Yes," Margaret said. "We can start you off at thirty one thousand after you complete your degree."

"You see." Cassandra glanced at Margaret, then at Bernard Hiller. "That's part of the problem."

"Thirty one thousand a year is a problem?" Dr. Hiller glanced at Cassandra, confused.

"Last year I made over sixty thousand at the detective agency, and I don't think half of that is much of a financial incentive," Cassandra quickly replied.

She didn't change her exterior blank expression, but the reaction of her major professor was not quite what she needed to see. Sixty thousand was about as much as he earned, and Hiller held an endowed chair in the department; she had admitted to making as much as the department chairman.

"Excuse me?" Bernard Hiller coughed.

"I'm sorry," Cassandra said softly

She knew she might have crossed a line she shouldn't have.

"I shouldn't have said that, but it was germane to the discussion."

"I think it's germane." Margaret grinned at Cassandra.

Margaret wasn't stupid, she knew exactly what Cassandra had done, and she thought it was humorous, although, Cassandra was beginning to regret it. First she verbally stepped on her major professor, now she admitted that she made as much money as he did. Academic egos are among the most fragile in the world, Cassandra knew that and began to regret this a lot, maybe that's why Margaret was smiling at her.

"I do want to use my degree; I spent years studying with the best minds in this field and I intend to use that knowledge forging a career in something related to it," Cassandra spoke a little louder.

"We thought this might be a good career path given your years of experience with the detective agency." Margaret said.

She looked at Dr. Hiller, his ego was still in shock and Cassandra couldn't bring herself to face him quite yet.

"I agree," Cassandra quietly replied. "I have committed to my husband to stay with the agency in Atlanta for at least two years, but, after that, I will most surely begin a career in my field."

"Well." Margaret stood up. "I hope you will consider us in two years. I think you and I could get along very well."

Margaret gathered her things up, arranged them in her briefcase, shook Cassandra's hand and let herself out. She didn't want to stay with Cassandra and the bruised Dr. Hiller.

"You made sixty thousand last year?" Bernard Hiller stared, slack jawed, at Cassandra.

"It was a good year." Cassandra attempted a smile.

"A good year?"

There was definitely an edge to that comment.

"Dr. Hiller," Cassandra gulped in a large breath. "For the first two years I worked there, I made only ten or fifteen thousand, and I've been arrested six times. Most days when I'm working a case, I work ten to twelve hours a day. I won't even tell you how many times someone has shot at me. And, a few years ago I was in a gunfight in San Francisco and I killed a man."

"You killed a man?"

This was becoming a bit too much for the poor man. The worst thing he had to contend with regarding one of his graduate students before was possession of pot, less than an ounce.

"The man I killed was an escaped murderer, he was trying to kill me at the time, so I'm not too unhappy about the results."

Cassandra knew she would have to draw this conversation to a close real soon if she ever hoped to graduate.

"A murderer?"

"We sometimes do high profile cases, they pay a lot, but they

34

tend to be more dangerous."

"I never knew."

Dr. Hiller was beginning to regain some of his composure.

"Why didn't you tell me before? Someone with a police record cannot matriculate at this school."

"I don't have a record."

Cassandra knew this was spiraling out of control.

"The police arrest me when they want me to leave a case alone, they hold me for an hour or two, until our lawyer gets there and threatens them. I have no real arrests for anything, not even a speeding ticket and I have never been convicted of anything."

"I guess this explains some of the people at your wedding." Bernard Hiller grinned, briefly.

"Yeah." Cassandra smiled broadly back at him. "That strange woman with all the tattoos and body piercings was an undercover policewoman. The four large men with no necks were FBI agents."

"You lead a strange life outside of class, Mrs. Katz."

Dr. Hiller was beginning to reassert his dominant position. This was his department, he was the top dog here, after all. Cassandra was happy he was climbing back out of the ditch he had been in for the past ten minutes.

"I know," she assured him. "It's been a strange life, but it's my life. I'm surprised you didn't read about some of my exploits in the newspapers."

"I didn't pay attention, I guess."

Hiller seemed a bit bemused which was a better emotion than anger.

"Most of my fellow grad students knew, they teased me about it all the time."

Cassandra got up to leave, Dr. Hiller followed her out of the room.

"I need to pay more attention to the metro section," Bernard Hiller commented. "Although, I don't think I'll have another graduate student quite like you again for a long, long time."

5

Zero is the loneliest number

"Mr. Katz."

"Yes."

"My name is Mr. Katzen," The voice on the phone said.

I didn't recognize the name at first, it sounded like a longer version of my name.

"You called me back and left a message with my secretary."

"Yes, I remember now, it was late last week, you said you might have a job for our firm?"

"Did you move to Los Angeles?" Katzen's voice seemed annoyed. "I thought your firm was in Atlanta."

"It is."

Maybe that's why he sounds that way, he wants a local investigator.

"I'm out here on business, but I can be there tomorrow if it is necessary."

"That's good." He relaxed a little. "You were recommended to me by someone I respect a great deal, and I would like you to work for us."

"Who was that?" I backpedaled a little. "It helps if I know where you heard of the firm for future advertising."

"I understand," he sounded annoyed, "it wasn't advertising, it was word of mouth. Your recommendation came from Mr. Mahoney, I met him at an insurer's conference in Germany two weeks ago. He works for Lloyds of London and you had finished a case for them and they were impressed with your work."

"Thank you."

Funny, I didn't work for Lloyds of London, I was actually working for the CIA on that case, but that didn't matter.

"What can I do for you?"

"There has been a death right here in Atlanta of a prominent businessman and he was insured by our firm for five million dollars."

"This is a recent death?"

"Yes sir, it happened about a week ago."

"Shouldn't the police be handling the investigation?"

I didn't want to piss of the Atlanta police since I hadn't made too many friends with that department yet.

"I don't think they will," Katzen assured. "The initial ruling was that it was from natural causes."

"What makes you think it was something else?"

Other than loosing five million dollars that is, I thought to myself.

"We think it's too suspicious," Katzen hesitated, this time the pause meant something; the silence between statements was becoming too long. "We must talk face to face."

"Why?"

"I can't be sure this conversation isn't being listened to." He took in a deep breath. "What's your daily rate?"

"Two hundred and fifty per day plus expenses."

It was like I was reading from a script by then. I did hate the business side of this whole thing, but one must be mercenary to eat I suppose.

"If we prove this is a false claim, what percentage do you pay?"

"For sums over one million, the company policy is that we pay two percent," he quickly answered.

"That's one hundred thousand."

Under the right circumstances, I can calculate real quickly.

"That is correct," Katzen replied. "Can you come back here tomorrow?"

"I think I can."

I thought quickly; Cassandra would understand. For the possibility of one hundred grand, she would certainly understand.

"If I can't get a flight for tomorrow, I'll get one the next day.

37

When I make a reservation, I'll call your office and leave my flight information."

"That will be satisfactory."

....

"How much do they pay?" Cassandra asked.

She didn't crack a smile. This meant our honeymoon was over for sure and I'd be heading back to our house in Atlanta sooner than we had expected. I was happy she didn't crack my head open like a piñata.

"Two percent on five million dollars."

"Assuming that it was something other than natural causes, some reason that the policy won't pay for," she said, calculating in her head. "With the way our luck has been running, this case might be like our infamous business sale."

"It can't be that bad, besides, the sale turned out sort of all right."

I was optimistic, sometimes I can be unrealistically optimistic, but optimism keeps the heartburn at bay.

"That sale hasn't turned out at all yet. Remember, even though we settled that lawsuit against the prick and his father who tried to screw us, the lawyers walked off with half of the settlement," Cassandra sighed.

"They deserve to get paid," I promptly replied. "They settled much quicker than any of the lawyers thought they would and the settlement replaced all the money our business was screwed out of, plus we came out with forty thousand bucks in cash, so it isn't all that bad."

"The lawyers got almost two hundred grand, we deserved more money for all that grief," she bitterly protested.

"Besides, I think our solution is a good one, anyway," I said. "Selling the Los Angeles Agency to ten of the PIs who work there will turn out fine."

"Assuming they can come up with the cash by the closing date, I suppose it is." Cassandra shook her head. "We didn't have to go down that much on the price, either."

"Hey, I dropped the price by fifty thousand, so with the forty we got from Peter and his father, we're only out ten grand." I shrugged. "And, given the sales price of two hundred and twenty five thousand, what's ten grand?"

"Ten grand is a nice new luxury car for Atlanta." Cassandra held her ground. "Lest you forget, I still think we need another car there."

"I agree, I agree."

I wasn't placating, I did agree with her.

"The gentleman buying Cheshire Agency from us are a good bunch of guys and we probably should have offered them the deal in the first place."

"I guess you're right," Cassandra reluctantly agreed.

"Well, at least this client back in Atlanta will pay two fifty a day plus expenses and if you haven't noticed we haven't had a paying client in going on three months."

"I've noticed."

She got up and paced the floor in front of me.

"Is there something else you want to say?" I observed.

"If you sign a temporary power of attorney I can close for the both of us and meet you in Atlanta in three days, that is, if everything goes all right."

"Think positive," I assured her. "It will."

"At least if this deal falls through, we'll still have the income from this branch and the income from your new client." She mused. "Something is better than nothing."

"By the way, what did your professor want? Is Hiller giving you fits again?"

I changed the subject, it was time to change the subject. That whole deal with our Los Angeles office still pissed me off a little too.

"He was once more trying to get me to stay in academia," Cassandra answered.

"Oh well."

I checked to see if I could notice a clue as to how well the plea worked.

"Actually, it wasn't a university job this time," she said.

"What then?"

This sounded interesting.

"He had some recruiter from the State Department who wanted me to be a Mid East analyst for them."

"That's peculiar."

My mind quickly went to all the possibilities.

"That's what I thought too," Cassandra sounded serious. "You don't suppose they know about me joining the CIA, do you?"

"I kind of doubt it. It's strange, I have to admit."

The State Department and CIA rarely cooperated on that level.

"The recruiter was a nice woman." Cassandra smiled at me. "I told her I had to help my husband with his business for a few years."

"How did your major professor take it?"

I knew he was the real problem for her, not some government recruiter.

"I don't want to talk about it."

She said that with such authority that I immediately backed off and changed the subject again, I know which side of the bed my bread is buttered on.

"I suppose it might be good if we checked in on our building in Atlanta. Mrs. Smith was only supposed to collect the rents for a month and she's done it for almost four," I said.

I looked carefully at Cassandra's face, she was calming down, which is a good thing.

"You know." Cassandra switched gears. "I like the widow Smith, but I think the women in the front apartment across from us would make good building managers, it would be less bother for them than it would for Mrs. Smith."

"Do you mean the lesbian couple in 2-A?" I felt like teasing Cassandra. "I think they both have the hots for you."

"You're not that appealing when you talk like a thirteen year old," Cassandra sounded sour.

"Ah, but I am a damned good observer of human behavior, and that's what I see." I left the grin pasted on my face. "Besides, Mrs. Smith likes collecting the rents and calling the repairmen when needed, she also likes the fact that we cut her rent for the job she's doing, and I think she needs the money more than 2-A does."

"I suppose you're right," Cassandra hesitated. "About Mrs. Smith, that is. Why don't you call around and see if you can get a flight back tonight."

"I will, but if I go back to Atlanta by myself, I'll be so lonely." I tried to appear hurt. "You know, one is the loneliest number."

"Maybe." She shot me an impious smile. "But when it comes to bank accounts, zero is a lot lonelier."

6

Till death do us part

"If your husband had died at a hospital, the death certificate would not be a problem, but seeing as he died in his car in the parking lot of a restaurant."

Detective Brown looked at the grieving widow. Something still didn't seem that right.

"There doesn't appear to be any foul play in his death, but we have to handle these things a little differently," he continued.

"I know there has to be a lot of paperwork, but the coroner said he already did sign a death certificate, but that you made him wait some more before giving it to me." Gladys Belchamp seemed anxious. "My son and I need to finish up my late husband's affairs."

"His accounts were in both your names, am I right?"

Gary Brown wondered if there might be other accounts that weren't in both their names; he couldn't find any when he checked a week ago, but one never knows.

"My husband kept everything in both our names, all right," Mrs. Belchamp sounded indignant at the question.

"So, what's the hurry?" Detective Brown carefully studied Mrs. Belchamp.

"I need to settle his estate," she insisted again.

"Estates take months to settle when they're small, but with your husband owning two businesses it could be a lot longer," Gary said.

He noted her non-verbal response. She squeezed her entire body tight for a second, then relaxed only a little.

"What I want to know is, why are you asking me about the death certificate?" Gary asked.

"The Coroner's Office said you were still investigating the case, and they wouldn't send it on until you cleared it," she stated. "They promised it to me when they released his body, then they won't tell me anything."

"I do apologize for any delay, but I had to set that case aside for awhile." Gary stared at the ceiling, then down to her glaring eyes. "I was waiting for some documents to get in, and they haven't yet."

"What documents?" She seemed hopeful now.

"Well," Gary replied, "if I remember right, I was waiting for the Army to send me a copy of his finger prints so we could verify that that was the right man."

"The right man!" Gladys Belchamp quickly regained her composure after the loud shout. "Who else could that be? That was my husband, I've lived with that man for thirty some years, and I ought to know it was him."

"Yes, Ma'am," Gary responded, noting that was a quick outburst.

What did she have up her sleeve? What was the real reason she needed the death certificate?

"I would much appreciate it if you could move the process on." Gladys completely regained her self-control. "If you need anything from me to help you in finishing your investigation, please ask me, and I'll give you whatever you want."

"Thank you, Ma'am."

Gary nodded, as if to tell her that she was through. She wouldn't get what she wanted right then. But, Gary knew he would have to tell the Coroner to give the widow the death certificate soon, no hard facts that would let him delay much longer existed.

....

"Something's fishy with that damned family." Gary leaned to one side in the metal chair. "I know what the doc said, but there had to be something other than a heart attack going on."

"What makes you think so?" Paul Mayer asked.

Paul was Gary's lieutenant, he was the man who could give Gary the go ahead to pursue this case, this case with no real evidence of foul play.

"It's a gut feeling, boss."

Gary glanced around the lieutenant's office. The office was Spartan, almost no pictures hung on the wall, and the old metal desk was almost devoid of clutter.

"If I'm not mistaken, you have nine active cases right now, and if I read the rotation right, you're due for number ten real soon." Lieutenant Mayer stared at Gary. "You're one of my best detectives, but I don't want you stretched too thin."

"I guess you're right," Gary said. "Can I have another day or two before I tell the Coroner he can give the widow the death certificate?"

"Two days."

Paul glanced at the door, Gary knew it was time to leave.

. . . .

"Hello," Gary greeted the next person on the phone.

This was the sixth large insurance company he had called. Detective Brown knew about three insurance policies on Simon Belchamp, all three companies had a request in for the death certificate. One policy, payable to his wife, was for two hundred and fifty thousand and the other two were for the same amount, payable to the business. Even taking all three into consideration, that wasn't enough money for murder, given the net worth of the family.

The value of Belchamp's car dealerships was several millions, income from them was also nothing to sneeze at. The wife and kid had an uncontested share of the car dealerships and nobody else was mentioned in the will, so those two were the only ones with a stake in Simon Belchamp's death. The wife got one half of both dealerships, the son got the other half and the wife got all his other assets.

"This is Mr. Katzen," The voice on the other end finally answered.

Gary had been placed on hold, and passed to three different people in this company.

"Thank you for speaking to me." Gary wound up for the same series of short questions with yet another person in this insurance company. "My name is Detective Gary Brown with the Atlanta Police Department." Gary let that sink in. "I am investigating the recent death of a Simon Belchamp of Decatur. I was wondering if your company had any policies in force for Mr. Belchamp."

After a ten second pause, Mr. Katzen answered, "Can you give me your number, and I will call you right back."

"Sure." Gary took in a breath. "555-3300, if I'm on the phone, leave a message and I'll call right back."

"It won't take but a second," Mr. Katzen quickly said. "I'll call right back."

He hung up.

"That was strange." Gary stared at the phone as he hung it up.

Within thirty seconds, the phone rang.

"Hello, this is Detective Brown," he said carefully.

"Hi," the same voice said. "I had the phone book open to the page of police numbers, and the number you gave me was in it."

"That's right," Gary said carefully. "Did Simon Belchamp have a policy with your firm?"

"Yes, he did," Mr. Katzen said quickly.

"Who was the beneficiary, if I may ask," Gary answered.

"Are you investigating his murder?"

"Why would you say that?" Gary was intrigued.

"The policy is for a large amount, and it is to payout to an offshore account," Mr. Katzen answered. "I'll ask again, is there an active murder investigation for Mr. Belchamp?"

"Officially, no."

Gary knew the legal implication of that question. He needed to find some hard evidence.

"Can you send me a copy of the policy?" Gary asked.

"I would love to, Detective, but our legal department is checking into whether we can or not."

"It's that big a payout?"

Gary knew it had to be, why else would an insurance

45

company say that to a policeman.

"Yes, sir, it's that big," Mr. Katzen said flatly. "What can you tell me?"

"I can tell you the truth," Gary answered. "The Coroner's office thinks it was a heart attack, and I don't have any real evidence to contradict that finding."

"So, there will be a final death certificate stating that?" Mr. Katzen asked.

"Within the next two days."

"Two days," Mr. Katzen sounded anxious. "Thank you, Detective. I have your number, and I will be in touch if anything changes."

"Sure," Gary sounded curious. "Bye."

That was strange, if anything changes? What was that about?

7

Here, there and every hare

"Can you tell me for sure when Mr. Lepus will be back?"
A large, older man seemed to slump into the well worn sofa just in front of the only window in the dark, musty smelling room Fred Lepus used as his office.

Lepus Detective Agency was shoe horned into what was once a working class home on twenty second street, not far from the Lee Highway in Arlington Virginia. Fred lived in the back bedroom, but used the living room as an office, of sorts. Today, Fred was out on a case, well, he was following someone who owed him three hundred bucks, if you can call that a case. While he was gone, his secretary, and sometimes girlfriend, Cathy, answered the phone and took the rare drop in client.

"He's out on a case, like I told you," Cathy insisted. "I can take a message for him, if you like."

"I would rather speak to him in person."

The man seemed to sigh instead of speaking normally.

"He may call in sometime today, and I can give him a message," Cathy sounded as if she actually wanted to help the man. "I could maybe give him your phone number."

"I'm not staying anywhere."

The man took in a deep breath, Cathy could see that he was nervous, he was more than regular nervous.

"What do you mean you're not staying anywhere?" She asked, a little skeptical.

"I don't have anywhere to stay, especially anywhere with a phone."

"Are you sleeping in the street, or something?" She asked.

"Well," The man replied, "not exactly in the street, but sort of near it."

"You're homeless?" Cathy shuddered for a split second. "Why are you here, and why do you want to see Mr. Lepus?"

"It's about a case he worked on for a relative of mine."

The man seemed hesitant to speak to her.

"What case?"

"I want to speak to Mr. Lepus," The man insisted.

"You tell me the case you're talking about or I'll call the cops,." Cathy insisted right back at him.

She cracked open the middle left drawer on the desk where she kept her twenty two caliber pistol.

"Why should I tell you?" The man's voice became less confrontational.

"Because I'm his secretary and I keep all of Mr. Lepus' cases straight for him, and I screen all his clients," Cathy became more insistent. "So, if you hope to speak to him, you'll tell me who you are and why I should let you stay one more second in this office."

The man, sitting upright in the sofa, took in a slow breath and let it back out gradually, he drew in another breath.

"The case was the Belchamp case, and I need to speak to Mr. Lepus on a matter of life or death."

"Who's death?" Cathy seemed interested again. "Mr. Belchamp's?"

"My death."

"In that case," Cathy thought quickly. "Sit down there and I'll be back with you in a minute."

Cathy Rumson had been employed by Fred Lepus for about ten years. She never did anything dangerous, nor did she travel; those were the two pre-employment conditions she had made, and Fred hardly ever asked her to do either. Cathy did do all of Fred's paperwork, and she did all the filing. The file cabinets were stuffed into what used to be the dining room of the house, along with every other useless piece of equipment and paper detritus. Cathy looked for the Belchamp file, she remembered the name, but not the exact case. Finding the thin file, she pulled it out and opened it.

"Are you Mr. Belchamp?" Cathy shouted towards the front room.

"No," The man answered quickly.

48

"Well." Cathy read the last of the meager file. "Who are you?"

"I'd rather speak to Mr. Lepus, if you don't mind."

"Suit yourself, but, you can't stay here all day waiting."

Cathy pushed the Belchamp file back into the file drawer.

"Can I sleep for awhile on your sofa?" The man seemed to beg. "Please?"

"Sure," Cathy sounded a little more at ease. "Just don't snore too loud."

....

"Hello, Lepus Agency, how may I help you?" Cathy caught the phone on the first ring, so the sleeping stranger might stay asleep.

"Hey, sweet cakes," Fred sounded chipper. "I've almost got the drop on this deadbeat."

"Fred, you need to get back here right now," Cathy sounded anxious.

"Why?" Fred whined. "I'm so close to my three hundred bucks that I can almost taste it."

"I've got a bum sleeping on our sofa here," Cathy spoke quickly. "He says he has to talk to you about that Belchamp case you did awhile ago."

"So, is he worth more than three hundred bucks?"

"How the hell do I know." Cathy shrugged. "He's right here in front of me and I want you back here, now!"

"Cool off a bit," Fred insisted. "Did he say why he wants me?"

"No," Cathy spoke quietly and slowly. "He only wants to talk to you, and since you put down in the file that the Belchamp guy had a lot of dough, I think you should come here now."

"You don't feel comfortable having the guy sleeping on my couch in front of you?"

"Now that you finally realize that, yes!" Cathy spoke loud enough to stir the man on the sofa.

8

Time travels when you're having fun

I was able to get a night flight back to Atlanta. The problem with going East on a nine PM flight from LA is that it's too early in the morning in Atlanta with no chance to catch up on the lost night of sleep when I get there. I did have time to get to our apartment and at least change my clothes and take a shower before my ten o'clock appointment with Mr. Katzen, it was good to be back in my own place again.

For the past three months in California, Cassandra and I had been living in her parents home. It is a very nice place, but we stayed in her old bedroom since she wasn't psychologically ready to sleep with me in her parents bed in the extra large master bedroom. I would be happy in three days when Cassandra was back here with me. We had a nice apartment; it was our home.

The building we owned on Euclid Avenue was divided into six apartments, four small one bedroom units were on the first floor. We had converted the lower left unit, 1-C, into our office. two large two bedroom units were on the second floor. Cassandra and I lived in the rear unit, 2-B. The inside stairs leading from the building entrance rose from the front hallway to a tiny landing on the second floor, with the doors to 2-A and 2-B leading off of it. As I opened the door to run down the stairs and see if my car would start after three months of inactivity in the garage, Cheryl opened her door. We stood silent for a second, staring at each other's expression, or lack there of.

"When did you get back, Katz?"

"Early this morning." I gave her my best neighborly grin. "How have you been, Cheryl?"

"Just fine." Cheryl cleared her throat, closed her door and walked to the stairs. "Is Cassandra back?"

Cheryl was about five foot two and solidly built. She wasn't fat, just muscular and on her small frame it didn't do her any good. Her dark blond hair was short cut and well coiffed. Cheryl wore little makeup, and, in my opinion, didn't need any.

I swear I could see her smile, even though I could only see the back of her head as we both descended the stairs.

"She'll be back in a few days." I considered my next utterance, but said it anyway. "You know, we got married two months ago."

"So I heard."

Cheryl spun around to stare at me as we both stood in the front of the door leading to the porch.

"Her dissertation was accepted, so all she has to do now is defend and she'll be Dr. Katz."

"She gave up her name?"

Cheryl seemed surprised, especially after I opened the front door for her, sometimes I can't help myself.

"It was her idea."

I stood on the front porch, waiting for the conversation to die down.

"She's sometimes a little old fashioned. You should have seen the wedding she and her mother planned out in such a short time."

"That would have been nice," Cheryl thought to herself for a second. "Actually, Anne and I would like to have the two of you over for dinner later this week after Cassandra gets back and you two get settled in."

"We would love to."

Sometimes the two women in 2-A can be a bit short with me, but they mean well, and I kind of like both of them.

"I'll tell Cassandra, and she can set up the day and time."

"Great."

51

Cheryl turned and walked down the front steps.

"Bye."

I stopped in our office to get the small box wrench; I had undone the negative battery cable before I left in hopes that the charge might last longer. The preset radio stations were gone, but that was better that than a dead battery.

I love the preciseness of German technology, its simplicity complements the ruggedness and reliability; my fourteen year old Porsche started on the second try.

. . . .

The Insurance office of Mr. Katzen was on Peachtree, inside Two Eighty Five. It wasn't the biggest building, but they occupied all six floors of it. Mr. Katzen was the Regional VP, and his office was on the top floor.

"Mr. Katz."

Katzen was a tall thin man, he seemed close to fifty years old and had a full head of short hair that was white on the temples. His secretary only accompanied me to his door, then she silently turned and waited for me to go into the office. As soon as I did, she shut the door behind me.

"Please." I extended my hand. "Call me Benjamin."

"All right, Benjamin."

He shook my hand; it was a firm business handshake. He was impeccably dressed, but he did have on a tad too much cologne.

"Have a seat and you can call me Allan."

His office was large, perhaps half the size of our entire apartment. I could see a wet bar tucked into the right rear corner and two large windows, with the blinds partly drawn, spread across the rear wall. I quickly tried to identify some of the many pictures which lined the walls. The photos of what looked like family were nearest his desk, but the wall near the wet bar seemed to be the place for famous faces. I caught a quick glimpse of him shaking hands with Gerald Ford; I hope he wasn't playing golf with him at the time.

"So." I dove right in. "Why do you think this death was suspicious when the police didn't?"

52

"You don't waste time, do you," Allan sounded quite pleased. "I'd like to ask you a few questions first."

"All right."

I thought I was the detective here.

"First, may I see your Georgia license?"

"Sure. Our firm also belongs to the Georgia Association of Professional Private Investigators and the Investigative Professional Association of Georgia."

I pulled out my wallet. I'm glad I remembered to cram all that stuff back into it when I was at our apartment.

"Here's the Private Investigator's license, and the company also holds a Security Agency license, the number is on my business card." I said.

"Thank you."

He checked them, quickly scribbling my PI number on the back of my business card, then handed the PI license back to me.

Both Cassandra and I took the test when we first came to Atlanta, it was easier than the California test, and a lot cheaper. Many other states don't even have an oversight board for PIs and we were surprised that Georgia did.

"So, why don't you think he died from natural causes?" I repeated.

"His beneficiary is a corporation that exists as a post office box in the Cayman Islands," Allan Katzen said. "We hired another investigator to locate any real person connected with the corporation and he couldn't find anybody. In fact, that investigator's life was threatened several times by unknown people, I even understand that he was shot at on one occasion. He dropped the case rather than be killed."

"That sounds like the police would be interested," I commented.

"I think the police detective assigned to the Belchamp case is interested, but he cannot find any hard evidence to indicate anything but a heart attack," Katzen said, with a note of regret. "The deceased left one widow, and one adult son, neither one of them appear to be beneficiaries to our insurance policy."

"Have you gotten a death certificate yet?" I asked.

53

"We haven't officially asked yet, but my contact said it will be ready in two days." Allen paused. "The legal firm for the Cayman Island corporation hasn't contacted us yet either."

"Who did the autopsy?"

"The Fulton County Medical Examiner's office."

"What did they find?"

"Advanced heart disease," Allan replied, sounding frustrated by this case already. "They said it appeared that he had a heart attack and that he probably died from it."

"Probably?" I asked. "That's a strange way to put it."

"That's what we think too."

"Didn't he have a physical before he was insured?" I asked.

I couldn't see a major company insuring a heart attack waiting to happen for millions.

"He did, but I think we might have a problem with that," Allan sounded grim.

"If he faked the exam, can't you cancel the policy?" I asked, knowing he couldn't for some reason.

"His physical description, and blood type is the same as the deceased, but the report didn't have any indication, or history of heart trouble, not even high blood pressure."

"And, I suppose the physician didn't take his picture?" I asked.

"Yes, the picture is of the deceased, but I have to think it was added after the exam by someone," Allan Katzen replied.

"Why is that?"

"Check the picture for yourself."

Allan nodded towards the folder he had on the desk in front of me.

"He appears heavier than the two twenty seven the exam says he is, and he seems like a physical disaster compared to the test results from the exam."

"Didn't your company request his medical records from his family physician?" I asked.

"We did, and they are supposed to be in there," Allan answered. "But, as you see, they aren't there any more."

"Did his widow ask for another autopsy?" I asked. "Even

54

though she wouldn't get the five million, she should want to know if her husband was murdered or not."

The man in front of me didn't seem nervous, annoyed.

"One might think so," he answered. "But, she had the body cremated within a day of being released from the coroner's office."

"That's quick, the undertaker shouldn't have done anything without a death certificate, it seems strange," I began to think out loud. "Maybe the widow, or the son set up the off shore corporation and killed the man for the tax free money?"

"That's the first thing we though of, but we'll have to prove it." Allan leaned forward. "There's no way in hell this company is going to send a five million dollar check to a post office box in the Cayman Islands, especially for a claim that seems so damned bogus."

"So, you want me to find out who's behind the post office box?"

"For that information, we're willing to pay you two fifty a day plus expenses." Allan leaned even more towards me. "But, for the hundred thousand, we want you to prove that his death was due to murder, and that this murder was for the purpose of collecting the five million payout. On the other hand, if you could prove that the man we insured was not, in fact, Mr. Belchamp, we would also be willing to part with the large fee. If either of those possibilities are true, we legally don't have to pay; I have this hunch that this is whole thing is some elaborate fraud."

"If your company doesn't have to pay the five million, I get one hundred thousand, right?"

"Is that a problem?" Allan sat back in his chair.

"Not at all." I smiled. "I do it all the time, it's legal, and it's even moral. But I have to tell you it won't be easy since the body is a pile of ashes right now."

"I have all the information you'll need in this folder." Allan tapped the plump folder on his desk. "I even got a copy of the Coroner's preliminary findings; it took some doing, but I know the right people. Please don't let that report out of your sight."

"You said the certificate will be signed and released in two days?"

"The word I have is that it was already signed when the

55

funeral home took the body, but the coroner decided to take it back for some reason and won't release it until tomorrow at the earliest." Mr. Katzen studied me carefully. "It might be advantageous if you can come up with something before then to cause the police to look deeper into this case."

"That's less than a day." I shook my head. "I doubt if I can have something that soon, maybe in a few days."

"The sooner the better."

"I brought our standard contract for you to sign."

I pulled one out from my inside coat pocket and handed it to him.

"Let me have our lawyer check it right away, I should be able to sign it before you leave today."

He took it and pressed a button on his expensive intercom. His secretary rushed into the office, he handed my contract to her.

"Please have George look at this right away, I would like to sign it now."

"While we're waiting, can we go over a few things?" I watched the secretary leave, then I turned to face Allan.

"What?"

"What do you know about the Cayman Island corporation?" I asked. "What connections to this country are there?

"Their lawyer is in Washington, DC." Allan Katzen replied. "And, the bank transfer is supposed to use a New York bank, all of that information is in the packet I gave you."

"Is that all?"

"As far as I know, yes." Allan seemed to study me for a second. "That's why we're hiring you, we need someone to find out more."

"Who was this alleged murder victim?"

I didn't even know that yet.

"His name was Simon Belchamp, he was fifty two years old. I think I already told you he was married and had one son, the son is twenty nine years old. All three of them live in Decatur. The son is married and has two children. Simon Belchamp owned two Chevrolet dealerships, one was in Decatur, and the other one was in Chamblee. The Chamblee dealership also sold Cadillacs. His son was the sales manager for both dealerships. His financials are in the information I gave you, but his net worth seems to be less than five hundred thousand, besides the house he lives in."

"That seems a little low, doesn't it?"

Actually it sounded high to me, but I don't own two car dealerships.

"It is, considering someone in his position should be worth four times that. The dealerships seems to be going well, but the profits were down over last five years. I'm not a car dealer either, but the profits seem awfully low to me."

"Why did he have that much insurance?"

"If the five million is really for the dealerships, I would assumed it was to cover the possible damage to the businesses if he were to die suddenly." Allan thought for a second. "Even if the Cayman Islands corporation is a front for the dealerships, that doesn't wash."

"Why?"

"The gross income for both dealerships last year was around eleven million which isn't that high; the profit margin was slim, but reasonable. If he were to die, the income wouldn't dry up, and if the family wants to sell, the price should not be affected at all by his death."

"Again," I continued. "Why the big insurance policy?"

"I don't know."

"Who sold the policy, and how long has it been in effect?"

"The salesman who wrote it is no longer with us, and it's been in effect for a little over one year."

"This would be the salesman who would have arranged the physical for Mr. Belchamp, right?" I asked.

"Exactly," he agreed.

"Where can I find this salesman?"

"We thought he had moved to Washington or northern Virginia, but we cannot find him there."

"I hope you have information on him in that envelope."

"Information and his picture," Allan replied

"What about the doctor who gave the physical?" I asked.

"The physician is right here in Atlanta," Allan said. "Our

last private investigator said the doctor was on vacation, but we have all the information on him in the file you now have."

"Sir." Allan's secretary came back into the room. "Mr. Wilson said there should be no problem with this contract."

"Great."

Allan Katzen took my contract, signed it and handed it to me.

"I'll get started right away."

I signed the contract, tore off the back page, and gave Allan the top two pages.

9

Call me when you get there

It didn't take me long to get back to our apartment building where I spotted Mrs. Smith sweeping the front porch as I walked around from the garage.

"When did you get back, Mr. Katz?" She asked.

Mrs. Smith lived in the front one bedroom apartment, 1-A. She was somewhere in her late sixties, about five foot even and always dressed in bright colors. Mrs. Smith was thin and had let her hair go completely white. Her husband had worked at the Doraville Ford assembly plant from the time they were first married, until he died of a stroke five years before. Since her only income consisted of some money from his retirement and a little from social security, she was forced to sell their home and move into that small apartment about two years ago, Mrs. Smith moved in before Cassandra and I took possession of the building. She always seemed to have a glass half full view of life which was making me grow to like that woman.

"I got in early this morning, Mrs. Smith." I smiled at her. "And, I wish you'd call me Benjamin."

"I suppose I should, Benjamin."

She glanced away from me for a moment, as if she was embarrassed to say the next phrase.

"Did Cassandra come back with you? I have to say I'm happy you two got married."

"Thank you, Cassandra will be back in a few days." I leaned against the front railing. "Did you have any trouble collecting the rents?"

"No, not at all." She propped her broom against the corner of the front porch railing. "The folks who live here are the best, I wouldn't expect any trouble from any of them."

"You know, Mrs. Smith, would you like to be the manager of this building? We would cut your rent down to twenty five dollars a

59

month."

Maybe I should have talked to Cassandra first, but sometimes I like making spur of the moment decisions; some of the decisions even work out well.

"Oh, what would I have to do?"

She sat down, a little suddenly, in the only chair on the porch which was an old rusty metal chair that she had wiped off not two minutes before.

"Just collect the rents and deposit them into the bank up the street. If something breaks, call the repairmen and tell us about it, we wouldn't want you to do anything else. We'll pay the bills, keep the books and we'll handle all the really bad stuff like evictions or legal things if necessary."

"I'll have to think about it," she sounded more cautious than usual.

"With the kind of work Cassandra and I do, we're gone a lot and you've been a godsend to us these past few months. I would rather have you do the management than pay an outside real estate firm to do it."

"Are you two really private investigators?" She asked. "That sounds dangerous."

"We're private investigators, and it's not all that dangerous." I tried to disarm her with my winning smile.

"Like in the TV shows?" She shook her head. "I could never do something like that."

"Trust me." I shifted slightly, the railing was pinching my butt. "Our work isn't anything like the detectives on TV, it's usually a lot more boring than that."

"Well, do you have a case now?" It seemed she was searching for something pleasant to say, more than being nosey.

"As a matter of a fact, we do have a case from an insurance company right now," I replied.

"What is it?" She asked quickly.

"Nothing unusual."

I thought for a minute; maybe she needs some excitement in her life other than the daytime soaps.

"We do these investigations all the time. Before an insurance company pays out a large settlement, they investigate the death more deeply than the police do."

"They want to make sure before they pay out that much," Mrs. Smith repeated the gist of what I had said. "How much is it for?"

"I can't tell you that, Mrs. Smith." I slowly shook my head.

"More than a million?"

"Maybe," I cautiously answered. "But, what about you being our building manager?"

"It hasn't been that much trouble for me so far." She appeared to be thinking out loud. "I could use the extra money, so perhaps I will."

"I'd love it if you did," I insisted. "You can think it over some more, maybe wait until Cassandra gets back, and tell both of us your answer."

"Thank you, Benjamin, thank you for thinking so highly of me."

She remained on the metal chair as I rushed back up to our apartment.

I dialed Cassandra's number in Huntington Beach quickly, maybe I could get her before she left for campus.

"Hi sweetheart," I brightly said.

"It must be my absent husband."

Her voice sounded extra good to me.

"That still sounds strange to me."

"How about, it must be my long lost lover," Cassandra chuckled.

"Now, that sounds more like it."

I did miss her after less than two days.

"What's happening?" I could hear her shift gears. "Does the case seem viable?"

"What happened to all the 'I miss you' stuff?"

I sort of wanted to dwell on the lovey-dovey part a bit longer.

"I have to meet with my committee, then I have to get to the closing for our sale."

"Your defense is today?" I asked.

Of course it was, I knew that.

"You know it is."

"I should have waited to come back here."

I could sense the nervousness in her voice.

"No, no, I'll do much better if you aren't there staring at me." Cassandra was certain about this. "I need to concentrate on the questions they'll ask. If you're there, I might not focus too well."

"You focus just fine." I grinned.

"That's what I mean," Cassandra sighed. "Take it as a complement that you distract me."

"You'll do fine." I was nervous for her. "They all love you anyway."

"I can always hope so," she groaned a little.

"You have a lot to do today." I snapped back to business quickly.

"Yes, I do." Cassandra sucked in a tense breath. "I have to leave in fifteen minutes to make it all on time."

"At least this means you'll be through after today is over." I smiled to myself. "And, we can have a nice long time together over the holidays."

"After you clear this case, that is," she sounded more nervous. "I need to get going."

"Right," I had to talk faster. "The insurance company signed a contract; they gave me a big file of information on the deceased. He was raised in Colorado Springs, so maybe you could fly there on the way back to Atlanta and do a little searching into his past."

"Can you get the information to me soon?" Cassandra asked.

"I can fax it to our soon to be sold, LA branch," I answered. "Do you suppose they could send the pages to the closing?"

"If you get off the phone quickly so I can call the office and beg for the favor right now."

"I'll give you a big wet kiss good bye over the phone, and hang up right now, I suppose."

"I love you very much too, Benjamin," Cassandra said. "I'll call as soon as I get to Colorado Springs, fax the stuff right away."

I spent the next ten minutes quickly pawing through the stack of information Allan Katzen had given me. I looked for anything Cassandra could use, stacked it up and fed it into the fax machine we kept on a low wooden table against the wall next to the window facing Euclid Avenue.

. . . .

"Congratulations, Dr. Katz." Bernard Hiller stood up and extended his hand to Cassandra.

Her defense was held in a large lecture room where she and her committee were seated around a long table at the front of the room. Depending on how important the major professor, or the subject of the dissertation, there may be from one to twenty other graduate students and faculty observing. Sometimes a faculty member from the audience would even ask a question; thirty seven people observed Cassandra's defense.

"Thank you, Dr. Hiller."

Cassandra stood up and shook his hand. At first a few observers were clapping, then the whole room applauded for a minute or so as Cassandra blushed slightly and glanced around the room. Up until it was over, she was afraid to focus on anybody other than her committee, but when she saw Mary Hatton sitting next to Albert and Annie, she smiled; friends from her other life did show up. She was sad Benjamin couldn't make it, but this was almost as good. The rest of the crowd were her fellow grad students and faculty she had known for years. A mixture of relief, excitement and contentment washed over her, life was very good then. This was one of those moments in a person's life that will remain on the top of the brain; this was a transition from a part time student to a full time, something. Cassandra mulled over the several transitions she had gone through in the past two months. She was now married, she had signed an ironclad contract with the CIA, she was no longer a student, she was Dr. Katz.

"We would like to take you to lunch." Bernard leaned towards Cassandra. "Sort of a celebration."

"I would love to but I have to go to a closing at two this afternoon and I have a flight leaving tonight."

Cassandra began to blush a bit more as fellow students now gathered around her to shake her hand and hug her.

63

"On the day of your defense?" Dr. Hiller seemed surprised.

"I didn't know you owned property in California?" George Placer stepped into the conversation.

Dr. Placer was the youngest member of Cassandra's committee, he was the only male member to have an obvious crush on her.

"It's our detective agency here in Los Angeles that we're selling today." Cassandra grinned at him. "The lawyers have more of a say in when the closing is than I do."

"Where are you going after the closing?" George asked.

"Oooh! Congratulations, Dr. Katz!" Annie ran up to Cassandra and hugged her.

"Thank you, Annie." Cassandra beamed and hugged back. "Let me introduce you to my committee."

"Hi." Annie smiled at the two faculty members in front of her.

"This is Dr. George Placer, and this is Dr. Bernard Hiller." Cassandra touched each man on his arm as she introduced them.

"And these are my friends Albert and Annie Chou, and, this is Mary Hatton."

"Annie Chou, the artist?" George stared at her.

"I have one of your paintings." Bernard stared at Annie.

"That must be me." Annie hopped a little bounce as she patted her chest.

"We'll wait back there." Albert pointed to the door. "It was nice meeting all of you."

"You know Annie Chou?" George seemed impressed.

"They're real good friends of my husband."

Cassandra didn't know Annie's reputation was that good.

"I'm continually surprised by you."

Bernard looked at Cassandra in amazement and shook his head slowly.

"I only wish I had known more of your other life sooner."

"Say," George interrupted. "If you ever need an aging, out of shape professor in your new agency, let me know."

"I take it Dr. Hiller told you about the money thing."

Cassandra slightly blushed. "It'll be awhile before our new agency is up to that level."

"Well, when it is, give me a call."

"I do need to get going if I expect to get to the closing in time," Cassandra said. "I'll be back here after the holidays and I expect to take the whole committee up on that lunch offer."

"That would be fine." Bernard nodded. "All of us should be here after the fifth or so."

. . . .

"That was a lot more interesting than I thought it would be."

Albert hugged Cassandra as she walked to the back door of the conference room.

"And, even I understood most of it," Mary said as the four of them walked into the hall. "You were crystal clear on so many of the answers."

"Thank you all, I want to plan a big party for all of you when I get back here in January."

"You and Katz are going to France for the holidays?" Albert asked.

"Yes," she answered. "But, we have an insurance case to finish before we leave."

"You need to slow down," Mary sounded worried.

"Finishing this degree will help that a lot," Cassandra sighed.

"I think you and Benjamin need to take six months off after all this." Annie tugged at Cassandra's arm. "I mean it."

"You're right," Cassandra acknowledged. "But, first the closing, then the case, then the holidays with my folks, then the big blow out in January with you guys."

"At least that won't be stressful." Albert smiled.

Cassandra appeared sad as well as hassled.

"I have to get to the closing in forty minutes, or Benjamin will soil his britches."

. . . .

It was a weekday, so the Medical Examiner's office was open and Dr. Jenkins had agreed to speak to me about Simon Belchamp. Many tidbits of information were in the packet the insurance executive gave me, except the final death certificate. Mr. Belchamp died in Fulton County, even though his home was in DeKalb county, so this is where the paperwork was. His body was discovered in the parking lot of a restaurant on Ponce de Leon near Peachtree; it might be a good thing to eat lunch there today. A new restaurant and the coroner in the same day, life is challenging sometimes. Dr. Jenkins didn't want to see me until three that afternoon, so why not go out for lunch?

Parking spots were scarce at Mary Mac's, but I found a spot on a side street that didn't seem too dangerous for my Porsche. It was eleven forty five in the morning, and this place had a reasonable crowd inside; the wait was only five minutes or so before being seated. The woman who led me to a table appeared to be in her early twenties, she was plain and wore her long hair spun firmly in a bun attached tightly to the back of her head. It was an older restaurant with many years and many layers of food smells. It seemed fairly clean and well stuffed with patrons at this time of the day, at least it wasn't awash with country music in the background.

"Can I ask you a question?" I stopped walking behind her.
"Sure."
She turned to face me; she didn't seem annoyed, yet.
"I'm investigating the man who died in your parking lot a little over a week ago, and I'd like to talk to the waitress who served him, if that's possible."
"So, you don't want lunch?" She asked me, like a good employee should.
"Yes, I do want lunch." I smiled my best smile. "If you could seat me on one of her tables, that would be great."
"I see," she thought for a second. "Are you a cop? Or a reporter?"
"Neither." I shook my head. "I work for the insurance company who might be paying someone a lot of money when I finish my investigation."
"Sure." She cautiously grinned back at me; I must have said

66

the right thing. "You can sit over there, near the window, I'll tell her you want to talk to her."

"Hi, I'm Luanne, Peggy said you wanted to talk about that guy who died in the parking lot."

The waitress came promptly. She was a middle aged woman with a pleasing face and a strong southern accent.

"Yes." I looked at a plainly printed menu. "But first, what's good to eat here?"

"Well." She studied me carefully. "You could try the Pot Likkers or the fried chicken, almost any veggie is good, and you simply have to have a yeast roll."

"I guess I'll take the fried chicken and potato salad and some of those rolls."

"No, hon." She pointed to the table. "You take one of those pencils and write what you want on that ticket and I'll get it for you. Let me know if you want a breast or three drumsticks too."

"Okay." I proceeded to do just that. "So, you served him that day?"

"Sure did." She nodded. "He had the cheeseburger, Pot Likker, green beans, mashed potatoes and rolls and a piece of apple pie with vanilla ice cream."

"You have to serve a lot of folks here, how did you remember him?" I handed her the meal order I had filled out.

"Oh, he's a regular." She smiled. "He owns a car dealership in Decatur and he came here at least once a week to eat lunch, sometimes twice a week. Sometimes he used to bring some of his employees here too."

"He was alone that day?" I asked.

"Yes, he was." She nodded. "What you want to drink? Tea?"

"No, water will be fine, thanks."

Southern tea tastes like sugar syrup, although I have to admit Moroccan tea tastes a lot sweeter, but at least it's mint tea.

"I gotta get back to work, maybe you can ask me some more questions when I bring your food." She turned and quickly darted towards the back of the restaurant.

I scanned the eating establishment, noticing lots of pictures

67

of what appeared to be important people were hanging on the walls of the several rooms. I observed that the Naugahyde coverings on the booth seats and backs were beginning to show wear; tears were in almost all of them I could see. Maybe this place had seen better days, but I hoped the food would be good, although it was hard to tell from the smells in the place; the overwhelming scent was that of fried chicken. I have discovered that the perfume of fried chicken seems to pervade the entire city of Atlanta, especially around the noon hour.

I was seated at one of the small tables near the row of windows facing out on Ponce. Seated in the booth, between me and the window, was a collection of four women who hotly discussed a party they had been to the night before. It seems that someone's husband was having an affair with a young bank clerk; who cares, besides the wife. At the table behind me sat three stock brokers discussing accounts of the rich and locally famous; remind me never to trust a stock broker.

"Here ya go, hon." My waitress didn't take long bringing my lunch.

The rolls smelled freshly baked, my palate appreciated the hot yeasty smell of the bread, it sort of cleansed my palate before I dug into my lunch.

"How long after he left here did somebody notice him in his car?" I asked the waitress.

I picked up a roll and took a bite which tasted good; I think they used real butter to make these.

"I guess it was an hour or so. A patron found him and got the manager to call the ambulance." She stood by my table, waiting for another question. "I went out on a smoke break and I saw all the cops around his car."

"Did anybody see him talking to someone while he was here?"

I tasted the potato salad which was also good; not great, but good. There was a little too much mayonnaise for my taste, and too much salt; I like New York style better than this.

"Sure," she agreed. "He came here a lot; most of the regulars know him, and all the lunch staff know him too, some of them bought cars from him. He always spoke to folks he knew

68

when he came in."

"I have to ask, who are all the people in the pictures on the wall around here?"

"Oh." She smiled as she looked at some of them. "They're famous politicians and local celebrities who have eaten here, this place is the best lunch in town and everybody who is anybody in Atlanta eats here."

"If you think of anything that was unusual that day, or anybody who acted strange, please give me a call."

I stuck my hand into my left pocket for my folding money and peeled off a twenty, I then pulled a business card out of my inside coat pocket and handed both to the waitress.

"I'll give it some thought." She stuffed both my card and the money into her pocket. "Thanks, hon."

She quickly walked back into her waitressing.

The chicken was not that good, but the price was fine; maybe in the next few years, I'll acquire a taste for this cooking. I left the waitress a nice tip, perhaps she would think of something. The twenty was an expense for the insurance company anyway.

10

And, then there were two?

Cassandra was able to close on our former Los Angeles agency. I was only slightly sorry to see it go, but Cassandra has always felt nostalgic about it. That was the business I had started when we first met, and where she and I grew our professional and personal relationship. I didn't like the last office space we rented there because it didn't have any character, it was a modern office on an upper floor of a big rectangular building with no character at all. Although, I think the reasons Cassandra liked the Los Angeles office were more metaphoric than otherwise.

The final amount we got in the closing check was a little less than we had expected, but the lawyer had to charge for six hours more, and we had to pay a bit more in our share of California taxes. We had to give a quarter of it back to the Company, but that could have been worse too. The government had wanted to keep all of my profits since they claimed I was an employee of theirs so the profit was theirs. Discussions on high levels arrived at the compromise that I could keep half of my share of the profits, and Cassandra could keep all her share since she wasn't a government employee while the profit accumulated. All in all, one hundred and ninety seven thousand dollars for the two of us is still a lot of money. The government had already taken their share from the deal on closing. Cassandra had the lawyer wire the gross proceeds to our bank in Atlanta, she always was the more practical one. I would have loved to carry that much cash around, even for a little while.

Finding a flight to Colorado Springs that night was impossible, but Cassandra was able to fly out of Los Angeles at six the next morning.

Cassandra wasn't able to concentrate on any of the papers I

had faxed her until after she arrived in Colorado Springs. She knew she couldn't check into her hotel room that early in the morning, but the hotel did keep her suitcases locked up until the room would be ready after lunch. She sat in the small lobby and read all the information I had sent her.

Simon Belchamp's parents had died years ago. He had a sister who still lived there, so Cassandra decided that would be a good place to start. The sister, Ellie Gumps, lived in a subdivision off Garden of the Gods Road; Cassandra loved that name, that would even be better than living on Easy Street. The hotel clerk was happy to draw a map to Ellie Gumps' house for Cassandra.

Driving up into the foothills with the morning sun shining on the eastern side of the mountains was a beautiful trip. The neighborhood was a relatively new one, all the houses were shiny and well maintained. Ellie lived close to the entrance of the neighborhood, only three houses up on the left. Cassandra parked her rental car on the street and walked to the front door. The morning was crisp, about ten degrees and only patches of snow were on the ground which was unusual for late November.

"Good morning," Cassandra said.

Her breath condensed on leaving her mouth. It was about nine o'clock in the morning and Ellie was still in her robe with a cup of steaming coffee in her left hand as she opened the door.

"Yes, may I help you?"

Ellie seemed curious as she stared at Cassandra through the storm door.

"My name is Cassandra Katz, and I'm a private investigator investigating your brother's death."

"Who?" Ellie stared blankly at Cassandra.

"I'm sorry, I thought someone would have contacted you by now, Simon Belchamp passed away about a week ago in Atlanta."

Cassandra guessed no one had told her. Why?

"Simon's dead?" Ellie took in a deep breath. "Who are you?"

"My name is Cassandra Katz, I work for the insurance company, your brother had quite a large policy with them and they have to investigate the death before paying out."

71

Cassandra shivered; it was cold, and she had just come from sunny California.

"Oh." Ellie noticed Cassandra shivering. "Please come in, you must be cold out there."

"Thank you." Cassandra pulled her identification from her purse. "Here's my ID, it's cold out there."

"You want some coffee?"

Ellie motioned for Cassandra to go into the kitchen.

"That would be great, I got in on a flight this morning."

Cassandra looked around Ellie's two story home. Walking through a small entrance hall, Cassandra glanced into the living room to her left, it was bright. Two large windows had a south easterly view. The stairs led straight up on the right side of the entrance hallway. Through the living room was the dining room, and off to the right was the kitchen. Ellie had many family photos hanging on walls and on tables in the living room. The house had a slightly stale odor to it; it was winter and homes were tightly sealed now.   A fresh aroma of orange juice, toast, and coffee hung over the stale background smell.

The large kitchen seemed less cluttered, perhaps this was the real public space in Ellie's house. Cassandra thought to herself that the floor plan left a lot to be desired, but she didn't live there so it didn't matter.   A bulky oval breakfast table with the remains of Ellie's breakfast and the morning paper on it hunkered in the back corner away from the large window over the sink. A door in the opposite wall seemed to lead to the garage.

"I could make you something to eat, if you want?" Ellie asked.

She sat in her chair at the breakfast table.

"No, thanks." Cassandra smiled at her again. "I have a lot to do while I'm in town."

"What did he die from?" Ellie put her coffee cup down.

"The coroner said he probably died from a heart attack."

Cassandra glanced at the woman in front of her; Ellie seemed sad, but not that sad.

"I'm not surprised." She shook her head. "I'm sorry, I was supposed to get you some coffee."

Ellie stood up and headed to the sink.

"Thanks." Cassandra needed caffeine. "When did you last see your brother?"

"The last time I saw him was at our mother's funeral."

Ellie grabbed a cup from a cupboard and poured coffee into it.

"That was eight years ago, before that I saw him at our father's funeral, and that was eleven years ago," she added.

"Did you two phone or write much?"

Cassandra wondered why the distance between them.

"Not much." Ellie put the cup in front of Cassandra. "We exchange Christmas cards, not much else. The sugar and cream are right there."

She pointed to them on the table.

"Thanks." Cassandra poured cream into her cup. "Does he have many relatives out here?"

"Our parents had just the two of us," Ellie answered. "We were both adopted, you know."

"No, I didn't." Cassandra stirred her coffee.

"I looked my real birth mother up five years ago."

Ellie seemed to want to tell this stranger the story.

"It was right after I divorced my husband and I thought I had cancer. It turns out I didn't but I was afraid I had a predisposition to cancer from my biological family. I guess that was my subconscious telling me I had to find my birth mother."

"How did you locate your real mother?"

"My real mother is the woman who raised me." Ellie seemed a little uncomfortable. "I don't mean to be short, but I loved my mom, the woman who raised me that is, the other mother was my birth mother. I have two separate places in my heart for each of them."

"Is your birth mother still alive?"

"She passed last year."

"I'm sorry."

Cassandra had to get the discussion back on track.

"How did you locate her?" Cassandra asked.

"Both my brother and I were adopted from the same

73

agency." Ellie straightened herself up in her chair, then stared directly at Cassandra. "That was fifty seven years ago for me, and the county welfare agency was the only game in town unless the adopting family knew the family of the pregnant girl."

"Were you adopted through the county?"

"Both of us were," Ellie said. "My adoptive parents were always up front with my brother and me, they told us that ever since I can remember so there wouldn't be any surprises when we grew up."

"Did they know who your birth parents were?"

"No," she thought for a second. "I don't think they knew, maybe they had an idea. This wasn't that big a town back then in the twenties, so maybe they had an idea but the welfare folks would never tell."

"Then, how did you find out?"

"There's a national organization that will help us find our birth parents." Ellie sank back in her chair. "You tell them what agency did the adoption, and the date of the adoption and they will do the rest."

"How do they get around the privacy rules?"

"They work with the agency and act as a third party. If the mother doesn't want contact, it ends there with me never knowing, but, if the mother wants contact, this advocacy group arranges a meeting."

"It must have worked out for you," Cassandra said.

"Yes, it did." Ellie smiled broadly. "I did write Simon and tell him he could find his birth family, but he never answered me."

"When did your brother leave home?"

Somehow the brother's birth family bothered Cassandra, it was one of those hunches that pulled at her gut until she did something about it.

"He was drafted for the Korean war."

Ellie stared at the ceiling, as if to remember the past better.

"He graduated from high school right after World War two was over, and he got a job at the Ford dealer in town as a mechanic. He was doing great, and he loved his job a lot. He had moved into an apartment in town, and he had a steady girlfriend. He didn't mind going into the army, though, he sort of felt bad about not being quite old enough to enlist during the big war."

"Did he marry his girlfriend here?"

"No," Ellie answered. "After he got out of the army in fifty three, he never came back here. He went to Fort Benning to train, and he liked Georgia because it was warmer in the winter, so he went there to live after the army."

"Did he visit you and the folks much after that?"

Cassandra wondered how much of a connection to Colorado was there for this dead man.

"He did for about five or so years, but he married a Georgia girl, and he sort of stopped coming back here after that."

Ellie noticed Cassandra's empty coffee cup.

"Do you want more?" She asked.

"No." Cassandra stood up. "I guess I'd better get going, I have to get a lot done today before I fly out tomorrow."

"Thanks for telling me Simon has died. I don't think that wife of his would have ever contacted me."

Ellie stood and followed her to the front door.

"You two didn't get along?"

This may be something.

"His wife is straight out of a trailer park," Ellie informed me, with her hand on the front door knob. "I know that sounds catty, but she has one huge inferiority complex. My ex-husband is a surgeon in Denver, and back then when they would come out for a Christmas visit, my sister-in-law would sulk about for a week and make snipping remarks about my husband, my career, his career or our house and cars, it was all about the status stuff."

"So, you think she's why Simon stopped visiting you and his parents?"

"Yes, I do."

Ellie seemed to be getting worked up about it after all these years.

"Well," Cassandra paused.

When you gotta go, it's best to leave on a good note.

"You have been so much help. And, I'm sorry I had to be the one to tell you about your brother," she added.

75

"I'm glad you did tell me or I might not have known for months," Ellie said.

She opened the door; it was colder than Cassandra had remembered and it was only November. What would it be like here in February?

. . . .

The same clerk was at the hotel when Cassandra got back from Ellie Gumps' house. Her room was ready, and they had already delivered her suitcases to it.

"Hello, Benjamin?"

"Sweetie," I blurted out. "Did everything go all right? Did you pass everything? I know you did fine," I couldn't shut up.

"Everything went fine."

"You're through with everything? No more hurdles?"

"I'm finished," Cassandra expelled her breath, relief.

"Congratulations," I beamed. "I'm both proud of you, and sad that couldn't be there."

"That's okay," she said.

From her voice I couldn't tell if it was all right, I needed to see her.

"No, it's not okay," I insisted. "I wanted to be there."

"No, it's really all right," she assured me. "It sort of hit home, the life I have with you is quite separate from my academic life. I'm no longer a student, I'm a real academic now, I need to integrate the pieces together myself over the next few years."

"You sound like you're giving this some serious thought."

"Yeah, I am."

"I want to mull it over with you," I insisted. "So many threads hold our lives together now, but, it's our lives, together."

"You say the right things at the right times."

"I hate to do this, but I would like to finish this case quickly so we can have a nice long holiday together."

"I'll be there tomorrow, most likely."

I could tell from her voice, she was missing me too.

"What've you found out?" I asked.

76

"I spoke to his sister, she doesn't have too must kindness for the dead guy's wife. You may want to talk to the widow yourself." Cassandra was ready for business. "Simon Belchamp was adopted, and I can't say why, but I'm gong to see if I can find out who his real parents were."

"That sounds like a good idea," I thought out loud. "Has he been back there recently?"

"Not according to his sister," Cassandra said. "She said he hasn't been back in about eight years."

"Okay," I said. "Let me know when your flight gets in and I'll meet you at Hartsfield."

"Love you a lot." Cassandra smiled into the phone. "And, I want to love you a lot."

"Love you too." I felt her warmth.

. . . .

"We're not going to tell you anything," The obstinate clerk insisted.

The woman straightened her skirt out as she sat bolt upright in her chair. The county worker was about thirty years old and seemed to be insulted that she was asked the question.

"Look." Cassandra smiled her professional smile. "Like I said, I work for an insurance company that underwrote a multi-million dollar policy on this man. He's dead, and most likely his birth mother is also dead. The insurance company thinks there might have been suspicious circumstances behind his death, and this might be a lead in a potential murder case."

"How do I know you work for an insurance company?"

The woman seemed to back down a bit; she leaned forward a little and lost some of her defiance.

"Here's the insurance company and their phone number." Cassandra handed her a sheet of paper. "The Vice President's name is Mr. Katzen, my company is Cheshire Katz and we are doing the investigation for him, my name is Cassandra Katz."

"Okay."

She stared at the paper for a full fifteen seconds, deciding on

77

what to do. She picked up the phone and dialed, luckily Allan Katzen was in his office. He figured out that Cassandra was a partner, and that our firm was hard at work for him.

"Will you help me?" Cassandra asked politely as the office manager hung up the phone.

"Will you promise that you will not reveal any of the information I decide to share with you?"

"Yes, I promise," Cassandra promptly replied.

The manager stood, and walked into a back room, reappearing in five minutes with an old folder.

"You're lucky that we haven't sent these files back to Denver for storage yet."

"So, you have his file? What can you tell me?"

It could be that today will be a lucky day.

"Simon Belchamp was born to a Mary Peavey on March twenty third nineteen twenty eight, no father is listed," The woman took a breath. "He was adopted by the Belchamp family when he was three months old."

"Anything else?" There had to at least some more information.

"The Belchamps already had one adopted daughter."

The office manager was reading the typed and handwritten sheets, flipping them in the folder as she finished each page.

"And, the boy had a twin brother."

"Simon Belchamp had a twin brother?" Cassandra repeated slowly. "Why didn't the Belchamps adopt the twin brother?"

"It doesn't say." The woman looked up at Cassandra. "That was a long time ago, and I haven't a clue as to why or how anything happened back then."

"Does it say who adopted the brother?"

"Not in Simon Belchamp's file it doesn't." The woman became defensive again.

"Is there any way I could get the name of Simon Belchamp's brother?"

"I don't see how."

The woman paged through the rest of the folder, stopping on the last page.

"His brother's name is George Blanchard."

"I thought you couldn't tell from that file."

"It appears that Simon Belchamp requested to find his birth mother about two years ago."

The woman pulled out the last sheet of paper in the file.

"I guess the person in this office then gave the finding agency the name of his brother since his mother was deceased."

"It says that?"

"Yes, it says that," The woman said sarcastically.

"Does it say where George Blanchard is?"

Cassandra knew her luck was gone.

"No, It doesn't." The woman's sarcasm increased.

"Well, what was the first names of his adoptive parents?"

How long would this woman answer any questions, let's find out.

"It doesn't say." The woman closed the folder and tossed it onto her desk.

"Can you see if the Blanchard file is still in your vault?" Cassandra forced a bigger smile. "Please?"

The woman leveled a hateful glare at Cassandra, but went back into the records room anyway. She came back out in two minutes with a scrap of paper.

"The adopted father's name was John, and the mother's name was Sarah, they were both from here, but the father was in the army; I guess they came back home to adopt a child. The family's permanent address was Washington DC, he was a captain in the army. No other information was in the records."

"Well, thanks for all the help."

Cassandra stood and left quickly. Leaving was a good idea before the woman took a swing at her. She was helpful, even though she didn't want to be.

City directories are a treasure trove of information. A quick call to the library led Cassandra to the old building next to the Penrose Public Library on North Cascade Avenue. Starting with nineteen hundred, she found a few Blanchards in Colorado Springs. After what seemed like forever at a microfilm reader, she found John Blanchard as a child in the nineteen hundred census records, then

79

back to the city directories to confirm where they lived, and how long they lived there. John Blanchard was twelve years old in the nineteen hundred census and his parents were John and Beulah Blanchard; his father was a carpenter for the city. After four hours in the library, Cassandra was able to narrow down the Blanchards left in town who might know anything about the couple who adopted the twin brother of the dead man fifty two years ago; not an easy task, but similar to what a graduate student goes through on a daily basis, at least she kept telling herself that.

....

"Can I talk to you about a John Blanchard who was born here in eighteen eighty seven?" Cassandra asked.

The woman in front of Cassandra was in her early sixties. She lived in a cramped apartment in a working class neighborhood near the edge of downtown. It was a little before three in the afternoon and the sun was low in the sky, close to the mountains and it was getting a lot colder.

"That's way before my time."

The woman didn't open the storm door, she peered through the glass at Cassandra.

"I think I remember a John in our family, but I don't know."

"Is there anyone who might?" Cassandra was hopeful.

"Maybe my mother," The woman cautiously answered her. "She's in a home up towards the hills; she's ninety two, but she's still sharp as a tack. She likes visitors and she'll talk your ear off."

It wasn't a long drive to the nursing home which was situated slightly west of town, into the hills. An aide pointed Cassandra to Ruth Johnston who was sitting in a wheelchair in the large recreation room of the home, in front of a large picture window with a view of Pike's Peak. The sun had set, a bright red glow of reflected sunlight off the evening clouds streamed through the picture window. Cassandra pulled a chair next to Ruth Johnston's wheelchair.

"I always come here to admire the sunsets." Ruth didn't turn to Cassandra. "At my age, you never know when it may be the last one."

80

"I don't think age has anything to do with taking in such a show."

Cassandra stared out the window with the old woman in silence for a full minute.

"Who are you?" Ruth turned to face Cassandra. "I don't know you, do I?"

"No, Ma'am, you don't."

Cassandra held out her right hand towards the elderly woman.

"I'm searching for relatives of John Blanchard."

"The son was my cousin, his father was my uncle." She gently shook Cassandra's hand, thinking of the past. "They were both John Blanchard."

"I know."

Cassandra moved her chair so she could see the woman better.

"I'm interested in the son, the one who was in the army."

"Yes, yes." Ruth turned back towards the window. "Could you move me to face you, I can't push this thing so well anymore."

"Sure." Cassandra positioned Ruth's wheel chair facing her seat. "I need to find the boy they adopted here in Colorado Springs in nineteen twenty eight or nine."

"John junior." Ruth started to become lost in her thoughts. "That's what we called him, he and I were born the same year. He graduated from the School of Mines, he was the first one in the family to go to college. We were all so proud of him, his dad was the proudest. John junior went into the army after college as a lieutenant, he was a horse soldier at first, then he went into artillery. He served in Texas, then went to upstate New York, then went to Washington, DC if I remember right."

"Was he in Washington when they adopted the boy?" Cassandra asked.

She had to get her back on track.

"I think so," Ruth pondered awhile. "Yes, they were in Washington, he and his wife came back home for their month vacation, they did that once a year back then. Like clockwork, they would spend a month each summer back here with the family."

"Did you know the boy they adopted?"

Stay on track, please.

"Yes," Ruth thought again for a full thirty seconds. "He would come back home with them for summer vacation until John junior was killed."

"When was that?" Cassandra asked.

"Sometime around nineteen thirty five." Ruth's expression turned sad quickly. "He died in a car accident, that was so sad. Sarah stayed in Washington after that, I think she married again, but I'm not sure; Sarah was John junior's wife, you know. Sarah couldn't have children, and they tried for so long to have one of their own, but they finally decided to adopt. John junior was almost forty when they adopted that baby, Sarah was ten years younger than John junior, you know."

"Yes, Ma'am."

That's enough information for now, please.

"You're a pretty young girl." Ruth sized up Cassandra for the first time. "Why are you asking about John junior? Are you a relation?"

"No, Ma'am." Cassandra slowly shook her head. "The adopted son had a twin brother, and that brother died a week ago; I am trying to locate his twin to tell him the news."

"Dead?" Ruth shook her head. "So young too, I am sorry about that. I hope I helped you."

"Do you know if Sarah Blanchard remarried?" Cassandra tried again.

"I think she did, but I'm not sure."

"Did she ever write to John junior's family after he died?"

"Not to me, but maybe to my mom." Ruth shook her head. "I don't know, she sort of went on about her business after a year or so, she wasn't blood kin after all."

"Did Sarah's folks come from here?"

Cassandra didn't want to start another all day search, but maybe she would have to.

"No, her family were ranchers out of Pueblo." Ruth seemed confused for a moment. "I never knew much about her family."

"Well." Cassandra stood up. "Thanks, but I have to get

ready to fly back east tomorrow."

"You can stay and have supper with me, they let us have guests you know." Ruth seemed hopeful.

"You have been a delight to talk to, but I do have an early flight, and I have three or four things to do before then. Thank you for talking to me."

Cassandra leaned over and hugged the woman.

"No, thank you." Ruth's expression lit up. "I don't get many visitors anymore. Most of my friends are dead and my daughter hardly ever comes by for a visit."

11

Come out, come out, wherever you are

I found a parking garage near the Medical Examiner's office and parked my Porsche next to a column, hoping for the best. It was a typical government office, and seemed well staffed. The glare of fluorescent lights greeted all as they entered the area. I was there promptly at three, but Dr. Jenkins was not. The Fulton County Medical Examiner's Center was near Grady Hospital and it was getting late in the work day, so foot and car traffic was picking up.

"I'm here for Dr. Jenkins." I smiled at what I assumed was the receptionist."

"Is he expecting you?"

"Yes," I answered, "it's about the Simon Belchamp case.

"And." she looked up at me. "You are?"

"I'm working for his insurance company, if that's what you meant."

I kept my pleasant expression plastered on for a little while longer.

"And, that company would be?" She grilled me more than a receptionist should.

"Here."

I showed her Katzen's business card; she wrote down the name and number.

"Please wait right here, and Dr. Jenkins will see you soon."

She got up and disappeared through one of four doors leading from the waiting area.

A stack of not so old magazines set on the coffee table in front of a row of uncomfortable chairs against the back wall of the waiting area. I pawed through them and picked up a Sports Illustrated that was three months old, at least I hadn't read it before. The strong stench of antiseptic cleanser filled my nostrils and after five minutes, my head began to hurt; it's for sure now, I can't work in a coroner's office. I could wait for a half hour more, then I would have to leave.

"Dr. Jenkins can see you now," The receptionist called out to me from the other side of a half opened door.

"Thanks," I mumbled as I walked through the door and followed her down a hallway.

She opened the third door to her left and motioned for me to enter.

"Mr. Katz." The doctor was standing in front of his desk. "The gentleman from the insurance company got off the phone with me, he asked if this department could cooperate with you in this investigation."

"That would be a big help."

I was still a bit pissy about having to wait forty five minutes, especially since I had gone through most of the normal magazines and was starting to read the collection of hunting magazines in the waiting room.

"I'm sorry you had to wait, but I do have a lot of cases to work on."

Dr. Jenkins was also a little miffed about having to talk to a pesky insurance investigator.

"Can we start over?" I smiled. "The main reason I am here is that a multi-million dollar policy is involved in this death, and we think there might be something unusual about it."

"What? The death or the policy?" Jenkins smiled back.

"Actually both, but maybe you could set me straight on the death."

I lost my super friendly expression, well, I tried to be nice.

"In layman's terms, he died of heart failure."

Jenkins sat down behind his desk and perused several papers in front of him.

"We check into every death in the county and issue death certificates, as well as notify the proper authorities when we suspect foul play in any death."

"Was there any suspicion in Simon Belchamp's death?"

"No." Jenkins looked at the papers. "It appeared to be a heart attack, and we did an autopsy and found damage to his heart as well as advanced blockage on several arteries. His blood chemistry was also consistent with that of a person who had recently had a heart attack."

"Too many pot lickkers, I guess."

I tried to see some of what was on his desk.

"I'll give you copies of some of this paperwork." Dr. Jenkins stapled a few pages together. "But, only because Mr. Katzen asked me to give them to you as a courtesy, and because Mr. Katzen seems to have some influential friends in the city government."

"How many bodies pass through this office a year?" I asked

I wanted to make friends with him since I was starting a business in this town, and the Medical Examiner can be helpful in my line of work.

"You're starting to see the problem." Dr. Jenkins sat back in his chair. "We handle over two thousand cases a year and our staff is quite small for that volume. Not every death is a murder, but even they can take days to work on not to mention all the follow-up paperwork. If this man had died at home in his sleep, or in a hospital bed, none of this would have happened, this office wouldn't have been involved."

"I know that," I agreed. "But, he died in a car in a public parking lot and, not every dead man has a multi-million dollar policy that pays out to an unknown corporation in the Cayman Islands."

"I didn't know that," he sounded surprised.

"That's the reason I suspect this death, and from the sound of what you said, that's the only reason," I said. "It's a good reason, though."

"It does sound suspicious," he slowly agreed.

"Were there any other marks on his body?" I pursued. "Maybe like he hit something, or something hit him?"

"No, just an old scar on his left arm midway between his

elbow and wrist." Jenkins thought. "No bruises or recent cuts, it appeared that he had a heart attack after lunch."

"Were there any needle marks on him?"

"No." Dr. Jenkins shook his head. "We searched his body for any such marks, and we didn't find any."

"Did you do a Toxicology screen? I asked.

"We did a brief one." Jenkins glanced down at a paper. "He had slightly elevated potassium, but nothing unusual given the circumstances. No toxins were in his blood."

"Did you look at his stomach contents?" I asked.

"Why?" Jenkins seemed curious.

"He supposedly ate at right before he died." I shrugged. "It might be of some use."

"We didn't do a detailed check of the contents," Dr. Jenkins said. "This was a clear cut case of an older overweight man dying from a heart attack from the start."

"I suppose if you had known about the large policy taken out on his life, that would have made a difference."

I studied him for a nonverbal clue; it wasn't his fault they didn't do a more thorough autopsy.

"The police or the insurance company should have been quicker in getting that information to you," I added.

Jenkins seemed concerned for a second.

"You're right, I suppose we assumed he had just eaten, that's what the police report said. He ate less than a half hour before, so stomach contents weren't that important compared to the health of this vascular system and his heart."

"I suppose not." I shrugged my shoulders.

"If we found anything that might indicate he was murdered, we would have told the police, Detective Brown was assigned this case," Jenkins replied.

"So, why did your department even bother with this case?" I wondered out loud.

"Detective Brown always was suspicious, that's why we did an autopsy in the first place, but the findings pointed to a heart attack, so we released the body and issued a death certificate."

"But you called that certificate back," I observed. "That's a little unusual."

"The police discovered the large insurance policy and requested that we look a little harder at the death."

"And, that's why I'm here too." I said.

Maybe the Medical Examiner would help me after all.

"This death does seem a little suspicious in light of the policy. Maybe it's the cynical nature of the police and the insurance company, but even I'm doubtful," I added.

"Without a body anymore, leads from this office may be sparse," Dr. Jenkins sighed.

"There may not be many, but I have to find leads and follow them until I'm sure this was just a heart attack," I said.

"Call me if you find something." Jenkins stood up and extended his hand. "I am the curious one in this office, if there was foul play I'd like to know, especially how they did it since I couldn't find anything."

I shook his hand and left. By the time I left the garage in my Porsche, rush hour traffic was in full swing. It was a long boring drive back home so I made the mistake of trying interstate twenty. I should have tried to go through town and get to Moreland, then up to little five points, I guess it would have been the same. First Los Angeles traffic, now this; I need to get a car with an automatic transmission.

. . . .

"You're home," Cassandra sounded annoyed. "I tried three times to get you."

"I was at the medical examiner's office."

I had rushed up the stairs to get the phone; I heard it as I opened the front door to the building.

"What did they say?" She quickly asked.

"They said he died from a heart attack, that's all." I took a deep breath; I needed some more oxygen after that dash up the stairs in what I assumed was a record time. "He gave me some of the autopsy notes."

"Well," Cassandra sounded excited. "I found out that Mr.

heart attack was adopted and had a twin brother."

"A twin!" I was astonished. "You mean that could have been his twin brother dead in the parking lot?"

"My thought exactly." Cassandra was proud of herself. "Simon Belchamp could well still be alive and waiting for his five million dollars."

"The coroner is waiting for Belchamp's Army records to identify the fingerprints," I added quickly. "If we can get prints from his twin, then it will be a slam dunk."

"I can tell the local cops where to get the birth certificates to prove Belchamp had a twin," Cassandra said.

"But, we need to find the twin, or at least where he used to live if the stiff in the morgue is in fact the twin," I replied.

I changed my plans immediately in my head.

"I'm going to get a plane ticket to DC; the lawyer for the corporation is there, and the salesman who wrote the policy is supposed to be there," I blurted out.

"Funny thing," Cassandra added, "his twin brother grew up there too."

"Maybe you need to fly to DC instead of Atlanta," I suggested

That would be nice, we could be together sooner.

"I'd love to, but I already have a flight to Atlanta tomorrow morning, and besides I need to dump my large suitcases at home," Cassandra sounded sad. "I miss you too, sweetheart, and, wild wet passion isn't the same without you there."

Oh, wild and wet, I hate dilemmas.

"Do I stay here and await the wild night, or do I go to DC and get this case over a day earlier so we can have a longer vacation together?" I asked.

"We've had almost three months alone together, so I suppose that's long enough for a honeymoon. No matter, I'll do the thinking for us on this problem, we'll celebrate when I meet you in Washington. I'll get a ticket tonight and meet you in less than two days, we'll have a party."

"Oh, speaking about a party, Cheryl wants to invite us to their apartment for dinner later this week. I told her to talk to you when you get in."

"I won't be there long enough," Cassandra thought out loud. "I'm going to try to get a flight out the same day I arrive, giving me enough time to dump my big suitcases, pack a small one and get back to Hartsfield."

"You can go to their book store, it's only two blocks away and one or the other of them is always there. Besides, they like you a lot better than they like me."

I didn't think they'd like to have me relay messages.

"Let's see," Cassandra started slowly. "Today is Tuesday, I'll be in Atlanta airport at nine or so in the morning, and I should be at the apartment by nine thirty or ten."

"If you book a flight out late afternoon or early evening Wednesday, you should have enough time to shower, visit our neighbor's bookshop and arrange a time for a dinner," I said, not wanting to do it myself.

"Okay, okay, I'll do it, but when do we have any time?" She sounded annoyed; at least she agreed to talk to them.

"We could try for Sunday," I proposed. "I think we should be finished in DC by Friday or Saturday at least."

"Okay," she said with a sigh. "I'll arrange it for Sunday, but, if we have to cancel, you call them and arrange for another day."

"That's fair."

I assumed we would be done in Washington by then.

"I'm going to call the widow and see if she'll talk to me this evening," I said.

"I'll see you in DC Wednesday night," Cassandra said. "Will you be in that expensive place in Crystal City like the last time we went to DC?"

"Sure," I answered. "I like that place, especially when we're on an expense account."

"Why don't you call the guy at the insurance company and tell him about the twin brother that Simon Belchamp knew about?" She asked.

"I don't know, maybe we should wait a day or two. We should wait until we have a chance to search for the brother, and maybe come up with some more definite proof" I took in a deep breath. "I love you and I miss you a lot. I guess we'd better get off the phone if I hope to see the widow tonight."

"I love you a whole bunch."

....

The first call I made was to the doctor's office where Belchamp supposedly got his insurance physical. All I got was the answering service who said he was away on vacation until Friday. It seemed he was a real doctor, but I had to check him out more closely as soon as I could find the time. The next call I made was to Allan Katzen.

"You're kidding," Allan Katzen said.

I could tell he was smiling through the phone. I decided to spill the beans, especially since our expense account was getting larger by the plane trip.

"I don't think I'm kidding. My partner found out about the brother after a day of searching in Belchamp's home town."

"That would be Colorado Springs?" Katzen asked. "Does she have proof?"

"Right," I cautiously said. "I'm sure she has something the police can use."

"I assume that Cassandra Katz is either your wife, or your sister," Katzen speculated. "She had some clerk call me to confirm she was working for my firm."

"Right," I said more confidently than before. "Cassandra is my wife."

"I like her work," Katzen said. "Do you two think that the dead man could be Belchamp's brother?"

"That would be good for you." I grinned into the phone. "But, I think it's a little soon to speculate about that; we need fingerprint records for both to be legally sure."

"Have you located the brother?"

Mr. Katzen seemed animated; here was a damned good possibility his company wouldn't have to shell out five million bucks, I couldn't blame him.

"Not yet, there could be other possibilities. Maybe

91

Belchamp's twin brother was attempting to kill him and take over his life and his money." I had to add another option; I don't know why, maybe perverseness. "Maybe the scheme went wrong and Simon's body was discovered before his twin could dispose of it."

"That's a little far fetched." Katzen didn't like being tossed from his euphoria.

"So was finding a twin brother," I added.

"I'm still glad you did."

"Me too," I added, "I have a good feeling about finding out what really happened in the next two or three days."

"I'm glad to hear that," Katzen said. "Where are you off to now?"

"First, I'm going to try to catch the first private investigator you hired, then I'm going to see the grieving widow," I said. "Then, we're going to Washington to search for the missing brother as well as speak to the lawyers."

"Very good." Allan Katzen didn't know what else to say. "Are you going to tell the policeman who investigated this case about the twin brother?"

"I don't think so." I thought for a second. "I'd like to have more details before I tell the police."

"That might be best," Katzen agreed. "If you can sort this whole thing out satisfactorily in a few days anyway, then waiting might be best."

Just two more phone calls before I went out on my appointed rounds. First, I called the state medical examiner's board who didn't seem too willing to give me Dr. Miller's home address; Dr. Miller was the doctor used for Belchamp's insurance policy. The secretary for the Medical Association of Atlanta was more cooperative as I spun my tale about a possible malpractice suit and my client wanting to calmly discuss the matter in private. She gave me Dr. Miller's home phone number, then my third phone call got the doctor's home address for me.

. . . .

The insurance company hired an investigator from one of the

larger agencies in the area, the PI's name was Andrew Holcomb. It took seven phone calls to locate Andrew; seven is, after all, a lucky number. Andrew was working a case close to our apartment, so the address on Peachtree was easy to find. After finding a parking place only a block off Peachtree and one block east, I walked by some of the less upscale establishments on that street to the address I had been sent by a secretary at the detective agency. Lots of red and yellow neon in the late afternoon spilled onto the sidewalk from the dive-like bar; loud thumping sort of country music oozed onto the pedestrians unlucky enough to be near it.

Stepping over one large questionable puddle, I pushed open the door into the bar which was dark; the smell of beer smashed me in the face as the door closed behind me, it wasn't even good beer. My eyes took a second or two to acclimate to the darkness. Directly in front of me was a long wooden bar with four customers slumped on stools in front of it and behind it was a bartender who was about thirty, wearing a bright red vest over a white shirt, standing about five foot six, and appearing to be around two hundred pounds. I leaned onto the bar, made from a blonde wood, I guessed pine with a thick layer of clear hard varnish on it..

"Hi, I'm looking for Andrew Holcomb," I asked the bartender.

I guessed that Andrew wasn't on a job since he was getting drunk at four thirty in the afternoon.

"He's over there, he's been there for better part of the day."

The bartender pointed to a small round table with one man seated at it.

"Thanks." I replied.

"Are you from his work?" The bartender asked before I headed to the table.

"No." I glanced back at the bartender. "But, the secretary knew where to send me."

"Hi." I stood over Andrew. "My name is Benjamin Katz."

"Yeah," Andrew slurred at me, still staring at the half empty glass of beer, at least from his miserable demeanor it was half empty.

"Your agency said you might be here."

I sat down but he still didn't look at me. Andrew seemed to

be somewhere in his mid fifties and notwithstanding a day of drinking too much, he seemed to be in fairly good shape.

"So?"

He finally visually acknowledged me.

"I'm working on the Simon Belchamp case."

I waited for a response.

"That's good for you." He attempted a smile. "I hope you have better luck that I did."

"That's why I'm here," I pressed on. "What did you find out that got you shot at?"

"Now, that's the point, isn't it." He seemed like he wanted to sober up some. "I never minded getting shot at before."

"I didn't say you did."

This conversation was heading somewhere else.

"This whole thing started me thinking about the whole thing," Andrew slurred out.

He was having trouble stringing words together.

"That's the thing about thinking," I tried to sound thoughtful, but I wanted to chuckle. "Sometimes it's difficult."

"I used to be a cop in Lawrenceville, you know." Andrew looked at me again. "I spent twenty years on the force and I only got shot at twice. Once was some husband who was drunk and pissed off at his wife and he didn't mean to shoot at me, the other time was three punks from Maryland who were on a crime spree. They held up a 7-11 on highway 78, and me and my partner were the ones who tried to pull them over, that was a short gunfight. My partner and I shot two of them and the other surrendered. I didn't think nothing of it, it was in the line of duty, I was thirty five when it happened. I became a grandpa last year, did you know that?"

"No, I didn't." I shook my head slowly. "Is it a boy or a girl?"

"She the cutest girl on God's earth."

He drank another long sip from the beer.

"Can you tell me who shot at you and what that had to do with Simon Belchamp?" I tried again, hoping not to get another trip down his memory lane.

"No," he replied, "I don't know who shot at me, they was

in a late model GM car, it was dark, and I couldn't see enough. I suppose it was two males, young men if I had to guess. One of them had a shotgun, and the other had a semi automatic pistol of some kind; one in the back seat and the other driving. They both open up on me as I was walking to my car. I dove for my car and crawled behind it. I got six pistol holes and four twelve gauge single ought blasts in my new car and the company says they ain't gonna pay for a bit of it and my insurance company is saying that I was using that car for my job and didn't tell them, so they won't pay neither."

"Wow, that's hard luck."

I thought about my insurance policy; I would have to call our agent out here and clarify some things.

"What do you think was going on?" I asked.

"I don't know." Andrew seemed to be getting a little more coherent. "My wife's daddy owns a used car place in Monroe, and I figured that Belchamp's two dealerships weren't making enough money, maybe he was skimming, maybe someone didn't like that, maybe they killed him for it."

"Did you find anything out about the skimming?"

I pieced together the two fragmented thoughts.

"I didn't have a chance to," Andrew replied.

He glanced at his beer. I didn't think he could take another swig without puking, at least not for ten minutes or so.

"Those punks shot at me after I started to question some of the workers at his Decatur dealership, I didn't find nothing out of place," he continued.

"Over half of our work consists of paperwork, like looking stuff up in court houses." I stood up and handed him one of my cards. "Doing that full-time is a lot safer, and there's no shame in it."

"Thanks, man."

Andrew stuffed my card into his shirt pocket, then turned to stare out the window.

Most of what he had told me, I had already read in his report to the insurance company. I hoped he would sober up and get back on the horse that threw him since, on average, being an investigator isn't all that dangerous.

95

12

Ready on the right, ready on the left

"Thank you for seeing me on such short notice," I politely spoke to the widow Belchamp.

Mrs. Belchamp had to be younger than her husband. She looked like she was forty, but I knew she was at least in her late forties since she had a twenty nine year old son.

"Come on in," she said.

She had a thick southern accent but she seemed friendly at least.

"Thanks."

I was directed to the living room. Their house was a nice two story brick in an upper middle class neighborhood. I guessed the construction to be sometime in the thirties, judging from the floor plan and the arched entrance to the living room. The interior seemed as if it had been completely redone within the last ten years. It was all done in pastel shades of white with thick wood framed furniture.

"I need to ask a few questions," I added.

"Are you from the insurance company? You want something to drink?" A younger man asked.

It must have been the son who appeared from one of the back rooms. He had a tall glass of ice tea in his hand.

Something was slightly different; ah, no musty smell. There had to be a class A air conditioning system in this house, and it must be kept very clean. As a matter of a fact, no smells were noticeable at all in the house; no dinner odor, no cleanser odor, no old people odor, no nothing; I bet Mrs. Belchamp has more than one maid cleaning for her.

"No, thanks, I won't be long."

I sat in a bulky chair next to a heavy brass floor lamp. The living room was large, maybe twenty by twenty feet. By an eyeball estimate, I calculated the square footage of her home to be around four thousand. Covering the center of the oak floor was a large oriental rug which appeared real.

"My manners, my name is Gladys Belchamp, and this is my son, Simon," Mrs. Belchamp put her hand on her chest as she spoke.

The woman was about five foot two, she was thin and well dressed for a stay at home wife at dinner time on a weekday.

"You're named after your dad?" I turned to face the son.

"Yes, I am," he sounded in a hurry. "You must tell us about this insurance policy, we knew nothing about it at all."

"No, sir, we did not. How much was the policy for?" Gladys sat in the sofa across from me.

The furniture seemed to be pre-war, maybe the twenties; whenever it was made, it was made well. Most of it had been reupholstered within the last few years. There was a feel to the décor which didn't seem like Mrs. Belchamp; I bet this was done by an interior decorator.

"Didn't the company tell you?" I responded with a question.

"No, they said it was a lot of money," Simon junior answered. "How much was it?"

"I can't say either, but it was a very large sum."

I could have told them, but maybe they'd be nicer to me if they didn't know yet.

"Well, I guess they'll tell us sooner or later." Gladys pasted on her southern charm for me.

"Why would your husband have a large insurance policy on himself and not tell you, let alone not have you or his son as beneficiaries?" I asked.

Let's throw the six hundred pound gorilla in the middle of the room and see what happens.

"That's exactly what has us so upset." Gladys stopped herself, I think she was choking up, but it was hard to tell.

97

"What do you think?" I looked from son to mother, then back to the son.

"I don't have no idea." Simon junior shrugged his shoulders. "If Pop was trying to insure the business in case he died, he would have told me. If that policy was for over a million, the premiums would have been real big and if he paid them from the company accounts, I would have seen them, and I didn't."

"Was it over a million?" Gladys' eyes got big.

"Of course it was," Simon answered quickly. "If it weren't, they wouldn't hire no private eye to investigate it."

"It was over a million dollars," I replied.

I carefully studied Gladys' face, she seemed to be delighted.

"Who's supposed to get the money?" She asked eagerly.

"We don't know," I answered, "it's supposed to be wired to an off shore account, not to a person, but to a post office box held by a corporation in the Cayman Islands."

"Where's that?" Gladys seemed confused.

"I think it's in the Caribbean, Ma."

How did he know that? It's not that hard, but Ma didn't know; maybe I'm reading too much into this.

"It is, but we still don't know the actual person who will get the money if the insurance company decides to settle it," I said.

"If they can't find nobody, do we get it?" Gladys seemed more eager than ever. "We're his only kin."

"I don't think it works that way." I shrugged my shoulders. "If the company settles, it will be with the corporation in the Cayman Islands."

"I still don't see how he could have paid for a big insurance policy?" Simon junior seemed truly puzzled. "The dealerships were doing good, just not that good. It was enough to live good, but no big vacations, or nothing like that."

"Whoever paid for the policy made quarterly payments, and they made their last payment on September thirty, it was the last day for that quarter," I said. "Did he make a large payment that month?"

"He kept the company checkbook at his office," Simon sounded excited. "I've brought it here, Ma has his personal checkbook too. Why don't we look at what he wrote checks for."

"Go get them," Gladys was still excited. "If your daddy was paying for that policy, we might be rich."

"Can I look at them too?" I asked.

These two weren't capable of plotting a complicated murder, besides they were in the dark as to the insurance policy. Without the five million policy, I didn't see a real reason for either of them to bump off the old man.

"Let's all have a peek," Simon said.

He plopped a large business checkbook on the coffee table in front of the sofa and opened it to the first page. It was a carbon checkbook, and it was mostly used.

The first date was March twentieth of that year. Simon turned the pages and he was too slow for me, but I guess they couldn't read that fast. There it was; I didn't stop them, but there it was. May fifteenth, a check for five hundred dollars made out to Fred Lepus, goddamn it! Cassandra shot the son of a bitch in the arm not three months before, and there he was right back in the middle of one of our cases.

Simon went all the way to the end of that book, and saw no checks made out to the insurance company although I did notice a check made out to a law firm every third month. It was for twenty five hundred dollars and it said legal fees. The funny thing was, the checks were made out to the same law firm that was connected to the post office box in the Cayman Islands. Neither Gladys nor her son thought anything of them, but I noticed it. I noticed some answers in the check book, and the dynamic duo didn't even see them; like hell I'd tell them.

"I didn't see nothing unusual," Simon sighed and opened the personal checkbook.

"Me neither." Gladys agreed.

She nodded and stared intently at the dead man's personal checkbook. I also glanced, but saw nothing unusual in there either, well, except for a check to a real estate company paid each and every month which claimed it was for storage, but my guess was that it was for a mistress. What storage area costs six hundred a month? I'd have to check into that when we got back from DC.

99

"Nothing there either," Simon sounded disappointed.

"Why don't you bring all his old books home from the office, and we'll look through them too." Gladys wasn't discouraged.

Gladys had a nice house paid for, the car dealerships were in her husband's name and she and her son had clear title to them. The strange thing was that her dress was nice, but definitely from the 'blue light special' fashion line and Junior dressed like a car salesman, rumpled and slick. That house and nice furniture had to be two to three hundred thousand, and if she sold the dealerships, she would be at least a multi millionaire. Why the cheap look when you're at the very least upper middle class? Class hopping isn't unheard of, in fact in American society it's encouraged. Maybe it's a Southern thing; I'll have to pay better attention to the locals from now on.

"I have to go now," I said. "You're right, I didn't see anything of use in those checkbooks, I'm sorry."

"Maybe we'll find something," Junior said.

Simon got up and walked me to the front door while Gladys stayed back, still staring at her late husband's personal checkbook. I wondered if she got the hint of a mistress from it, probably not. They can't be stupid, Simon had two car dealerships, and the son had to be able to manage them too, maybe I'm looking at two of the three stooges.

"He did have another insurance policy, didn't he?" I whispered to Simon as we got to the front door.

"Yeah," Simon answered. "He had two quarter million dollar policies the company carried, then he had the same kind of policy so Ma would have something if he died."

"So, who do you think took out that big policy on him?" I had to ask once more before I left.

"I wish I knew." Simon shrugged his shoulders. "I'd like to make a deal with them for some of the action, it sounds like it's a butt load of cash."

"That it is." I smiled as I walked off to my car.

Junior shut the door behind me. My car was parked one house down from theirs since I had found no space in front of the Belchamp house. It was not that cold an evening, the temperature was in the low fifties and the sky was clear. Someone on the block must have thought it was cold since I smelled the odor of a wood fire in a fireplace.   Even with all the street lights, the stars shone plentiful and bright. A line of almost leafless trees lined the street on both sides. It was quiet except for two barking dogs in the distance.

As I approached my Porsche, I heard the squeal of tires. I glanced quickly to my left and saw a car peel from the curb, it must have been waiting for me to show up. I checked my surroundings to assess cover since I knew it wasn't teenagers on a joy ride. This felt like what the retired policeman had talked about in the bar that afternoon.

I saw the back window open, and a barrel stick out; I've been through this before. The trees lining the street appeared to be at least forty years old, large enough for cover, so I ran for the nearest one as I pulled my revolver from its holster. The loud bang echoed through the neighborhood and I could hear shotgun pellets hit the tree in front of me, as well as sheet metal and lawn.

Sheet metal? Shit! I caught a glimpse around the tree at the car racing away, it didn't appear as if they were going to turn around so I stared at my car. Yes, I had heard the sound of several large lead pellets slicing through an expensive German sports car, my expensive sports car, damn.

"Was they shooting at you?" Simon shouted from his front porch.

"Maybe you'd better get back inside and call the police," I shouted back at him. "They might come back for another shot at me."

Simon jumped back into his house. The police made it there in five minutes proving to me that these cops are certainly faster than the ones in Los Angeles. I had glimpsed the license plate of the car as it sped past me, and I remembered most of the number. Colors don't show up too well in the dark, so I couldn't tell them the exact color, but I did recognize a seventy eight Impala which was remarkably like the description of a late model GM car Andrew Holcomb had given to me.

"Sir, can you think of anything else?" The uniformed DeKalb County cop asked me.

By then three other police cars had pulled up next to my

Porsche; one of the cop cars was parked askew in the street, blocking one direction. Most of the neighborhood had meandered into their front yards to gawk at the show and finding nothing of much interest anymore, all of them had trundled back in to watch television.

"I can't think of much else," I thoughtfully replied. "I gave you the partial license plate, the make and model of the car, and I think it's a seventy eight, not an seventy nine."

"Were you a police officer, sir?" The cop asked.

"No," I said cautiously.

"You noticed a lot more than the average citizen would." he glanced up from his notebook and smiled at me. "A lot of the local private investigators around here are retired policemen."

"If it helps find those two, I'll be happy," I said. "Do you need me any more?"

"No." he glanced towards Simon Junior pacing about his mother's front yard. "I guess I'll talk to that gentleman now."

"Thanks."

I started to leave, then stopped. The policeman was still writing notes on his pad.

"I have to go out of town tomorrow, I hope that won't be a problem?" I asked.

"No." he looked at me again. "I don't think we'll need you anymore until we catch them."

Those cops were nice and I would have liked to stick around town and searched for those gunmen myself, but I had to go to DC and see my new wife as well as slap Fred Lepus around for old times sake.

13

Where have you been all my life

"It's about damn time you got here," Cathy Rumson snorted as she stood up from her chair behind the metal desk.

"I got here when I got here," Fred Lepus tossed the cavalier phrase into the faintly lit room.

"I was about to give up on you're getting here and throw the bum out on his ass," Cathy was exasperated by Fred's lateness.

"Well, who is he?"

Fred glared at the man asleep in the sofa under the front window.

"And, why is it so dark in here."

Fred flipped on the main light switch for the living room office.

"What!" The older man jumped up from the sofa. "What happened!"

"Oh, it's you, Mr. Belchamp," Fred said in a matter of a fact way as he stared intently into the man's face. "What do you want from me?"

"My name isn't Belchamp." The man took stock of where he was and wiped the sleep from his eyes. "I'm his brother, you were paid to find me, remember."

"Yeah, I remember that, but you look more like Simon Belchamp."

Fred studied the man's face more carefully.

103

"My brother took me from Washington and brought me to Atlanta and cleaned me up, he fed me and bought me new clothes, and took me to a doctor and fixed me up." The man sat back down on the sofa. "Now, my brother's dead and someone wants me dead too."

"Really." Fred glanced at Cathy, then back at the man on the sofa. "Why?"

"I don't know."

"If you're in that kind of trouble, why don't you go to the cops?" Fred asked.

"Well," The man's voice faded.

"Well, what?" Fred insisted. "Does it have to do with money your brother was hiding?"

"Why would you ask that?"

"Why else would you see me instead of the cops?" Fred shot Cathy a brief grin.

"It has to do with money, but my brother didn't hide it."

"What kind of money?"

"Uh," The man nervously hesitated. "Insurance money, I think."

"How much insurance money?"

"Over a million, but I don't know for sure."

"So," Fred relaxed into this conversation. "What can I do for you?"

"First, I need to find a place to hide."

"Where are you staying now?"

"Well," The man thought for a second. "I don't have any money on me, so I'm back on the street where you found me before."

"That's a good place to hide for now," Fred heard plain and clear that he had no money right then. "What else do you want?"

"The lawyers at Smith, Smith and Heywood are the ones who are handling the insurance claim," The man said. "I think I should get the insurance money, and I would like to hire you on a contingency basis to make sure I get it."

"What kind of contingency?" Fred asked.

"Ten percent."

"forty," Fred quickly answered.

"Twenty."

"Thirty five."

"Twenty five, and that's final," The man insisted.

"Look, even lawyers don't do contingency work for less than a third." Fred shook his head rapidly.

"Okay, a third, but no more," The man reluctantly agreed.

"Which lawyers?" Fred asked.

"I think the second Smith and the only Heywood."

"I'll check into that and get back to you in a day or two," Fred replied.

He looked at Cathy, who had a broad grin by now, even she knew what a third of a million dollars was.

"What do I do?" The man asked.

"Go back to the place I found you, and I'll get back with you there in two days," Fred answered.

"On the street?" The man seemed uncomfortable.

"You supposedly spent decades as a homeless bum, a few more days won't kill you," Fred sounded annoyed.

"I suppose not."

The man got up and walked out the front door with his shoulders slumped more than before.

Fred stared out the front window and watched as the man walked down the sidewalk towards the bus stop.

"Do you know how much dough that is?" He turned to the smiling Cathy.

"You bet your ass I do!" She leapt towards Fred and hugged him tightly. "We're going to be rich!"

14

Home is where the suitcase is

Tonight Cassandra and I will be back together after what seems like forever; actually, it's only been three days. Before any of that, I had to locate Fred Lepus and beat some information out of him. If he would tell me what I want to know I wouldn't have to, but he never has up to this point.

Lepus has been falling into my cases over the past several years. At first, I kind of wanted to slap him around, but he's kind of grown on me over the years. Well, a tumor kind of grows on a person too, but Lepus is a benign tumor at least.

Maybe I should wait until Cassandra joins me; she shot him the last time we met, so maybe she'd like to get in on some of the action, that would be a nice present. Okay, it's settled, I'll talk to the lawyer and search for the mysterious corporation first, then we can slap Lepus around together.

My plane touched down in National Airport at five past one in the afternoon then I walked quickly to the baggage claim and pulled my bag off the merry-go-round. Parking myself and my suitcase near the exit gate, I unlocked and unzipped the main compartment; there it was, my revolver and holster. In nearly six years of traveling by air with it, it's never been stolen. It has to be in a checked-in suitcase, not a carry-on and as long as I tell the folks at the check-in counter that it's there, there's no problem.

I stopped by the car rental booth and arranged for a car. Although the insurance company was a large international business, I rented a compact car anyway. By the time I dumped my suitcase in the suite at the expensive hotel it was almost three in the afternoon. Hey, I rented a cheap car, but the room had to be nice, after all, I hadn't seen Cassandra in three days and I felt we deserved a top class love palace. Although we had been married for a few months, it continued to feel like a honeymoon to me. Well, maybe when she showed up it might feel more like a honeymoon. I told the front desk to issue a key to Cassandra as soon as she showed up.

A call to the law firm of Smith, Smith and Heywood got me an appointment the next morning at nine sharp. I decided to kill some time walking around that shopping mall below the hotel. I could scout out the restaurants since Cassandra was supposed to be in later that evening, and I assumed she would not have had dinner. I got back in the room at quarter to five in the evening and finding the local news on the television was depressing, and the reruns of old sitcoms was even more depressing, I fell asleep on the king sized bed.

. . . .

"Well, well, well," A voice in the dark shocked me awake.
I jumped to my feet as I heard the door open.
"If it isn't sleeping beauty," Cassandra's voice teased.
"I fell asleep a second ago." I rubbed my eyes. "What time is it?"
"It's eight thirty, how long have you been out cold?" Cassandra asked.
She shoved her two small suitcases next to mine in the closet. She kissed me and boy, that felt good. It was a long kiss; actually, it was an hour long kiss, but I don't need to carry on about the details.
"Did you have dinner?" I asked as I opened my suitcase and searched for something to wear.
"No." Cassandra stuck her head out of the bathroom. "They didn't feed us a damned thing on that flight except peanuts and juice."
"It might be too late for that French restaurant I found in the mall downstairs." I replied.
"We could eat at the hotel restaurant," she shouted over the sound of the hair dryer. "I bet they're open late."

. . . .

"You've got to tell me all about the defense," I insisted.
She had told me some at the hotel room, but I wanted to hear more.
"Well, I told you about everything," she insisted. "I

107

thought they would be harder on me than they were, but the questions were kind of softball."

"Maybe you thought they were softballs because you knew the subject backward and forward."

"What meant the most to me was Mary, Annie and Albert showing up," Cassandra said. "I've been to a few defenses and I've never seen relatives or friends there."

"Did you want me to be there?" I thought I sensed disappointment.

"Not at all." She patted my hand. "I think if you were there I would have been too nervous to have done so well."

"That's sort of what I thought too," I meekly replied. "It's more important to be there for the actual graduation."

"I don't know if I really want to do that," Cassandra sounded thoughtful. "I didn't go to the ceremony for my masters."

"This is a lot more important," I insisted. "When is it, June?"

"Yeah," she replied. "Some time the first week, I think."

"Hell or high water," I insisted again. "You, me, and at least your parents will be there."

"I love you." She wanted to change the subject.

"How's your salad?" I was willing to oblige a change in subject.

"It's not bad," she replied while smiling at me. "How's your tuna steak?"

"It's very good." Even small talk was fun. "Since you want to change the subject, how did the closing go?"

"Better than I expected." Cassandra sipped her water. "All I had to do was sign a bunch of papers and it was done."

"The money was wired all right?" I asked

I guess I was mercenary after all.

"Yes." Cassandra nodded her head. "I checked it while I was in Atlanta,. We really do have to put that money somewhere else, there's over two hundred thousand in that one account right now, and the federal insurance is only good for one hundred thousand."

"What do you suggest?" I asked.

"Maybe we should invest half of it." She seemed to be plotting something. "At least it might get more than sitting in a bank."

"I agree."

I always trust her with the money side of our relationship.

"What about a few blue chip stocks like Coke, IBM and GM and maybe some government bonds and some mutual funds."

"That sounds good," she thought for a second. "We have to save some of it aside as cash to pay for all the stuff like this, you know the big companies wait at least thirty days before they pay us for these expenses. Sometimes they wait longer to pay us, so we have to have enough saved up to cover it all when the credit card bills come to us."

"I'll trust you, divide up the money and set up a brokerage account somewhere."

I held her hand over the table for a moment. She always did have good instincts in financial matters.

"You never did have a hard time with the money." Cassandra grinned at me. "A lot of men are picky about sharing assets in a marriage."

"Given the real nature of our business, I think money is the least of the things I need to worry about." I smiled back at her. "Besides, you always struck me as being much better handling money than I am."

"Just to let you know, I was impressed that you suggested we have a joint account when we weren't married, and you had all the money in our relationship." She patted my hand on the table.

"I guess I've always trusted you." I shrugged. "I assumed you always trusted me."

"You've found out how much I trust you lately."

She slowly drew her hand from mine and grasped her water glass, taking a slow sip.

"I have."

I stared into her eyes, it's a nice place to get lost.

"What did you find out from the grieving widow?" Cassandra took another bite of her salad. "Not to change the subject or anything."

"From the reactions I was getting from the widow and her son, I don't think they had a clue about the five million dollar policy."

I guess business conversations are somewhat necessary, sometimes.

"What about overall impressions?" She asked.

"The wife seems like a good old girl." I took a bite of food. "She's very interested in money and keeping track of as much of it as she can. It also seems like she's trying her best at social climbing, but hasn't quite gotten the hang of it yet. The son appears like a typical car salesman, slick and not too bright."

"Did they say anything?"

"Not directly." I thought for a second. "But they let me glance through the dead man's company and personal check book while they were desperately searching for possible payments to insurance companies."

"Were there any?"

"No." I cracked a grin. "But, I noticed a five hundred dollar payment to Fred Lepus."

"That's what that big grin was all about." Cassandra smiled back at me. "So, do we go visit him tomorrow?"

"Just visit him?"

"Oh." Cassandra knew I was feeling playful. "I know your game, we'll go slap him around tomorrow."

"That's why I love you so much," I chuckled. "We share so many hobbies together."

"All kidding aside, I kind of like that Lepus guy," Cassandra said. "He can be a pain in the ass at times, but he's still likeable."

"You forget that the last time he trotted through one of our cases he kept hitting my head with the butt of his revolver." I rubbed the spot on my head.

"Yeah, but I shot him in his arm, so we should be even."

"I'll have to think about that," I replied.

"Did you find out anything else about this case when you spoke to the grieving widow and son?"

"Regular twenty five hundred dollar payments to a law firm here in DC, and what appeared like apartment rent for a mistress," I replied.

"So, there might be another reason to murder the car dealer," Cassandra said. "I guess the insurance company was right, there are plenty of reasons to believe this was not a natural death."

"A greedy mistress, an angry wife, a greedy wife," I took in a breath. "There could indeed be lots of reasons for someone to kill Simon Belchamp."

"Also, the son could be greedy, and the guy could have been into some shady folks for extra cash," Cassandra joined in the speculation. "But not much of that would negate the insurance company paying out unless the murder was for the express purpose of collecting on the policy, or unless the body wasn't that of Simon Belchamp."

"You know my watch words," I interrupted. "Things are not always as they seem."

"You're too cynical sometimes," Cassandra chided me. "Sometimes they are exactly as they seem."

"Sometimes, you're right." I had to agree with her. "But maybe my cynicism has to do with getting shot at as I left the Belchamp house."

"Shot at?" Cassandra seemed worried for a second. "Obviously you're still a failure as a target, for which I am eternally grateful, but, who did it?"

"I don't know, I was able to give a partial plate number to the police, so maybe we'll know when we get back to Atlanta," I answered. "It has to do with this case since I was shot at outside the Belchamp house."

"Why do you think Belchamp was paying Lepus?" She pushed her salad bowl away from her. "You don't think Belchamp or Lepus had anything to do with the shooting, do you?"

"I think Simon Belchamp hired Lepus to find his missing twin brother," I replied.

"That makes sense," Cassandra agreed. "I wonder if Lepus found the brother?"

"We'll find out tomorrow when we visit our favorite pretend detective."

15

Hi, Don and Mike

Cassandra and I were in the lobby of Smith, Smith and Heywood at five minutes of nine in the morning. I thought it strange that a lawyer would agree to see someone, especially not a client, before ten as the secretary disappeared into the back sanctuary to announce our presence.

"They will see you now," The secretary said.

The secretary was twenty five years old, and looked as if she belonged on a fashion runway, not a law office. Cassandra noticed my keen interest in the secretary and jabbed me in my ribs as we passed her on our way to an open door two down and to the left of the door to the waiting area.

"Hi," The shorter of the two men standing in the large conference room said. "My name is Don Smith and this gentleman is Mike Heywood." Both men seemed to be in their mid forties and were dressed sharply in gray business suits. Don was about five feet eight tall and a little stocky, Mike was about three inches taller and even stockier.

"My name is Benjamin Katz, and this is my partner Cassandra Katz." I shook each man's hand. "We're private investigators working for an insurance company which has a policy on a Mr. Simon Belchamp, who died a short time ago."

"Hi Don." Cassandra also shook their hands. "Hi Mike."

Both men smiled at her; Don smiled a bit too much.

"The policy for the deceased named a corporation in the Cayman Islands as beneficiary, and the deceased made regular large payments to your firm." I took in another breath. "While not

112

wanting to break any attorney client confidentiality, we would like to know if Mr. Belchamp was using your firm to defraud the insurance company?"

"Right to the point and insulting to boot," Don huffed.

He sat down in the chair at the head of the table which gave us a big clue as to who was the senior partner. This had to be a problem for this firm since two of the three senior partners were meeting with us at nine on a Thursday.

"We will be more cooperative than you might expect." Mike sat down to the right of Don. "We were unaware of what was happening."

"This is a large firm and we uncovered a small part of this three days ago," Don interrupted his partner.

"Uncovered what?" Cassandra asked.

She sat down opposite Mike, I sat next to her.

"Can we see some identification, please?" Don demanded.

He glanced at Cassandra, then at me; we produced our PI licenses.

"Thank you." Mike passed the IDs back. "We called the insurance company yesterday and they confirmed that you were working for them."

"All the transactions with Simon Belchamp were handled by an associate who disappeared two weeks ago," Don said.

Don stared at Cassandra, sizing her up; clearly he was the reason the secretary was sexy. Judging from the sloppy grin on his face, Cassandra more than measured up to his standards.

"Who was that associate?" Cassandra sounded upset.

Don wasn't being too subtle, and Cassandra didn't like it.

"Her name is Kelly Chalmers," Don replied.

He was quick to see that he was annoying Cassandra and shifted his eyes from her boobs to me.

"She's worked for the firm for under two years and as of two weeks ago she's nowhere to be seen," he added.

"It's really strange," Mike interrupted. "Her apartment is empty, and no one in the building remembers her moving, she had to have done it in a hurry in the middle of the night."

"Furniture and everything?" Cassandra asked Mike.

113

"She had a furnished apartment," Mike answered. "But all of her personal things were gone."

"The information about her parent's address and her education and everything on her job application have turned out to be false," Don added, becoming more serious.

"We checked her school references and her license to practice when we hired her, but on closer inspection the person behind the transcripts was not the person we hired," Mike said.

"How much background checking do you do when you hire someone?" I glanced at Don.

She must have been a looker if he didn't check her background that carefully.

"She was a junior associate," Don became defensive. "We checked her transcripts, and her license to practice law, it all seemed okay."

"But obviously it wasn't legitimate, so what made you start carefully investigating your employee?" Cassandra asked.

She wanted to slap the sexist pig at the head of the table, but she held it in well.

"It was when she didn't show up to work and didn't answer her phone." Mike replied.

He seemed to still be a little worried, maybe he had a crush on her.

"One of the other junior associates and I went to her apartment, and the manager let us in after we knocked for a long time. That was when we all became worried that something bad had happened to her," Mike added.

"That's also when we started checking the cases she was working on," Don interrupted.

"Was Simon Belchamp a client?" I asked.

"No," Mike stuttered a second. "He wasn't an official client, but we saw an envelope with his return address stuck behind one of her desk drawers, it was addressed to Kelly."

"Was there anything in the envelope?" I asked quickly.

"Only a note saying that he would be late with the next payment, and the note referenced his last payment of twenty five hundred dollars," Mike answered.

"Did you check your books to see if a twenty five hundred dollar payment was posted?" Cassandra asked.

"Of course we did, but none that we couldn't account for from legitimate clients," Don answered. "After checking ten banks in the area, the eleventh bank had an account in our company's name that none of us knew about."

"That makes sense," I observed. "Belchamp made the checks out to your law firm, so she would have to have an account in your name to get the money."

"I assume the account is closed?" Cassandra asked.

"No." Mike shook his head. "But, there's only thirty some dollars left in it."

"I'll bet that's how the insurance policy was paid for," Cassandra commented.

"I'll bet you're right," I said. "But, if we can't find this Kelly Chalmers, what good does that do us."

"Do you have a picture of her?" Cassandra asked Don.

"I do," Mike answered.

He pulled out his wallet and produced a trimmed snapshot of him and Kelly standing in front of the Washington Monument. He must have had a crush on her, his expression as he gazed at her in the picture spoke a thousand words.   In the photograph she was wearing a short dress which showed off her long shapely legs; she was good looking and had a trim figure and the tight pullover proudly showed off her ample chest. Next to her, with his arm around Kelly, was Mike with a big grin plastered on his face. He seemed so happy to be there.

"Can we keep this?" Cassandra sympathetically asked Mike.

"Only if you give it back when you're through." He seemed so melancholy.

"I assume you had something going on with Kelly Chalmers?" I glanced at Mike.

"Yeah." Don smiled at me. "He was hoping that she would be the next Mrs. Mike Heywood."

"That's not funny." Mike shot a harsh glance at his partner. "We were only friends."

"What else have you found in her records?" Cassandra

115

asked.

She stared at Don; she was still annoyed at him, I saw it in her expression.

"We've been looking carefully at all the cases she worked on for the last two years, but have found nothing unusual." Don glared at me. "She wasn't supposed to work on any cases by herself until she moved up the food chain a few notches, so if she was doing something on the side, it was really outside this firm."

"None of the other lawyers here knew of anything like that," Mike sounded sad. "She only worked on the cases we have files for, even the secretaries and paralegals didn't know of any outside stuff she could be working on. We've asked all of them and we believe them."

"Have you reported any of this to the police?" Cassandra asked.

"Only her disappearance," Mike replied. "They said that since she gave us false information about her past, that they couldn't treat her as missing in the sense that they would try to locate her, but they said we should check to see if she stole from us, and that if she did they would become involved again."

"That makes sense," I agreed. "Have you told them what you have discovered?"

"Like what?" Don stared at me.

"Like the fact that she set up a bank account in your firm's name and has taken all the money?" I answered.

"Now, what would we tell them about that?" Don glared at me. "That one of our employees was doing work off the books and keeping all the money? That's not a real crime; it pisses me off a lot, but it's not a major felony."

"That depends on what the twenty five hundred dollar payments to her were for," I observed. "They might have been extortion payments, for drug deals, payment for a murder, or any number of illegal activities. How do you know for sure what it was for?"

"That's the whole point, we don't know exactly what the payments were for, do we?" Don continued to glare at me.

"And, I suppose felonious activities wouldn't look good to

116

your other high paying customers, would they?" Cassandra verbally jabbed him.

"I think we're more interested in why she lied to us for two years," Mike interrupted. "I mean, think about it, she set herself up in our firm for two years on a false identity to do something illegal. Two years is a long time to lead a fake life just for part of an insurance payout."

"I have to agree with Mike." Cassandra smiled at him. "What cases or clients do you have that might be financially or politically big? I'm talking about a two year investment big."

"We do business with a lot of rich clients, companies and more than a few important politicians," Don proclaimed.

He leaned back in his chair, he was proud of that statement.

"The partners are checking carefully all the cases Kelly had access to since she started work here."

"What have you found so far?" I asked.

"If it has to do with the possible insurance fraud, we'll share that information with you, but if it doesn't involve that, we'll tell you nothing," Don insisted, he wasn't exactly angry, just insistent.

That sounds fair," I replied. "Is there anything that could relate to the insurance fraud?"

"Like we've been trying to tell you, not that we've found yet," Mike answered me. "If we do find anything, we'll give it to you, and to the police."

"I assume you'll let the police investigate any fraud you actually do come up with?" Don teased me.

"Of course we will." I smiled back at him. "If we find actual evidence, our client will want us to give it to the appropriate authorities; we get paid for proving it, not prosecuting it."

"Could we have the address of Kelly's old apartment, and any other information that might help us find her?" Cassandra asked Mike.

"I'd be glad to," Mike replied. "I'll go gather it all up right now for you."

He glanced at Don, who nodded his head, then stared at the table in front of him. Mike then got up and walked down the hall to his office.

"If we do find her, I'll let you know where to locate her," I said. "Even if it's in a prison somewhere."

"I would appreciate that."

Don seemed to be interested in what we could do to help him.

"I guess we do have similar interests in this woman."

"I suppose so." I agreed.

I stood, Cassandra also got up and headed to the door first. My interests in the well shaped Kelly Chalmers was not exactly the same as Don's, I wasn't a letch.

. . . .

"Two years?" Cassandra stared at me as I put my seat belt on. "Two years is a long time to settle into someone else's life. That sounds like a government agent, maybe even a police woman."

"I don't think so."

I glanced around the parking lot, observing that the law offices were in a nice building by itself on Columbia Pike near the National Cemetery.

"It appears that she was taking money under the table for a shady deal with Belchamp. Real government agents don't do that, they don't like attracting too much attention to themselves. It sounds like this Chalmers woman initiated the blackmail scheme, undercover cops don't do that, well, not unless they're stupid greedy cops."

"Maybe," Cassandra sounded skeptical.

"If we find more information that leads to her being a government agent of some kind, I guess I can leave a message for the agency to contact us, but I don't think we'll need to."

I pulled out of the parking lot and turned left towards the intersection with Glebe Road.

"Maybe." She still didn't agree with me. "You're going to Lepus' office?"

"Right now."

16

Hear no evil, tell no evil

Lepus had to be in his office since his rusted old car was parked beside the dilapidated building on Twenty Second Street.

"Why don't you wait by the back door in case he tries to run out that way when I go in the front," I suggested.

I parked our rental car across the street from his office and waited until Cassandra had walked to the side of his building before I got out of the car and walked slowly to the front door of his office. A wind picked up from the north and it was in the high forties, looking like a cold rain may start by nightfall. The bare trees around the mix of commercial and rental properties made the scene appear even more bleak.

"Hello Fred old pal, old buddy," I spoke loudly as I walked in the front door which was unlocked.

I assumed he didn't see me get out of the car across the street. There he was, sound asleep leaning back in his wooden desk chair with his feet propped up on the edge of the desk.

"Yes sir, can I help you," he sputtered before he realized it was me.

"I think you can," I chuckled.

I moved quickly to the space right in front of him as he then stepped sideways and turned to the entrance to the back room.

"Hi, Fred," Cassandra said as she walked towards him. "He left the back door unlocked, that's not a smart thing to do, Fred."

"What the hell do you two want?"

Fred began to turn red in the face which contrasted quite nicely with the tufts of his white hair. He had finally gotten a decent haircut so the tufts were at least neatly trimmed now.

"You have come up in another one of our investigations," Cassandra said.

"Yeah, I remember the last time that happened, you shot me." Lepus sat back down in his chair. "What is it this time? You come to finish me off?"

"Simon Belchamp." I flatly said.

I sat on the corner of his desk and stared at him.

"Yeah." Fred's eyes darted to Cassandra, then back to me. "He was a client of mine, but he finished paying me last spring and the case is closed."

"What was the case?" Cassandra asked.

"I can't tell you that, you should know better."

He blinked quickly, then looked at me; at least I hadn't shot him, yet.

"Simon Belchamp is dead." Cassandra said.

She leaned against the door jamb behind Lepus.

Lepus' office was in a rundown one story frame house that he converted into an office. What used to be a living room and dining room he converted to an office with a large desk towards the back with a wooden secretary chair behind it. Under the front window was an old almost worn out couch. The rest of the space was taken up with an assortment of chairs and a coffee table with a few magazines on it. That front space had two doorways, the one near Lepus' desk led to what laughingly can be called the kitchen then a door out to the back driveway, the other doorway led to the two small bedrooms and the only bathroom.

"Was he murdered?" Fred asked Cassandra.

"We think he was," she answered him. "Now, I repeat, why did he hire you?"

"Every time I see you, somebody's been murdered." Fred shook his head. "What is it about you two?"

"It's some of the cases we take." I shrugged. "You're the lucky one who finds the murder cases and sticks his nose into them."

"Tell us about Belchamp and we'll be out of your ugly hair," Cassandra slowly walked in front of him and spoke forcefully.

"Every time I see you two, you want me to tell you something about one of my cases." Fred stared at Cassandra. "Why?

120

If you want me to do your work for you, pay me."

"He has a point." Cassandra shot me a glance.

"She's right, what's in it for me?"

That seemed to be Fred's words to live by.

Cassandra rummaged around in her small purse and pulled out a handful of money.

"One hundred and twenty three dollars," she said as she handed it to Fred.

"Sounds better than a bullet."

Fred nodded to her, not wanting to smile at all. The wound wasn't fully healed yet, I guess.

"So?" Cassandra said in a much louder voice.

"He hired me to find his long lost twin brother." Fred replied as he took the money from Cassandra.

"And, did you?" She kept the volume high.

"It took me a little over six months, but, yeah, I found him," Fred sounded proud of finding the missing brother. "And, thanks for the dough."

"Where's the brother?" I had to ask.

"The hell if I know," Fred insisted. "Last April he was a bum sleeping on a grate in front of a bagel place a block or so from the Air and Space Museum, I think it was near a Holiday Inn. Where he is now, I don't know and I don't care."

"Did Belchamp ask for any other information?" I pressed. "This is a murder we're investigating and we'd hate to send the cops after you."

"Send the cops after me?" Fred huffed. "Big fucking deal! The last time I met you two not only did that woman shoot me." He pointed to Cassandra. "But you two had the FBI on my ass, so don't think the local cops will scare me at all."

"So what." Cassandra leaned closer to Fred. "They were on our ass too."

"Tell us the truth, if he did ask for more stuff from you." I moved back from him a little. "She actually did pay you this time for any help you might give."

"Say." Fred stared at Cassandra. "I kind of enjoyed your wedding reception, the food was great."

121

"Thanks, why are you changing the subject?" Cassandra cocked her head slightly as she stared at him.

"You never did give us anything," I added. "I'm disappointed."

"You didn't actually invite me." He turned towards me. "You really should have."

"It was a small wedding." What else could I say.

"Will you two stop that." Cassandra was irritated at our side trip. "I asked you a question."

"I guess as a wedding present, I could tell you that he asked me to find someone who could do some legal stuff for him, kind of on the QT." Fred winked at Cassandra.

"Who did you send him to?"

I think I knew the answer.

"Well, this woman lawyer I used to know who had been disbarred, but she still could do some mighty fine work for the right price."

Fred turned and smiled at me showing that he was trying too hard to be nice to us.

"What is her name?" I asked.

"Paula Thorpe." Fred thought for a second. "She was quite a good looking broad too."

"Was this her?"

Cassandra stuck the snapshot of Mike Heywood and Kelly Chalmers in Fred's face.

"Yeah, that's her. Who's the fat dork she's with?"

He reached for the photo but Cassandra stuck it back into her purse.

"The dork's a real lawyer," I answered. "Do you know where she is now?"

"Yeah, I have it here somewhere." Fred mumbled.

He opened his desk drawer. I put my hand on the butt of my revolver as he pulled out a ragged notebook. He flipped a few pages.

"Here it is," Fred proudly announced.

He slid it on the desk so I could write the address down in my own notebook. Cassandra quickly compared it to the information the lawyers had given her.

"That's the address she went missing from," Cassandra said.

"She's skipped town?" Fred seemed surprised.

"Looks like it."

I noticed his expression.

"Do you have any idea where she might go?" Cassandra asked.

"She has friends in Atlanta, and her ex-husband also lives there and she has some friends in New York too," he admitted. "I guess she might go to one of those places."

"What's her ex-husband's name?" I asked.

"Gilbert Thorpe." Fred glanced at his note book. "I think."

"Well." Cassandra got up. "I think this went well, we're leaving without shooting you, and I don't think you hate us so much this time either."

"Not so much this time." Fred smiled at Cassandra as she walked to the front door, I followed her out.

"Gilbert Thorpe." I said as I stopped on Lepus' front steps and looked at Cassandra.

"Yeah." she glanced back at me.

"Gilbert Thorpe was the agent who wrote the five million dollar policy on Simon Belchamp."

"Now," Cassandra paused for effect, "isn't that strange."

"Can you tell me why we didn't shoot Lepus?" I asked as we crossed the street to our car.

"Because I already shot him? Well, maybe I felt sorry for him." Cassandra shrugged. "I don't know why, besides, I don't think he knows any more than he told us."

"I guess not." I moved the rear view mirror to see the car behind us. "That's strange."

"What?"

"There's a Crown Vic behind us with three goons in it." I readjusted the rear view mirror. "They're sitting in the parked car, staring at us."

"Not to subtle." Cassandra started to turn around.

"Don't turn around," I quickly said. "Let's see if they want us, or Lepus."

"Okay." She put her seatbelt on.

"It must be us," I remarked.

I saw them pull out behind us and make the same turn on George Mason Drive.

"They have to want something we may know. So, how do we avoid this without getting killed?" Cassandra asked.

She checked her holster for her gun, and her pocket for her extra clip.

"Only three of them are in that car," I thought out loud. "We should be able to get the drop on them if we plan it well."

"We could rush them in front of a police station," Cassandra suggested. "It would be safer."

"Since when did that ever motivate me?" I shrugged my shoulders. "Besides, we would never get anything out of them with cops everywhere."

"I suppose not," she said with a loud sigh. "But there's something to be said for safety."

"I have a plan." I grinned.

17

I had a plan

"You've got to be joking." Cassandra shook her head. "That's not much of a plan."

"We need to search for a deserted place so no one else can get shot." I started to go back over my master plan.

"We need to find a place where WE won't get shot," Cassandra insisted.

"I can turn around and get to Route Seven and head to Loudoun County," I was conversing mostly with myself. "If we go out far enough, we can put our plan in motion."

"What do you mean OUR plan?" Cassandra pushed my shoulder. "I think we would do better going on into the Capital."

"Too many people, besides it's easier dealing with the Virginia cops than the DC cops," I took in a breath. "The DC cops don't like us carrying guns, remember?"

"I remember," she acknowledged. "I suppose."

"Could you reload my revolver?" I pulled my Smith and Wesson from it's holster and handed it to her.

"What with?" She opened my revolver and dumped the cartridges into her left hand.

"This." I handed her a speed loader from my coat pocket. "They're extra hard cast bullets, they'll go through a car door."

"These others won't?" She shoved the cast bullets into my revolver, then put the other cartridges into the now empty speed loader.

"No, they won't."

I glanced in the rear view mirror noticing the Crown Vic, still three cars back, was sticking to us like a bad debt.

"Those cast loads are made from linotype and they're hard enough to make a good sized dent in the engine block as well as passing right through the car door."

"The others are expanding bullets, right?" She asked.

125

"Right," I agreed. "With forty one caliber, the problem is little choice in bullets. I had to cast those myself, and I don't have the equipment anymore."

"You left it in Los Angeles?"

"Right," I said. "I sold my share in all that stuff to the other guys in my old apartment building."

"Do you want to set up more of a reloading system in our apartment?"

She was being nice to me but I knew she wouldn't like that very much.

"It's too much trouble, too messy and it takes too much time." I replied. "Maybe I should change the caliber I carry."

"What to?" She asked. "Forty four?"

"Probably, I guess I'll change when we get back to Atlanta."

I guessed it made the most sense since I already owned a few of those anyway.

The black Ford followed us as I drove past the exits to Dulles Airport. About five miles down the road, I took a left turn on a paved country road. Not five hundred yards down that road, rose a high embankment with bare crumbling rocks protruding from it. I couldn't see any houses or much of anything else around indicating human habitation.

"There." I pointed ahead. "We'll do it there; I'll charge them, and you take cover behind the car and fire at them before they have a chance to get out of their car."

"What a plan," Cassandra said sarcastically as she pulled her pistol from its holster. "Just remember, it's a rental car."

I spun the rental car sideways, parallel to the embankment rising from the left side of the road. Cassandra and I both jumped from the car at the same time as the black Crown Vic slammed on it's brakes; the driver pointed the car directly at ours. Cassandra fired two quick shots at the black Ford, hitting the driver's side mirror and grazing the top where the windshield met the roof. I moved quickly to the driver's side of the car, pausing only long enough to see Cassandra's bullet pass through the driver's side mirror.

The driver, who was portly and appeared well over six feet tall, shoved his door open and I could see him reaching for a pistol

126

tucked in his waist band; my original descriptive use of 'goon' seemed appropriate. He stumbled on one knee behind the open driver's side door and from my vantage point of ten yards and running closer, his pistol seemed to be a well worn Charter Arms thirty eight, less of a real, useable gun, and more of a mobster's throw away piece. I took quick aim and fired at the same time as he did. His aim was poor and my aim put a forty one caliber hole in his abdomen. He shouted a profanity and crumpled to the ground, tossing his pistol five feet away from the car.

The man in the passenger seat took a longer time to stumble out of the car with his revolver drawn. He fired twice, but didn't take time to aim at all. I could hear both slugs thud into the embankment above Cassandra's position which gave Cassandra enough time to put two bullets into him, one in each leg above the knee.

As the second large man fell to the ground amid loud profanities I shouted. "Get out of the car right now slowly and with both hands where I can see them!"

After five seconds of reflection, the man in the back of the car raised both hands and pushed the back car door the rest of the way open. It was already partially open as he had been preparing to join the gun battle. Cassandra stood up and pointed her pistol directly at the man emerging from the car while I quickly moved to the revolver the driver had dropped. I picked it up by the trigger guard with a pen from my inside coat pocket and placed it on the hood of our car.

"Would you please step away from your car," I said sternly to the man holding his hands in the air.

"Who are you, cops?"

The man stared at me as I walked to pick up the revolver from the man laying on the ground holding his leg wounds and still cursing.

"We'll tell you who we are in a minute." I replied.

I set the other revolver down on our car hood, then checked the two wounded men for other weapons. One had a large switch blade, and the other one had brass knuckles and a knife which I also set on the hood of our rental car.

"Why don't you tell us who you are?" I asked the uninjured

127

man as I motioned for him to lean onto the trunk of his car.

"Not until I know who you are," he insisted as I pulled a pistol from a holster strapped on his belt and hanging down his right side.

"This is interesting." I set his pistol onto out hood. "This is a twenty two semi automatic with a silencer, it's a Colt Woodsman Sport model." I glanced back at the pistol on the hood of our car. "The serial number is on the front grip strap so it's a pre war gun."

"What the fuck're you talkin' about?" The man leaning on the car shouted. "You wanna buy the damn gun or what?"

"It's worth more than you might think." I blankly stared at him. "Although this homemade silencer stuck on it might lower the value a little. I'll bet it's loaded with subsonic cartridges too."

"So?"

The only goon standing glared at me as he spoke; he seemed confused and quite angry.

"So, that's the sign of a hit man," I said with certain authority. "Subsonic ammunition and a silencer means no one would hear you killing us. Using a soft lead twenty two means the cops can't trace the slug to your pistol and this pistol is old enough to not have any paper trail attached to it. All this means that someone hired you to kill us for some reason."

"The mob?" Cassandra sounded surprised.

"That's right," I concurred.

I walked close enough to the man with his hands still up so that I could put the barrel of my Smith and Wesson closed to his head.

"We're not cops, and we don't give a damn if you have a good lawyer or not. I'll blow a big hole in your head if you don't tell me who wants us dead," I slowly said, in my best G-man voice.

"Don't fuckin' tell the son of a bitch nothing!" The man with bullets in his legs shouted.

"I don't know nothing," The standing man answered nervously as he stared at the wounded man on the ground. "Tommy G hired me to whack you this morning, and that's all I know."

"You fuckin' moron," The wounded goon shouted. "Tommy's gonna have you whacked now, you and your big

128

goddamned mouth!"

"Shut the hell up." I insisted.

I walked to the man shouting from the ground who had his legs spread so he could place a hand over each leg wound. I aimed at a space near his crotch, but away from his legs and hands then fired one round into the ground; the concussion was enough to cause him to move his hands to his crotch, he shouted even louder for a second, then fell silent.

"Benjamin!" Cassandra was surprised.

"He was pissing me off."

I shrugged my shoulders and tried to convey that these were real mobsters who wanted to kill us and that I was acting extra tough to get them to talk before the cops arrived, but I don't think it was working.

"Don't kill him," she insisted.

"I wasn't."

I gave her the look again, this time I think she got it.

"At least not yet." she quickly grinned at me.

"What the fuck do you two dip shits want?"

The standing man glimpsed at the wounded man on the ground, trying to hold two wounded legs and his crotch at the same time.

"Before the cops get here, I want to know who exactly hired you three to kill us, and why," I insisted.

"Like I said," The man grunted. "Tommy G paid us five thousand now, and ten after it was done. And, Tommy G don't need to give nobody a reason why he wants someone whacked."

"You're a bundle of help," Cassandra butted into the conversation. "Do you know anything about a law firm, Smith, Smith and Heywood?"

"They ain't my lawyers," he insisted.

"How about a real beautiful woman lawyer named Kelly?" Cassandra added.

"Now, that sounds interesting to me," The standing goon added. "You got her number on ya?"

Two county cop cars from two different direction sped up to us without their sirens blaring. Three cops jumped out from their

129

cars, two from one, and one from the other.

"Drop your weapons!" One of the cops shouted as all three leveled their pistols at us.

"We're detectives," I shouted back as I slowly placed my revolver on the ground in front of me. "These are wanted felons."

I didn't know that, but it was a good guess.

"What jurisdiction are you from?" One of the other cops asked me as he began to handcuff the three of us left standing while another officer checked the wounded and the third called for backup and an ambulance.

"We're private investigators," I answered softly.

That was never a good answer in situations like these.

"Well, private investigators, you're both in a world of shit right now." The not so friendly cop patted me down.

"They shot at us first, and they admitted they were hired to kill us," Cassandra said.

She was adamant as the cop gingerly patted her down; he did make an effort to not be too fresh about it.

"We'll take statements from all of you," he assured her.

"Those crazy fuckin' shit heads forced us off the road and started tryin' to kill us," The man holding his wounded legs shouted at the policemen.

The cop handcuffing me looked at our car, then at theirs. He slowly shook his head as he realized we couldn't have forced them off the road since their car was behind us, and blocked our car from the main road.

"Those guns on our hood are theirs, and I didn't handle them so you can get fingerprints from them," I spoke quickly. "I'll bet they've been used in other crimes if you check them through the FBI."

"We'll be sure to do that, as well as check your weapons," The cop said.

The county cops were actually very nice to us as all of us waited until two emergency vehicles arrived to take the wounded men off. Right after that, two tow trucks arrived to take the cars back to wherever the cops took cars involved in shoot outs. They took our IDs and hauled us off to their jail in handcuffs after reading

130

us our rights, but at least we rode together in the back seat of the same squad car. They didn't slap me around at all and they treated Cassandra quite well, calling her ma'am the whole time, they didn't even push her once.

"I wonder if Smith, Smith and Heywood would defend us," Cassandra whispered to me.

"We already have a good DC lawyer." I smiled back at her. "It's all part of my master plan."

"You and your plans!" She complained as she jangled her handcuffs behind her back.

"I'll bet we can find Tommy G in New York," I said.

"When will we get to New York?" Cassandra sighed. "In five to ten years?"

"We didn't do anything wrong," I whispered back to her. "We were defending ourselves, they shot at us first."

"We actually didn't shoot first," she whispered back. "That's our story and we're sticking to it."

"How was the guy with the gut wound?" I asked the policeman driving.

"He seemed all right, you shot him to his left side, through his ribs. He for sure has a few broken ribs and some internal damage, but he was stable when they took him off." The cop glanced at me briefly in his rear view mirror. "All this would be a lot messier if you had killed him.

"Like I told you back there," I answered. "They were hired to kill us, and we would have been a lot worse off if we had lost that gun battle."

"We'll let the district attorney sort it all out."

The policeman driving us to jail didn't want to have a conversation about any of this.

"Did you see the twenty two back there?" I asked. "If that isn't a hit man's gun, what is?"

"You might be right, but we have to figure out who it belonged to first."

"You're dusting all the guns, aren't you?" I had to make sure.

"Yes, they are," he agreed. "We should have some answers by the time the DA talks to the both of you."

131

It took over an hour for them to book us as we got some nifty photos taken and our fingers smudged with black ink. Cassandra had been through all this many times since she started working with me and she was holding up much better than the first time. The police station was small, so we were able to stay together the whole time, they even put us in the same holding cell together before they pulled me out and stuck me into a small interrogation room.

"Are you the District Attorney?" I asked the man in the suite waiting for me in the interrogation room as the cop that brought me in unlocked the handcuffs and took them off me.

"No, I'm not." The man stood and pointed at a chair for me to sit in. "I am agent Thomas Russo."

He stuck an FBI identification badge in front of me.

"They must have been mobsters," I replied.

I studied his identification for a second, it seemed like the real thing; I should know, I've used real fake FBI identification several times, well, the ID was real, I was fake.

"Good guess, Sherlock," he scowled, my guess was that he wasn't too happy with our shooting the gangsters.

"They did say that Tommy G hired them, but I'm afraid I don't know who he is," I said in my most friendly voice. "Who is he?"

"He's a punk."

Agent Russo glared at me; I knew he'd never crack a smile, but I hoped he at least would lose the sour expression.

"So, he's not a boss?" I thought I might as well ask.

"Not hardly, he's a punk who works for the scumbag we're trying to bust for extortion, money laundering and a bunch of other crimes."

Agent Russo was still pissed at me, but why? I didn't kill any of the bad men, and I didn't even shoot at the nice FBI man.

"I suppose this also has to do with the fake woman lawyer who worked at Smith, Smith and Heywood?" I asked.

I threw that question out for a reaction. There had to be more to his sour mood than the shootings.

"Do you know where she is?" He asked quickly.

132

Ah, maybe this is why he's pissed at me; I'm crashing in on his investigation. I wondered what all this had to do with a New York mob family.

"Her ex-husband is in Atlanta, and she has friends in New York." I shrugged my shoulders. "That's all I know."

"The District Attorney has declined to press charges, so as far as the Loudoun County authorities, you and your partner are free to go." Agent Russo kept glaring at me. "They bought your self defense story given the backgrounds of the men you shot."

"From your attitude, I take it you don't want to let me go," I said.

This could be a big problem, it would put a hell of a crimp in our dinner plans with the lesbian neighbors this Sunday.

"I don't, but you have a friend in the Bureau," he scowled again. "Someone at the assistant director level."

"It must be a Marine buddy."

I faintly smiled at him; I didn't know who he was talking about and I was sure that Billy Sullivan wouldn't interfere since it might compromise my cover story; hell, that cover story was my life. I wondered, who my friend was at the FBI?

"You're free to go, but stay the hell away from our investigation," he still wasn't letting up.

"All we care about is uncovering what is obviously an insurance scam." I tried to assure him. "My assumption that the ones that want us dead are in New York."

"Don't go there," Agent Russo pressed.

"If the insurance scam leads us there, why can't we travel to the big apple?" I asked.

I wasn't about to be shoved away from my case that easily.

"Because if you show up in the middle of my case again, I'll shove the big apple up your ass." Russo continued his angry tirade. "I don't care what the brass say."

"Well, you do seem a little tense about this."

I was starting to enjoy the absurdity of this pissing contest.

"You might not have any better luck than the hoods did, I'm kind of hard to mess with, you know."

"Just watch your back. You can count on me being there if

you set one foot in New York."

He got up to walk out of the interrogation room.

"Maybe you won't have to worry for awhile, my partner and I will head back to Atlanta as soon as we can get a plane out of here."

"That'll suit all of us just fine," Agent Russo snorted.

Cassandra was waiting for me in front of the police station, she had collected our stuff, including our pistols. One of the county cops that arrested us was waiting with her.

"Benjamin, this is officer Bowman." Cassandra smiled at me as I stood closely beside her.

"Call me Jimmy." The policeman nodded at me. "Your wife was telling me how you two did so well at the shootout."

"All it takes is a good plan," I said.

Cassandra jabbed me in the ribs, again.

"Whatever it was, I wanted to tell you two I admire what you did, it took lots of guts to face those three down." Jimmy beamed at Cassandra.

I could tell she had yet another admiring fan.

"That FBI agent wasn't to forthcoming with information," I said. "I told him that Tommy G put the contract out on us, but he didn't seem too impressed."

"Oh, they don't care about him, his boss is someone called the Roach," Jimmy replied.

He shook his head, he had yet to stop staring at Cassandra, who was playing along.

"Willy the Roach?" I said.

I knew the name, he was an old style mob boss from New York, strictly a small time hood. He had to be in his mid sixties by now.

"The Roach?" Cassandra sounded disgusted.

"Not the bug, the dubie," I chuckled. "He got his start trafficking drugs."

"Oh." Officer Jimmy finally noticed me.

"I guess we'd better get going if we want to get a flight back home." Cassandra tugged at my sleeve.

"Well, it was nice talking to you, Jimmy." I shook his hand. "And, I'm very happy that your county DA decided not to throw us in jail."

"Not at all." Jimmy resumed smiling at Cassandra. "He wouldn't dream of taking your case before a grand jury. Shooting a bunch of New York mobsters out to kill you? You two are from the South, and, hell, the DA would never win another election out here if he did that."

"You made friends with the right sort of fellow."

I winked at Cassandra as she got into our rental car. By some miracle, none of the whizzing bullets hit our rental car so I knew I lead a charmed life after all.

"He's a nice guy." she grinned back at me. "Besides, he did tell us who actually wants us dead."

"The FBI guy told me to stay the hell away from New York," I said as I started to drive out of the parking lot. "But, you know, I haven't seen my uncle in along time."

"Benjamin!" Cassandra shot me another one of those looks.

"Why not?" I shrugged my shoulders.

"Well, I'd like to know what Willy the Roach has to do with the missing woman lawyer and the five million dollar insurance claim." Cassandra held my arm.

"Me too," I agreed. "When do we have to be in Atlanta?"

"It's Thursday, our neighbors are expecting us in three days, so I suppose we could do some quick checking before we head back home," Cassandra replied.

She glanced at her watch which was a nice Rolex I bought for her the last time I was in Italy; it had the day and date on it as well as the time.

"Where do you want to go first?" Cassandra asked.

"Maybe we could search for the twin brother," I paused for a second. "At least until we give it a try."

"It's too late, isn't it?" Cassandra glanced out the window. "It's almost dark."

"The clock on the dash says it's five o'clock." I looked at my wrist watch. "That's about right."

"I guess we could check out the street where Lepus said he was." Cassandra continued to take in the countryside out the window.

135

18
Don't call me, and I won't call you

"How the hell did you find me?" Paula Thorpe's voice sounded very angry.

"Let's say that we have mutual friends, Paula," Fred Lepus replied.

He shifted the phone to between his right shoulder and the side of his head so he could grab a pen to take notes.

"So," Paula asked, "what the fuck do you want?"

"No need to be so hostile," Fred replied, holding his sarcasm at bay. "All I want to talk about is the deal you made with Simon Belchamp."

"What deal?"

"That's what I asked you," Fred replied. "I sent him to you because he wanted some legal work done under the table."

"When was that?"

"Last April." Fred took in a deep breath. "You can deny all you want, but I know you and I know there's a lot of money up for grabs since the Belchamp guy's taking a dirt nap right now."

"I don't know what the hell you're talking about, Fred. Have you been drinking?"

"The brother that Belchamp guy hired me to find paid me a visit and told me about some insurance scam you and the dead guy were up to, so don't give me the brush off so quickly," Fred sounded annoyed with this woman.

"So?" Paula asked.

"So, he offered me a third of the payout to make sure the brother would inherit, and I was wondering if you and I could come to some agreement."

"Why would I know anything about an insurance policy?" Paula asked in her most innocent voice.

"You can act above suspicion all you want, but I know you, and this smells like a Paula Thorpe scam all the way," Fred spoke more forcefully.

"You don't know shit, you little worm!" Paula became angry again. "Take my advice and walk away from this before you get dead real quick."

"You never scared me that much, Paula." Fred smiled to himself.

"It's not me you have to be worried about, it's my new boyfriend."

"And who would that be?" Fred kept his grin. "A big bad wise guy?"

"No," Paula paused for effect. "A big bad Columbian drug lord."

"You're shitting me." Fred lost his grin.

"No, but you'll be shitting lead if you keep bugging me about this."

"I still like to keep my options open," Fred said a little softer than before.

He wildly mulled over all his options and none of them seemed too fruitful, but all that money was still out there and he wanted some of it for himself.

"Your options are limited to keeping your distance, or staring up at six feet of dirt," Paula flatly declared.

"Where can I get in touch with you?" Fred meekly asked.

"You can't," Paula thought for a second. "Who else knows about this hiding place?"

"Just me, I think," Fred answered.

"I'm taking off for places even you don't know about, so drop this whole thing," Paula was adamant. "I mean it, Fred, I don't want to see you dead, but other people are in this that would rather kill you than see anything leaked, do you understand?"

"Yeah," Fred reluctantly said. "I guess so."

19

Oh where oh where did the missing bum go?

We got back to the hotel at six that evening and after quickly showering, we changed into more comfortable and clean clothes then headed down to the Metro. I called the airlines and made reservations for a quick one day trip to New York. Expensive last minute tickets can always be cashed in if we decide not to go, so it isn't that big a deal, besides, it's another expense for the insurance company.

It was a quick ride to L'Enfant Plaza, the closest stop to were Lepus had said the missing twin hung out. It was a little confusing, but we managed to make it to Ninth Street and headed North towards the Mall. The neighborhood seemed a little rough as we walked under a train bridge which made me glad I was carrying a gun. Within a block, we were back in safer territory as we turned East on C Street and walked past the Holiday Inn. A Roy Rodgers hunkered at the end of the block, and the breakfast place Lepus had mentioned which was closed this late in the day.

"Button your coat so he doesn't see your gun." Cassandra pointed to a policeman slowly walking towards us.

"Excuse me, sir." I approached the policeman,

Cassandra couldn't believe I was doing that, not after all the cops in our life that day.

"Yes, may I help you?"

The officer regarded both of us carefully. I could see him assess us as harmless tourists.

"We're searching for a Korean Vet."

I pulled out the picture of Simon Belchamp from my outside coat pocket.

"His brother was supposed to be a twin, so the missing

138

brother had to look something like the dead one."

I'm glad I didn't put the picture in my inside pocket, the one next to my revolver.

"He's a relative we're searching for and we had a report that he liked to hang out by the grates around here when it was cold."

The beat cop took the picture, moved closer to the light coming from Roy Rodgers and studied the picture for half a minute.

"He looks familiar, but not exactly like this," The cop replied.

"He may appear a lot more ragged than the man in this picture," Cassandra added.

"Yeah." The cop handed the picture back to me. "That sort of looks like old George, I don't know his last name."

"George is his first name, his last name is Blanchard," Cassandra sounded sad. "Do you know where we could find him?"

"He usually does hang around here when it's cold." The policeman pointed to one of the grates in the sidewalk. "But that's only when it's colder than this outside."

"Where might he be now?" I asked like the long lost relative.

"He usually works the trash cans in the Mall for food this time of day." The cop pointed towards the Air and Space Museum. "He stays at this end of the Mall as a rule."

"Thanks a lot," Cassandra said.

"Be careful, you two," The cop shouted after us. "Don't stray too far away from this area."

"Like I have Benjamin's death wish," Cassandra muttered in my direction.

"It wasn't that bad," I defended myself, sort of.

"I don't enjoy getting shot at as much as you do."

She stopped and glowered at me; I knew we had to have our little fight first.

"We didn't have many choices," I began. "Those mobsters would have followed us no matter where we went, and they were paid to kill us."

"I know, but we could have called the cops for some help," she insisted.

"I didn't see a phone in our car," I replied. "Besides,

wherever we stopped for a phone, they most likely would have started shooting at us."

"Not if we drove to a police station."

"You're mad because you thought I didn't listen to you, right?"

"Well." She stared at the sidewalk, then back up at me. "Yes."

"I'm sorry." I put my arm around her waist.

"You have to know I'm ready for almost anything, especially after I agreed to join you in your government jobs." She slipped her arm around me. "But if we're going to be a team, you have to pay attention to me, at least acknowledge what I say."

"You're right." I squeezed her tighter. "I'm getting better about it, aren't I?"

"Sometimes, you are." She kissed me. "Let's get going, I'm getting hungry and I sure don't want fast food so let's find him before all the good restaurants close."

It was a warmer night than the last one, the sky was completely overcast and a few drops of cold rain started to fall. The late November night could have been a lot worse to walk around in. This wasn't exactly the height of the tourist season and all the museums were locked tight for the night. A smattering of evening joggers scampered on the Mall, and a few tourists walked towards the Washington Monument which was open for night visitors, but that was a long walk away and I guessed that a bum wouldn't want to waste the effort and would be searching the garbage cans close to home.

"So," Cassandra started to talk, then fell silent for a second. "Do you think Simon changed places with his brother?"

"Yeah, I think he did just that." I turned to face her. "If for some reason Simon wanted to change places with his brother, he'd have to be here."

"Why?" She asked.

"If Simon is now supposed to be his brother, he'd have to hang out where his brother hung out," I thought for a second. "Besides, if he tried to stay at a classy hotel, he'd be an easy target for someone trying to kill him."

140

"What if he was the one who killed his brother?" Cassandra liked playing the devil's advocate.

"If he did kill his brother for the insurance money, he would be long gone by now," I mused. "Probably somewhere in the Cayman Islands waiting for his five million, but I don't think he did, and I think Simon Belchamp was the murder target, and I think he knows it so he's here taking his brother's place trying to figure out what's happening."

"I tend to agree with you about the bum brother getting killed instead of Simon, but I still don't see why Simon would be here, living on the street," Cassandra observed.

"My guess is that he knows about the insurance, and he wants it for himself." I stopped walking. "And, if he's asked Lepus to help him do it, he has to hang around Washington for awhile, looking like his brother so he can hide in his brother's old life."

"So, you think Lepus sent him out here on the street to hide in plain sight until he could get some useful information?" Cassandra asked.

"Yes, I do."

"It seems logical, but how do we prove it for sure?"

"We find the bum on the mall." I pointed to the Air and Space Museum.

"I still don't think either the brother or Simon will be there," she commented as we waited for the light to change.

"Well, let's look at this from another angle," I thought out loud.

"What angle is that?" Cassandra asked.

"Maybe Simon Belchamp didn't start the insurance scam."

"What?"

"Maybe all Simon wanted his brother for is to change identities with him for some reason. If Simon changed places with his poor lost brother, he would have to hang around all the bum brother's hangouts to make the switch seem real. He would have to come up here to hide in his brother's life at least for a while." We started to cross the intersection, heading for the Mall. "If it's the real bum brother up here, then he'll be here because this is his home."

141

"Why would Simon have to come up here and play like a bum?" Cassandra asked yet again. "It still doesn't make that much sense to me."

"Assume he was being blackmailed, or that someone wanted him dead," I thought for a second. "Maybe he wanted to leave his wife, maybe he had a ton of gambling debt."

"Yeah," Cassandra said. "I thought about some of those things too."

"If Simon needed to duck out of sight and wanted to switch identities with his twin, where could he go after the switch?"

"Judging from the picture we have of him, he like to go to a hunting cabin."

"Well, the hunting cabin I can believe," I agreed.

"So, why aren't we searching for a hunting cabin instead of hunting bums?" Cassandra wasn't in a mood for bum hunting.

"For one, the hunting cabin is too obvious, and for another, because we're already here." I stopped walking and faced her. "Why not? Beside, we may get lucky and find the remaining twin here."

"A lot of homeless are out here." Cassandra gazed up and down the Mall as we walked past the Air and Space Museum

"I know." I also scanned at the territory. "There has to be a lot of irony in all this, but I don't have time to think what it is."

"Let's start up at the Art Museum, then work our way down." Cassandra pointed towards Congress.

Pulling out a half eaten hotdog, the bum in front of us sniffed it, then downed it. Cassandra stared at the ground for a second, I don't think she believed what she saw.

"Excuse me." I walked towards the man as he fished for dessert.

"You talking to me?" He stood up and stared at me as I approached. "You got some change on you?"

"Maybe." I stopped three feet from him, pausing because he smelled fairly ripe, even though it wasn't that warm outside. "We're looking for old George."

I held up the photo of Belchamp.

"I seen him tonight." The bum stepped closer to me and studied the photo. "That don't look much like him, though."

142

"Where is he?"

I held my ground and asked, thinking it would be insulting to step back or hold my nose.

"Down by the castle, last I saw. I saw him from a distance, but it was him," he sounded slightly nervous. "Where's my change?"

I handed the bum a five dollar bill, which made him happy; I guess he could buy a whole bunch of forties with that much change.

"Did he mean the old Smithsonian?" Cassandra asked as the happy bum trotted off towards a liquor store on Pennsylvania Avenue.

"That's what I'd guess." I pointed down the Mall towards the museum.

There seemed to be one homeless man wandering in the vicinity of where the missing twin was supposed to be, across from the castle, near the Natural History Museum. He seemed kind of plump to be long term homeless. The bum stopped walking as he noticed us approaching, I observed that his behavior seemed nervous.

"We want to talk to you for a minute," Cassandra said in a kind tone. "Are you George Blanchard?"

"Who are you?" He seemed more startled than a bum should be. "Are you cops?"

"No." Cassandra stopped. "We're from your family."

"I don't recognize you," he sounded hesitant, like he wanted to run away.

"Did you know you had a brother?" I asked.

I moved closer to him, he was kind of fat, it was hard to tell from the coat he was wearing, but he was plump; also, he didn't stink. As a matter of a fact, I smelled after shave coming from him which was odd in a bum.

"I don't want to talk to either of you." He backed up a few steps.

"Are you George Blanchard?" Cassandra asked again.

"Yes, I am." He stood still for a second. "I like my life the way it is, leave me alone."

"We want to talk to you about your brother," Cassandra

143

spoke softer. "Did he try to contact you in the last few months?"

"That's not George, that's Simon for sure," I whispered in Cassandra's ear.

"How can we be certain?" She whispered back.

"What are you two talking about," The man in front of us shouted.

"Nothing," I tried to calm him down. "We need to talk to you about your brother; can we go somewhere, we'll buy you dinner."

"No," he almost shouted. "I don't have a brother, and I don't know what you're talking about."

"I think you do," I insisted.

Walking around from the Constitution Avenue side of the museum came two cops, I guess they heard the loud shouting and wanted to investigate. Whichever one of the brothers it was saw them and took out running towards the Washington Monument end of the Mall, one of the cops took out after the running bum and the other one came towards us.

"What now?" Cassandra asked.

"Wait." I was busy staring at the running overweight bum who couldn't outrun the cop. The bum took a sharp right and headed up Twelfth Street, I hoped he wouldn't get lost in the crowds.

"What's the problem here, folks?" The cop walked up to us.

"We were trying to contact a George Blanchard for his family," I quickly answered.

"We think that was the right man, but he became quite upset and ran off when he saw you two policeman," Cassandra added.

"Who did you say you are?" The cop repeated.

"We're private investigators and we were hired by the family to locate George," I replied.

"Here's my identification." Cassandra pulled her PI license out of her purse.

"Georgia?" The cop carefully checked the ID. "Do you have another picture ID?"

"Yes, sir." She pulled out her driver's license.

"You got two different names, lady." The cop looked at the two cards Cassandra had handed him.

144

"I got married and haven't had a chance to get another driver's license." Cassandra blushed slightly.

"Okay." The policeman glanced at me.

"He's my husband." Cassandra grinned at the cop.

"We're here to locate George Blanchard," I interrupted.

We needed to get the focus of this conversation away from us and back on the running bum.

"I know old George." The cop smiled at Cassandra as he handed the IDs back. "Does he have relatives in Georgia?"

"Yes, he has a brother," Cassandra said.

"It's sad for their families." The cop shook his head. "I don't know what got into George, though, he's about the most harmless bum around here."

"Is he a drunk, or does he do drugs?" I asked the cop.

"He's drowning his liver," The policeman replied. "I don't think old George has enough of a mean streak to afford a drug habit."

The other cop slowly walked back towards us, alone.

"Looks like you lost George," The first cop said.

"I don't suppose he'll be back either." I shook my head. "But maybe we can get that bottle he was handling and see if the fingerprints match, at least we could tell the brother we actually saw him tonight."

"You can have any trash you want," the cop answered me. "Good night, and stay out of trouble."

"I think you're right, that was the dead man we talked to," Cassandra said as I carefully picked up the empty root beer bottle George, or Simon had dropped when he saw us approaching.

"We can tell soon enough."

I pawed through the trashcan until I found a bag big enough for the bottle.

"Should we stay here tomorrow, maybe catch Simon Belchamp?" Cassandra asked as we walked quickly towards the Smithsonian Metro station.

"I don't think so." I shook my head. "He seemed like a deer in headlights."

"He was afraid, but of what."

145

"My guess is that he'll head back to Atlanta now that we've uncovered him here," I said. "If he's scared enough to live on the streets, he'll crawl down a hole and try to figure out another safe place; he'll want to hook up with his mistress and head out of the country if I'm not mistaken."

"I guess you may be right," Cassandra reluctantly agreed.

"I'd like to talk to Lepus to see if Simon Belchamp contacted him in the past few days."

I had a hint that Lepus had been visited by the alleged dead man.

"Shall we eat first?" Cassandra wanted me to answer correctly.

"I guess we can." I raised my hands as if to surrender to her wish. "Why don't we go back to the hotel and stash the bottle and try to get Lepus on the phone, then we can go out to dinner."

"I love the idea."

. . . .

"Hello, is this Fred Lepus?" Cassandra asked in a sweet voice.

I had convinced her that Lepus might respond better to a cute female than to me but she reminded me that it was she who shot him, she agreed to call anyway.

"Yes," Fred answered hopefully.

"This is Cassandra," she said. "I spoke to you earlier about a case I'm working on."

"Oh, it's you," Fred sounded disappointed, I guess he didn't have a date for the evening after all. "What do you want?"

"By any chance, did your old client, Simon Belchamp contact you recently?"

"Yeah, funny thing about a dead man visiting me," Fred agreed. "He saw me right after you guys left. He was real interested in the insurance thing you two must be working on."

"What did he say?" Cassandra asked.

"He asked me to kill you two," Fred chuckled, he always did like yanking our chains. "You think I should take the job?"

146

"I don't think so," Cassandra purred. "We're such good friends now, and I would hate to have to shoot you again."

"Very funny," Fred snapped. "Whenever you figure out that dope you married is a looser, please call me up."

"I don't think you'll live that long." Cassandra hung up the phone.

"What did he say?" I asked.

"Let's talk over dinner."

"Actually, we'll have to get a late dinner in New York." I glanced at my watch. "We have a flight in two hours."

20

I'll be an uncle's monkey

"Who were you talking to on the phone." Cassandra blinked her eyes several times as she focused on me as I was sitting on the edge of the bed, not dressed yet.

"I was talking to my Aunt." I replied.

"What time is it?" She glanced around the dark room.

"It's six thirty in the morning."

"You idiot." She flopped back down under the covers. "We didn't even get into this bed until three this morning."

"I know," I firmly said. "It's time to get up, though."

....

"Is your Aunt still mad about the wedding?" Cassandra asked as the cab crossed the Williamsburg Bridge.

"Not since I told her we were coming out for a visit."

I picked up her hand and wrapped mine around it .

"We can't stay that long," Cassandra sounded concerned. "We have to look into that Willy the Roach mobster."

"I know," I said. "But, my Uncle will also be there."

"The Assistant Chief?" Cassandra seemed too serious. "He ought to know about our mobster."

"My thought exactly."

"I've met your uncle," Cassandra changed the subject. "What's your aunt like?"

148

"Aunt Ruth?" I remembered. "She's about five foot even, a little plump and the last time I saw her she'd let her hair go white."

"I mean, what's she like?"

"She loves her family," I continued. "And, now that you're part of it, you'd better get used to lots of hugging and kissing and dishing the dirt about all your other new relatives; she's kind of stand offish with non-relatives."

"She sounds like fun," Cassandra sounded anxious.

"Excuse me for sayin' somethin'." The cab driver quickly darted a glance at the two of us in the back seat of his cab.

"What?" I glanced at him in the rear view mirror.

"I heard you mention Willy the Roach."

"We did," Cassandra answered. "Is he a friend of yours?"

"Me?" The cab driver sarcastically laughed. "Not likely."

"So, Alphonse Rassetti," I said.

I noticed the copy of the hack license posted on the back of the plastic separator between us and him.

"Are you interested in Willy the Roach for some reason?"

"Not for nothin' good," Alphonse chuckled. "I think he's a pig bastard."

"So, why the concern?" I asked.

"He 'n his old lady lives up a block or two from my mother," Alphonse said.

The cab driver still stared out the front window at the traffic and I preferred he do that since the traffic was a little heavy that early morning.

"Then, you know him?" Cassandra asked.

"Yeah, I know the scum ball," The driver said flatly.

I swear I could see his jaw muscles churning as he said it.

"What did he do to you?" Cassandra asked.

"His goons broke both my brother's legs five years ago."

"What can you tell us about the Roach?" Cassandra asked.

"Why?" Alphonse turned around quickly to stare at Cassandra.

"We're detectives investigating one of his deals," I carefully said. "And, he's got a contract out on us."

"No shit!" Alphonse punctuated the phrase with a laugh.

"You ain't cops, then."

"No." Cassandra looked at me, then at the back of the driver's head. "We're private investigators."

"What do you wanna know?" Alphonse asked.

"Where does he hang out most days?" I asked.

"He's got a two bit club in a back room of a bar down in Queens." Alphonse quickly glanced back at me. "It ain't far from where he lives."

"Could you pick us up at eleven and take us there?"

I peeked at Cassandra and shrugged; she didn't object, at least not right away.

"What you gonna do?" The driver asked

"All I want to do is ask him why he wants me dead." I smiled at the driver in the mirror.

"Are you carryin'?"

"A forty one magnum."

I opened my coat to show the butt of my Smith and Wesson model fifty eight.

"You bet your ass I'll take ya."

"Will that leave us enough time?" Cassandra wondered out loud.

"It should." I shrugged. "Our flight leaves at five, we should be through by then."

"If I can stay 'n watch, I'll take you guys to the airport myself." Alphonse glanced into the rear view mirror at me.

. . . .

"She's a tall one, Benjamin."

Ruth Rosenblum hugged Cassandra again. Aunt Ruth came up to Cassandra's chest and Cassandra had to bend over slightly each time Aunt Ruth grabbed to hug her so she could get her around the neck for a proper Rosenblum hug.

"Not so tall for me, I think," I chuckled.

It was so easy for me to fall back into those speech patterns; the time I spent here as a child was happy and I liked being reminded of them.

150

"So." Uncle Benjamin slapped me on my back. "What's this about Willy the Roach? I'm glad you waited until after breakfast."

Uncle Benjamin was an Assistant Chief in charge of the patrol services for the Bronx. He was dressed in his uniform with two stars on it, and he was late for work.

"He's involved in an insurance fraud case we're working," I replied.

I kind of didn't want to get back to work either.

Cassandra and Aunt Ruth had bonded, they bonded better than I could have hoped for. Once it sunk in that Cassandra was a doctor, Aunt Ruth beamed brighter than a spotlight at a Hollywood premier even though Cassandra wasn't a hospital doctor.

"Insurance fraud?" Uncle Benjamin scratched his chin. "I'm not surprised, but that's not his usual game."

"What is?" I asked.

"Lately, it's drugs, prostitution and bootleg cigarettes. He's not exactly a big mob boss, he's more of a mid-level schmuck." He looked straight at me. "What are you going to do?"

"Am I stepping on anybody's toes?" I raised my eyebrows in a question.

"Not mine," he answered me without expression. "I don't think the organized crime or detective divisions are any more interested in him than usual."

"I think the FBI has him bugged for some reason or other," I observed, remembering my FBI warning not to come here.

I followed Cassandra and Aunt Ruth into the living room and Uncle Benjamin followed me. Cassandra and my aunt were engrossed in some unknown conversation as my uncle and I were having ours.

"What gives you that idea?" He asked me.

"An agent told me to stay away from New York in general and Willy the Roach in particular."

"And, you always do the opposite of what the FBI tells you?"

He motioned for me to sit in the comfortable chair in the back living room which was the room for family, not formal guests.

"I usually ignore them if I need to find out who wants me dead."

"So, Willy has a contract out on you?" Uncle Benjamin didn't seem that worried. "He has a lot of contracts out on a whole lot of folks."

"It must be a hobby," I said with a smile.

"Luckily for you, it's not a successful hobby," he took in a deep breath. "He has quite a temper but I don't think he could afford as many hits as the word on the street attributes to him."

"There's a cab driver picking us up in about thirty minutes," I continued. "He says he knows where Willy the Roach is this time of day."

"That would probably be a bar named Smiley's." My uncle sounded thoughtful.

Smiley's was in Queens, not his borough, but I'd bet he'd make a call and have several cars full of cops standing by in case Cassandra and I got in trouble; he must love me. He's never given me a hard time about being a private investigator, and he's helped me out several times in this city without yelling at me once, I suppose he hasn't objected to any of my investigations here.

"That's probably it," I concurred. "I can't figure out what he has to do with all this, but I'd sure like to know."

"What's the case?" He asked for the first time.

"We think a car dealer in Atlanta faked his own death for a five million dollar policy. He had a twin brother that no one knew about, and we think his brother is the dead body."

"Yeah." Uncle Benjamin leaned towards me. "That doesn't sound like Willy the Roach at all."

"There has to be some angle in it for him, since he put a hit out on both of us," I thoughtfully said. "It appears as if he does have his hand into this scam somehow."

"Be careful," he warned.

"Is there something you'd like me to ask him?" I shrugged. "As long as we're taking the trouble?"

"If you could get him to tell you where all the bodies are buried." He smiled broadly at me.

"I'll ask," I chuckled.

"It's settled." Cassandra and Aunt Ruth walked back into the living room.

152

"What's settled.?" Uncle Benjamin stood up.

"We're going out to Los Angeles to see Cassandra graduate." Aunt Ruth beamed at her husband.

"When?" He asked quickly.

"Oh, don't worry." She patted her husband's arm. "It's in June, and your secretary said you could take a week off then with no problem at all."

"I've got the itinerary all set up for their visit," Cassandra added.

She stepped up to my side and put her arm around my waist.

"They'll stay in the big guestroom at the end of the hall across from my folks room."

"But," I paused. "don't we have something scheduled out of town?"

"That's the first week of March, and they'll be there the first week in June." Cassandra smiled back at me. "It'll be fine."

"And," Aunt Ruth continued Cassandra's sentence. "we have all the places Benjamin and I want to see worked out, and when we'll see them."

"You know what I want to see?" Uncle Benjamin glanced at his wife with a twinkle in his eyes.

"Better than you do."

"You little monkey," My uncle chuckled. "Look at all the trouble you've gotten me into."

Uncle Benjamin rubbed his knuckles in my hair. He never stopped doing that, even when I got as tall as he is.

153

21

Stop monkeying around

"I'm glad to see you're a man of your word," I said as I threw our suitcases into the trunk of Alphonse's cab.

"Hey." he smiled at me as he slammed the trunk closed. "I wouldn't miss this for anythin'."

"Where's Willy the Roach?" Cassandra asked as Alphonse slipped into the driver's seat.

"He's at his hang out in Queens," he answered.

"A bar called Smiley's?" I asked as the cab pulled out into traffic.

"How'd you know?" Alphonse glanced back at me quickly. "I bet it was that cop you was talkin' to back there in front of that house."

"It was," I affirmed.

"Who was he?" The cab driver continued his questioning. "Clinton Hill's a ritzy section, and that was a big old building back there, is he the only one that lives there?"

"Just he and his wife," I replied. "What's all the questions for?"

"You told me you wasn't a cop, and that cop back there had a bunch of stars on his uniform." Alphonse squinted at me in the rear view mirror. "What's goin' on here?"

"He's my uncle, and I was paying a social call on him," I grunted. "It has nothing to do with my business with Willy the Roach."

"Just so," Alphonse said, "cops that big give me the willies."

"We just got married, and his Aunt hasn't met me yet," Cassandra added.

"You two just got married?" Alphonse seemed more at ease.

"Right." I cast a sideways glance at Cassandra. "I said my

visit to my aunt and uncle didn't have anything to do with this trip to Queens."

"Got ya." The cab driver nodded. "So, lady, are you a private dick too?"

"I wouldn't use that particular word, but yes, I am," Cassandra laughed.

"How many men does Willy the Roach keep around him most of the time?" I needed to work this meeting out a little before we got there.

"Oh," Alphonse thought for a second or two. "Maybe he's got three or four of his boys around at all times, they like to hang out and shoot the breeze a lot."

"That sounds like a tough life." Cassandra shook her head. "Shoot the breeze in between shooting people."

"Something like that."

I was busy thinking.

"You have a plan?" She shook her head as she grinned.

"I do."

"I hope it's better than your last plan." She stopped smiling and glared at me.

"I hope so too."

"Does it involve shooting?" She asked.

"I hope not." I shrugged; we were silent for the rest of the ride to the bar.

. . . .

"We're here," I pronounced.

Cassandra looked out the back window of the cab. This crowded neighborhood was definitely the Italian section of this borough, so many shops selling Italian food and the odor wafting through my nostrils was a combination of rank city smells and irresistible cooked and baked goods; so many good eatables and so little time. The buildings on the block ranged from ten stories to three and most of them seemed a century old with lots of character, kind of like it had been planned by a set designer for a gangster movie. But wait, this was going to be a gangster movie, staring

155

Cassandra and Benjamin Katz in their classic rolls of simple but honest private investigators; they're doing their job, fighting for truth, justice and the American way. No, wait, that's another superhero.

Alphonse the cab driver pulled into the single vacant parking spot across the street from the bar which was very convenient, it was almost as if the director of this mobster movie had set it up.

"Well," Cassandra said.

She patiently looked at me as I scanned the whole scene from the back of the cab.

"I think the FBI are in that building across the street from the bar." I nodded in that direction.

"Why?" She asked.

"Above that liquor store are three floors of apartments, and that's where I'd put a camera and listening equipment."

"So, you work for the FBI?" Alphonse butted in.

"No, we don't," Cassandra insisted.

"We don't even like them," I added, which was true in general, but not always true.

"Do you think any of them are out on the street?" Cassandra opened her door.

"Not yet." I opened my car door. "But, I'll bet two minutes after they spot us, there'll be a bunch of them out here."

"So, what's your plan?" Cassandra asked.

She walked up beside me as I leaned over the front passenger window so I could talk to the driver.

"We'll leave the suitcases in the trunk," I said to Alphonse through the open front window. "This shouldn't take more than ten minutes or so."

"You gonna shoot the bastard?" He seemed delighted to say that.

"I'm going to try not to," I replied. "A lot of cops and FBI will be here very soon, and I'd rather not have a big gun battle right before a long plane trip."

"Me too." Cassandra squeezed my arm. "So, what's the plan?"

"The plan is that you're going to go into the bar and tell the bartender that you work for the insurance company and that Willy

156

the Roach has been named beneficiary on a five million dollar policy and that you have to talk to him and have him sign some papers."

"Me?" Cassandra pointed to her chest. "You want me to go in there and face down five or six mobsters all by myself?"

"I'll be right there in the bar." I tried to assure her. "Some guy in a suit asking for him would alert him to trouble, besides this pistol kind of sticks out in a crowd."

"Yeah, but," Cassandra stammered. "If I'm supposed to be an insurance claims person, I'd have to know Willy's real last name."

"Right." I leaned down to the front window of the cab again. "What's his real last name."

"Deluca," Alphonse spoke softly as he leaned towards me. "Willy Deluca's his real name. I can't believe you're sendin' in the broad."

Deluca, that name sounded familiar, but from where?

"She's the A-team, sport." I winked at him. "Wait right here with the cab; I'll give you a fifty dollar tip for all this when I'm through."

"Not that I think you ain't all that good, but," Alphonse said.

"Here's twenty five, I'll give you the rest when I get back," I said as I pulled off a twenty and a five from my pocket cash.

"Follow me into the bar in a few minutes." I patted Cassandra's arm. "First, give me your gun, clips and your PI identification."

"They'll frisk me, right?"

She handed them to me. It took her a minute to remove her jacket and pull off her shoulder holster.

"Right."

I stuffed the pistol into my pocket, and tossed the other items into the back of the cab before we walked towards the bar.

Like most drinking establishments, this place was poorly lit, mostly to hide the dirt and scampering rodents. The dimness also made the chronic drunks look better to themselves and their companions, besides, bright light kills the alcohol buzz fairly quickly.

This was a small place; the room couldn't be more than twenty five feet wide. The bar ran down the left side of the room with a row of red Naugahyde upholstered bar stools lined up in front of it. Lined up against the wall behind the bar was a large mirror behind row after row of small shelves.

Somewhere in that establishment was an industrial deodorant dispenser because I could smell it predominating the other scents; beer, mixed drinks, peanuts, undisguised body odor and beer farts. Bottles of every imaginable kind of hard liquor filled those small shelves and in the center of the bar were four large beer taps. Only one row of small round tables clung along the left side of the room. Even though it was before lunch time, every bar stool was occupied, and half the small tables had people sitting at them.

Where would be the best place to wait for the mobsters? I scanned the whole room over several times; the only place I could pick was the far left side of the room, two tables from the back. No one would be behind me, the wall was beside me and I could see the entire room from there.

Two doors were visible at the back of the long narrow establishment, and each one was marked as a restroom. The bar ended ten feet short of the back of the room. I walked to the bar and ordered a bottle of Labatt, the bartender stared at me since I wasn't a regular, and this bar was only used to serving regulars. He kept his stare as I paid for the beer and wandered towards the second table from the back, near the restroom doors.

An unmarked door stood alone in the middle of the blank wall beyond the bar, where I assumed Willy the Roach and his friends were holed up. As Cassandra entered the bar, I sat down at the third table from the back and kept a close eye on her as she explained to the bartender about the insurance policy.

"Just a minute, lady," he answered her.

The bartender turned around and picked up the receiver to an old black rotary phone sitting between rows of shot glasses.

"Sure thing," Cassandra replied.

She scanned the bar area, making note of the door beyond the bar and the two bathroom doors; she was becoming very good at this job.

"Willy says to wait right here," The bartender spoke directly to Cassandra. "He'll be here in a minute."

When a large man came through the door just down from the

bar, I knew that I had guessed the right place for the Deluca gang. Several drunks at the bar glanced up and considered the hulking man as he walked towards Cassandra. He was only about twenty five years old, and looked like a bodyguard, not the actual Willy Deluca.

"Lemme see your purse," he demanded as he pushed into Cassandra's personal space.

"Excuse me?" Cassandra asked in her best 'I'm a professional insurance agent and you're a scary bum' demeanor.

"You heard what I said," The massive man insisted. "Mr. Deluca don't like no one to surprise him."

"Are you going to rob me?" Cassandra indignantly replied, handing him her purse.

"No, I ain't gonna rob you."

The man dug through her purse, fishing out her wallet then handing her purse back to her.

"So, you're Cassandra Pales?" He checked her driver's license.

"That's right," she replied.

She hadn't changed the name on her license yet, which was a good thing since Willy the Roach had a hit on Katz and if the license had said Cassandra Katz, there might have been a problem.

"Wait here," the man said.

I could see the door open again, and another, much older man stuck his head out.

"She's okay," the hulking man said. "Tell Willy he can come on out."

Willy did come out, accompanied by two men in their late forties or early fifties. The last man out of the back room left the door open. I couldn't see the entire back room, but I had the impression that it was empty now.

Everybody at the bar silently slipped off their bar stools and headed to the tables, damn. Now two men were behind me so I got up and let two men sit at my table as I walked slowly towards the bathrooms. I could see more of the back room now; no one was left in there. I slowed my pace towards the men's room. Luckily for me, one of the bar stool crowd beat me to the door so I hovered near it, as if I were waiting for my turn. One of Willy's henchmen stared at me for a long time, he didn't recognize me, but he assumed I had to pee very badly, at least I kept crossing my legs and showing great pain as I gazed longingly at the closed men's room door.

"You got something for me?" Willy asked.

Willy the Roach was a balding man in his middle fifties, pleasantly plump, but not as fat as the two older men with him. Willy sat on a bar stool next to Cassandra. Well, maybe he was as fat as the two other men; his butt took up more space than the bar stool offered. Two of his men sat between Cassandra and the front door, and the other man sat behind Willy.

"Yes," Cassandra cleared her throat. "But, are you going to hurt me?" She asked nervously.

"Not if you don't piss me off to much," Willy playfully responded. "You're kind of pretty, ya know."

"Thank you, I guess."

Cassandra didn't look at me, which was a good thing.

"Well?" Willy was becoming impatient. "What's your deal?"

"Do you know a man named Simon Belchamp?"

She waited for his reaction, none was forthcoming.

"No," he shrugged. "Is he the hump who left me a pile of dough?"

The man who was in the bathroom opened the door right then. I stared at him, as did all the henchmen seated at the bar, then they also looked at me. The man leaving the men's room all of a sudden knew he was the center of attention so he quickly walked to the front door and left. I tried not to stare at the men near the bar so I turned to go into the bathroom. Before I went in, I pulled my pistol from its holster with my right hand, and pulled out Cassandra's 380 automatic with my left hand; I quickly turned and faced the men at the bar.

"He's got a piece!" One of the henchmen shouted as all the other patrons either fell to the floor or ran for the door.

"Freeze!" I shouted. "Keep your hands on the bar!"

Cassandra hustled for the nearest table as I tossed her pistol to her as she seemed to fly to the table less than ten feet from the bar. She caught her pistol in mid-air; I don't think we could repeat that trick in a million years if we tried, it was a beautiful sight to see.

160

"The broad's with him," the large hulking younger man shouted as he reached for a pistol in a waist band holster.

I shot the man reaching for his pistol in his right upper arm; the impact of my 41 caliber slug made his arm snap back, throwing the small 38 revolver against the wooden bar and onto the floor by the front door.

"I said keep your hand flat on the bar, and I meant it!" I shouted.

"What the hell was that?" Willy demanded. "What the fuck did you shoot him with!"

"It is a forty one magnum," Cassandra replied as she pointed her pistol at the three men. "Let me re-introduce myself, my name is Cassandra Katz."

"Katz!" Willy sputtered. "Katz!"

"That's right," I replied.

I stayed near the men's room and shot a quick glance towards Cassandra which made me feel better. Everyone standing near her had fled the bar, so she was alone with no one near her.

"My name is Benjamin Katz and you have a contract out on me, so if you don't want to be splattered all over your slimy bar, tell me why you want me dead?"

"I don't have to tell you nothin'!" Willy shook his head.

"You already told us you don't know Simon Belchamp, but I'd like to know if you know his brother, George Blanchard?"

"Who the fuck are they?" Willy became more irritated. "What the fuck are you talkin' about?"

"Okay," I continued. "How about Paula Thorpe?"

"Now, I finally know who you're talkin' about," Willy said with renewed conviction. "I know that bitch, she used to live in this neighborhood."

"What does she have to do with your wanting me dead?" I asked, wanting to get to the sixty four thousand dollar question.

"Not a goddamn thing!" Willy shouted. "She used to hang out with one of my boys, but I hear she's into some big shot spick now."

"So, why did you put out a contract on me?"

"You stole a hundred grand from my brother, you fuckin'

161

bastard."

"I what?"

I thought for a second; Deluca, that's why I know that name.

"Your brother's Tony Deluca?" I asked, finally having a clue to this problem.

"Yeah, that's my brother." Willy glared at me. "After you took his money, you got him arrested and I'm gonna destroy you for that."

"So." I thought more clearly now. "You hired three men to kill me?"

"Yeah," Willy said, slightly calmer than before. "I was gonna give them ten grand when the job was done."

"So," I said again for clarity. "You made a contract with three men to find me and kill me because I sued your brother for one hundred thousand dollars."

"What're you, deaf?" Willy rose slightly from his stool. "It ain't the hundred grand, it's the twenty years in the slammer that gets you dead."

"Wait just a minute, you moron," I shouted. "You almost had my wife and I shot because you think I had your dumb ass brother sent to prison?"

"Yeah, you fuck head, that's what I said!" Willy shouted back at me.

"First of all, your stupid brother was selling his two bit casino to a legitimate company." I felt I had to start at the beginning for this idiot.

"So!" Willy demanded.

"So, the corporation hired me to find out how mobbed up this rinky-dink casino was so they knew what they were getting into if they did buy it." I was a bit calmer by now.

"What's this got to do with why you fingered my brother?" Willy was also a little calmer.

This was a good plan, I needed the bad guys to be calmer.

"I went to the Vegas cops and asked them about your brother's casino."

"So, you did go to the cops!" Willy ramped up his foul mood.

162

"They told me they were investigating your brother about fixing the games and skimming," I spoke in a calm and even voice. "They told me they thought the feds were after him for tax evasion too."

"So?" Willy calmed down again.

"All I did was identify all the crooks who worked for the casino and give that report to the corporation so they knew who to fire the first day, if they bought the place."

"Like I said, you built the case that put my brother away," Willy sounded intent on killing me.

"Like I'm trying to tell you, I didn't build any case against your brother and I didn't turn him over to the cops." I shook my head. "The Las Vegas cops had him under surveillance for three years, the lieutenant out there told me all about it right after I won the lawsuit. Didn't your brother's lawyers tell him that?"

"You're shittin' me," Willy insisted.

"No, I'm not," I insisted back. "If I remember right, the lieutenant's name is Wilson, Ronald Wilson is his name. Get your lawyers to ask the cop himself."

"You're shittin' me." Willy sat back down on his stool. "Son of a bitch."

"Why, son of a bitch?" I asked. "Didn't your brother tell you any of this?"

"My brother didn't own that place, the Gambino Family owned it, he was supposed to run it for a few years, then sell it for a profit," Willy said in a much lower voice. "He told everybody that you set him up with the cops, he swears that he never skimmed nothin'."

"Those weren't trumped up charges," I insisted. "Find out from the cops, and the lawyers about that, did you even ask them?"

"What?" Willy laughed. "Me ask the cops anythin'?"

"Does that mean the contract on Benjamin is off?" Cassandra asked.

She stared at Willy and his friends still on the stools. The man with a hole in his arm didn't seem in that much pain, he had wrapped several large rags around the hole and the bleeding was greatly diminished.

"Stealing a hundred grand is worth a good beatin', not a good shootin'." Willy glared at me. "But, stormin' into my funckin' bar and shootin' my friend here is worth killin'."

"I didn't steal your damn money, I won it in a legitimate lawsuit. Your stupid brother hired a goon to kill me; I couldn't prove it to convict anybody, but I had enough evidence to convince a jury that he did."

"He hired the wrong guy for the job." Willy shot me a wicked grin.

"You know damn well he put a contract on me. The only stealing involved in that whole thing was the lawyers who stole most of the hundred grand from me in fees." I smiled back at him. "Are you through with the contracts on my life or do I have shoot you?"

"I ain't lettin' this shit go."

Willy didn't seem happy, he had to at least save face.

"So?" I kept my revolver trained on Willy's head. "You're a big talker, but I've never heard of any good clean hits in the past ten years from you."

"Benjamin," Cassandra said with a good bit of trepidation in her voice.

"Those three stooges you sent after me couldn't kill a half dead fly with a dozen tries." I smiled at the fat mobster. "With no planning at all, I got the drop on you, what kind of mob boss are you?"

"You piece of shit!" Willy hissed.

"You haven't had a decent hit in years, you're too old and too soft to be afraid of," I continued my taunts. "Why the hell shouldn't I blow your head off now and put you out of our misery."

"Iggy's widow don't think we're so tame," The fatter of Willy's boys spoke up.

"Iggy who?" I demanded. "Iggy Pop?"

"Iggy Benedetto, you ass hole!" The plump mobster shouted.

"Oh, I'm so impressed," I mocked. "You whacked a two bit street hustler."

"And I'm gonna have you and the bitch's heads on a pole by the end of the day," Willy sounded very serious now.

"Yeah, like you're a real mobster," I continued my ridiculing.

164

"What's your game? Stealing apples from street vendors? Scaring little children with your ugly faces?"

"Da boss runs all the dope in twenty blocks, all the whores and all the numbers, you ass hole," Willy's other buddy piped in.

"I'm so impressed, I tell you what I'm going to do." I studied all the men by the bar.

By now, no one but the two of us, plus the mobsters by the bar were left in the room.

"I won't shoot you, if you promise to stay right there until we leave the neighborhood."

"We're through for now." Willy looked at his henchmen. "Let 'em go."

Cassandra and I held our pistols on the men as we left the bar, putting our guns away as we ran towards the cab. Even with the loud shot, the crowds didn't notice anything, at least they knew better than to notice anything. The commerce went on as usual, the throng of humanity pressed on their way down the streets and sidewalks as if nothing had happened.

Not unexpectedly, agent Thomas Russo was in middle of the back seat of our cab as Cassandra and I hopped in on either side of him.

"You two are under arrest," he scowled. "I told you not to come here, and I wasn't kidding."

"I assume you were listening?" I asked him.

"It's kind of crowded in here," Cassandra commented.

She tried to expand her small space on the left side of the backseat.

"Listen to what?"

"Willy Deluca confessed to paying money to get me killed." I kept grinning at him. "His boys also admitted to hiring a hit on someone named Iggy Benedetto. Also, they admitted to lots of illegal activities in the neighborhood."

"He did?" Agent Russo glared at me, then at Cassandra.

"Go ask your people in that building across the street." I pointed to the apartments above the liquor store. "They should have it on tape."

"How did you know?" Agent Russo seemed confused.

165

Two beat cops walked slowly to the cab and rapped on the window. Being on the side nearest the sidewalk, I rolled down the window.

"Are you all right?" One of the patrolmen asked. "You're uncle asked that we check on you."

"I'm fine," I answered him. "Tell Uncle Benjamin, thanks."

"Will do."

The two policemen kept walking past us.

"Who the hell are you?" Agent Russo asked.

"Like you haven't done a background check on me?"

I tried to turn towards him, it was kind of crowded in that back seat.

"Yeah, but I don't believe it." he stared towards the front of the cab.

"Why don't we get out of this cab and stretch a little bit." I opened the door and spilled out onto the sidewalk.

"What's your real story?" Agent Russo followed me out of the cab and glared at me. "I've had an assistant director tell me personally not to arrest you, but I may ignore him."

"I'm not kidding," I said with my most sincere voice. "He's a Marine buddy and we Marines stick together. And, can I help it if my uncle is an assistant chief here in New York?"

"You wait right here." Russo insisted.

He pushed me back towards the cab. I saw a man walking from the building we were parked in front of walk towards us. FBI agent Russo walked to meet him at the entrance of the building and after conferring with the man for a second, the man walked back into the building; Russo came back to me.

"He says we have all of that on tape," Russo said with a sigh. "You were right."

"I know I was." I smiled at the FBI agent. "And, here's a little piece of advice for you."

"What?" Russo was clearly more annoyed than ever now.

"Willy and his four henchmen are staring at us right now, and they know what you look like and what that idiot who came out to talk to you looks like and that he came from that building across from his favorite hangout," I took in another deep breath. "So, if I

166

were you, I would go pick him up right now and make whatever case you have against him. Please make it stick, because I don't want to have to come back up here and mess with him again."

"Well, you aren't me, so mind your own damned business," Russo growled.

"I know I'm not you, and I'm glad of it too," I happily agreed with him. "Because your eavesdropping operation has been blown for sure, I don't think your assistant director will appreciate it either."

"It's your doing, you know," he steamed.

"I don't think so." I kept my ever so clever smile. "If I had been you, I would have followed this cab until it was out of the neighborhood then pulled it over to arrest me or talk to me or whatever. That way, Willy wouldn't have made you, or seen where your spies were. As it stands now, the whole neighborhood knows."

"You son of a bitch."

He was about to hit me, I guessed.

"Calm down." I opened the cab door. "At least you know me a little better now."

"You son of a bitch."

Agent Russo wanted so badly to grab me and start pummeling me. I wasn't sure what stopped him, but I jumped into the back seat of the taxi and shouted to the driver to start driving to the airport.

"What the hell happened back there?" Alphonse, the cab driver, asked.

"Not much," I said as he stared back at me in the rear view mirror. "I put a hole in the younger of his associates, but I didn't shoot Willy."

"That would be Mickey." Alphonse nodded. "Mickey's the muscle, he's the one who beats the crap outta who Willy tells him to."

"Well, Mickey's got a big hole in his right arm right now." I slowly shook my head. "I guess his crap beating will have to wait for a month or so."

"So, the FBI's got a bug on Willy the Roach." Alphonse smiled as he negotiated heaver traffic. "Dat's great news."

167

"So, all that shooting back in Virginia had nothing to do with the Belchamp case," Cassandra said.

She seemed tired, and a bit disgusted with the past thirty minutes.

"No, but maybe now that mobster will have more to worry about than putting a hit out on me." I leaned towards Cassandra. "I have a feeling that he's about to be drained of most of his funds, power and friends, he'll no longer have the means to come after me."

"I guess that's worth it, since they might have missed you and shot me instead." She took my hand and held it.

"Let's sleep late tomorrow and do nothing this weekend but go to the party next door." I kissed her cheek.

22

The hound and the hare

"Mr. Smith will see you now." The smartly dressed, fashion model secretary led Fred Lepus into the large office

"You must be Mr. Smith." Lepus extended his hand.

"Why are you here?" Don ignored the gesture.

"I understand that a Paula Thorpe works for you." Lepus dove right into his topic.

"No," Don said flatly.

"Maybe she had a different name, seeing as how her law license was revoked." Lepus tried a smile on for size, it didn't fit this situation well.

"Go on." Don looked up at Fred for the first time.

"It has come to my attention that she arranged for a large insurance policy on a Mr. Belchamp." Fred kept trying to arrange a grin to fit the situation, it still didn't.

"Are you working with those Katz people?" Don carefully studied Lepus.

"Why, yes, I am," Fred replied quickly.

"No." Don stood up. "I don't think you are."

"What makes you say that." Fred cleared his throat. "Benjamin and Cassandra have been dear friends of mine for years. As a matter of a fact, I was at their wedding in California not three months ago."

"Yeah, yeah." Don walked towards Lepus. "I don't know a

damn thing about any insurance scam that woman was up to, and I don't care about it anyway."

"You don't?" Lepus gulped in a breath. "I think you do."

"Well, think what you want, just think it somewhere else," Don huffed as he moved into Lepus' personal space.

"What do you mean?" Fred wanted more from this conversation than he was getting.

"I mean, get out of my office right now," Don insisted.

As soon as the secretary shut the door behind Fred Lepus, Don sat back down and reached for his phone.

"Mike."

"Yeah," Mike Heywood answered. "What's up?"

"I had a low rent private eye in here, and I got some good news from him."

"What?" Mike seemed hopeful. "Does he know where Kelly is?"

"I told you, you're going to have to cool your hormones about that broad," Don said.

"Well," Mike sounded irritated. "What did you find out?"

"Her real name is Paula Thorpe."

"What else?" Mike asked.

"I think you should go visit this Lepus fellow and see if he can locate her for us," Don said.

"What about The Katz detectives?" Mike seemed apprehensive.

"This Lepus guy said he's working with them, but I get the impression he's trying to horn in on the case for his own agenda," Don said. "Try to work that angle and maybe we can get to that bitch before she can damage us any more."

"How have you been doing with your current cases?" Mike seemed eager to find out.

"I finished my pile of them and I found only two possibles."

Don spread out a small stack of folders on his relatively clean desk.

"Both of them are senators, what about you?"

"I've got two also," Mike answered. "One is a section head at the DEA, and the other is also a senator."

170

"So, if that bitch stole any of the information in any of these four cases, she could be blackmailing them as we speak," Don sounded angry.

"What are we supposed to do?" Mike was worried.

"Why don't you see Fred Lepus, and see if we can locate whatever her name is, and then we can figure out what to do then," Don said. "I've got Lepus' address and number, I'll have my secretary get that to you right away."

. . . .

"I knew your firm would come around on this insurance matter." Fred seemed to gloat at the fact that a senior partner in a big law firm was now in his office.

"As my partner told you, we don't know or care anything about any insurance policy." Mike checked out the dingy living room Lepus used as his office.

"Then, why are you here?"

"I need to locate my missing friend, Kelly Chalmers," Mike sounded eager.

"Who?" Fred seemed confused.

"I think she's the same woman you know as Paula Thorpe." Mike continued to glance around the dismally appointed room.

"Oh, Paula," Fred acknowledged. "Why?"

"She's my close friend, and she's missing."

"That's not a good enough answer."

Fred leaned back in his old desk chair, it creaked slightly as he did.

"I'll pay you a thousand dollars to find her."

"That's still not a good enough answer." Fred now smiled, he could sense money.

"How about two thousand dollars." Mike started to stare at Fred.

"That's a better answer, but," Fred pressed, "why?"

"How about three thousand dollars and you stop asking stupid questions." Mike's irritation bubbled to the surface.

"So, when do you need her address?" Fred sat back up in his

171

chair.

"Now would be nice." Mike glared at Lepus.

"Have a seat over there." Fred pointed to the sofa. "And I'll confer with my secretary."

"You have a secretary?" Mike glanced at the sofa, deciding not to sit there.

"Yes, and she's right here."

Fred stood up as Cathy walked in from the kitchen.

"Cathy, this is Mr. Heywood."

"Hiya, sweetie." Cathy smiled at Mike.

"Ms. Rumson knows Paula Thorpe." Fred glanced at Cathy, then at Mike.

"You know her?" Mike seemed eager at first; he took in a deep breath and let it out slowly as he spoke. "I need to find her soon."

"Are you in love with her?" Cathy noticed Mike's expression. "Yeah, you are."

"No," Mike quickly answered. "We're good friends."

"I think you wanna be more than that," Cathy drawled with a grin.

"How do you know her?" Mike wanted to change the subject.

"Oh," Cathy laughed. "A good friend of mine was her girlfriend," she paused for a second. "And, Fred investigated her."

"What did you investigate?" Mike seemed agitated.

"Do you want the long story?" Fred asked. "That'll cost extra."

"No."

"She was stealing from several clients, and one of them hired me to do a background on her," Fred took in a breath. "I found she was stealing, and I gave the report to her client, and she sued Paula and that's how she was disbarred."

"Oh," Mike sounded sad. "Who was this boyfriend you knew."

"She wasn't a boyfriend, she was Paula's girlfriend." Cathy carefully studied Mike's reaction. "Didn't you know?"

"Know what?" Now, Mike seemed shocked for the first

172

time.

"Well," Cathy continued, "Paula sort of swings both ways, if you know what I mean."

"Can you tell me where she is?" Mike asked.

His expression said it all.

"Yeah," Cathy sounded eager. "I made some phone calls before you got here."

"Well?" Mike was truly eager.

"The Weston Hotel in Atlanta."

Cathy was proud of finding Paula, it was semi-difficult, but she did it in six phone calls.

"Now, how about my money?" Fred cleared his throat.

"Fine ." Mike pulled out a checkbook from his inside coat pocket as he stared at Cathy. "How do you spell your name?"

23

Home sweet home

Late night flights are better than mid-morning flights, at least I've noticed they're less crowded; when I said late night, I meant one o'clock in the morning. I liked the hotel we were staying at in DC, but our apartment would feel better because it's home. This would be the first time we were there together as a married couple, and we had a dinner date with our neighbors the next night. This flight was at least a direct flight into Atlanta so it wouldn't be that long until we were home; I think it's obvious that I was looking forward to being alone with Cassandra in our own home, in our own bed, together at last.

"I hope we'll have some time together after this case is done," she said.

Cassandra patted my leg as we sat together in the plane. She had the window seat, and I had the middle; luckily, no one was on the aisle seat this time.

"When is your graduation?" I asked.

"The first week of June," she answered. "I guess I can't skip it, now that your aunt and uncle are signed up for the show."

"You know this is something that you need to go to, it's the public front to what you've worked so hard and so long for." I stroked her hand.

"I guess."

"Plus, you're the one who invited my aunt and uncle to the graduation. Besides, do you really want to call your mother and tell her not to come to your graduation?"

"No."

"At least we'll have a good Christmas together." I was happy at the thought. "Even though we're supposed to go to Paris and be with your folks."

"It won't be that bad, you know," Cassandra said with a happy look on her face.

"I thought we could stay home for our first real holiday as a married couple." I gazed at her. "But, maybe a trip to Paris won't be that bad."

"Speaking of my Mom." Cassandra turned toward me. "That comment she made after the wedding, you know, the one where she almost said outright that she knew I joined the CIA."

"I know," I said. "Like I said before, she's got to be a sharp woman to figure you out with not that many clues, I see where you got your brains."

"We've always been close, but I never would have guessed she could deduce that secret." Cassandra leaned closer to me.

Her father hinted that he suspected his wife knew he had worked for the Company, so I guess Cassandra's mom was ready to put two and two together about her daughter. Cassandra had to suspect that her father at one time worked for the Company; she was smart enough to put the bits of information together correctly, but maybe she didn't want to think about it. I wasn't ready for that conversation with her, not yet.

"She won't talk about it at all any more." Cassandra shook her head.

"She's an army wife, she knows the drill." I gave Cassandra a grin and a shrug. "I like your Mom."

"I do too." Cassandra put her hand on my cheek. "Daddy's a nice man too."

"I get the feeling it takes a little more effort to get on his good side, though." I kissed the palm of her hand.

"This year, you can start the process."

"Maybe next Christmas we can go somewhere else?" I asked.

"Maybe," she sounded serious. "We could visit your brother, or maybe your aunt and uncle in New York."

"Or your uncle in Chevy Chase, or your other uncle in Framingham?"

I didn't want to share her with anyone else for the holidays, but I guess that wouldn't work in the long run.

"Your aunt and I hit it off, you know." Cassandra seemed to wake up a little more. "I'm looking forward to their visit in June."

"I am too." I tried to find a comfortable position in the small seat. "I do like them a lot. Uncle Benjamin has been more like a father to me than my own was, but I was eager to have more time alone with you before you go for your training."

"I see your point," she answered, now looking out the small window. "I guess we could have a quiet time alone at home sometime in the future, but I do want to get to know your family better."

"Not to change the subject or anything, but, do you have the same feeling about the supposed dead Simon Belchamp?"

I also glanced out the small window; I could see some lights on, mostly street lights in the occasional parking lots and urban streets. There weren't that many cars on the roads. From thirty thousand feet one can get a broad view of civilization.

"If you mean do I think he's still alive and his brother's ashes are in the urn, yes." Cassandra turned towards me. "I guess he's behind the Cayman Island scheme to get the money."

"That would be the obvious guess," I postulated, "But, remember, things are not always as they seem."

"So, you think something else is going on?"

"I think that bum we saw in Washington was Simon, but I don't think he may necessarily be the mastermind behind this five million dollar scam."

"What makes you think that?"

"After checking into his past, and his mediocre business acumen, I don't think he could come up with a complicated plot like this, nor do I think he would have the balls to pull it off," I said.

It was hard to concentrate on work, she is a beautiful woman.

"Maybe his mistress could be the brains behind a scheme like that," I speculated.

"It could be more simple than that," Cassandra observed.

176

"You saw a check written to a real estate company from his personal account. That says he did have a young cutie on the side, and maybe he wanted this tart for his main dish, maybe that was Simon's only scam, and the five million dollar insurance thing was somebody else's doing."

"I know, he concocted this elaborate scheme to disappear and run off with his sweet thing to Tahiti; perhaps the five million was the traveling money."

But, even as I said it, I didn't believe it, I wondered if Cassandra did.

"Why don't we check with the real estate company and try to find his side dish and at least check her out," Cassandra replied. "At least if we find her, we may find our dead man."

"That sounds like a plan, we can get to it first thing Monday."

I looked back out the window.

"What did Cheryl ask us to bring for dinner?"

"Just ourselves." Cassandra lay her head on my shoulder. "I thought we could bring a bottle of wine, though."

. . . .

Our flight got in after three in the morning on Saturday so the traffic wasn't all that bad; the cab got us to our house around four. All was quiet in the neighborhood that early. We set the alarm for one in the afternoon and tried to get some sleep, we mostly slept.

24

Where oh where did my missing girl go?

"What's that?"

Cassandra shoved my shoulder. I was dead asleep, I don't even remember what I was dreaming about, or if I was dreaming at all.

"Wake up!" She shouted louder.

"Why?" I was almost conscious.

"Don't you hear all that racket?" Cassandra forcefully asked.

She bolted from the bed and was fumbling around in her closet for her robe.

"Get your ass out of bed before we get invaded," she insisted.

"Invaded? What day is it?"

I checked the clock on my bed stand; it was eleven in the morning.

"It's Saturday," Cassandra sounded annoyed.

She tossed a pair of boxers, a tee shirt and some jeans on the bed as she rummaged around in her dresser drawer for her pistol.

"It might be a delivery man," I commented.

I pulled on my underpants. The last mundane thing I remembered doing before I crawled into bed last night with the love of my life was that I tossed my revolver under my side of the bed. There it was, I pulled it out of the shoulder holster and followed Cassandra into the living room. Cassandra had managed to put on my tee shirt and pajama bottoms, I liked the look.

"Why don't you answer the door before everyone in the building calls the cops," Cassandra said.

She stepped aside and tried to focus her sleepy eyes on the door, whoever was out there, wasn't going to give up knocking loudly on our front door.

"Okay," I agreed.

I snapped the front door open and shoved the barrel of my revolver at Mike Heywood who jumped back a pace, surprised.

"Hi, Mike." I lowered my revolver. "Where's Don?"

"Are you going to shoot me?" Mike still sounded shocked.

"No." I smiled as best as I could, given that I was essentially still asleep. "Not yet."

"Come on in, Mike," Cassandra added.

She stepped around where he could see her; Cassandra still held her automatic pistol in her right hand.

"Do you two always greet people this way?" He was becoming a little more at ease.

"Come in," Cassandra insisted. "Why are you here?

"Kelly Chalmers met me here last night in Atlanta," Mike sounded so dejected as he said that.

"You flew here with her?" I asked.

At least we knew where the woman was, at least where she was last night.

"Sit down."

Cassandra pointed to our couch. She stepped back down the short hall and tossed her pistol on the end of our unmade bed then she closed the bedroom door so she could put some more clothes on.

"We got to sleep about five this morning, and you woke us up."

I sat on the upholstered chair facing the sofa.

"I'm sorry." He glanced at me. "I didn't know where to go, you two are the only people I know in this town," Mike almost pleaded.

I knew that couldn't be true, a big DC lawyer knows somebody in all the major cities on this coast. He must have had some specific reason to bang on our door this early on a Saturday, well, it was early for me.

"Could you get some more clothes on, please," Mike said.

I guess he didn't really want to stare at me in my boxers and nothing else.

"I'll wait until my partner gets back so she can keep an eye on you," I replied.

"Well," he said, "I like her better anyway."

"So, tell me what happened," I asked.

I was curious. Cassandra came back out into the living room, still barefooted and wearing cut off jeans and an old work shirt. Actually it was one of my old shirts that had one too many stains on it for me to wear outside the house but she liked it and took it for a shirt to paint or fix things in.

"Kelly and I had a heart to heart yesterday and said she was in a lot of trouble that wasn't her fault at all." Mike seemed to be winding up with this story. "She said the police thought she was involved with something really bad, but that she wasn't; someone had set her up and she had to find him."

"I think I'll get some pants on, if you don't mind."

I got up from the chair and headed back to our bedroom, setting my revolver next to Cassandra.

"I appreciate that." Mike stared at Cassandra, not me.

"Did Kelly say who set her up?" Cassandra asked.

"Yes," Mike replied, still facing Cassandra. "She said her ex-husband set her up."

"What was she supposed to have done that would send the cops after her?" Cassandra asked.

"She wouldn't say," Mike answered, now looking at the floor. "I have to find her."

"You lost her?" Cassandra asked; she was trying to lose her sloppy grin. "Where did you leave her?"

"We were both in the Weston Hotel last night," Mike answered.

He looked at Cassandra, he appeared so bleak, it seemed that he was here only because of his crush on the woman he thought was Kelly Chalmers.

"She wasn't there the next morning?" She asked.

Cassandra glanced at me as I walked back into the living room with pants and a shirt on. I saw the faint smile flash on the right corner of her mouth.

"No, she wasn't," Mike slowly answered.

"You want us to find her and bring you two back together?" I asked.

"Yeah." Mike stared back at the floor.

"Kelly Chalmers is not her real name," Cassandra added.

She stared at me. I was giving her a harsh look; I didn't want her to tell him the right name for Kelly Chalmers.

"It's not?" Mike acted confused.

"No, it's not," I answered. "We're not sure what her real name is, but we did find out that she's been disbarred in at least one state. And, we're not even sure she graduated from law school."

"I don't care." Mike glanced up at me. "Can you find her and make sure she's all right; I want to see her again."

"I don't know if we can do that," I answered.

My bullshit detector was beginning to flash red, what was he up to?

"Where are you staying?" I asked.

"I still have a room at the Weston," Mike answered. "Leave a message for me, my room is 1168."

"Okay," I said. "How about you let us get dressed for work and we'll see what we can do for you."

"I'll pay you three thousand dollars to find her and let me talk to her again," Mike said as he got up and headed to the front door.

As Mike left and I shut the door behind him, Cassandra stared at me and motioned with her head for me to follow her to the bedroom, which was okay with me.

"Did you buy his story?"

Cassandra started to make the bed as I joined in on the other side.

"Not for a second," I emphatically said. "What the hell is he up to?"

"I did get the impression that he had a crush on the woman, but not that big a crush."

181

Cassandra finished making the bed, then began searching for something more presentable to wear.

"My question is, how did he know where to find us?"

I looked for some socks and shoes.

"This address isn't on our business cards, and the phone number is our answering service, he had to do some checking on us to find our apartment," I added.

"I know, but it isn't that hard to find us." Cassandra said as she pulled up her full length jeans. "We're actually in the phone book. Maybe we should get an unlisted number."

"I'll call the Weston and see if he came in with a girl, and who else might be there with him," I said.

"Good idea," Cassandra agreed. "But, how about I go out and get something to eat for the next few days? Have you noticed that there's not much food around here?"

. . . .

"What did you get at the Farmer's Market?" I asked as Cassandra walked in.

"Some French table wine for tomorrow and some cheese. I also got a few staples for the next few days."

She closed the front door behind her and walked to the kitchen as I followed her there.

"We do have to get another car," I said. "You're right about that."

"So, you're finally the one without a car and you had to pay for the cab rides." She smiled at me as she put the food away. "So, how did it go downtown?"

"I had some luck at the Weston," I replied as I sat at the kitchen table.

"Did Mike check in with Paula Thorpe?" Cassandra asked.

She sat down across the table from me.

"No, he didn't, she checked in two days ago, and he got there last night," I answered. "But, guess who else checked into the Weston yesterday?"

182

"I don't know, who?" She didn't want to guess.

"Don and Mike are back together again, right here in Atlanta." I kept my smug expression.

"Well, I'll be." Cassandra seemed to be turning over a few possibilities. "Why is that woman so important to them?"

"Do you think it has something to do with the insurance scam?" I asked.

"No."

"Me neither." I nodded in agreement. "Those two didn't appear that worried about our insurance case when we talked to them, they seemed more uncomfortable about something else to do with Paula."

"So, what do we do about them?" Cassandra asked. "Do we confront them? Do we threaten them? Do we work for them?"

"Work for them?" I was confused.

"He did offer to pay us to find the Thorpe woman," Cassandra answered with a grin. "We can pump her for information, give her to the cops, then call Mike and collect the reward."

"You're joking, right?"

"Of course I am, you idiot," she laughed out loud.

25

Steak out

"When are we supposed to go next door?" I asked as I finished getting dressed.

"Six," she replied.

Cassandra turned off the hair dryer, then she stepped out of the bathroom so she wouldn't have to shout.

"I think we should go to the grocery store again; I got some stuff, but not enough. Since we've been gone from here for months, we're out of about everything."

"Why don't you take the car again." I kissed her as she sat down on the bed with me. "I want to arrange all the notes we've taken on this case, I'll be in the office."

"You know," she said, "I've been thinking about another car again."

"That's better than thinking about another man," I chuckled.

"It's too soon, and I'm still too fond of you to start thinking about another man." She patted my arm. "I think we should have something besides your Porsche to drive around town and get groceries, you sort of agreed with me yesterday."

Cassandra had used the only company car Cheshire Katz agency owned while we lived in Los Angeles. But that car, along with the agency, had been sold, so we were down to one car.

"And, I agree with you today too." I nodded. "The last time I checked in the newspaper I saw a BMW Bavaria."

"What is it with you and German cars?" She slowly shook her head in bewilderment.

"It's a damned good car, it looks cool and it goes fast," I answered emphatically.

184

"Now it makes sense," she laughed. "How much does it cost?"

"Too much for a four year old car, but maybe I can get the price down. At least we can depreciate it for taxes."

I got up and started to gather together all the notes from our investigation.

"You aren't going to get all huffy about parking it in the mall or anything, are you?" Cassandra asked.

"Not if I can keep my 911 in the garage," I replied. "It's a classic 1965 Targa, that's the first year they made them."

"The garage is fine for your old Teutonic toy," she said with a grin.

....

"Hi, Cassandra." Cheryl gave her a big hug. "It's good to have you back home."

"Come on in." Anne, Cheryl's partner, motioned for me to come back to the kitchen. "You didn't have to bring anything, but why don't I open the bottle and we can have a drink before the main dish is done."

"I forgot to ask either of you if you were vegetarians," Anne spoke loud enough for everyone to hear.

"We're not." I glanced at Cassandra to show solidarity. "But, it doesn't matter what you fix, we like almost everything."

"Benjamin is sort of like a human garbage disposal," Cassandra had to pipe up. "I've never seen him refuse anything."

"Well." I peeked back out the kitchen door at Cassandra. "That's not entirely true."

"Good." Anne seemed to want to end this discussion. "We made squash casserole and cooked four t-bone steaks."

"We sort of covered every possibility," Cheryl added.

"Can you help me put some of this stuff on the table," Anne spoke to me in a quieter voice.

"Sure." I grabbed a bowl of mashed potatoes and a bowl of green beans while Anne accompanied me to the dining room with

185

the casserole.

"So, Benjamin tells me you're finished with your degree." Cheryl said.

She plopped down in the only sofa in the living room.

"That's right, I'll be going to the graduation ceremony in June."

Cassandra sat in one of the two stuffed single chairs facing the sofa.

"Do you have to move back there for another quarter?" Cheryl asked.

I guessed she's the one with the crush on Cassandra.

"No." Cassandra smiled at me as I sneaked a glance at her from the kitchen. "I'm completely done with everything. All the hurdles are jumped over, and the hoops jumped through. I have to go back there in January for a week so I can pack all my junk up and ship it back here along with me. We're going back out there in early June for the graduation ceremony, but that'll be it."

"That's great," Cheryl said. "Will you be searching for a teaching job around here, I know the chairman of the political science department at Georgia State."

"Thanks for thinking of me, but I think I'll stay with our business for a while." Cassandra smiled at her.

"I think everything's on the table now," Anne announced.

Anne stood at the archway separating the living room from the dining room. Cassandra and Cheryl got up and joined Anne and me in the dining room. The cooking was nothing fancy, but the scents of well cooked steaks and a good collection of side dishes steaming through their apartment was a comfortable smell. A lot of food rested on the table; I guess planning for meat eaters, and non-meat eaters can make for a plentiful feast.

"So, where do we sit?" Cassandra looked at the four chairs around the table.

"Wherever." Anne shrugged her shoulders.

Cassandra sat on the left side and I sat across from her.

"I think it's exciting as hell." Anne sat down at the end of the table nearest the kitchen. "Being a private investigator has got to be more exciting than teaching."

186

"I think so," Cassandra chuckled. "That's why I like doing it."

"Me too."

I was feeling estrogen challenged all of a sudden, well, maybe I was feeling left out.

"Are you working on a case right now?" Cheryl sat at what appeared to be the head of the table.

"As a matter of a fact, we are." Cassandra settled into her chair. "We're working for an insurance company investigating a death claim."

"So, something's not quite right," Cheryl mused. "Is it murder?"

"He died of a heart attack," I flatly replied as I passed the bottle of wine to Anne.

"But that's what the Medical Examiner's office said." Cassandra was amused about all this somehow.

"That's not what you think?" Anne sipped the wine. "This is good."

She cast me a glance as she passed the bottle to Cassandra.

"Thanks," I answered. "Cassandra picked it up from the Farmer's Market yesterday."

"What about the dead guy?" Cheryl said, glancing at me for two milliseconds, then back to Cassandra.

"We think we saw him in Washington last night," Cassandra replied.

She winked at me while I was eying the largest steak on the platter in front of me.

"Then, he isn't dead after all?" Anne sounded confused. "So who was the guy that the Medical Examiner said had a heart attack?"

"I know." Cheryl got a bit more excited. "He must have a twin."

"I take it you have a big mystery section in your book store?" I asked.

"Yes, we do," Anne interrupted. "It's Cheryl's favorite genre."

"I'm right, aren't I?" Cheryl peeked at Cassandra.

"We think you are." Cassandra smiled back at her. "We have

187

to check out some finger prints tomorrow."

"That's not all we have to do tomorrow." I glared at Cassandra.

I wish she wouldn't discuss cases with our neighbors, but I guess it won't harm anything this time.

"Right, we also have to search for that Thorpe woman," Cassandra replied.

She raised her eyebrows, I don't think she agreed with me about not telling them.

"I know a Thorpe woman." Cheryl became even more excited. "Is her name Paula Thorpe?"

Cassandra and I stared at each other for a full ten seconds in silence.

"I'll get the photo," I shouted as I got up quickly and headed to our office.

"What was that all about?" Anne asked Cassandra as I left their apartment in a rush. "Was it something I said, or did he not like the food?"

"That's the woman you're searching for, right?" Cheryl stood up. "I can't believe it!"

"Believe it." Cassandra shook her head. "That's the name of the woman we're looking for."

"You know her too." Cheryl spoke to Anne . "She moved away three years ago, remember?"

"Yeah, I think so." Anne searched her memory. "Was she the prissy one who had dumped her husband?"

"That's her." Cheryl sat back down, shaking her head.

Still huffing from the mad dash to our office on the first floor, I sprinted back to the dining room table. I had left the front door to our neighbor's apartment ajar so I could come back in without knocking.

"Is this her?"

I handed Cheryl the snapshot of Paula Thorpe and her alleged lawyer boyfriend.

"That's her," Cheryl answered quickly. "What did she do? Did she kill the man?"

"No," Cassandra answered. "We need to ask her a few

188

questions about the dead man; she knew him, it seems."

"Does she live here in Atlanta?" I asked.

"Not in three years," Cheryl answered. "She dumped her husband, came out of the closet and left Atlanta all in the same year."

"She was gay?" Cassandra took a bit longer to catch on.

"I got the impression that she was more bi than gay," Anne sounded lost for a second in a recollection.

"She was one prissy dyke for sure." Cheryl smiled and nodded.

"Be a little more civil, please." Anne shot her partner a glare. "Can you pass the potatoes down here."

"Sorry." Cheryl handed the bowl of mashed potatoes to Anne. "She likes me to be civilized in front of company."

"Don't mind us, we're just your friendly neighbors." I grinned at Anne.

Cheryl had taken the largest t-bone while I had run downstairs for the picture of Paula Thorpe. Well, he who hesitates eats less.

"Where did she like to hang out when she lived here?" Cassandra asked.

"Before she came out, I don't know," Cheryl quickly answered. "But lately, she loves the 688 club."

"Is that a lesbian club?" Cassandra asked.

"No, not really," Anne answered. "It's a new club, it opened last year and they have great live music and a great dance floor."

"Yeah." Cheryl brightened; maybe that was a favorite place of hers also.

"They started playing the punk music and I don't like it so much," Anne said in a distracted tone.

Anne dropped a large spoonful of squash casserole on her plate; ah, she was the vegetarian here. Judging by the steaks on the three other plates, Anne was the only vegetarian here.

"They have other bands there." Cheryl shot Anne a disgusted look. "A lot of really good bands from Athens come up here."

"I don't know much about punk music," Cassandra interjected.

189

"Oh." Cheryl gave Anne one more glance, then moved her eyes to Cassandra. "You know, bands like the Ramones and the Sex Pistols."

"I guess I've heard them." Cassandra shrugged, giving me a questioning look.

"Don't look at me," I replied. "That's not my brand of rock."

I finished swallowing the food I'd been chewing; it was good.

"It's better than Disco," Cheryl sounded a little hurt.

"Anything's better than Disco," Cassandra observed.

"The club has threatened to play disco one night a week," Anne added.

I don't think Cheryl liked Anne adding that, judging from the expression it elicited.

"We both like classical music better anyway." Cheryl glanced back at Cassandra.

"Now, that's my speed," I added.

I put another helping of squash on my plate. Maybe Cassandra was right, I do eat almost anything.

"Have you been to the Atlanta Symphony yet?" Anne asked.

"The first thing I did after moving here was to buy season tickets," I answered.

"Maybe I could go to the club and learn something about punk rock tomorrow." Cassandra shot me a worried look. "Do you want to go too?"

"Hey," Cheryl interrupted. "You can go with me."

"Maybe." Cassandra glanced at Cheryl. "Why?"

"You're looking for Paula and I know what she looks like and who her friends are." Cheryl continued building the case to accompany Cassandra; I was amused by the whole thing.

"Okay," Cassandra sounded out slowly. "I'll get in touch tomorrow about the details."

26
The Katz Cradle

Contrary to my prior expectation, we enjoyed the dinner with our neighbors the night before. The steaks might have been better if they were grilled, but I didn't have that much of a problem with the one I ate. The squash had a combination of spices that made it more palatable than it should have been. After the main course, the conversation moved away from our detective work and on to more interesting discussions of politics, local job markets and the local music scene. Anne and Cheryl are fun folks; Cheryl is the more gregarious of the two, and the skinniest. High energy people often burn more calories even when standing still. While Anne dressed in billowy earth tone dresses, Cheryl dressed in sharp hues of red and blue. Anne had a masters in English from Emory, and Cheryl had a degree from Georgia State in political science. They met five years ago and must have hit it off well since they are still together.

Anne always wanted to own a book store so she and Cheryl bought out a book store in Little Five Points four years ago and have transformed it from mostly a comic book shop to quite a good used book store, specializing in women's studies, big surprise.

"You don't suppose it would hurt if I use Cheryl as a lookout for the Thorpe woman tonight," Cassandra asked.

She checked herself out in the full length mirror attached to the inside of our closet door.

"Since you're asking, I don't think it would be a good idea," I answered. "I don't like involving paying tenants in hazardous doings, at least not on purpose."

"She should go with me tonight." Cassandra stayed on the same course. "If the woman shows up, Cheryl could introduce us since she already knows the Thorpe woman."

"That makes better sense." I stopped tying my shoes. "Not a lot of sense, but better sense."

"Where are you going?" She asked.

191

"I think I need to see the doctor who allegedly gave Belchamp the clean bill of health for the insurance policy."

"Where else are you planning on going?"

"I'm taking the bottle down to the Medical Examiner's office to give it to Dr. Jenkins."

I checked my shoes to make sure I got both of them tied.

"Maybe I can interest him in turning the whole thing over to the police if we got Simon Belchamp's fingerprints in DC several weeks after he supposedly died."

"I guess if the police believe Simon is still alive and his brother is in the urn, then the insurance company will be happy and we'll get our money."

"I guess so."

I stood up and glanced at my self in the mirror, it was still early and I could have put my trousers on backwards and not known it.

"I'd like you to see Katzen and give him the report and expense sheets I typed up yesterday, also see if he wants us to go any further into the Cayman Island corporation and who is behind it as well as locate Simon in the flesh," I said.

"Sure," she sounded a bit nervous. "I have something to do at eleven."

"What?" I was not calm.

"Well, I'm more than two weeks late, and I didn't know how to tell you."

She sat down on the bed and I thought she started to cry.

"I wanted to tell you when I first got back in town, but I wasn't sure and I wanted to find out first before I said anything. I'm always on time, I can almost set my watch by my periods. It could be all the pressure I've been under, or it could be something else."

"You mean, you could be pregnant?" I was in shock.

"Maybe." She stared at me as I sat next to her on the bed. "I've been on the pill the whole time, but I just don't know."

"Maybe you shouldn't have gone with me to DC and New York." I hugged her. "That was a little dangerous."

"Now you admit it." she didn't appear too happy right then. "If I'm pregnant or not, this is my job and I am going to do it."

192

"Okay." I didn't know what to say. "I love you, and I guess that's all I can think of right now. This isn't something I never thought of happening."

"We have talked about it," Cassandra reminded me. "We both decided to wait, maybe forever."

"If you are, we can adjust our plans." I hugged her again.

"Maybe it's my nerves," she said. "This dissertation stuff on top of our last few cases has me about to jump out of my own skin."

"That sounds like a long vacation for the two of us may be needed." I kissed her. "After we finish this case, we'll take a long vacation."

"Don't forget I have that thing to go to in March," Cassandra whispered into my ear as she hugged me back.

"Right."

"See what I mean about too much on my plate at once."

"March is a long time away," I answered in a calm voice, at least I was trying for a calm voice. "You're finished with school now, except for the graduation and March is three months from now. We have plenty of time for a vacation, and we have the money now."

"I don't want to spend that much money on a vacation," she spoke up. "We have to pay capitol gains tax on it and we need to have some savings, especially if we're going to have a kid."

"Let's rock that cradle when the time comes," I replied. "Right now, let's get through this one day and see what the next has in store."

"You're right," she paused, a possible pregnant pause. "What's the plan?"

"You take the Porsche and drop me off at the car dealer," I said.

I gathered up my stuff from the dining room table.

"What?"

"I called and the BMW is still there," I clarified myself. "Unless it's a complete dog, I was going to buy it this morning so we both can have a car."

"But, it's around seven thirty in the morning," Cassandra sounded confused. "They couldn't be open this early, could they?"

"The service department was open at seven, and they told me

193

the BMW was still there, and, the salesmen get in between seven thirty and eight."

"Okay." She seemed to be rising from the baby funk. "I guess if you don't buy it you can cab it around town like you did Saturday."

"Do you feel like seeing Katzen before you go to the doctor?" I asked.

"No," she thought for a second. "I'd rather wait until this afternoon to talk to him."

"Okay, I'll meet you back here with the new car around lunch time." I smiled at the love of my life. "We can both go see Katzen then; will we know by then?"

"We should know before I leave the doctor's office." She sounded happier.

"Where is it?"

"Northside Hospital has a women's clinic," she said as she picked up her purse. "You know we need to pick out a regular doctor for the two of us."

"I suppose so."

I guess I'm not immortal after all.

"Where is this car dealership?"

"It's in Decatur."

"That's not too far," She said, not knowing what else to say. "I'll drop you off there and you meet me back here at noon."

. . . .

I hate car dealerships and I hate car salesmen, especially I hate used car salesmen. There's too much hate in the world. Why can't this be like buying a can of tomatoes at the supermarket? I've never had to argue about the price of a can of tomatoes.

Once I agreed to a price and it was firmly chiseled in stone, my helpful used car con man balked at my request to drive it home right then. I guess I don't open the can of tomatoes in the store, but this was a damned car.

"What haven't you done to it?" I was clearly annoyed. "Are you telling me it isn't ready to be sold? What's the matter? No brakes? Why did you let me drive it around for thirty minutes?"

"No, sir," he hemmed for a bit longer than I thought he

should have. "We need to clean it up before you take it home."

"It appears clean to me." I stared at him. "The mechanicals seemed fine, I drove it to a service station on Ponce and had them check the obvious. Are you telling me there's something not so obvious wrong with it?"

"No, no sir," he insisted, waving his right hand in the air this time. "We need to clean it inside and out before it leaves the dealership."

"How about we knock off three hundred for the superb wash job and the new muffler you were going to put on it." I watched as he tried not to squirm.

The mechanic told me it would need replacement muffler soon, but it should last for a few months more and he didn't see anything else wrong with it. He was a good sport to check over the car with no notice.

"Okay," he sighed loudly. "I have to get the manager to approve the new deal, though."

He got up and rushed to the back suite of offices; I bet he never spoke to anyone, it's all just a game anyway. The back office must have been empty since my salesman made it back to his desk in less than five minutes, solitude isn't this salesman's forte.

While my salesman was contemplating his belly button in the back room, I used his phone to make a call to the physician who preformed the insurance medical exam on Simon Belchamp, well, allegedly he did the physical on Simon Belchamp. After some pressure, the receptionist let me speak to the head nurse who was even more reluctant to let me speak to the doctor. It seemed, however, that Allan Katzen had already raised enough questions about this case to get me an appointment with the doctor later that morning.

"Can I ask you a question about another dealership near here?" I asked as I wrote a huge check to the dealership.

"Certainly." He pointed to the spots on the contract I was to initial.

"Simon Belchamp." I initialed the paperwork.

"The Chevy dealership?" he asked.

"That's right." I nodded. "What's their business like?"

"He's not a high volume dealer," he answered. "I think Chip used to work for them, let me see if he's here."

He stood up and peered over his office partition.

"Hey Chip, can you come over here for a second."

"Yeah." The slack-tooth salesman stuck his head in the opening to the office.

"This gentleman wants to know about the Belchamp dealership," My clever salesman asked.

"I worked there over two years." Chip wasn't too talkative; he guessed I wouldn't buy a car from him anytime soon.

"What kind of dealer are they?" I asked. "Are they a high pressure outfit, or a mom and pop outfit?"

"Simon Belchamp was not a high pressure kind of guy," Chip answered with a salesman smile. "Now, his wife more than made up for that."

"She's involved in the business?" I asked innocently. "I met the son at a party a few months ago and I got the impression that he and his dad ran the business."

"You got the wrong impression there."

Chip took a step into the office after I had finished signing all the papers. My salesman slipped past Chip on his way to the business office where I'm sure he was going to call the bank to make sure I had the funds in there to cover it; after all, I was going to drive off in the car.

"You mean the wife runs the business?" I acted surprised.

"She don't put her name on nothing, but if you work there long enough you find out the old lady hires and fires and sets the work conditions." Chip shook his head slightly. "I honestly think old Simon would rather have spent the rest of his life in his bass boat and at his hunting cabin in the mountains."

"Why was she so active in the business?"

There had to be a story there, somewhere.

"Well." This good old boy was about to dish some dirt. "The scuttlebutt around the office was that she didn't get enough money to fly in the higher circles."

"You mean she wanted to hobnob with the rich folks?" I understood him.

"Yeah," The salesman said. "If she couldn't be a real socialite, she wanted to buy her way into the life style. They belonged to the most expensive country club, and she gave big bucks away to the charities, and then there was all them big parties."

"But, wasn't Belchamp rich enough to afford all that?"

"Not for the past five years or more." Chip shook his head. "It seems Belchamp was taking home less and less of the profits."

"Why was that?" Ah, I was getting closer to a real clue.

"I don't know for sure, but the finance manager thought the old man was skimming," Chip lowered his voice as if he were about to reveal a state secret.

"Did anybody raise the issue with Belchamp?" I asked.

"What?" Chip stared at me like I was a dunce. "And get fired? Who cares if he steals money from himself as long as he paid all his bills, and we got paid."

"What about his son?"

"He's the spittin' image of his old man," Chip said. "Why are you so interested?"

"Nothing important, really," I replied. "I was shocked to see he died so suddenly. I had met them socially and didn't know that much about the family, I was curious, that's all."

"Yeah." Chip scratched the back of his head. "I didn't know he had that much heart trouble. He was kind of fat and he did like the greasy food too much, but it still was a shocker."

"Yeah, for me too."

"Hey, what's that plastic bag with the old bottle in it?"

Chip seemed like he was dying to ask me a question and I guess my pumping him for information on Simon Belchamp gave him the push to ask me the burning question.

I couldn't help the large grin that spread over my face.

"I'm a private investigator and that's evidence in a case I'm working on. I'm headed to the police to get them to check the fingerprints on it," I replied.

"Oh," he paused for a second. "I guess that explains the gun you've got under your coat."

"I guess it does." I nodded.

"What is it?" He asked.

197

"A revolver." I grinned again.

"No, I mean what kind." He sounded annoyed.

"It's a Smith and Wesson model twenty nine," I answered.

I did change my carry gun to something a bit more mainstream. It would be a lot easier to feed the forty four with different kinds of ammunition than my forty one. Too bad, I liked the old model fifty eight Smith.

"Yeah." Chip smiled at me. "My brother's got Super Blackhawk in forty four with a long barrel, he's scoped it and hunts deer with it."

"Here's your keys," My salesman interrupted my conversation with Chip; I was kind of glad he did. "We'll mail your title and tag as soon as we get them. The temporary tag is good for over a month, just keep the sales agreement in the glove box until you get your paperwork."

"Thanks for the information." I shook Chip's hand. "Maybe we can do business again." I added as I shook my salesman's hand.

. . . .

The BMW wasn't that bad a car, it only had thirty five thousand miles on it and the interior was in immaculate condition. I know it wasn't the proverbial little old ladies car but I saw the old title in the salesman's office and the name of a leasing company was on the old title, but that didn't help with who actually drove the car. Maybe I could look into that when I had some more free time; what free time was I talking about?

A little after ten in the morning, I drove my shiny new car into Dr. Miller's parking lot, well, it was a new car to me. The doctor's office was tucked into a commercial development and strip mall north of the two eighty five perimeter on Buford Highway. On my northward journey on Buford, I noticed what seemed like a big old fashioned army surplus store. When I had some free time, I'd have to visit the Old Sarge; there I go again with this fictitious free time.

I was five minutes early, but the nurse led me into an examining room. I wasn't there to be poked or prodded, so what was the deal with the examining room? I was there to examine him, not the other way around.

198

"Hello, my name is Dr. Miller."

A middle aged man with graying hair scanned the room, then settled his eyes on my face.

"My name is Benjamin Katz and I'm working for Mr. Katzen." I stood up and faced him as I shook his hand. "I'm investigating the Belchamp case for him."

"Yes, yes, I know all about that problem," Dr. Miller sounded disgusted. "Allan has called me incessantly since I got back from Florida this weekend."

"Then, I take it you know that the man you examined probably wasn't the man who was insured," I carefully said.

"I'm damned sure he wasn't."

"What makes you say that?" I was curious about his insistence.

"Well." He sized me up. "For starters, my office was burgled a week after I gave that man the physical and nothing valuable was stolen except a handful of patient records."

"Let me guess," I interjected. "The Belchamp files were stolen."

"Among six others, yes," he expelled a half lung-full of air. "I make a good part of my income from insurance companies in the Atlanta area and the last thing I need is some minor problem turning into a big scandal."

"I take it Mr. Katzen has sent you the picture of the dead man?" I asked.

"Yes, he sent it by courier to my home on Saturday," Dr. Miller cautiously replied. "You know, if the exam had taken place more than a few years ago, and if there hadn't been the burglary to make me keep that man's face in my mind, I might not have been able to categorically say the dead man was not the man I examined."

"Did the man you examined even look like the dead man?" I had to ask.

"Yes," The doctor replied. "They both had the same build, height, hair color and eye color."

"So, you'd testify in court the man you examined was a plant?"

"You bet I would," he said emphatically.

Ahead of time, I was almost sure this man didn't have any part in an insurance scam. That alone would give the insurance company reason not to pay up.

Our new car had a lot more room in it than my 911 and it was almost as much fun to drive, almost. At about noon I found a parking place on Euclid Avenue near our house, the parking place was only three houses down from ours and I considered myself lucky for finding it. Cassandra was not there yet, so I went up to our apartment and fixed tuna on toast for her and me; she was right, our cupboards were bare. I put the sandwiches in the refrigerator until she got back.

. . . .

"Well?" I asked as she walked in.

She had a half grin on her face which I could not read.

"The answer to the burning question is, no." Cassandra sat in the rocker in our living room. "It's ninety nine percent, no."

"Ninety nine percent?" I shouldn't have said that.

"Nothing is a sure thing in this world." She didn't sound happy. "Ninety nine percent is what you'll have to take for now."

"How do you feel about that?" I asked.

"I feel a bit relieved," she took in a deep breath and let it out slowly. "How do you feel about it?"

"The same as you." I was relieved.

I have to admit, I wasn't ready for the pitter patter of little Katz feet quite yet.

"So, it's all the tension and worry about our work and your school?" I asked.

"That was her diagnosis."

Cassandra seemed to relax, she seemed to melt into the rocker. It was a big wooden rocking chair we bought together on an impulse right after we moved into the apartment and we both liked it since it had enough room to curl up in and even tuck your feet up.

"The most important thing is that you're all right," I said. "We need to take a long vacation as soon as we're through with this case."

I was a little worried about her then.

"Believe me." She lay her head back in the chair. "I want

200

that too, it's kind of a relief that all this happened."

"How so?"

"It was my body telling me that I've been trying to do too many things at once." She took in a deep breath and let it out slowly. "First I'm a private investigator, then I'm a doctoral student at UCLA, then I've signed my life away to god only knows what, then I'm married, then I think I may be pregnant."

"I guess that's enough to make anybody a nervous wreck. Although, I have to say I wasn't that upset by the possibility." I got up and headed to the kitchen. "I've got our lunch, I'll be right back."

"Are you telling me you wouldn't mind having kids?" Cassandra sounded surprised and irritated at the same time.

"No," I reflected, trying to avoid landmines. "We agreed to hold off on that decision for a few years. I love you, no matter what happens, and that you can count on over and above anything else."

"Was that our new car parked on the street?" Cassandra wanted to change the subject. "The silver BMW?"

"Yeah." I came back in and handed her the sandwich. "It wasn't that bad a deal, although I never know what is and what isn't a good deal when doing business with a car salesman."

"I called Katzen and he'll see me at two thirty." Cassandra took a bite of her lunch.

"You don't have to continue on this case," I spoke between bites. "I can finish it all up in a day or so."

"No such luck, sweetheart. I'm into this case and I'd like to finish it. Besides, I feel great now that I know, for now, a little Katz isn't in our future," she said.

"Okay, I'll go see Dr. Jenkins this afternoon while you see Katzen," I said. "One of the car salesmen where I bought our new car used to work at Belchamp's dealership, he said the wife really ran the business."

"Really?" She sounded as surprised as I had been. "What did he say about Simon?"

"Simon Belchamp and his son both sound like good old boys who like hunting and fishing more than getting rich," I said. "And, he thought that Simon was skimming cash from the business."

"Interesting," she said as she got up from the rocker. "Did

201

you get a chance to call the real estate company about the place Simon was renting?"

"Yes I did, while I was waiting for you I called the company and pretended to be the lawyer for the estate."

"They bought that?"

"Trusting and naïve souls are here and I was lucky enough to find her," I said as she put her dish in the sink. "The real estate secretary gave me the address he was paying for, and a few more calls got me the name. The other woman's name is Elsa Peterson."

"How about meeting back here at four and heading over to the mistress' apartment together," she said as she walked to the living room and got her purse.

"Here's your key." I handed her a key for the new car. "Which one do you want to take?"

"I'll take the new one." She patted my shoulder. "Yours has a hole in the passenger's door and I found buckshot in the driver's seat."

"I forgot."

Damn it, I had to find a decent body shop sometime in the near future.

27

What do I do when I get there?

D r. Jenkins was able to see me at two that afternoon; it was a rush to get there, but the traffic wasn't that bad. I had to love the address, 50 Coca Cola Place; only in Atlanta would such an address exist; I hadn't gotten used to the glory that is Coke in this town.

The building was a gray stone color government building with tinted windows looking out on the crowded street, only a block away from Grady Hospital. Grady was the largest hospital in town, and it had a fair reputation. Atlanta Police headquarters was on one side of Grady, and the Medical Examiner's building was on the other side, with the hospital in between; there has to be some sort of balance in that.

The blue Fairmont that followed me from our apartment, followed me into the garage and parked not that far away. I figured it was either Don or Mike, or some cheap gumshoe they paid to follow me but I was too busy to stop and find out who it was, that would have to wait. I assumed that they wouldn't give up, and that they should be waiting for me when I got through with the Medical Examiner.

. . . .

"Did you find out anything interesting?" Jenkins asked.

This time Dr. Jenkins was in his office at the appointed time so I did an attitude readjustment. A tall, lanky black man in a suit who looked like a cop was with him, he had to be the detective Brown Dr. Jenkins had told me about the first time I spoke with him.

"Yes, I did."

I handed him the root beer bottle that I had transferred it to a large zip lock bag.

"We got this bottle in the Mall in Washington, DC this last Thursday night at around seven in the evening."

"And, what does this prove?" Detective Brown asked.

"Hi." I extended my hand. "My name is Benjamin Katz and I assume you are Detective Brown."

"I'm sorry," Dr. Jenkins sounded flustered as he took the bottle from me. "This is Detective Gary Brown."

"Good to meet you." I greeted him. "If my suspicion is right, we met the deceased, Simon Belchamp, in Washington more than a week after he died here in Atlanta, if his finger prints are on that bottle."

"How do we know those finger prints aren't from months ago, even if they do wind up belonging to Simon Belchamp?" Gary asked.

He didn't crack a smile; no policeman ever cracks a smile, at least none that I've met on duty.

"You'll have to take my word for it, and the word of my partner." I managed a small grin. "I have a complete report of what we've uncovered so far."

"Thanks," Gary replied as he took the folder from me. "Can you only tell me the highlights."

"Simon was adopted," I began. "He had a twin brother he found out about a short while ago. We spoke to the investigator he hired, and that detective said he spoke to his client, Simon, last week."

"So, you think the dead man was Belchamp's twin brother?" Dr. Jenkins interrupted.

"Yes, I do," I concurred. "I think I can even find Simon in the next day or so, that is if the insurance company wants us to."

"We still don't have Mr. Belchamp's finger prints from the Army yet," Dr. Jenkins said.

"Speaking of finger prints," I asked Detective Brown. "have you taken prints from his office and home?"

"We're not stupid," Gary Brown replied. "We did."

"Do they match the deceased?" I had to know.

"Some of the prints in his office match, but none of the prints in his home match," Gary sighed. "That hints at your conclusion, but doesn't prove it."

"Once you have the real Belchamp prints from his Army

records, or if I actually find the real Simon Belchamp," I stated, "that will prove my conclusion."

"I still don't think there's a provable murder here," Gary spoke up, shaking his head. "Maybe if you can prove Simon Belchamp is alive, this might be insurance fraud, but the doctor here still says that the dead man died from a heart attack, whoever he was."

"The possible crime might be murder," I added. "If Simon Belchamp's ashes aren't in the urn, who's are they? If the Medical Examiner is right, and that man died from a heart attack, then why was he passed off as another person?" I took in another breath. "Maybe a drug that's not that easily detected was used to induce a heart attack."

"You might be right," Gary reluctantly agreed, his expression was noncommittal.

"Do you have any of Simon's blood left?" I asked Dr. Jenkins.

"Of course we do," he replied thoughtfully. "We'll do a more complete toxicology screen but I still think whoever that was died from a heart attack. I spoke to the doctor who did the autopsy. He noted a large amount of blockage around his heart. He pulled a huge plug of plaque three inches long from an artery near his heart and he also noted plenty of damaged heart muscle in several areas."

"Even if this dead guy was a heart attack waiting to happen, if someone killed him for five million dollars, that's still murder." I looked at Dr. Jenkins, then at Detective Brown.

"I suppose it is," Dr. Jenkins agreed with me. "If we can prove it."

"I don't mean to be a pain in the ass, but if you have a detailed record of stomach contents for the dead man, it might prove the body wasn't the same person who ate in the restaurant a half hour before."

"You mean the pot lickkers and apple pie?"

Detective Brown grinned at me; he had interviewed the waitress too.

"Right," I said. "When are the fingerprints due from the Army?"

205

"He was in the Army when he was younger." Gary felt he could tell me some things, which made me happy. "It took a while, but they did finally locate them and I should have them very soon."

"Very good."

"I'll check this stuff you gave me." Gary shuffled through some of the pages. "If the insurance company wants you to go further, call me."

Gary and I exchanged cards and I was happy he didn't go into the 'this is an active case, get the hell away from here now' speech. He seemed to be all right; I was new in town, and any friendly cop was a good cop.

....

Okay, I don't want a tail on me for the next few days. Maybe he didn't move his car while I was in the Medical Examiner's office, he didn't. I carefully surveyed the level my car was on, noting that the blue Fairmont was parked at the other end of the level, near the ramp to drive to the next level up, three cars down from the stairs. I stood on the elevator, looking out at the parking garage before I took the elevator to the next level up.

I got out at level three and headed to the stairs to walk back to level two. Luckily for me, no one was in the stairwell as I cracked the door. There he was, it was Don Smith sitting by himself in the small blue Ford. I wish I had noticed if more than just the driver was tailing me, but I didn't.

Someone came up behind me in the stairwell so I glanced at my watch and acted upset until he stepped around me and walked through the door. I could see Don Smith check out the man as he left the stairwell; it wasn't me, so he stared for a second more, then turned around to stare at a car that was driving to the next parking level. I took that moment to jump from the stairwell door and dash behind the nearest car. I was two cars away from the man in the blue Fairmont as I crouched behind a silver Mercedes and pulled my revolver out of its shoulder holster.

Don Smith had moved his attention to the elevator across from where his car was parked as I approached him quickly and tapped on the driver side window with the barrel of my revolver.

206

"Open the door, we need to talk," I insisted.

As Don was lowering his windshield, I heard the stairwell door open again. Decisions, decisions, decisions; I had to turn quickly to see if my back was in danger, it was.

"FBI!" Two men shouted as they pointed their weapons at me.

What is it about them and this case?

"Don't get too excited," I loudly replied.

I carefully checked their badges, they were real. I turned and cautiously placed my Smith and Wesson on the roof of Don's car, then turned to face the agents.

"We don't want you, sir," The larger of the two men grunted at me. "Why don't you move along, Mr. Katz."

"I assume you've located the other member of the dynamic duo?" I asked. "No?"

"That's all, Mr. Katz."

His eyes were beginning to form formidable slits; I knew it might be best if I gathered my pistol and left.

28

Can I help you find something?

"I was expecting Mr. Katz," Allan Katzen said.

He was pleasant, but obviously not excited to see a woman in his office talking about an important case, a five million dollar case.

"I'm his partner," Cassandra answered with the company smile.

"And, your name is?"

He stood to shake her hand; it was a little late, but he did it anyway.

"Cassandra Katz."

"You're…"

"I'm Benjamin's wife." she enjoyed saying that.

"He's a lucky man."

"More than he knows," Cassandra quietly replied as she sat down in the chair in front of Alan's large desk. "This is the report to date." She pushed the folder towards him. "We believe that Simon Belchamp is not dead."

"You what?"

"Simon Belchamp has a twin brother. Well, we believe he had a twin brother who now is in an urn on his sister-in-law's mantle," Cassandra said while Alan was busy skimming the report. "The law firm handling the Cayman Island corporation doesn't appear to know a thing about the possible insurance fraud. It seems a woman who has disappeared did the insurance scam on the side, we think she may be in Atlanta and Simon may also be here."

"Holy shit." Alan set the folder down. "Your husband told me about the twin a few days ago, but I have to say you guys do one hell of a job."

"Why, thank you." Cassandra flashed her real smile for a second. "My question is, do you want us to go any further?"

"What else will you do?" Allan asked.

"Well, first look at our expense account." She pushed a second folder towards him.

"This is fine." he quickly glanced at it. "I can cut you a check today, what else will you do?"

"You have to know that if the man who took the insurance physical wasn't the man insured, you're off the hook," Cassandra replied. "Also, if the man in the urn isn't the insured, you're off the hook."

"I know that," Katzen insisted. "What else can you do?"

"If you like, we could try to locate Simon Belchamp. We can also try to locate the two people responsible for the insurance fraud in the first place," she said with a bigger grin, this conversation was making her feel a lot better.

"I'd pay good money to have the sons of bitches behind this scheme sent to jail," Allan Katzen sounded more serious than ever. "Sorry for the language."

"No reason to be sorry, and, I'll be glad to get paid to do it," she joyfully replied.

. . . .

"Hi." Cassandra greeted me with a warm smile as I walked into our apartment. "How did it go with the Medical Examiner?"

"I think he's interested in the case." I kissed her. "Even a cop was there who might be interested; he says he isn't interested that much, but I bet he is."

"That strange look you have tells me that something else happened," Cassandra said.

She stared at me as I walked to the large comfy chair across for the sofa and sat down.

"Well," I began. "Don Smith was following me in a rental car."

"Did you confront him?" Cassandra was interested, I knew she would be. "What did he say?"

"I was about to ask him some pointed questions when the FBI crashed in and took over," I said with a sigh. "That's too bad, I think he might have shed some light on the other scams Paula Thorpe was involved in."

"I guess we won't know, will we?" Cassandra shrugged her shoulders.

"It has to have something to do with the client list for Smith, Smith and Heywood," I surmised. "Something that would interest the FBI."

"Are they mob lawyers?" Cassandra speculated.

"I don't think so," I thought for a second. "I bet it has to do with government workers, maybe congressmen."

"That makes sense," Cassandra replied. "They are in Washington."

"How would the FBI be interested in the Belchamp insurance thing?" I thought out loud.

"The common thread." Cassandra knew the answer, and was proud she did, "Paula Thorpe."

"We have a good idea where Paula might me, and maybe the FBI doesn't," I said.

"If we find her first, we can ask the questions," she agreed.

"How did your meeting with the insurance guy go?"

"Katzen gave me a check for our expenses so far, and he wants us to find Simon Belchamp and Paula Thorpe, and he'll pay us to do it." Cassandra's smile grew larger.

"It must have been a good meeting with him. I can't believe they paid the expenses the same day you gave them the bill," I said, basking in her good spirits. "You seem a lot happier than when you left."

"I am," she sat back down in the rocker. "That was quite an ego trip, Katzen was overflowing with praise about our work so far, I loved being the recipient of all those good vibes."

"Then, I'm glad you went there."

I moved to the sofa, next to her, taking her hand, I gently squeezed it.

"How about we go to the girlfriend's apartment and snoop around before dinner?" Cassandra asked.

"What about the club," I asked, "what was the name?"

"Club 688, somewhere near Spring Street."

"Right." I stood up. "Maybe we should go to our neighbor's book store and you can arrange a time to go down there with her."

210

"Sure." Cassandra stood up. "Which car do you want to take?"

"One guess," I answered. "Which one do I mind getting shot at more?"

I parked the 911 in the garage. Besides, it already had holes in it.

....

"Are both of you here?" Mrs. Smith asked.

She stood in our doorway, looking determined as she tightly clutched a small wrapped gift. I assumed it was for us, but she didn't hand it to me right away; I guess she wanted to wait for Cassandra to join us.

"Yes." I nodded.

"I'd like to say, yes."

Oh, that's what this was about, I had forgotten my offer to her about being a building manager for us. As a matter of a fact, I had forgotten to discuss it with Cassandra; I wondered how well this would go.

"Sure." I stepped aside to let her into the living room. "Great, come on in."

"Thank you." She stepped into our apartment and looked around.

I could see her checking out all the furniture and where we had put it, she had never been in here since Cassandra and I moved in. Maybe we should have had a party or something for all the tenants, but I never think of those kinds of things. Cassandra has had an awful lot on her mind lately, too much on her plate to plan a party for our renters too.

"Have a seat anywhere." I nervously pointed to the sofa. "I'll go get Cassandra."

"Who was that?" Cassandra asked, she was still in her underwear and rummaging around in her closet deciding on what to wear to the night club later.

"Mrs. Smith is in the living room." I moved closer to her and put my arm around her bare waist. "I kind of asked her to collect the rents and call the repairmen when we're out of town."

211

"You did?" She turned to face me.

"Yeah," I sheepishly answered. "I forgot to tell you about it."

"That's okay." She patted my cheek and turned back to the closet and pulled out a blouse. "She's probably the best person to do it anyway."

"Thanks." I stepped back so she could put on the shirt and the jeans she had also pulled out of the closet. "I'm sorry I forgot to tell you before."

"No problem." she pulled her jeans on. "I hope you cut her rent for the job, right?"

"I was thinking about twenty five dollars a month," I answered. "I thought about letting her stay for free, but I thought we should charge something. There has to be some official reason for that somewhere in the legalistic part on my brain, like free rent equals a salary and paying taxes on it and the alleged salary reducing her social security payments and the like."

"You thought this out," she commented as she walked into the hall and into the living room. "Hi, Mrs. Smith."

"Hello dear." She stood up from the chair she had decided to sit in.

"No, sit back down." Cassandra sat in the sofa across from her. "I'm sorry I took so long, but I was changing my clothes."

Mrs. Smith warmly greeted Cassandra, "I told your husband I will manage the apartments when you two have to be out of town, I think the arrangement will be fine, more than generous."

"I'm glad you agree to it," Cassandra warmly said. "We think you'll do a fine job."

"You've already done a fine job,." I added. "For the past three months, everything has run very well."

"Well." Mrs. Smith glanced at the front door. "I see you're getting ready to go out now, so I do want to congratulate the two of you on getting married." She handed Cassandra the small wrapped gift in her hand.

"Thank you, Mrs. Smith." Cassandra took the gift. "You didn't have to."

"I know," she cleared her throat. "But, I like you two,

212

you're a nice young couple."
....

"Hi," Cheryl eagerly greeted Cassandra. "This is the first time you've been to our store."

"Yes, it is and I love the place," Cassandra replied as she glanced around their store on Euclid, on the west side of Moreland Avenue.

Our building is on the east side of Moreland; Euclid kind of takes a jag when it hits Moreland. The book store wasn't that far from the intersection, on the left, it's a short walk from our building. Cheryl and Anne had done a good job of making the small space a going concern. Most of their stock was books dealing with gender issues, although towards the back, between a little literature and even less humor, was a good twenty shelves of mystery.

"So, did you decide to let me help in your investigation?" Cheryl sounded enthusiastic.

"Yes," Cassandra answered. "Would you take me to the club tonight and see if you can find out if Paula Thorpe is in town, and where she might be?"

"It has to be done subtly, otherwise she might disappear and we'd never find her," I added.

"Sure." Cheryl glanced at me, lost her smile, then looked back at Cassandra. "I know what to do; that'll be a blast, I love a good mystery."

In the meantime, I noticed Anne walk past with a customer. She acknowledged us, but kept talking to the woman searching for a book on natural healing.

"Okay," Cassandra replied, nodding her head. "What time does that club get going?"

"About ten or eleven. How about I pick you up at ten?"

Cheryl moved us back towards the door to the storeroom to get us away from the four new customers that walked into the small store.

"That'd be fine," Cassandra answered.

Cassandra glanced at me, but I was pointedly glancing around the area, looking for a way out of this conversation. My eye was

213

caught by a small display case, the case had a locked glass front, inside it was a small collection of strap on dildos, vibrators and assorted sex toys. I don't embarrass easily, but I began to blush. Cassandra noticed me, glanced down and saw the same thing; she had a hard time not laughing. I was so happy to be her amusement de jour.

"See you then." Cheryl didn't notice.

We walked to the front of the store and said our goodbye to Anne who was working the register.

"Thanks for not busting a gut laughing at me," I said as soon as we hit the sidewalk.

Cassandra couldn't stop laughing until we made the intersection.

29

Put the insect aside

"What's in the box?" Cassandra asked.

She slowly circled the kitchen table. Sitting on top of the table was a brown cardboard box, tightly closed with clear shipping tape.

"Oh, it's something Billy promised me a few months ago," I replied as I walked into the kitchen from the living room.

"Well." She smiled at me. "What is it?"

"It's an electronic device that can locate almost any bug in a room." I started to cut the tape holding it shut. "We're supposed to sweep our apartment and office every week or so, just to make sure."

"Ah, the life of a spy," she whispered to me. "I'm not quite used to it yet."

"Not so loud until I sweep the room," I whispered back to her with a grin and a wink.

"How did it get here?" Cassandra sounded curious. "That's not the sort of thing one mails to us, is it?"

"Not hardly." I pulled the device out of the box. "I met one of Billy's minions after lunch today, while you were at the bank."

"Who?" She sounded interested. "Do I know him?"

"No," I answered semi-evasively. "Her name is Nancy, and you'll meet her soon enough."

"Nancy?" Cassandra straightened her back up. "Maybe I should meet her sooner than later."

"She's a courier," I said with a teasing grin.

Nancy was a nice looking woman, about forty five and kind

215

of plump. She had been a secretary at the agency for years before she started doing pick-ups and deliveries. I think she had a thing for one of the operations officers who lived in Alexandria, but I wasn't sure.

"She looks like the average American house frau which is why the agency uses her to deliver stuff on this coast," I added.

"Anyway, speaking of the bank." Cassandra sat down at the table and began fiddling with the electronic gadget. "We now have a brokerage account and two large certificates of deposit."

"Then, we're rich, beyond all dreams of avarice?" I chuckled.

"Not hardly," she replied, glaring at me. "I also paid our last quarterly tax payment for the feds and the state."

"I bet that wasn't fun."

I visually checked out the gadget in Cassandra's hand, it was a new model, about ten inches long, in the shape of a tapered cylinder, with what seemed like a base to stand it up on its end. The base had the antenna in it and on the opposite end was the meter, indicating that a bug was in the room, hidden under a screw off top. These things came in all sorts of shapes and sizes to hide in plain sight. This one sort of looked like a piece of modern art to sit on an end table; to me, it seemed like a bad piece of modern art one might buy in a store devoted to post modern Scandinavian crap.

"It wasn't fun at all," she said with an expression of disgust. "I had to give the state and federal governments all too much of the money we got."

"We'll get some back, though?" I was always hopeful.

"I hope so." She seemed to be fascinated with the device in her hand as she held it by the base and closely inspected it.

"Well, if we get the hundred grand from the insurance company won't we have to pay some more in taxes?"

"No," she said as she looked up from the device. "I figured our taxes on the premise that we'd be getting the money. If they pay us after January, we can apply any refund towards next year's taxes, so it'll be fine no matter what."

"You're good with this stuff, you know." I reached out to take her hand.

"Where's the on switch?" She turned the device over in her hand.

"Mine or that thing's?" I grinned a playful grin.

"It does kind of look like a vibrator, you know," she teased back. "Maybe you got it from our neighbor's store."

"Very funny." I leaned towards her.

"Very nice." she teasingly rubbed her face with the narrow end of the apparatus.

"Well then, let's find the on switch." I reached for it.

"No, I want to find it." She pulled it back towards her.

"Well?" I paused.

"Well, what?" She turned it over and over, looking for anything resembling a switch.

"I think you need to unscrew the top part to get to anything." I patiently observed, at least I tried to be patient.

"Here it is," Cassandra said.

She took the rounded top cap off, noticing a small light and an even smaller switch. She pushed a small black button next to a small red light which immediately came on.

"It's on, but it's not vibrating," she added.

"Move it around." I insisted.

I was instantly snapped back to work mode; I much prefer play mode, but the red light had me worried.

"What?" When she pointed it at me, the red light went out.

"Don't say anything else," I whispered loudly and took the electronic device from her.

She cocked her head, looking slightly worried as I moved the bug detector around the kitchen. The signal strength meter led me back into the living room, Cassandra followed me in silence. In the living room, the signal strength was fluctuating until I walked towards the hallway leading to the bedrooms. My worst fear was confirmed as the two of us walked into our bedroom.

A small transmitter was hidden somewhere in the lamp on Cassandra's side of the bed. She stared at me in disbelief for a second, then gave me an exaggerated shrug. I pointed the antenna of the detector in every corner of our bedroom, then walked from room to room in our apartment; the only bug was in the lamp in our bedroom.

"Hey," I finally spoke as we stood in the middle of our

217

bedroom. "I feel like a nice fat burger."

"Luckily, you don't look like one," Cassandra replied, still with an anxious expression on her face.

"Very funny," I answered. "You know what I mean."

"They're not good for you, you have to know that." Cassandra shrugged again.

She assumed we would make casual conversation, then leave our apartment to talk about the bug in our bedroom.

"I don't care." I nodded towards the door to the hall. "Every once and a while, I want a juicy, dripping with fat burger, and deep fat fries."

"What about the Varsity?"

"Just the place for the craving."

I led us out the front door of our bugged apartment.

. . . .

"What the hell's that all about?" Cassandra demanded as we got into our car, parked in the rear of our building.

"Let's get to lunch," I insisted. "I really need my grease fix."

"Okay." Cassandra answered.

She sullenly slumped in the passenger seat as I drove out onto Euclid, then turned onto Moreland.

I picked up the bug detector, which was still on, from the edge of my seat and handed it to Cassandra. I pointed to the back seat, wanting her to sweep the car for any listening devices; she understood and did it.

"According to this thing, we're alone in the car." Cassandra switched the device off.

"Good." I took in and let out a big breath of air. "We do have a problem."

"No shit, Sherlock." Cassandra made a sour expression out the front window. "Someone has been making tapes of our more intimate moments."

"That's the least of our worries." I glanced at her. "If this bug isn't from the creepy lawyers Don and Mike or from Willy the Roach, we have a security problem that could be much worse."

218

"The Russians are on to us?" Cassandra tried to be flip.

"Something like that," I reluctantly agreed. "It could blow our cover for good, you know."

"Why would the commies suspect you all of a sudden?" She sounded confused. "I'd believe the mob bugging our bedroom before anything else."

"The only way to make sure is to send the lamp to a lab and find out who made the thing," I said.

"And, how do we do that without letting whoever is listening realize we know there's a bug in the lamp?" Cassandra looked back out the front windshield.

"I don't know," I thought for a second. "Maybe one of us could accidentally knock it over and break it, then we could put it in a trash bag and throw it out."

"If the bug is still working, won't they know we didn't throw it out?" She asked.

"If we do throw it out, and have our people pick the trash up, they could isolate it and take it from there," I said. "That might work."

"It might," she replied. "But, how can we fake an accident and have whoever is listening believe it?"

"In the throws of wild sex, one of us knocks it over and smashes it against the wall?" I laughed.

"Or, you piss me off so much, I throw it at you," she said with a grin.

"How about the two of us flip our mattress and accidentally knock the lamp into the wall and break it." I moved my concentration back out into traffic. "Although, I like the wild sex thing better."

"Well," she paused. "Maybe later, and we don't have to break a lamp."

30

Shot in the dark

"I see a parking place up there," Cassandra said.

She pointed to the next block; we were on Juniper, not far from Piedmont Park. The apartment buildings were nice looking, they seemed upper middle class. Lots of brick homes were split into apartments and the building we wanted was a square brick apartment building with a parking area in the rear. The rent Belchamp was paying for his side dish was low average for the area, especially for such good off street parking.

"Do we go up to the door and knock?" She asked.

"Why not?" I said as I locked the car. "She doesn't know who we are. Simon does, and if he's there, then we've got the hundred thousand in the bank."

"I guess so." Cassandra looked up and down the street. "Did you notice that old Oldsmobile before?"

"If you mean the one parked on that side street with two men in the front seat staring at us," I acknowledged; at least it wasn't the Impala that drove by me the other day with two shooters in it. "Yes, I noticed them."

"What did Billy say about the bug in our bedroom?" Cassandra put her hand on my arm to keep me in the car for a while longer.

"Like I said before, he'll have someone come by tomorrow morning and pick up the trash." I took in a breath. "It's the regular pick up day, so no one will be surprised. We have to break the lamp

220

sometime today, and take the bag with the lamp in it out to the dumpster at seven in the morning."

"Did he seem concerned?" She seemed to be getting a little concerned herself.

"No more than usual," I reassured her as I patted her shoulder. "When our people get a look at it, we'll all know more about who put it there."

"How long do you think it's been there?" She asked. "I've been going over in my mind what we've done in that room over the past year or so, it's embarrassing to think someone was listening."

"When we did that case for the agency three months ago, Billy had his people sweep our whole apartment building and they found nothing. We haven't been back too long since we both left three months ago, so whoever it is can't have heard too much of the good stuff." I slipped my hand down to hers, holding it loosely. "It's best not to be too paranoid."

"No, it helps me to be paranoid," Cassandra said.

She checked her holster for her pistol. Silently, we left the car and walked to the front door of the apartment building.

I opened the front door to the building, it wasn't locked. It was a little after four in the afternoon on a late November day, the sun was low in the sky. The light in the small entrance was off, although we could still read the names on the row of mailboxes.

"There she is." Cassandra pointed to the box with the name tag, Elsa Peterson on it. "What a coincidence, she's in 2-B like us."

"I don't like this."

I stared up a narrow flight of narrow stairs. The carpet was frayed and it smelled faintly of mold since it was an un-air conditioned space. Since it was a tad too dark, either someone had turned out the lights, or some had burned out. I did not have a good feeling about this place.

"You don't like what," she asked. "that car outside?"

"Yeah."

I peeked out the window in the entrance door; I couldn't see them. I stepped out and looked down the block, they were still there.

"What?" Cassandra was half out the door as she whispered to me.

221

"Go back inside for a minute." I pointed to the door. "I'll be back soon."

I walked slowly towards the mysterious dark red Oldsmobile. It was light enough to see the license plate, but in this state there's only a rear plate so I had to walk around the block to see it. The men in the car became agitated and started the engine. I put my right hand on the butt of my revolver and began walking faster. A small ally lead to the parking area behind the apartment; I took it and ran around to the front door.

"What was it?" Cassandra asked as I ducked back into the entrance way.

"That car." I pulled out my note book and wrote down the license number. "Did they drive by?"

"I didn't see them," she answered.

"Let's get up to 2-B." I headed up the stairs as she followed me.

We both paused outside the door to 2-B; light shone under the door and we could hear the muffled sound of a television set inside.

"It's the Flintstones," Cassandra whispered to me.

I knocked softly; no answer, no footsteps so I knocked louder, nothing. I turned the knob; the door was closed, but it was unlocked. I glanced at Cassandra, then I pulled my revolver out. I opened the door slowly with a handkerchief in my hand as I stepped to one side, Cassandra was standing behind me in the hall with her pistol out. I could see into the living room off to the left, the television was there and Cassandra was right, Barney and Fred were up to no good I'm sure.

A floor lamp shone near the opening between the entrance hall and the living room. The floor was wood with a big mostly red oriental carpet on it. I stepped in slowly; from what I could see, the apartment was very neat.

"Don't touch anything," I whispered to Cassandra.

We both walked in, leaving the front door slightly ajar. As I stepped into the living room I could see Elsa's body laying on the floor; she was dressed in a nice white blouse and a calf length dark blue skirt. Elsa had tossed off her shoes before she was surprised.

222

She appeared thirty years old, maybe a bit younger with dark blond shoulder length hair and darker roots. Although her face still showed the shock of being shot, she was a beautiful woman. It appeared as if she had been standing against the wall to my right when she was shot in the head; a small red dot punctuated the center of her forehead where the bullet had entered her skull and I could clearly see the bullet hole in the wall with blood spattered all about it. She had crumpled down to the floor; her legs twisted by her weight, and her arms had flopped off to her sides. Her face was staring straight at the ceiling and her eyes were open wide. Elsa didn't seem like a home wrecking mistress as she lay on the floor. I didn't see any breathing movement so I knelt down beside her and felt her neck for a pulse, none was evident but her body temperature hadn't fallen that much. I glanced all around the room; it didn't seem as if they disturbed anything in the room. I checked my watch for the exact time, it was seven minutes after five in the afternoon.

Cassandra stared at the body for fifteen seconds, then she walked to the window in the far wall. She looked out, then turned to me and said, "The car's still there, but the men are gone."

"If they're the ones who killed Elsa, they'll be here soon."

"I'll go next door and see if somebody's home." Cassandra carefully walked back to the front door. "I'll call the cops."

"Wait." I handed her my notebook. I followed her into the hall to provide cover, if she needed it. "Call Gary Brown, his number is towards the back, he's the cop assigned to the Belchamp case."

Hearing someone answer next door I went back into Elsa's apartment before the neighbor opened the door to her apartment for Cassandra. I quickly searched in Elsa's bedroom, nothing was out of place. I took out my handkerchief and opened her dresser drawers one by one, nothing unusual. I went to the kitchen and also found nothing unusual, then I went back to her living room. Drawers were in both the end tables on either side of the sofa. Shuffling through them with my ballpoint pen, I saw a bank book for the C & S bank proudly declaring she had one hundred thirty thousand and change which is a lot for a kept woman; she could have kept someone herself with that bank balance. Next to the bank book were two airplane tickets to Brazil dated to depart in one week; one was in her name,

223

the other in Simon Belchamp's name. An extradition treaty between the US and Brazil doesn't exist, I surmised they also knew that.

Why would Simon run away? I know he had a pushy wife, but he also had a sweet deal with those two car dealerships, plus he also had a son and grandchildren which I assumed he liked better than he liked his wife so why toss that life away? Was Elsa that first-rate? I went back to observe the dead woman more closely; she was pretty, but I couldn't tell if she was worth Simon Belchamp dumping his current life, never having met the mistress while she was alive.

Suddenly I heard a slight noise come through the still open front door. Turning quickly with my revolver drawn, I caught a blur as someone ran down the stairs; they must have seen my large revolver. I ran to the door and noticed a man in the dark vestibule fire a shot up the stairs at me which sounded like a muffled bang from a small caliber handgun. At the same instant I heard a loud thud as a small projectile sunk into the door frame a few inches from my face. I didn't want to fire my revolver in the stairwell, but I did point it at the man near the front door to the building who grabbed the door, opened it, and burst outside. I sprinted as fast as I could down the stairs and exploded onto the sidewalk where I found him, running like a madman towards the red Oldsmobile still parked on the side street. Not taking any time to steady his hand, he turned and fired again at me. I have no idea where the slug went, but it landed no where near me. Should I return fire, or not? Too many people were on the sidewalk trying to scramble out of the way so I kept running after him.

The mystery man jumped into the back of the Oldsmobile which I now could clearly see was idling by the curb. Loud squealing tires accented the busy sounds of going home traffic as the red car turned on Juniper headed directly towards me. I assumed he would try to hit me with the car, so I jumped into the front yard of some apartment building. A spindly tree that may or may not have slowed the car down was my only hope, so I headed for the far side of it. He didn't drive at me, but the man in the rear seat did begin shooting at me; this time I did return fire. My Smith and Wesson was very loud as I shot twice at the trunk of the car as it sped away. I was fairly sure both of my slugs hit the trunk, and if I was lucky, the gas tank, making their getaway shorter. I was shooting round nosed lead bullets, loaded to a relatively slow velocity compared to what the forty four magnum is capable of, so they still make a large hole in what they hit, but they didn't ricochet or travel too far after they hit their target.

Most of the people on the sidewalk had scrambled for cover by the time I shot, and several of them cautiously approached me as I stuck my revolver back in my holster.

"Are you a cop?" The first man to come near me asked.

"No." I shook my head. "They're coming right now, did you get a look at either of the men in the car that raced by?"

"Just a glance." He glared hard at me. "They were both white guys, and one of them had a big moustache. And, I swear I heard the driver shouting in Spanish as they drove past me."

"Do you live around here?" I asked him.

Spanish, how did that fit into any of this?

"No, I'm here to meet my girlfriend," he sounded like he badly wanted to leave.

Was this a neighborhood of other women? I was beginning to wonder.

"I live here," Replied a woman in her early forties who stood about ten feet behind me. "Who the hell are you and who were you shooting at?"

"My name is Benjamin, and those men in the car were trying to kill me for some reason." I turned around to face the woman. "Where do you live?"

"Are you a cop?"

"No, I'm a private investigator."

I pulled out my ID and shoved it in her direction; she took two steps forward and took it.

"I guess you are Benjamin," she replied after studying my ID for a few seconds. "But, I still don't know who the hell you are."

"Do you live in that building at the end of the block?" I pointed to Elsa Peterson's apartment building.

"Yes I do." She shot me a weary gaze.

"Did you know Elsa Peterson?"

"Why?"

225

"Those men who sped off probably killer her in the past hour or so."

"Elsa's dead?"

"The police should be here in a few minutes," I thought quickly. "Would you please wait right here for them, I'm sure they'll need to talk to you."

"Sure," she said as she began to slightly shake.

"What can you tell me about Elsa Peterson?"

Maybe I could get something before the cops stopped me from asking anything.

"She's a nice woman." The neighbor calmed down a little, talking seemed to calm her down. "She moved in a little over a year ago. I don't think she had a job, Elsa was home a lot and she never did say anything about work, she was always quiet. I don't think she ever had a party; I live right under her."

"Did she have a boyfriend?" I asked in a nice calm voice. "Maybe an older man, a little pudgy?"

"Yeah," she said. "She introduced him to me as Steve something, I don't remember the last name, that wasn't her only steady though."

"Oh?" Something interesting. "Who else came calling regularly?"

"I'm at work until five every day, so I don't know much about daytime visitors, but, she did have a nice man her own age who visited two or three times a week at night."

"What did he look like?"

"Maybe late twenties, and real tall," she thought for a moment. "He had to be a few inches taller than you are, he was real nice looking and seemed like he worked out a lot, lots of muscles."

"Anybody else?" I began to wonder about the true profession of Elsa Peterson.

"No," she answered. "But you might want to talk to the lady in 1-C, she's home all day and she notices everything that happens here, although she is a bit deaf."

Too late, four police cars with flashing blue lights screamed up Juniper and an ambulance from Grady followed them ten seconds later. Gary Brown arrived a minute after the original gathering of cops. I walked towards him as he got out of his car.

"Excuse me, sir." One of the cops stuck his hand in my chest. "This is a crime scene, you'll have to get back."

"I'm part of the crime scene," I firmly spoke to the policeman. "The assailants shot at me, I need to speak to detective Brown."

"Let him in." Gary motioned for me to join him.

"Did you read what I gave you?" I asked as I walked up beside him.

"Yeah," he sounded more curious than when I had last seen him.

"The woman who was probably Simon Belchamp's mistress is in her apartment, shot in the head. I think the men who did it were the ones who took a few shots at me, and I do have their license plate number."

"Very good, at least you're helpful," Gary replied.

He didn't want to put me in cuffs, maybe this will turn out to be a good cop.

"The man who shot at me was using a thirty eight, or maybe a twenty five, I didn't get that good a look at the gun. There's a slug in the door frame of Elsa Peterson's apartment on the second floor," I continued to be helpful. "It did have a silencer and I find that kind of strange, don't you?"

"It does sound unusual." he scratched his chin.

"If you read my report, you should recognize that this is the second time we've had a run in with hoods with a silencer in the past week," I continued. "This is getting old."

"I don't think they were after you. The real question is, why would they kill that woman?" Gary questioned me. "It must be something about that man who died with the five million dollar insurance policy."

"That's what I'd guess." I pointed to the neighbor woman, patiently waiting on the sidewalk twenty feet away. "You need to talk to her, she lives downstairs from the victim. You need to get that guy in the blue suit walking away too, he saw the hit men as they drove away and he said they were speaking Spanish. And, you might want to talk to the lady in 1-C."

227

"Spanish?" Gary stared straight at me, then pointed to the man in the blue suit; one of the uniformed cops went after him. "Did you see which way the gunmen turned?"

"They went towards Peachtree," I answered. "That's not too helpful, but I did put two shots in their car, and I think I got at least one in their gas tank."

"That wasn't too bright," he sounded disappointed. "You could have caused a lot of trouble doing that."

"That idiot emptied a whole clip at me as they were driving away." I was a bit exasperated; after all, I was the one shot at. "If I shot back, they might not stick around and keep shooting at me, I thought putting a slug in their car was better than risking any of the pedestrians walking by."

"I suppose," he said. "But if the gas tank had exploded, there might have been a lot of casualties."

"I don't think gas tanks explode that easily," I said. "My thinking was that they couldn't get that far if they were out of gas."

"Maybe." Detective Brown glanced sideways at me, I don't think he believed me.

"My partner had already called you guys before any of this happened," I added. "Can I go see my partner?"

"Why don't we both go up there." Gary motioned for me to follow him.

"Cassandra?" I smiled at her, she was waiting by the open door to Elsa's apartment, having finished talking to a uniformed policeman. "This is detective Brown, this is my partner."

"Hi." Cassandra extended her hand to Gary. "I'm the one who called you from the neighbor's apartment."

"Good to meet you."

We spent the next hour on the scene telling the detective about the Belchamp case, at least most of what we knew. He was calm, and seemed to accept everything we said. He also seemed happy we had done so much work up to that point, and that we were willing to share most of it with him.

"Oh." I put my hand on Detective Brown's shoulder to stop him from walking away. "I forgot something, the neighbor occasionally saw a younger man visiting Elsa Peterson so you might want to locate him."

"That I might," he said. "One of the uniformed policemen already told me about it, but thanks anyway."

"Do you need us any more?" I asked; it was nearly seven o'clock. "We'd like to get some food in us soon."

"Go on ahead," he said with a noncommittal expression. "You know, I have to say you two are quite refreshing for private investigators."

"Thanks," Cassandra sounded taken aback.

"Most of the ones I deal with are so stupid they probably couldn't find their way out of an outhouse." He glanced at his watch. "The rest of them I practically have to throw in jail to get them to tell me anything."

"We aren't that way." Cassandra looked at me. "You can bank on that."

31

A date in the dark

Cassandra and I decided to try a vegetarian place near our house, that way we could park the car in front of our house and walk there. The food was adequate but the ambiance left a little to be desired, it left a lot to be desired. Our waitress should take more than one bath a week, and although Cassandra says I can be a little old fashioned sometimes, I still think that some women should not try the braless look; sometimes it seems too National Geographic to me. Actually, Cassandra told me to mind my own business and stop staring at her. It was like watching a train wreck over and over again, I couldn't stop looking.

"Can we talk here?" Cassandra leaned towards me, over the small table.

"No," I whispered and shook my head slowly. "Remember, not that stuff in a public place."

"Okay," she agreed, "in general terms, what do we do after we find out?"

"A pest control company will call us with an estimate," I chuckled. "Sometimes I think those guys actually have a sense of humor."

"So, we call them back?" She asked.

"Yeah," I answered. "It'll be obvious what to do when they call."

"Okay," she agreed. "I wanted to know in case I was the one to take the call."

"Oh shit," I sounded maybe a little more exasperated than I really was.

"What?" Cassandra quickly turned around and checked out

the entrance to the small restaurant. "Oh, shit."

Mike Heywood was almost to our table and he seemed upset. He struggled out of his rumpled overcoat and threw it over the vacant chair at our table then sat down and stared at me for a second.

"Did you find her?" He insisted.

"Who?" I playfully asked.

"Kelly, or Paula that's who," he sounded eager.

"Aren't you more concerned with your partner?" I kept my smug grin firmly on my face. "Don got arrested by the FBI earlier today."

"Yeah, I know," he collected his one thought. "But, did you find Kelly yet?"

"What is it about that woman?" Cassandra joined the conversation.

"You may have the hots for her, but that doesn't completely explain your focused attention on getting to her," I observed.

"Maybe we could guess why Mike wants to find the mystery lady so badly?" Cassandra playfully asked. "It might make a good after dinner game."

"I'd have to say it has to do with their law practice," I started.

"Do you think she could have been blackmailing Don and Mike?" Cassandra took her turn at a guess.

"Ah." I felt a revelation coming over me, "she was blackmailing their clients."

"That makes more sense," Cassandra continued as Mike became even more angry. "They did tell us that some of their clients were important politicians."

"Nothing is more dangerous than a pissed off politician," I laughed. "If one class of citizen can get the FBI to take notice, it's a senator or representative."

"That's not funny at all," Mike steamed.

I swear I could see smoke coming from his ears, no, that was the squash linguini the waiter was serving to the table behind him.

All three of us looked up to the front door of the restaurant as three large men in suits and dark brown overcoats walked into the place like they owned it. They seemed to be wearing uniforms of a

231

sort, they were uniforms, FBI uniforms, the agency seemed to be our partners in this case but I wasn't going to share a dime of the fee with them.

"Excuse me," The first large government employee to reach the table said.

His voice was expressionless, although I detected a slight irritation to it. My guess was that they were tired of seeing me in the middle of whatever case this was. This case was an insurance fraud to me, but neither Cassandra nor I was exactly sure of what this case was to the FBI.

"I think these large men are for you," I said to Mike, who seemed so dejected right then; I kind of felt sorry for him, kind of.

"I think you and Mrs. Katz can leave now," The second large agent said, staring directly at me.

It was no mistake, they were pissed at me; I felt so rejected by the whole thing. Cassandra and I obligingly got up and left Mike to deal with the FBI agents after dumping what I thought would be enough money to cover the meal and tip; I guess that's the way it should be.

. . . .

"Do you think we guessed what the problem was?" Cassandra glanced at me as we waited for the light to change so we could cross the street. "I mean why the FBI wanted those two?"

"Yeah," I said as we walked across Moreland and headed to our apartment. "I think Paula Thorpe was blackmailing politicians and the FBI is trying to find her. I think Don and Mike were trying to find her first so they could do some damage control for their law practice."

"How could they do that?" Cassandra asked. "She'd eventually get caught by the FBI and spill the beans anyway."

"I don't know," I answered. "And, since I don't think it has a thing to do with the insurance fraud, I don't care."

"I guess you're right," Cassandra agreed. "We should only stick to the case at hand."

. . . .

It was nine thirty by the time we got back home and I was tired. Cassandra seemed to be game for the late night partying, she was three years younger than me, after all.

"What are you going to do?" Cassandra asked.

She stared at herself in the full length mirror. She looked beautiful in anything, and in nothing; I can't say that too often, too bad we didn't have enough time.

"Maybe I could revisit the grieving widow, or maybe I could call detective Brown," I mused. "But, I think I'll sit here at home and wait for you."

"Good."

She noticed me sitting on the bed admiring her.

"I'll call you if we find the woman," she added.

"Hey." I stood up and smiled a broad grin. "How about we flip the mattress before you go out on the town? It'd be nice to do it before I take a nap waiting for you to call from the club, besides, we haven't done it since we moved in, and it's overdue."

"Sure." She walked to her side of the bed. "Now?"

"Why not." I affirmed.

She was standing next to the suspect lamp, and I was on the other side.

"Okay." She moved out of the way. "You lift your side up and I'll guide it."

I lifted the bottom half of the mattress up and shoved it towards the night stand with the lamp on it. She set her side down on the bed and moved out of the way while I gave it a hard shove. Surprise, surprise, the lamp slammed against the wall, cracked somewhat and teetered on the table. Cassandra leaned over towards the lamp, shoving it with some force to the bare wooden floor; crash, it was broken.

"Look what you did!" Cassandra shouted. "I liked that lamp, and it was a perfect match with the one on your side of the bed."

"I'm sorry," I replied.

I sheepishly walked to the pile of lamp parts on the floor. I couldn't see anything unusual, it must be a small bug.

Cassandra pointed the bug detector at the pile of ceramic on the floor; the red light came on. She shook her head and studied the

233

mess.

"Well, I have to go now, so you clean this mess up and try to find another small light for tonight," she spoke towards the broken lamp.

"Maybe we can go shopping for another one tomorrow." I motioned for her to speak to me, not the floor.

"Sure," she said. "If there's time although I might have to wait until this case is finished."

"I think I have a small lamp in the office we can use," I replied as I sat back down on the bed.

"Okay, but I have to go soon."

"Don't stay out too late," I said.

She was overacting a bit; maybe I was too, but I couldn't tell.

"Don't worry," she said as she sat next to me. "I'm probably as tired as you are, maybe more."

"Let me get that mess up."

I got up and searched for the broom and dust pan in the kitchen. I swept up the mess and placed it into a plastic trash bag. As I emptied the first dustpan of broken lamp into the bag I saw a small metal gadget with a short bare copper wire dangling from it, a bug was in that lamp and the detector was working fine. It was a small apparatus, quite sophisticated. I doubted it could have been put there by the mob, damn. I ignored it and filled the bag, tied it up and dumped it in the small closet in the kitchen.

"What do you think of this?" Cassandra asked.

She stood in front of me wearing a plum colored dress which was tight fitting from her chest to her waist, then flared our a bit, ending above her knees.

"I think you look sexy as hell," I replied with a lecherous grin.

"No, really," she sounded exasperated.

"Really." I stared at her, feet to head. "You look like a very hot woman."

"I take that as a compliment," she grinned broadly at me as she spoke.

"I have one question."

"What?"

"Where is your holster?"

"I'm taking my pistol in my purse."

"It's a little out of reach there, isn't it?" I shrugged.

"Look closely at my dress," she lightly demanded.

"Believe me, I am."

"So, where can I hide the thing in this tight a dress?"

"I see your point."

"I'm beginning to see yours, too," Cassandra chuckled.

Cassandra primped some more in the bathroom mirror. The door bell rang; I greeted Cheryl, dressed in a tight mini skirt which shimmered and glistened as she walked into our apartment. She didn't sit down, I don't think she could sit down.

"You look sexy." Cheryl scanned Cassandra up and down slowly.

I guess I'll have to get used to this. They seemed like good neighbors, and they always pay their rent on time. I kind of hoped they weren't the ones who had bugged our bedroom.

"Am I under-dressed?" Cassandra studied Cheryl's outfit. "I can dress different if I need to."

"Don't change a thread on your body," Cheryl insisted.

. . . .

"Wow," Cassandra shouted into Cheryl's ear. "This place is loud."

"Let me introduce you around."

Cheryl dragged Cassandra past the empty stage and towards the bar. An assortment of strangely dressed people with multi colored hair appeared to be attempting to dance, or rather flail about in time to the driving loud music; disco was dead here. Mixed in were the upwardly mobile twenty somethings who wanted to be cool, but had to hold down nine to five jobs. Booze and music seemed to make the whole crowd coalesce. The place smelled like a crowded bar; lots of booze, perfume and body odors competing for space.

"This is my friend Amy, Amy's a graduate student at Emory," Cheryl shouted as she pushed Cassandra towards the end of the bar.

Amy was a twenty five year old woman who stood just under

five feet tall and was quite petite with long black straight hair and big brown eyes.

"Hi Amy," Cassandra said in her social voice.

"Cassandra got her PhD at UCLA," Cheryl sounded obliged to add.

"She's hot." Amy winked at Cheryl.

Cassandra swallowed and glanced around the room; she felt a little embarrassed, a little out of place. She was only twenty six, but her discomfort there made her feel a lot older.

"Cassandra's my landlady." Cheryl pushed Amy's shoulder. "She's married."

"Oh." Amy blushed a bit.

"We're looking for Paula Thorpe." Cheryl moved much closer to Amy. "You remember her, right?"

"Of course I do." Amy grinned as she remembered. "We had a thing for a couple of months."

"Right," Cheryl continued. "Did she some back to town?"

"She's here tonight," Amy said.

Cassandra quickly forgot her embarrassment.

"Where is she now?" Cassandra leaned towards Amy.

"She went to the can." Amy moved closer to Cassandra. "I think she went in there for a snort or two, are you sure you want Paula? You're too good looking for a skank like that."

"Excuse me?" Cassandra tried to be polite.

"I can give you the best ride in town if you're interested." Amy leaned into Cassandra to kiss her.

Cassandra dodged and missed her. I'm married, Cassandra thought, off the meat market, besides this is the wrong market anyway.

"Back off." Cheryl stepped in front of Amy. "She's with me."

"No problem." Amy raised her hands up briefly. "I had to try."

"She'll try to jump anything without a dick." Cheryl pulled Cassandra off towards the women's room. "She's not that bad, just forward."

"Could you do me a favor?" Cassandra leaned over and

236

spoke in Cheryl's right ear.

"What?"

"Call Benjamin and tell him to get here as soon as he can." Cassandra drew in another breath. "Also, how many exits are there besides the front door and that emergency exit?"

"That's it." Cheryl looked around.

"When I go into the bathroom, could you keep an eye on the two exits. If she gets past me follow her if you can do it safely."

"Sure thing."

Cheryl was getting excited at the prospect of actually participating in a real case. As Cheryl shoved her way to the small bank of public phones at the back of the large room, Cassandra walked to the women's room which was smallish for an establishment of this size.

A row of five stalls stretched along the left side wall. The floor and walls were covered with medium sized pale blue ceramic tiles and on the opposite side of the restroom were six sinks with at least fifteen women either primping or waiting for a stall to empty. Given the fact that a lot of beer was being consumed, Cassandra thought this was a small number of women in the rest room.

Gathered around the far sink were four women, Cassandra recognized Paula as one of them, this was easy. Paula was right in front of her and it didn't take any great sleuthing to find her, it took luck. In the back of her mind, Cassandra wondered when the FBI would come falling into the women's room like the keystone cops.

Cassandra slowly walked towards the four women; the closer she came to the group of women, the more it was obvious that they were snorting coke from several open compact mirrors. She wondered if they were accidentally snorting as much makeup as they were coke, but she couldn't tell from her angle.

Now for the decision, should she try to nail Paula Thorpe right there, or should she wait until Paula tried to leave. Although right at the moment, Paula seemed to be quite coherent, Cassandra surmised that Paula wouldn't be coherent for long, judging by the amount of white powder flying up her nose, but Cassandra decided to wait.

Ten minutes dragged on, Cassandra got her place in front of

237

a mirror, and adjusted her hair, and spread on some makeup so she could keep a good eye on Paula from the reflection in the mirror. The group moved closer to the sinks, and kept on snorting cocaine.

The four woman at the end sink hung around enjoying the drug taking affect, talking much louder, laughing hysterically at times. Cassandra could make out several conversations about men, women, sex, and clothing. Paula Thorpe and her friends then gravitated towards the middle of the bathroom as more and more women stuffed into the small area. As the number of women needing the use of the facilities grew, Paula Thorpe and two of the women migrated to the door; Cassandra followed them.

Paula and one of the women turned right, towards the bar as they left the bathroom, Paula had to steady herself several times before she made it to the bar.

"Gin and Tonic," Paula shouted at the closest bartender as she leaned on the only unoccupied three inches of the bar.

Cassandra moved within two feet of Paula Thorpe and remained as still as she could. Many more people had come into the club, so not that much free space was left. Cassandra was constantly bumped and shoved by people trying to move and dance.

"I called him about fifteen minutes ago," Cheryl spoke right behind Cassandra, pressing up against her. "What do we do now?"

"We wait."

Cassandra turned sideways, then whispered to Cheryl, "She's headed to the door."

Cheryl pointed to the bar where Paula and the other woman had moved towards the exit. It was very hard to move in a straight line, and Paula and her friend were squeezing their way through the crowd towards the front door.

"You wait here." Cassandra put her hand on Cheryl's shoulder. "I'll follow her into the street; you wait inside here for three minutes and then come outside."

"Three minutes?" Cheryl didn't like that idea at all.

"Yes," Cassandra insisted. "Check your watch and wait three minutes."

Cassandra shoved her way towards the door behind Paula Thorpe and her friend, keeping a very tight hold on her purse. She had put her three eighty automatic and a pair of handcuffs in it before she left home and she didn't want to lose them. Leading with her right shoulder, Cassandra plowed her way to the exit.

The street in front of the club was crowded with people. It wasn't all that cold, and the wind was almost nonexistent. Wafting in from the side alley, a strong scent of urine slapped Cassandra in the face. The loud pounding of the club music bass line agitated the night air outside the club. Men, women, casual conversation and mating rituals filled the night air as Cassandra spotted Paula, who seemed to be alone.

"Aren't you Paula?" Cassandra walked up to her as she leaned against a parking meter.

"Who are you?" Paula tried to focus her blurry gaze on Cassandra. "You're a tall one, aren't you?"

"I'm a friend of Amy."

Cassandra wanted to keep the conversation light; she was trying to stall until I got there with the car so Paula could be escorted to the police.

"Amy?" Paula asked, confused. "Listen, I'm waiting for my friend to get here with her car, we're going to her place for some fun. Would you like to join us?"

"I've got a better idea." Cassandra thought fast. "I'm waiting for my friend, would you like to have even more fun?"

Paula observed Cassandra from her head to her feet slowly. "You might be a lot more fun, after all."

"Here's my ride now." Cassandra pointed to our new BMW slowly driving down the street.

I was looking for a parking place, realizing that there wasn't a chance in hell for street parking when I spotted Cassandra and Paula talking near the end of the block. As I slowed to a stop next to them, I caught a glimpse of something familiar hovering around the entrance to an alleyway. It was familiar and yet it was revolting at the same time; it was Fred Lepus who had his eye on Paula Thorpe.

"You're talking about a man?" Paula squinted towards the inside of our car.

"It's fun," Cassandra said with an encouraging tone. "If you like, he'll mostly just watch us."

239

"I guess so." Paula carefully checked out Cassandra again. "You're kind of sexy, it might be interesting."

Cheryl was a woman of her word, it was three minutes to the second when she burst onto the sidewalk from the crowded club. Paula Thorpe was in the process of getting into the back seat of our car when Cassandra saw Cheryl and waved at her. Cheryl clearly saw what was happening, stopped in her tracks, then slowly walked in the other direction.

As soon as both Cassandra and Paula got into the back seat of the car, I sped off. I could hear Cassandra pull handcuffs out of her purse; I also saw Lepus run to the curb, all too late, which was the story of his life.

"Oh, that's kinky." Paula said.

She put her right hand on Cassandra's bare cleavage, then slid it down and around Cassandra's waist.

"Let's wait a while before we try that kinky stuff."

"I think I'd like to try it right now," Cassandra insisted.

Cassandra grasped Paula's hand that was pulling her towards Paula's lips and clamped the handcuff around it. She quickly placed Paula's other wrist in the other cuff and locked it.

"Gee." I smiled into the rear view mirror. "It was getting interesting back there."

"Shut up and keep driving."

"I got a call from Belchamp's son," I said as my eyes turned to look back through the front windshield.

"What did he have to say?" Cassandra grabbed Paula's small purse.

"Belchamp?" Paula's mind centered for a second on what was happening to her. "Who the hell are you two?"

"We're here for a good time," I said, keeping a straight face.

"She doesn't have a gun." Cassandra tossed Paula's purse in the front seat.

"Belchamp Junior said his old man called him from the dealership, he's scared shitless and I think the son wants us to help his father," I said. "He wants to meet with us tomorrow morning, early."

"I thought I heard you say Belchamp." Paula slurred.

She squinted, trying to concentrate on the conversation but concentration wasn't in the cards for her yet, the cocaine blast was still too fresh.

"What do you want to do?" Cassandra asked me.

"I'd like to know who's behind the Cayman Island corporation." I checked back in the rear view mirror for a second.

"That's a good question," Cassandra added. "Who paid you to set up the Cayman Island scam?"

"What?" Paula tried to slap Cassandra, then quickly realized she was in handcuffs.

Cassandra blocked Paula's blow but when Paula kept on trying, Cassandra hit her once, hard with her fist, forcing a small trickle of blood to ooze from Paula's lip.

"I asked who were you working for in Washington, at the fine law offices of Smith, Smith and Heywood. Who had you set up that corporation in the Caymans?" Cassandra asked again.

"Ramón Gutierrez."

Paula wiped the blood from her mouth with the back of her hand as best she could with the handcuffs on.

"Will you stop hitting me," Paula demanded.

It was obvious that Paula was still flying on the dope, and she didn't care that much about telling us the truth.

"Who's Ramón Gutierrez?" Cassandra asked.

"He works for some big wig in Columbia, but he never did tell me who," Paula answered, not coming off her high, even considering the smack Cassandra gave her in the face.

"What does that have to do with Simon Belchamp?" I asked from the front seat; I was so happy she was a babbling idiot right then.

"Nothing." Paula struggled a little with the handcuffs.

"What do you mean nothing?" Cassandra asked.

"Nothing is what I meant." Paula almost shouted.

She reached for the door handle as I stopped at a red light. Cassandra jerked Paula back to the middle of the seat, then pasted Paula again with her fist.

"I said, stop hitting me!" Paula shouted in Cassandra's face.

"Stop trying to get out of the car, then," Cassandra forcefully

241

replied.

"You don't have the right to hold me." Paula became more coherent by the second.

"Yes, we do," I said. "You're a fugitive, you're wanted for fraud and several other charges in Washington, and in Virginia and the FBI seems real keen on finding you too."

"Are you cops?"

"No." Cassandra smiled a wicked smile at her. "So, we can beat the crap out of you and you can't cry police brutality."

"What the hell do you want?" Paula demanded.

"If no connection existed between Gutierrez and Belchamp, then what were you doing with Belchamp?" Cassandra asked. "We know he was sending you a few thousand every other month, what was that all about?"

"I was doing a scam on the side," Paula replied, a bit more reluctantly than before. "Simon Belchamp used Smith, Smith and Heywood for a liability lawsuit a few years ago. When he was in town for the settlement last year, he asked if I could set up a limited partnership in Brazil for him and his girlfriend, it seems he was skimming quite a bit off the top of his car dealerships and he didn't want to stash the money in a local bank anymore. he wanted to skip out on his wife and live like a king with his new woman."

"Was that what he was paying you for?" Cassandra asked. "Or were you blackmailing him?"

"A little bit of both, I suppose." Paula shrugged her shoulders, Cassandra could see the glaze still in her eyes. "He said he would turn me into the cops if I didn't stop. I figured he would, so I was planning on stopping soon anyway."

"What about the five million dollar policy on Belchamp?" I asked.

"That was something Gutierrez and I cooked up," Paula said, then softly laughed. "I needed to keep Simon quiet about me, so I thought up this five million dollar policy. I took it out on him, and Ramón and I would wait six months or so, then kill Simon and collect the five million. He could make it look like a heart attack, some druggist in Columbia had a concoction that would bring on a heart attack, besides old Simon was about ready for one anyway. It

242

was a great idea, Simon did stop sending me money last month, and threatened to uncover me, so I had Ramón put the drug in a box of doughnuts to kill him."

"How did you get him to eat the doughnuts?" Cassandra was curious.

"Ramón had some street guy hang around the restaurant and offer Belchamp a box when he came out to get into his car. The guy would say he had sold all but this box that morning, and he had to unload it before he went back to the store, he sold it for fifty cents."

"Too cheap for a fat guy to pass up," I surmised.

"That was the plan," Paula confirmed.

"You do know now that that the fat guy who bought those doughnuts and died wasn't Simon Belchamp." Cassandra stared at the drugged woman.

"No," she glared at Cassandra as she spoke. "He was, the newspapers said he was."

"I take it your boyfriend killed Belchamp's girlfriend because you two planned to not only collect the five million dollar insurance, you also planned to steal his stash in Brazil."

It was kind of obvious now.

"No comment." She was beginning to loose her buzz.

"What were you doing for Gutierrez?" I asked. "I mean, besides plotting to kill Simon Belchamp."

There had to be more to this, something besides stealing all that money. She said her boyfriend worked for someone else, what was that all about? Whatever it was had to be the reason the FBI was all over Don and Mike.

"Ramón's boss, some drug king back in Columbia, wanted me to dig up dirt on officials in Washington so that he could blackmail them. I think the Feds were putting to much pressure on his business." Paula stared out the window. "I guess, all I know is that I made a bundle of cash for two years work."

"One thing I have to know." I turned around quickly to face Paula.

"What?" Paula sounded pissed off, I think she was in and out of her drug induced honesty.

"What happened to the drugged doughnuts?"

243

"The bum was supposed to hang around and wait for Belchamp to keel over, then he was supposed to get the doughnuts back, wipe Belchamp's mouth and throw the doughnuts down a sewer." Paula shrugged. "I suppose he did what he was paid to do."

"Where are you driving?" Cassandra asked.

"We're here," I answered as I pulled up to the curb. "I called Gary Brown before I left and asked him to meet us on the street in front of police headquarters."

"Good thing we finished with her before we got here," Cassandra said as she opened the back door on her side and stepped out.

"Why do you think I drove so slowly the last mile or so," I chuckled.

"Did Benjamin tell you who we had?" Cassandra asked Detective Brown, pulling the key to the hand cuffs off her key ring and giving it to him.

"He did." Gary looked in the rear of our car. "Is that the Thorpe woman?"

"It is."

Cassandra opened the back door to the car and pulled Paula out and to her feet.

"She's whacked out on coke right now so talking about everything seems to be her favorite pastime, so read her rights and have fun."

"I think you'd better call the FBI as soon as you finish with her," I advised the detective. "I think they've been looking for her too."

"This woman has been punching me around," Paula verbally stumbled.

She pointed to Cassandra, then finally noticed that she was almost at the front door to police headquarters.

"I want you to arrest her, now."

"She punched you around?" Gary continued to stare at Paula.

"Yes, she did."

"Good." Gary winked at Cassandra. "I guess I don't have to do it myself now."

244

"You can give me back those handcuffs later," Cassandra said as she grinned back at the detective. "Be sure to ask her about the poisoned doughnuts and a street guy who sold them to the dead man for fifty cents."

"What?" The detective sounded confused for a second.

"We should be in possession of the alleged dead man by tomorrow," I said to the detective as he began pulling Paula towards the police station.

If I had told Detective Brown about Simon Belchamp's whereabouts, the sight of cops might have scared him away.

"I like you're doing all this work for me, but I wish you'd do it at a reasonable hour," Gary said as he pulled Paula to police headquarters.

32

Good night sweet Katz

It was nearly two in the morning when we got back home so I let Cassandra take the first shower since she had all that cigarette smoke to get rid of.

"I'd like to know why this damned case has to be so complicated." Cassandra jumped into bed and pulled the sheet up.

"It's not that complicated," I replied, sitting on the end of the bed. "If we can believe that Thorpe woman, the plot to kill Belchamp involved only Thorpe and her boyfriend. Other than his being the victim, it had nothing to do with Belchamp."

"I still would like the alive dead man to tell us what the hell he was planning with his girlfriend." Cassandra sat up in bed and stared at me.

"The five million dollar insurance policy had nothing to do with Simon Belchamp's scheme of running away with his girlfriend." I shook my head. "That is, if Paula Thorpe wasn't lying."

"I guess so." Cassandra shrugged. "The girlfriend didn't look that good to throw away everything he'd built up here in Atlanta."

"We don't know the whole story," I added. "All we'll get is Simon Belchamp's side, Elsa is dead. She may well have been worth all the trouble to him, we'll never know."

"Okay." Cassandra lay on her side, facing me. "The five million dollar insurance policy maybe has been explained, and maybe Simon Belchamp is still alive, and maybe the policy and Belchamp aren't related, but, what about the three times one or both of us has been shot at?"

"Well, the shooting in Virginia wasn't related to this case, it was an old vendetta against me, but I'm not completely sure about the other two."

"My point exactly." Cassandra nodded her head

emphatically. "And, do you really believe the Colombian shot Belchamp's mistress?"

"It most likely is the Colombian, or it could be Mrs. Belchamp."

I was too tired to squeeze another coherent thought out.

"And you said it was simple," Cassandra said with a smile.

"Right now, a good night's sleep seems simple enough."

"Are we sure it had nothing to do with his wife or son?" Cassandra asked.

"I don't think so, but we'll talk to Simon and his son tomorrow."

I wanted to take my shower and begin my long due, refreshing slumber. Too bad I had to set my alarm for six in the morning since that trash bag had to be out in the dumpster at seven on the dot, and we had to visit the living Belchamp rather early. Before I did anything else, I swept our apartment for bugs, and confirmed the bug was still active in the plastic sack tucked away in the kitchen closet. It was still there, and nothing else seemed to have been put in our apartment while we were away that night, at least that was a good thing.

"We have given Paula to the cops, and she's the one who tried to defraud the insurance company. If we can also produce Simon Belchamp to the insurance company, won't our job be done?" Cassandra asked. "We shouldn't care about any of the other stuff going on."

"I suppose not." I shrugged my shoulders. "But for my own peace of mind, I'd like to know more about all the plots."

"A lot of plots," Cassandra agreed.

"I have to admit, there appears to be a lot of seemingly unrelated stuff going on here," I said as I walked into the bathroom.

"I still think some of them are related," she said. "It would take a lot of serendipity to throw a dumb car dealer into the middle of all this intrigue."

"Maybe everything is related, I don't know." I stuck my head out of the bathroom. "I want to get clean and go to sleep right now.

"I agree." she lay back down. "Good night, sweetheart."

. . . .

"Wake up." Cassandra said.

She shoved my shoulder, I thought I was dreaming even though she had been shoving my shoulder for about five minutes. It was part of a dream about us mud wrestling, or was it real? We were naked, so at least on the surface it was an enjoyable dream.

"What time is it?"

I was awake now; it must have been a dream, I wasn't muddy.

"It's a little before seven."

She was almost dressed, and there I was still in my Katz pajamas.

"Okay."

I got out of bed more quickly than I thought I could have. I trundled to my dresser and pulled out some clothes, hoping that I'd matched the socks. What happened to my alarm clock? I looked at it and realized I had set it for six in the afternoon, damn.

"I toasted a bagel for you." Cassandra pointed towards the kitchen. "We're almost out of juice, but I gave you the last of it."

"What about coffee?" I peered at her through somewhat open eyelids. "And what about the garbage?"

"That, we're out of," she bluntly informed me. "Not the garbage, but coffee."

"There's always the seven come elevens," I mumbled. "Did you put the trash out?"

"Right at seven," she calmly answered me. "I didn't have the heart to wake you up any earlier, you looked so sweet sleeping there."

"Thanks."

I trundled to the bathroom, then attempted to shave; I got most of the whiskers and I did manage to brush my teeth without missing my mouth.

"What time do you think we'll have Simon if he is alive and with his son?"

Cassandra adjusted her dress as she glanced in the full length mirror in our bedroom.

"Simon junior said he'd meet us at his house at eight." I replied. "We should have him in tow by nine if he's really there."

248

I drank the last of the juice; it wasn't coffee and I wasn't awake.

"Good." Cassandra walked back into the kitchen. "I'll call Allan Katzen and tell him I'll see him at ten to finish up this case."

"Is that why you're wearing a dress?" I glanced at her as I hastily threw on my clothes. "Not that you don't look great, but don't you think a pair of jeans will work better, especially if we have to chase after someone?"

"Who?" Cassandra asked. "A fifty something overweight slob?"

"I see your point," I agreed.

"I'd like to look presentable and professional when I go to the insurance office to settle this case with them," Cassandra thought out loud. "Besides, look at you, a coat, tie and jeans?"

It was early in the morning, and neither one of us had gotten enough sleep, so the logic sounded good to both of us.

"It's the fashion statement for the exhausted." I would much rather have been in bed than dressed anyway. "Restful, and casual."

"The only problem I see with this outfit is that I have to carry my pistol in my purse again since there's nowhere to hide a holster with this dress." She patted her left side, where she would have been carrying her pistol. "I need to project a professional look so he'll hire us again for the next job his company has."

"Well, while you're being a professional, I need to look at a map to see where Ansley Street is, that's where Junior lives."

I got up and left for our downstairs office.

"So, what happened?" Cheryl popped out of her door at the same time I opened mine.

"Hi," I greeted our neighbor. "We took her to the cops. Isn't it a little early after such a late night?"

"It's never been a problem for me." Cheryl smiled back at me.

I must be moving to the A list now, a smile is a good thing in the morning.

"Can you tell me what the case is all about yet?" Cheryl inquired.

"Maybe later," I cleared my throat. "We have to get

somewhere right away."

"Is this for the same case?" Cheryl sounded especially eager for this hour of the morning.

"Yes, it is," I confirmed.

"Well, what is it?"

"I can't say yet," I reluctantly answered.

"Yes, you can." She was becoming irritated at my unwillingness to spill the beans.

"I have to get to the office right now and look something up. Why don't you ask Cassandra, she's up and on the phone right now."

The truth was that I needed coffee very soon.

Cheryl walked into our apartment as I ran down the stairs and opened up our office. The map was in the center drawer; unfolding it, I realized we needed another one because this one was beginning to tear from use. I found the street quickly and made a mental note of how to get there.

"Hi."

I walked back into our apartment, wondering if Cheryl was still there, she wasn't.

"Let's get going." Cassandra pulled me by my sleeve back into our bedroom.

"Remind me to ask around about body shops." I sat down on the edge of our bed.

"What?" Cassandra began brushing her hair; she seemed irritated. "Right, your Porsche and the holes in it."

"By the way, why are you in a bad mood all of a sudden?" I asked.

"You didn't have to send Cheryl in here," she chastised. "I'm not in the mood to talk all that much this morning."

"What did you tell her?"

"I said I'd tell her the whole story later tonight."

"You think we'll know the whole story by tonight?"

"Very funny."

A soft knocking at our front door grabbed both our attention.

"What the hell is it this time?" Cassandra glanced at me, then stared towards the front door.

250

"It can't be Don or Mike, unless they got away from the FBI," I replied as I grabbed my revolver.

"I'll open it, you stand over there." I pointed to my left.

"Lepus!" Cassandra shouted as I opened the door all the way.

"What the hell do you want?" I stridently asked.

"You owe me, Katz." Lepus barged in.

"What now?" Cassandra lowered her pistol.

"What, are you going to shoot me again?" Lepus flopped onto our sofa and quickly checked out our apartment.

"It's not as nice as your folks place, but it's kind of cozy." Lepus smiled at Cassandra. "You two screwed up my case real good this time."

"What case would that be?" I stared at him. "You wouldn't be talking about our case, would you?"

"Your case, my case," Lepus said with a shrug. "All I care about is that everyone who could have paid me is either lost or in jail, except you two."

"How do you figure somebody would pay you anything?" Cassandra sounded intrigued.

"Smith and Heywood are real hot about locating Paula Thorpe," Lepus began. "Simon Belchamp seems real interested in convincing me that he's his twin brother, and, then I find out that Belchamp has a million dollar insurance policy ready to pay out, so I figure there's a case in there somewhere for me."

"The FBI picked up Smith yesterday, and we dumped Thorpe in the city jail late last night." Cassandra glared at Lepus. "So, where's the case for you?"

"Heywood's still out there." Fred grinned.

"No, the FBI picked him up yesterday too." I started to become annoyed. "So, why are you here?"

"Don't tell me you're broke again?" Cassandra laughed.

"Well, yes, I am." Fred glanced at the floor, then back at Cassandra.

"So, what do you want us to do about that?" Cassandra was still enjoying this.

"More to the point, what do we have to do to get rid of

you?" I added.

"I'd like to get a flight back to Washington, and, well, I don't have any money."

"Why not?" I started to see the humor in this. "Didn't one of the lawyers pay you to locate Paula Thorpe?"

"Well, that would have been Mike Heywood," Lepus spoke softly, as if he didn't want to say this. "But, he paid Cathy and she wouldn't give me any of the dough."

"If we give you three hundred bucks for the flight, will you leave?" Cassandra tried not to face me; she was still grinning.

"Okay." Fred sounded thankful.

Between the two of us, we had two hundred and ninety six dollars, and Fred Lepus seemed happy with that. I had the feeling that his exit would only be temporary, but at least he was gone for now.

. . . .

After dropping by our bank for some ready cash, we had enough time to drink coffee, so we used a drive through on the way to Decatur; at least drive through coffee is better than drive through food. The smells at those places are discouraging because the predominant odor is of the plastic containers for the food which is not a heartening thought.

Simon Belchamp junior lived in an upper middle class neighborhood, his house was a brick two story. By its appearance, it must have been built within a decade after the second world war. Hanging onto the left side of the house was a recent addition, which, from the outside I guessed was a family room. The one story addition balanced the one story two car garage on the right side of the home and the new construction seemed well thought out, whoever did the work matched the bricks quite well to the original house.

"I don't see any car on the street directly in front of the house." Cassandra scanned the street.

"Why don't we park there?" I pulled up to the curb near their driveway.

"Do you see the kids staring at us out the upstairs windows?"

252

Cassandra pointed to them as she walked to the front door of the house.

"That could be us in ten years." I nodded.

"What, we're going to regress in ten years?" She said with a tinge of whimsy. "Don't start up with me right now."

The front door opened as soon as we stepped onto the front porch; Simon junior was there and I could see his father hanging back in the front hallway.

"Come on in quickly." Simon Junior practically grabbed Cassandra as she approached the front door. "Someone's been circling the house for the past hour."

"Are you really Simon Belchamp?" Cassandra asked.

She studied the older man now standing right in front of her. He was wearing old jeans, a blue sweatshirt and leather boots and his entire ensemble was worn and old, which didn't smell bad, so I assumed it was at least washed. He had a minimum of a four day stubble growing on his face and his countenance was drawn and sad, he appeared as if he had gotten less sleep than we had.

"That's me," he said softly as he cleared his throat. "Do you two know why someone has been trying to kill me for the last week or two?"

"As far as we can put all this together, Paula Thorpe and her boyfriend are the ones who took that insurance policy out on you." I took in a short breath. "We think Paula's boyfriend is the one after you; if you're dead, he and Paula get the big payout."

"I remember you two." Simon studied Cassandra, then me. "You're the ones I ran away from in DC."

"Yeah, that's us." I took a step toward Simon senior. "Maybe if you'd come with us and told us the whole truth, your girlfriend might still be alive."

"What?" Simon's jaw dropped to the floor. "Elsa?"

"Last night." I put a hand on Simon's shoulder. "We went there hoping to find you."

"She was supposed to meet me at the airport next week," Simon whimpered.

I could see a small tear forming in his eye.

"Who is Elsa, Daddy?" Simon junior joined the

conversation.

"Just a friend of mine, son."

He seemed a little embarrassed but Junior could see from his father's expression that Elsa wasn't just a friend.

"Is that what this was all about?" Simon junior became indignant.

"Let it go," The father pleaded with his son.

"I hate to break up this family moment, but we need to know why Ramón Gutierrez wants you dead," Cassandra interrupted the tension between father and son.

"I don't know who Ramón Gutierrez is," Simon senior insisted.

"He's Paula Thorpe's boyfriend," I answered.

"Who the hell's Paula Thorpe?" Simon Senior demanded.

"That's Kelly Chalmers' real name," Cassandra answered. "You remember her, the one who was blackmailing you from the law firm in Washington."

"Oh, her," Simon's voice trailed off.

"That's right," I added. "Like I already said, if you're dead, Paula and her boyfriend get the insurance money."

"I don't get it," Simon stammered. "What did they have against me?"

"Paula seems to think you were going to turn her in for blackmail." Cassandra watched the older man's face go through several quick contortions.

"Well." Simon glanced at his son. "Maybe I was, I was tired as hell paying her twenty five hundred four times a year to keep quiet about me and my girlfriend."

"That's where that money was going?" Junior shook his head as he shot his father an expression somewhere between anger and sadness. "I figured you had some woman on the side, but I wasn't sure."

"Did mom suspect?" Simon acted like a lost puppy now.

"I don't think so," Junior looked sad as he answered his father. "She was worried about the business, the cash flow has been off for years and neither one of us could figure out how. You always said it was a slow business and you didn't care a lot."

254

"I didn't take that much, it was only a few hundred thousand a year, maybe a little more these last few years," Simon Senior said as both Cassandra and I stood there.

It appeared that Simon needed to confess and we were surprised that he hadn't told his son before, but it appeared as if he waited for us to arrive to spill the beans.

"How long have you been skimming? When did you start?" Junior was beginning to get mad.

"About five or six years or so." Simon blushed a lot, it was obvious he was lying, but Junior didn't push it.

"How did your brother get killed instead of you?" Cassandra interrupted the father-son confessional.

"I spent a lot of time and money finding my twin brother." Simon was glad to change the subject. "He was a homeless bum in Washington, I paid to clean him up and bring him to Atlanta. I thought I could help him rehabilitate, maybe work at my business."

"Why didn't you tell us about all this?" Junior interrupted.

This was yet another irritation and a probable falsehood; an uncle he didn't know about? Maybe someone else he'd have to share the inheritance with, could this be another angle? No, I didn't think so.

"I was going to tell everybody as soon as he sobered up, and I could get him presentable," Simon insisted, although it didn't sound too convincing to me yet.

"So, how did he get killed instead of you?" I wanted him to get to the point quicker.

"I put him up in a hotel not far from Mary Mac's where he was sobering up just fine for the first month or so, but he was getting real nervous about it all." Simon stopped, becoming a little emotional. "I asked him to meet me after lunch there, and I guess he got to the parking lot a little early. When I went outside to wait for him, I noticed someone in my car, he had been shoved into the driver's side where he was slumped across the front seat. I checked for a pulse, and there weren't none."

"Was his body warm?" I asked.

"Yeah."

I could see a tear forming in the corner of Simon's right eye again.

"Did you see anybody else anywhere around there?" Cassandra asked, seeing if he had noticed the derelict that poisoned his brother.

"No," he stopped and thought for a second before he continued speaking. "Just some street bums hanging around on the corner, I could barely see them."

"Daddy?"

Simon junior seemed confused; he pulled at his father's sleeve to get him to look him in the face.

"That dead man who was in your car was your real brother, my uncle, then that poor man did get killed because someone thought he was you?"

"You and your family can sort all this out later, but we'd like to take you somewhere safe right now," Cassandra interrupted.

"That car is back," Junior almost shouted as he pointed out the window.

I glanced out the large window in the living room and noticed the red Oldsmobile I had seen yesterday, the one I had put two slugs into; I guess I missed the gas tank. They had taken the tag off it and put a temporary tag from a local dealer on it. It would have been ironic if the temporary tag had been from Belchamp's dealership, but it wasn't. I pulled Simon junior back from the window and pushed him towards the kitchen.

"Call the cops right now, tell them there's a gunfight going on in your front yard," I spoke slowly and softly. "Tell your family to hide in the upstairs bathroom right now."

"There isn't a gunfight in my front yard." Junior was shocked.

"There's about to be one, so get moving and call the cops," I spoke louder as he ran off.

"Where should I go?" Simon asked. I turned around to answer him and saw a large twelve gauge pump shotgun in his hands.

I pointed to the back of the entrance hallway. "You go there with her, and give me that shotgun."

Simon handed me the shotgun, a twelve gauge pump action Savage Arms, maybe twenty five years old but in very good

256

condition.   Cassandra had already pulled out her pistol as she and Simon positioned themselves behind a bench at the rear of the entrance hallway.

"I've got sight of the back and front entrance," Cassandra said to me. "Are you going out the back?"

I sneaked a glance out the front window, clearly seeing one man exit the car with an automatic pistol; it looked like a nine millimeter pistol. The other man was still in the car holding a long gun, probably a shotgun. I pumped the shotgun I was holding and picked up the ejected shell; it was double ought buckshot, very good. I shoved that shell back into the shotgun.

"Do you have any more shells?" I called back to Simon who threw me a box of five more shells.

"Be careful," I heard Cassandra shout to me as I ran for the back door.

I raced as quietly as I could out the back door, damn, they had a huge in ground swimming pool; he had no reason to bitch about lost money, Junior wasn't hurting that much. I raced to the right side of the house and paused before I peeked around the corner. I set the shotgun down and pulled out my revolver. I then emptied the revolver, stuffed in six rounds of full metal jacketed loads and put it back in the holster. Picking the shotgun back up, I looked carefully around the side of the house.

The shrubbery surrounding the house had been there for a long time and had grown thick. Junior kept it trimmed so that it was only four feet tall. While on my knees, I saw the man who had left the car stop and gaze at the house carefully, he was tall, maybe he was Paula's boyfriend. The other man was still in the car and I could still see him fairly well; he seemed to be staring directly at the front door. He had opened the front car window and had pushed the barrel of his shotgun out.

The man staring at the front of the house turned and began slowly walking directly towards me, he had decided to enter through the back door. I had to assume he hadn't seen me yet, so, as he got to within ten feet of my position, I stood up, pointing the twelve gauge at his chest.

"Stop!" I shouted.

I quickly positioned myself behind him in relation to the man in the car. If the shotgun in the car fired, it would kill the man in front of me, and hopefully not hit me.

The man paused, then swung his pistol towards me. I fired one shot at his knees; one pellet struck his right knee, another pellet tore through his left upper leg, and a third through his right hip. He fired once before dropping his pistol and falling to the ground in shock and bleeding; his shot went somewhere into the grass beside me.

The man in the car didn't do anything for a second, but as soon as the first man hit the carefully manicured lawn, he fired at me. I had also fallen to the ground and I pulled my revolver, firing once at the man in the car. My bullet went through the car door and through his upper abdomen, then it was deflected downwards by the rear portion of one of his ribs, passing through the other door and lodging in the street. His shotgun was a semi-automatic so he fired it twice more before falling into unconsciousness.

I checked the condition of the man in front of me; he was out cold and loosing blood fast. I ran into the house through the back door, reaching for the phone in the kitchen, I dialed 911 and summoned an ambulance. I then grabbed several dish towels, and, rushing to the bleeding man in the backyard, I tied off as many blood flows as I could. He was still unconscious, I assumed he had passed out from the shock of being plastered with twelve gauge buckshot.

"Thank you for saving my life." Simon was very effusive as I walked back into the hallway.

"What do we do now?" Cassandra asked.

"You take Simon to Katzen's office," I thought quickly. "Do it now," I insisted.

"Hey," I shouted up the stairs as Cassandra rushed out the front door dragging Simon after her. "It's safe for now, come down here."

"What happened?" Junior led his wife and two kids down the stairs.

"The wife and kids need to go to the garage and take the car and get the hell out of here for a few hours," I insisted.

I glanced at his wife who was in her late twenties and good

258

looking, not a raging beauty, but pleasant on the eyes. She had the appearance of middle class or higher; Junior married into the class his mother aspired to.

"I'll go to my mom's." She nervously glanced at her husband, then at me. "Is Daddy Belchamp all right?"

"He's fine," I assured her. "My partner's taking him somewhere safe right now."

"Let's get going, dear," Simon junior's wife insisted.

"I want him to stay with me and wait for the cops." I pointed to Simon junior.

"Why?" Junior whined.

"Because I saved your father's life and the cops will be here in a few minutes. You need to explain to them what went on in the past half hour or so."

Damned straight he'd stay there with me to explain to the cops what two bodies were doing in his front yard.

Junior's wife and two kids ran to the garage and I could hear the car start; I also heard sirens in the distance. As I glanced back at Simon junior, I saw a hammer in his hand and I saw it flying towards my head. I was able to get my revolver out before the hammer struck but I wasn't able to move completely out of the hammer's way. I did get one shot off, the one shot hit Simon junior in his hand but it was too late, the hammer crashed into my skull. The slug from my revolver passed through Junior's right hand, through the ceiling, the ceiling of the next floor, the lower brace of the roof truss and burrowed into an upper rafter.

33

Wake me when it's over

Cassandra broke several traffic laws on her way to the insurance offices in midtown; she didn't get stopped so I guess it was more or less legal. Sometimes I go by the adage that it's only against the law if you get caught, actually that only applies to parking meters, the victimless traffic crime.

Simon Belchamp sat nervously in the front seat beside Cassandra as she sped to her meeting with Allan Katzen, not saying anything. Cassandra tried a few questions, but Simon didn't say anything, other than the occasional complaint about her driving.

Pulling into a loading zone in front of the insurance building on Peachtree, Cassandra jumped from the car; she came close to being hit by a passing truck which would have been sad, our new car without a driver's door. Simon also quickly departed the car seconds before Cassandra scampered to Simon's side and grabbed his left arm.

"We need to go into this building and up to the top floor."

Without saying a word, Simon shoved Cassandra hard as he jerked his arm from her grip; Cassandra tumbled to the sidewalk with a thud, knowing then and there it was a mistake to have worn a dress that day. The throng of workers milling about, late for work or on their first coffee break, could all see the fine pink daisies on her panties. At least one gentleman attempted to pull her back up. 'I will destroy that fat pig' was her mantra as she scrambled to her feet and took off running after Simon.

Simon was fat and Simon was old, but it took Cassandra a

block and a half to catch up with him. His coat was flapping behind him as he ran, snaking his way through the crowded sidewalk. Cassandra got a hold of his coat tail first; that slowed him down enough for her to grab his shoulder. She got enough of a grip on his coat shoulder to pull him off balance and shove him to the ground, in the process, Cassandra yanked Simon's coat half off his shoulder. She was running too fast to keep her balance, so she fell on top of Simon; the two of them tumbled for a few feet before coming to a stop. Cassandra was more or less on top of the large man and, again, her dress blew up and revealed a bit too much of her under parts; pants should have been more of a fashion possibility for a day like this, Mr. Katzen would have understood.

Modesty was not Cassandra's primary concern as Simon pushed her off him and back onto the sidewalk. Cassandra swung her leg around quickly and toppled Simon as he was standing up, the training Cassandra had begun in the martial arts gym was paying off now. Cassandra jumped to her feet while Simon tumbled to the sidewalk. The morning multitude on the sidewalk began to open a wider and wider arena for Cassandra and Simon to fight and no one yet seemed willing to step in.

As Simon got up from the sidewalk again, Cassandra was already standing over him with her fist drawn back. She had made the decision not to dig through her purse for her pistol since far too many people were around, besides, her purse had fallen ten feet away. As Simon rose to his feet, Cassandra punched him as hard as she could, her fist landing on the right side of Simon's face. The blow was enough to daze him, but he made it back to his feet. Cassandra punched him again as hard as she could in his large stomach; this time he doubled over and loudly expelled all the breath in his lungs. She didn't wait for him to try anything else, stepping back a half pace, she then kicked him in his balls, this time, Simon fell to the sidewalk and assumed the fetal position.

About a dozen women in the ever enlarging crowd began to applaud while expressions of great pain and sympathy crossed over the faces of most of the men close enough to see. A woman had picked Cassandra's purse up and held it for her. After the fight was all over and Cassandra had recovered her purse, a street cop calmly

261

walked up to Cassandra.

"What seems to be the problem here, miss?"

"I want you to arrest that man." Cassandra pointed to Simon, still crying in a ball on the sidewalk.

"Why?" The cop asked as he stared at Belchamp. "It seems he should be the one complaining."

"He assaulted me," Cassandra replied quickly. "He assaulted me as we left my car together."

"Like hell I did." Simon seemed to recover enough to speak.

"Can I have some ID from you two?" The policeman asked.

Cassandra pulled her wallet from her purse and fumbled two IDs from it.

"You're a private investigator?" The cop carefully studied Cassandra, he scanned her from head to toe. "Are you carrying a weapon?"

"Yes," Cassandra sounded disgusted as she handed the cop her purse.

"You've got some nasty scrapes on your knees and arms, do you need some attention for those?" The policeman sounded sympathetic as he took her purse and pulled the pistol out of it.

Cassandra quickly checked herself, nothing was wrong and more importantly, no skin showed through the rips in her clothes. She brushed herself off, and tried her best to readjust her dress and blouse. "I'm fine, I think; thank you for asking."

"Do you have any identification?" The cop stared at Simon who had sat up by then.

"No," he said flatly.

"Can you tell me what's going on?" The cop looked at Cassandra.

"I can tell you everything." Cassandra glared down at Simon, who was attempting to stand up. "We need to go to the top floor of the insurance building down the street and talk to the vice president."

"Why do we need to do that?" The cop sounded skeptical.

"The insurance company can identify this man," Cassandra forced herself to speak slowly. "I believe this man is involved in a murder case that Detective Gary Brown is working on."

"I know Gary." The cop's expression changed.

262

"Radio him to meet us at the insurance office and you and he will find out who this man is."

"All right, lady," The cop complied, "I will."

Within five minutes eight cops and two squad cars were on Peachtree, luckily one of the squad cars had a good sized first aid kit. They bandaged all of the more serious cuts on Cassandra and one female cop had pointed out a small, but reveling tear in the back of Cassandra's dress. Fortunately, Cassandra had a coat in the back of our car which the policewoman retrieved for her.

As a matter of protocol, both Simon and Cassandra were wearing handcuffs. The sergeant in the second squad car had taken command of this situation, and had decided to take both of the prisoners to the insurance office. They had called Allan Katzen and he begged them to bring Cassandra and Simon Belchamp to his office; Detective Brown was on his way to the office to meet them all.

"Why did you try to run away from me?" Cassandra asked.

Cassandra sat next to Simon in the second squad car. The building was only two blocks away, but they rode to it anyway. It wasn't that cold outside, somewhere in the upper sixties, which is why Cassandra didn't wear a coat while she was driving Simon to the insurance company, if she had one on, her scrapes wouldn't have been as bad.

"All I ever wanted is to run away with Elsa," Simon said in a resigned voice. "I loved her so much."

"She's dead." Cassandra had lost all her sympathy for the man. "What's your plan now?"

"I want to get away from here." Simon began to breathe deeper. "I want to get away from my wife and son and start over, I can't face Gladys, I can't face my friends." Simon burst out in tears.

"How much money have you stashed away?" She asked.

"I don't know what you're talking about," Simon replied.

He wiped his face with his right shoulder, then with his left; they were both handcuffed with their hands behind them.

"Don't bullshit me." Cassandra glared at him. "You admitted it back at your son's house, it's just that I don't completely believe you. You skimmed a whole bunch more than you confessed

263

to."

"No, I didn't."

"Tell me or not, it doesn't matter." Cassandra faced the front of the cop car. "The feds will find out and charge you with tax evasion, and the wife you hate so much will get everything that's left."

"I'll deny I'm Simon Belchamp," he insisted.

"Your fingerprints won't lie." Cassandra turned and faced him. "And, you have to know you won't get away anytime soon."

"The cops don't have my finger prints," he insisted. "The Army lost my records and I they don't exist anywhere else."

"You can't be that stupid," Cassandra observed.

"What do you mean?"

"Your house and office are full of your finger prints, besides, the Army found your records with your official finger prints."

"Well," Simon sounded more nervous, "all I did was try to get away to Brazil with my girlfriend."

"You covered up the murder of your brother." Cassandra watched a cop get into the car and start it up. "You skimmed off money from your business and hid it overseas. Maybe Paula Thorpe, or as you knew her, Kelly Chalmers can come up with a few more of your little schemes."

"They have her?" He sounded excited.

"Like we said before, my partner and I found her last night." Cassandra glanced out the front windshield; they were now in front of the insurance building. "She's with the Atlanta police, and I guess she'll turn you over in a heartbeat for anything and everything she can think of if the district attorney offers her any kind of deal."

"Oh, shit," Simon whispered.

The police pulled Cassandra and Simon out of the car and led them into the building; no one spoke on the elevator ride. All the office workers stared as the convention of police officers led Cassandra and Simon Belchamp to Allan Katzen's office.

"Mr. Katzen, I'd like you to meet Simon Belchamp," Cassandra was the first to speak as she and the entourage walked into the large office.

Allan Katzen and Detective Brown were standing in front of

the large desk and two police officers waited by the open door to the office while Simon and one officer followed Cassandra in.

"Dammed, you do good work. I heard about your fight with the alleged dead man," Allan smiled at Cassandra as he spoke.

He still hadn't gotten over how such a good looking woman was a real private investigator, let alone how she had solved his case so quickly.

"Well, dead men fight no fights," Cassandra replied as she turned to face Allan. "But this creep sure did, so I guess he's no dead man."

"Are you Simon Belchamp?" Detective Brown asked.

"What if I'm not," Simon stuttered.

"We have the file on Simon Belchamp from the Army, and we have his official fingerprints." Detective Brown winked at Cassandra, then glared at Simon. "Why don't you try answering my original question, are you Simon Belchamp?"

"Yeah, yeah," Simon replied as he glanced at Cassandra; if he had continued to deny it, she would have beaten him to a pulp. "I'm Simon Belchamp, but I didn't kill no one, I swear."

"Why did you really bring your brother here to Atlanta?" Cassandra had to know.

"I was going to pretend to leave my wife, move into an apartment, then I was going to set my twin up as me for a while at the dealership so Elsa and I could make our escape; he could have passed as me for a few days at least. I gave it a try once at my dealership and no one noticed. Elsa was going to pay my twin fifty thousand dollars to pretend to be me for as long as he could while we flew away to Brazil."

"Paula Thorpe has filled in some of the details too," Gary brown added. "It seems that Simon has skimmed off over three million dollars and has it stashed in Brazil."

"You lying weasel," Cassandra glowered at Simon, then turned toward Gary Brown. "Did Benjamin call you?"

"No, he didn't." Gary nodded at the cop next to Cassandra. "Could you take the cuffs off her."

"What happened?" Cassandra asked quickly.

"The Dekalb police called me," Gary gingerly replied. "It

seems your husband is in Grady Hospital with a mild concussion."

"He's all right?" Cassandra's jaw dropped a few inches.

"They said he was fine, just a possible concussion," Gary continued. "We have to sort out what happened, but the Dekalb police have Simon's son under arrest, and those two men your husband shot are alive and one of them is talking non stop."

"But, Benjamin is all right?" Cassandra barely heard the rest of what the detective said.

"Just get going," Gary replied, his expression not giving Cassandra a clue. "I'll talk to both of you later."

34

It's better than an exclamation point

Cassandra got to my hospital room in less than twenty minutes from leaving Allan Katzen's office. Although she still hadn't gotten a speeding ticket, she did get a ticket for parking in a loading zone. I wasn't in the room when she rushed into it. A woman at the nursing station told her that I was in X-ray, and that she should wait in my room for me.

A short muscular orderly pushed my bed back into my room, a Dekalb policeman had stayed by me in X-ray, and he followed my rolling bed as I was pushed back to my room. He waited outside the door after I whispered that the cute woman in the room was my wife. Cassandra was waiting for me, I loved seeing her there; she did appear a tad disheveled, but still beautiful. My head hurt like someone had hit me with a hammer, wait, someone did hit me with a hammer.

"They said you went to get your head X-rayed." Cassandra smiled at me.

"That he did, Ma'am," The orderly answered for me.

"Did they find anything up there besides a vacuum surrounded by bone?" Cassandra winked at me.

"I don't know, Ma'am," The orderly chuckled. "You'll have to talk to the doctor about that."

"Why is the cop outside the room?" Cassandra pulled a chair next to my bed as the orderly left the room. "Are you under arrest?"

"As a matter of a fact, I am." I scrunched around in the bed so I could see her better. "What happened to you?"

267

"Simon tried to run away."

She kissed me several times, luckily she stayed away from the bandaged area of my skull.

"Did he?"

"No, I beat the crap out of him for messing up my new dress." She kissed my cheek again.

"Are you all right?"

"I'm better off than you are, evidently," she stroked my face as she spoke to me.

"How long have you been waiting for me?" I asked.

"Not that long." She glanced at her watch. "Maybe an hour or two."

"That long?" I looked confused, hell, I was confused. "They said I was out cold for quite a while, the first thing I remember is being in X-ray."

"Gees," Cassandra sounded worried. "That's a long time, are you sure you're all right?"

"Take off your dress and get in here with me," I teased. "I'll show you all right."

"You sound fine to me," Cassandra laughed. "Before you pass out again, I need to tell you something."

"What?"

"I started my period this morning, so I guess I'm not pregnant for sure."

"I'm too groggy to make up a bunch of punctuation jokes, so you fill in the blanks," I replied as I held her hand. "I love you so much."

"I love you too." She squeezed my hand.

"Did anything happen that I should know about?" I was thinking about the hundred thousand dollars, I have to admit.

"Our answering service got a call from the pest control company," she sounded somber.

"Oh," I said, "you take care of it, will you?"

"I've already done it." She squeezed my hand again. "I'll be meeting with one of their representatives at three this afternoon."

"Come back and hold my hand as soon as you're finished," I somewhat apprehensively answered.

"I hear you still have most of your faculties." Detective Gary Brown walked into my hospital room.

"I didn't know I was an institution of higher learning," I attempted a bad joke, I must have been feeling better.

"He's delirious." Cassandra stood up and extended her hand to the policeman. "What's happened?"

"The Dekalb District Attorney's office said they wouldn't press charges against your would be comedian husband." Gary shook her hand.

"That's a comfort." Cassandra looked from Gary to me, then back to Gary Brown again.

"You might prefer it if the District Attorney were after you." Gary smiled at me.

"Why?" I asked.

"The FBI here in town seems to think you're a real big problem."

He sat down on the edge of the other bed in my room; the guy who was in that bed had been discharged at eight that morning, I was told, and nobody had yet been assigned as my roommate.

"Why would the feds be on my case?" I asked innocently. "I found the woman they were searching for."

"Well," Detective Brown sounded like he was ready to dump something on us. "They told me about the two men you shot in Virginia, and the man you shot in New York City. Then, there's the three men you shot here in Decatur, then there's Simon Belchamp's girlfriend who was shot, also, I'm not forgetting Belchamp's brother who was poisoned."

"So, did the Medical Examiner did find something in the man's blood?" I tried to focus on the conversation.

"Yes, they did," Gary sounded concerned, I wasn't sure if he was thinking about me, or the case. "The Thorpe woman sort of helped by telling us something about the poison that was used."

"So, I didn't shoot the girlfriend, nor did I poison his brother." I tried to smile. Again, it hurt, so I stopped; a smile shouldn't hurt.

"Yeah, I know," Detective Brown said with a muted grin. "I shot the sheriff, but I did not shoot the deputy."

"Are you trying to tell us something?" Cassandra asked.

She got that worried look on her face, the same worried look she has when she has to tell me something bad, like she might be pregnant.

"No," he replied. "I called the Loudoun County Sheriffs office and they told me you were defending yourselves from some hoods."

"The guy in New York was a mobster," Cassandra added. "They were ones who had a hit out on Benjamin."

"I know," Gary acknowledged. "I spoke to your uncle, he's an assistant chief and that's impressive."

"So." I glanced at Cassandra; she seemed better. "you're not going to bust our balls about all this, are you?"

"A friend of mine who's an FBI agent here in Atlanta told me that they all want to bust your heads for interfering in one of their cases, but their boss said to leave you two alone since you actually found the Thorpe woman for them." Gary took in another breath. "He said, however, that the local cops can throw you two in the slammer for all the trouble you caused."

"Is that what you're going to do?" I had to ask.

"No," he answered, "we figure the cracked skull you got is enough punishment."

"I promise not to shoot as many people in my future cases." I raised my right hand, as if taking an oath. "At least I'll try not to."

"That would be nice," Gary said, taking on a friendly sarcastic tone. "We're trying to lower the shooting statistics in this city and you alone have blown this months count."

"Okay." I tried to grin again, it didn't work. "I'll spread the shootings out more in the future."

"Will you two stop it." Cassandra put her hand on my arm, she wanted to get back to the case, and stop me from trying to think too much. "What about Don and Mike, the two DC lawyers?"

"I don't know about them," Detective Brown sounded confused. "Who were they?"

"They employed Paula Thorpe for two years," Cassandra said. "The FBI picked both of them up here in Atlanta over the past twenty four hours."

"Why?" He asked.

"We don't know for sure." Cassandra shrugged. "I was hoping you would."

"Well, I don't," Gary sounded a little frustrated. "The FBI would like a copy of your final report. They're questioning Ms. Thorpe, her boyfriend and some of his associates about drug trafficking, extortion and a whole bunch of other things they won't even tell us about."

"I suppose we'll all find out when they start to prosecute them for whatever," Cassandra observed.

"Did they take the Thorpe woman away from you?" I asked.

"Not yet," Detective Brown said. "They're trying to, but the District Attorney is fighting it because she's wanted here as an accessory to the murder of Belchamp's brother."

"That won't stop the feds," Cassandra added.

"What about the two I shot this morning?" I tried to sit up but I grimaced.

"Take it easy." Cassandra gently placed her hand on my shoulder.

"Neither one of them was Gutierrez," Gary answered me. "We have them cold for the murder of Elsa Peterson, their three eighty was the one that shot Elsa. Besides that, and that they're here illegally, we don't have much else on them."

"That's a lot," Cassandra remarked.

"What about that other man who visited Elsa Peterson?" One more loose end I had to know about.

"That was Elsa's brother," Gary said.

"I guess Cassandra will have to write the final report for the FBI, the insurance company and you guys," I said.

I pushed the button to raise my bed, I still couldn't sit up without getting dizzy and my head was still hurting like someone hit it with a hammer; that's right, someone did.

"I'll do it," Cassandra said with a sigh.

"You have to tell me why Simon junior hit Benjamin with a hammer." Cassandra glanced at me, then at Gary. "The nurses told me he was hit with a hammer, and I assumed it was by Simon junior."

"Yes, he did," Gary Brown confirmed. "It seems his father told him about the three million bucks he had socked away in Brazil, and I guess the son wanted at least part of it; he assumed his old man was headed to jail and the opportunity to get all the money wouldn't get any better."

"He knew about the three million bucks, but didn't know about the mistress?" I asked. "Maybe Simon Junior was pissed at his father and took it out on my head."

"Why did he want to kill Benjamin?" Cassandra asked again. "His father had the money."

"He didn't want to stick around with me and wait for the cops," I speculated.

"That sucks." Cassandra pursed her lips.

"Don't feel like Junior got away scot-free." I turned toward Cassandra. "I'm pretty sure I shot him in the hand before he smashed my skull."

"Yeah," Gary Brown verified. "And, he's in the same hospital as you."

"I love irony like that," Cassandra said with a grin.

"I bet the son wanted to get away from mother Belchamp too, I bet the mama held the purse strings pretty tight," I replied.

It wasn't hard to see greed, especially when it hits me in the head like a hammer. No, wait, it did hit me in the head like a hammer.

"Mr. Katzen at the insurance company also asked me to tell you that your check will be ready for you Wednesday next week," Detective Brown paused near the door to the room. "If you don't mind telling me, how much is he going to pay you?"

"It's a percentage of the five million dollars we saved his company," I answered.

"It's one hundred thousand," Cassandra added.

I wondered why; she later told me she liked him and wanted to be honest. I guess being honest pays off over the years.

"That's a lot of money," Gary said, seemingly shocked by that amount.

"That's before taxes," I added, not wanting to sound too rich.

"Those kind of taxes I wish I had." Gary's expression showed sadness and envy for a brief second.

"Are you married?" Cassandra changed the subject quickly.

"Yes, I am," The detective sounded confused.

"As soon as Benjamin gets back on his feet, we'd like to take you and your wife out for dinner, you pick the place," Cassandra asked. "You've been remarkably kind to us in the past few days."

"You two have been remarkably cooperative with me, and I think I actually like you two," Gary answered as he left the room. "My wife and I would be happy to have you buy us dinner, and we'll pick a place commensurate with the fee you just got."

35

Hello there

It was kind of a cryptic message, but Cassandra found the building on Peachtree, downtown Peachtree that is. In Atlanta, more roads are named Peachtree than anywhere else in the world. This building was seven stories high and appeared disheveled; it had a light green façade with big square windows staring out onto the heavily traveled downtown street. The windows were all outlined with black, although, with all the accumulated dirt, the green and black colors sort of blended together. That ten block area of Peachtree is the only place Atlanta has a big city feel, all the really tall buildings are stuffed into that stretch.

This building housed several US government offices and as Cassandra stared at the large black sign with moveable white letters in the front lobby, she could see who occupied offices here. The US attorney occupied the second floor, and the FBI had offices on the next floor up; she was to meet someone in room 238.

Pausing at the closed door to room 238, Cassandra looked up and down the hall. Very little activity was going on here, she could hear typewriters clacking away two doors down. The office opposite 238 was dark, but the loud discussion in the room to the left of that one was quite noticeable; some one thought Johnny Carson's monologue was good enough to loudly repeat it between slurps of coffee, although it lost a lot in the retelling.

Cassandra softly knocked at the door. The light was on in the office in front of her, but she heard no reply to the knock so she again tapped on the opaque glass pane in the door, nothing.

Cassandra tried the knob, it was unlocked so she stuck her head into the room as she slowly opened the door.

"Hello there, Mrs. Katz." It was Margaret Stanley.

"This is a surprise." Cassandra tried not to look too

surprised as she sat down.

"I know," Margaret answered. "I affect a lot of people that way."

"You're not with the State Department, are you?" Cassandra began to put one and one together. "You're with the Company, right?"

"And, which company would that be?" Margaret asked Cassandra with a curious tone.

"The one I signed my life away to, that one." Cassandra tentatively kept her grin.

"Sorry." Margaret looked at Cassandra for a second. "I'm yanking your chain, I'm your contact person at Langley."

"I thought I would have the same one Benjamin has," Cassandra sounded confused.

"No," Margaret replied. "well, some times you two will have the same person coordinating your assignments, but for now I've been assigned to you."

"Oh." Cassandra was confused. "What about the bug in the lamp, I thought that's what this meeting was all about?"

"It is." Margaret pulled a folder in front of her and opened it. "Come on over here to this side of the table so we can view this together."

"Sure." Cassandra got up and sat on Margaret's right.

"Did you check the surroundings before you came into this room?" Margaret asked.

"No guards in the front lobby, lots of FBI agents walking around."

Cassandra checked out the ceiling, then the four walls of the room, then looked back at Margaret.

"The hallway outside here is deserted, the office across the hall is vacant, and there's a lot of slack government employees in the other nearby offices this hour of the afternoon."

"Okay," Margaret hesitantly said.

"And, my guess is that this conversation is being recorded." Cassandra pointed to a large smoke detector hanging on the back wall. "We're probably being video taped too."

"Why would you say that?" She asked.

275

"Smoke detectors in commercial buildings have to be on the ceilings." Cassandra leveled at glare at Margaret.

"The bug was made in France." Margaret pointed to an eight by ten color photo of the listening device. "It's a relatively new gadget."

"So, it wasn't the mob?" Cassandra searched Margaret's face for a clue. "Was it one of ours?"

"I know it wasn't put there by our agency, but as to who actually did place it in your bedroom, the evidence is inconclusive." Margaret put the photograph aside. "You two have caught someone's attention all right, what we have to do is figure out who's bugging you and how much they know and why they suspected you in the first place."

"Well," Cassandra interrupted, "I've been thinking about that."

"And?" Margaret asked Cassandra.

"The only person to visit our place who could possibly arouse suspicion was Billy Sullivan, he visited Benjamin to give him an assignment about three months ago."

"We know," Margaret said. "He had the whole building swept clean, but somebody could have seen Billy there and waited to plant the bug since both of you have been gone from there for quite a while."

"Yeah," Cassandra added. "It could have been almost anybody. Supposedly no repairmen came into our apartment. We do, however, have the place sprayed for bugs every three months, I recognize the irony, so don't bother."

"Right," Margaret chuckled. "Were your jokes that bad before you met Benjamin?"

"You know my husband?"

"We've met several times," she replied, losing her smile. "Uh, what about your tenants?"

"I guess we don't know that much about them, all of them were there before we moved in."

Cassandra shook her head, why didn't she think of doing a background check on them before?

"Don't worry." Margaret shuffled some papers from the

276

middle of the stack in the folder. "Benjamin did the background checks eight months ago."

"He did?"

Cassandra was surprised, why didn't he say anything to her?

"That was before he got permission to tell you anything, remember?"

It was as if Margaret could tell what Cassandra was thinking, although that question wasn't that hard to figure out.

"Right," Cassandra said, "are any of them not what they seem?"

"Not that we can tell right now," Margaret replied. "But, these reports were preliminary, and a lot could have happened since then."

"It could be anybody," Cassandra took in a deep breath. "It could be someone in a neighboring building, it could be a client we've had, and it could be someone from California."

"I know," Margaret agreed. "We've already started doing backgrounds on everybody you two have had contact with for the past six months."

"That's a lot of people, you know."

"As well I know," Margaret chuckled again.

"What do we do in the meantime?" Cassandra asked.

"Sweep your apartment several times a day and keep a close watch on who comes and goes. If we're lucky, whoever is spying on you will return to replace the bug that's gone," Margaret said.

"We have to leave for France in two weeks." Cassandra shuffled in her seat. "We're spending Christmas with my folks there."

"I know." Margaret moved her chair to face Cassandra. "You have a friend from graduate school who is in town and will spend that week in your apartment."

"Good idea," Cassandra said, not as surprised as she thought she should be. "Do I even know this person?"

"You've never seen her before in your life, but that's not a problem is it?"

"My life long buddy," Cassandra replied calmly. "No problem at all as long as she doesn't make a mess."

"She's applying for a job in Atlanta and you're loaning your apartment to her while you and Benjamin are gone," Margaret handed Cassandra the correct party line.

"Not a problem."

Really deep down, Cassandra wasn't that comfortable with a stranger living in her house, but she accepted it anyway.

"When is Benjamin getting out of the hospital?" Margaret asked with a concerned look.

"I pick him up at five this afternoon," Cassandra replied. "That is if the doctor thinks he can stand up without shaking so much."

"He still has balance problems?" Margaret still sounded concerned.

"No, he was a lot better when I left, but the doctor wanted to wait until five to make sure." Cassandra wondered about the concern Margaret was showing. "Where did you two meet?"

"Benjamin and I?" Margaret caught the undercurrent. "He's a friend of my husband."

"Does your husband work for the agency?"

"No." Margaret smiled. "My husband works for the State Department."

"I see." Cassandra knew not to ask anything else along that line.

"An answer to one of your unspoken questions is, not many real husband and wife teams are in this field," Margaret said. "Although most all of the real couples are contract employees like you and Benjamin."

"Thanks," Cassandra replied.

That was one of her questions, it was one of a thousand questions she had. Real husband and wife teams, what was that all about? Cassandra felt it might be better to wait to ask them until she knew Margaret Stanley a little better.

"You and I will have more time to get to know each other when you go for training this coming March," Margaret said.

"You'll be there?"

"Yes, I'll be there off and on the whole time," Margaret answered her. "You and Benjamin are well suited for each other; you two already make one hell of a team."

"Thank you."

Somehow, that swelled Cassandra's pride.

....

"Benjamin," Cassandra said.

"You have that look."

I was sitting up in my bed after having changed into my street clothes. I had put my coat on, even though it did have some of my blood splattered on the back of it. Since I had my revolver the cops had given it back to me strapped back on, I kind of needed the coat to hide it.

"What look?" Cassandra sat next to me on the bed. "How are you feeling, by the way?"

"I'm doing fine," I struggled to say as I hopped off the bed. "I can stand and move around without falling or puking."

"That's encouraging," she tried to hide her nervousness with a pasty smile.

"Anyway, you're acting like you've had a semi-stressful afternoon."

"Oh, that." She slid off the hospital bed and stood facing me. "I'll tell you all about that on the way home."

"The doctor said I could go home whenever I want."

"I take it now is a good time."

Cassandra took my hand and led me out of the room.

....

"Margaret?" I still couldn't believe it. "They assigned you to Margaret Stanley?"

"That's what I've been saying ever since we left the hospital." Cassandra sounded curiously at me. "Where did you meet her husband?"

"We did a case together three years ago." I tried to remember as much as I could even though my head still hurt. "He's with the intelligence service of the State Department, and we did a joint assignment in Turkey."

"I put the bug detecting dildo back in your gun safe,"

279

Cassandra said. "Sweeping the whole apartment and office so often will be a drag until we catch whoever's after us."

"Yeah," I acknowledged. "The price of anonymity."

"What's his wife do?" Cassandra asked. "Is she an operations officer?"

"She didn't tell you?" I stared at her.

"No." Cassandra shook her head. "I didn't feel comfortable enough to ask all the questions I wanted to."

"I understand." I really did. "The last time I knew, Margaret was an analyst for the Mid-East section, I kind of doubt she's a field officer now."

"So." Cassandra sat down in a kitchen chair. "That's how they want to use me?"

"Looks like," I agreed. "But, if you object, I think they'll understand."

"What I want to do is work cases with you."

"Then, we'll not let them push us around," I firmly said. "Right?"

"Damned right!"

"Did you get a look at the information on our neighbors?" I sat down across the kitchen table from her.

"I did," Cassandra responded, sounding tired. "Both our neighbors in 2-A have an arrest record, but no one else has anything unusual in their background."

"Yeah, I remember," I said. "Both the women were arrested in a protest against the war, that's not bad."

"The woman in 1-C seems okay," Cassandra sounded serious. "The couple in 1-D are odd as hell, but I kind of doubt they're any problem."

"I kind of like having hippies around who refuse to acknowledge that the world has passed them by," I said with a grin. "It's entertaining and the older they get, the more entertaining they'll be."

"I don't think the women in 2-A are a problem, and Mrs. Smith isn't either." Cassandra shook her head. "A sixty five year old woman isn't that much of a threat to anybody, besides, if she's the spy, who'll collect the rent when we're out of the country?"

280

"You know, I always say things aren't what they seem," I tried to sound playful.

"What the hell does that mean?" She was annoyed. "I know it could be any of them, or none of them."

"Exactly," I agreed.

"So, we have to wait until one of them shows their hand?" She asked.

"I guess so," I answered. "Also, I can only assume that each and every one of our neighbors is being bugged, showing their hand will be a lot easier that way."

"I kind of like that." Cassandra smiled. "Payback for bugging us."

"Right." I glanced around the kitchen. "We didn't get any coffee, did we?"

36

Odds and ends

"Why are you here, Mr. Katz?" Andrew Holcomb looked hard at me through his screen door.

It had been a week since I got out of the hospital and my head still hurt, they took the ten stitches out yesterday. At least they didn't shave a large patch of my hair off, I suppose I could have done a decent comb over, but, anyway, hair grows, at least so far it does on me.

"I see your car has still got some holes in it." I pointed to his Ford in the driveway.

"So?" He still sounded confused.

"Well, mine does too." I pointed to my car parked in front of his house.

Andrew Holcomb lived in a small one story ranch east of the town of Between, situated about two hundred feet from highway seventy eight. A pasture with three cows in it lay to his west, and a mobile home about a quarter mile to his east; this was a pleasant place to live, fresh air and lots of room.

"So?" He was becoming annoyed.

"I remember you telling me that some relative of yours was in the car business, and I kind of hoped you might know a good body shop I could use."

"You drove all the way out here to ask me that question?" Annoyance was turning into curiosity.

"Well." I was a little embarrassed about this, "that and tell you that my partner and I solved the Belchamp case."

"I read about some of it in the Atlanta paper." Andrew kept staring at me through the screen door like I was a bible salesman. "Was it all about the mistress?"

"Not really," I said. "He was being blackmailed and he threatened to turn them in, so they took out a big policy on him and killed him, or at least they thought they did."

"They killed his long lost twin brother," Andrew said, smiling for the first time. "That's the most unlikely thing I would have ever thought of, not even in a bad movie."

"Yeah," I agreed. "Kind of strange, wasn't it."

"So, the best shop in these parts, especially for your foreign job out there, is in Lawrenceville," Andrew kept talking through the screen door; I wondered when I might get invited in.

"Actually, I also wanted to ask you for a favor," I added.

"What?" I could see the annoyance rising a bit.

"If you and I both drove our bullet ridden cars to this repair shop, could you talk them into a good price?"

"I can't afford to get my car fixed yet," he insisted.

"So you told me the other day, but the insurance company paid us a pile of cash for finding the dead man alive, so I'm gong to pay for your car to get fixed too."

"Why?" He asked, expressionless.

"Because it isn't fair that they won't pay to have your car fixed, and that your insurance company won't pay either," I said. "Besides, I figure that the life insurance company's paying for this anyway, just in a different way."

"Come on in while I get my wife to follow us out there."

He opened the door for me to come in; the coffee and bacon smelled real good.

. . . .

"I do wanna thank you again for fixin' my car." Andrew Holcomb smiled at me, then stared back out the front windshield.

"Me too," his wife piped up from the back seat. "It'll be a whole lot better when we have two cars we can actually use again."

"The insurance company owed it to you," I said as I watched the traffic on highway seventy eight as we approached Atlanta. "I made sure they made good on it."

"But, it did come out of your own pocket," Andrew insisted.

"I'm still new here." I wanted to change the subject. "Can

283

you tell me about the Atlanta Police Department?"

"What about it?" Andrew asked.

"Do you know a detective Brown, Gary Brown?" I asked.

"No," he shook his head slightly as he spoke, as if he were trying to shake loose some recollection. "Yeah, wasn't he the one who had the Belchamp case?"

"That's him," I confirmed. "Did you know him at all?"

"No," he looked quickly at me as he spoke. "I only met him once when he came around and asked me a few questions about the case. That was the week after I got shot at, and I was a little out of it."

"I was kind of wondering how they treat us?" I asked with a shrug. "How they treat private investigators."

"Oh," Andrew replied, "they act like we don't exist most of the time."

"I suppose that could be a blessing sometimes." I turned to glance at a row of large delivery trucks on one of the side roads.

"I suppose so." He wasn't eager to talk about it.

"What about detective Brown?"

"Like I said." He glanced sideways at me. "I don't socialize much with them."

"The Atlanta cops have changed a lot since the Coloreds took over the city," Andrew's wife offered her opinion from the back seat.

"I was only curious." It was best I let this go.

"As far as rumor and reputation, Detective Brown is a fair man." Andrew could tell I was uncomfortable with his wife's remark.

37

Could I see the whine list?

"How'd it go?" Cassandra was on the sofa, next to the floor lamp reading a book when I walked in the front door."

"Fine," I sounded disgusted. "What're you reading?"

"Clan of the Cave Bear." She put the book down and smiled at me. "I just got to a sexy part."

"Oh?" I grinned. "That's encouraging."

"You seem upset," she observed.

"It's eighteen sixty three."

"Pardon me?"

"It's eighteen sixty three and the emancipation proclamation has been signed and there's a bunch of pissed off white folks down here."

"Was it that detective guy who dropped you off?" She patted the sofa for me to sit next to her. "It's actually nineteen eighty one, but this is the deep south, you know."

"Yeah," I said. "I know, it was his wife, I think Andrew has a little more couth than that."

"Gary Brown called while you were out."

"A date for dinner?" I asked.

Maybe that would cheer me up. Andrew Holcomb's wife wouldn't approve of us having dinner in public with a black man and his wife.

"Tonight," Cassandra stroked my leg as she spoke to me. "He wanted to wait until the week after Christmas, but I told him we'd be in France."

"I bet he loved that."

"He did kind of laugh a little," she said with a smile. "He

285

said his wife wants to go the Abbey."

"That's an expensive place." I took her hand in mine. "Sounds like fun."

"I did a sweep after you left," Cassandra informed me. "Still nothing."

"I've been thinking." I didn't want to go on to serious subjects, but since she brought it up. "I think I know who's spying on us, and I think I know how to prove it."

"Are you going to share?" She glanced at the coffee table in front of us for a second. "Oh, I forgot, we got a special delivery package this morning."

"A real one, or something from Washington?"

"I went downtown and picked it up; it's the new and improved versions of everybody's background checks." Cassandra pointed to the large envelope on the table.

"They sent it home with you?" I sounded surprised.

"I guess so."

"I take it you read it?" I asked, knowing something was up. "They know who it is, right?"

"First," Cassandra replied, "who do you think it is?"

"Mrs. Smith."

I looked at the envelope, then at Cassandra.

"Why?" She asked.

"It was Andrew's wife."

"The bigot?" Cassandra sounded surprised. "How did she give you the clue?"

"When Andrew finally realized I wasn't playing him for something, he invited me into their house and offered me some breakfast."

"I bet you liked that," Cassandra sounded a bit jealous.

"I sure did." I began to relive it. "Eggs, bacon, toast, coffee and grits, man, were they good too."

"Enough of the menu, get on with it," she sounded slightly annoyed since all she had for breakfast was the last stale bagel and water.

"Right after she asked me what I wanted to eat, Andrew's wife asked me where I was from, and what church I went to," I said.

286

"That seems to be the first two questions people ask you around here."

"I noticed that too."

"Well," I continued. "Mrs. Smith is supposed to be a good old girl, and married to a good old boy for forty years, she never asked us once where we were from or what church we went to. Her accent never did sound right, either."

"I didn't notice that," Cassandra said thoughtfully. "Your observation sounds right to me though, but I don't notice anything wrong with her speech patterns."

"She doesn't swallow enough vowels," I said.

"You're right." Cassandra picked up the package and pulled out the report. "They did a check on her husband who worked for the Ford factory; he did work there, but his wife died two years before he did. The real Mrs. Smith and our Russian spy are real look-alikes. I guess the KGB took some time to find an average citizen who was a physical match for their agent."

"That was kind of careless, even if she is a look-alike, there's the problem with the family of the real Mrs. Smith, plus what story did they come up with for what happened to the persona the KGB spy had before," I observed. "Why is she here?"

"I had a long talk with Margaret Stanley," Cassandra began. "She told me that the FBI has been searching for that woman pretending to be Mrs. Smith's for three years."

"Why?" I shook my head. "She's a good background person, but she's not exactly in a position to provide critical information sitting in that little apartment."

"Margaret said her real name was Ida Kreugel and she worked in the White House as a cook's assistant for twenty eight years. The FBI was tipped off three years ago by a defector that she worked for the KGB for the whole time but, up until now, they haven't been able to locate her."

"So, she was set up with a phony name and background in Atlanta so she could retire?" I asked. "Isn't that nice of the KGB."

"She also let me see some of the transcripts from the bugs they had on her," Cassandra added. "It's good for us, but kind of sad."

"Can I see?"

"No," Cassandra answered, "Margaret said I couldn't take those with me, all she'd let me take for you to see was a couple of summaries on Mrs. Smith's real past."

"So, what were in the transcripts?" I was dying to know.

"Well," Cassandra took in a deep breath as she wound up to tell all. "Mrs. Smith is really seventy one years old, her handler is a KGB captain and he's kind of exasperated with her. It seems she recognized Billy Sullivan when he came out here to visit you and she thought you and he had to be CIA cronies. Her handler kept telling her that you and Billy were marine buddies and that you never showed up on any list as a spy."

"So," I interrupted. "The young KGB captain didn't believe the old lady?"

"Apparently not," Cassandra confirmed.

"That's good for us." I felt a great deal of relief, I think it showed through on my face.

"She was pissed off," Cassandra continued. "All the captain wanted her to do was stay retired and stop annoying him."

"She missed being part of the game?" I asked, feeling kind of sorry for her; not really, but in a very abstract way, never mind.

"That's not the real good part, though." Cassandra threw a teasing smile towards me.

"What?" I asked, surprised; I thought the KGB Mrs. Smith was enough of a bombshell.

"Guess who put the bug in our bedroom?" Cassandra kept her grin.

"I'm supposing it wasn't Mrs. Smith, judging from your silly grin."

"And, right you are," Cassandra laughed a little. "It was our friends, the FBI."

"What!" I was both pissed off and surprised. "Well, I guess it kind of makes sense."

"How so?" She asked.

"It had to do with Paula Thorpe blackmailing some senator or congressman, right?" I asked.

"Right," Cassandra didn't want to say more, she wanted me

to keep guessing.

"They thought we were hiding her?"

"And?"

"And, maybe we were part of the conspiracy?" I replied. "That doesn't make any sense, why wouldn't they have arrested us, especially after we blew their Willy the Roach stakeout?"

"Maybe one hand didn't know what the other was doing?" Cassandra continued to tease me.

"Right! The blackmail investigation team wanted us to be on the loose to show them the way to Paula Thorpe," I answered, finally getting it.

"They didn't count on us discovering where the Thorpe woman was by talking to our neighbor, in an apartment they didn't bug." Cassandra nodded quickly.

"I suppose our people discovered the court order to wire tap our place," I asked.

"Right," Cassandra agreed.

"So, because of us finding the bug, we found a retired KGB spy?" I asked. "Who, ironically, didn't put the bug in our apartment."

"I suppose the FBI will arrest her now," Cassandra assumed. "Who will we get to collect the rent?"

"Didn't Margaret tell you?" I asked.

"Tell me what?"

"No one will arrest the old lady."

"Why?"

"By the time we get back from France, Mrs. Smith will have died in her sleep."

"No!" Cassandra sounded shocked for a second. "That's not right."

"I know it isn't, but it has to work that way."

"Why?"

"The Company has put a lot of time and money in me as one of their assets, and they won't risk it for that retired KGB woman." I didn't like what I was saying, but I knew it was going to happen. "If she's arrested, there'll be press all over the two of us, and we'll be worthless to the government from then on, besides, think of all the

289

Americans she's indirectly responsible for having killed, and all the secrets she gave to the Russians."

"But, can't they come in the middle of the night and take her away?" Cassandra insisted. "She might be able to give us some good information on who is and who isn't a Russian spy."

"Don't you think that would be a big giant tip off to the Russians that the two of us are CIA?" I asked. "Especially after she blabbed all that stuff to her handler."

"Yeah," Cassandra reluctantly agreed. "That's what Margaret said too."

"Since we got back from Los Angeles, all Mrs. Smith has heard from us was all about our insurance case, and how we need to have someone collect the rents while we're out of town."

I could see Cassandra was upset by this.

"Besides, the only cases we've done around Atlanta are non-government cases," I added.

"I've been replaying everything we talked about in my head for days." Cassandra nodded. "You're right, that's all we talked about, we never even implied anything except our regular cases like the insurance one we just finished."

"I know," I agreed. "If we had said or done anything suspicious, the KGB captain would have given Mrs. Smith tons of bugs to plant all over our apartment; think about that, the FBI and the KGB bugging our apartment."

"Margaret said we shouldn't do anything," Cassandra reported. "I want to do something, I want to know who all her handlers are, not just that captain. I want to know what she told them about us, I want to know why she was a spy for Russia."

"If either one of us gives the slightest clue we even know who she really is, we're busted." I held her hand. "Don't worry, I'll bet there's a dozen cameras in this neighborhood right now, and when the old lady dies, whoever comes by to pick up her stuff will be nailed by the FBI."

"Arrested?"

"Hell no," I answered, "that would finger us as much as arresting Mrs. Smith. They'll have a new face to follow and see who he talks to. If they didn't know about the KGB Captain before this, they do now, that's how it's done. Our side will bug that person, and hopefully they'll find out if we're still suspected by them. Besides, one spy uncovered can lead to many others, all you have to do is follow them and keep track of phone calls, letters, and stuff like that."

"I still don't like the idea of killing that old woman," Cassandra muttered as she looked back down at the floor again.

"I don't either," I sadly agreed. "I don't either."

Damn.

. . . .

Cassandra was in the shower and I was in the process of getting dressed for our dinner date with Detective Brown and his wife when the front doorbell rang.

"I'll get it," I shouted towards the closed bathroom door as I hurriedly pulled my pants on.

"Hello, Benjamin," Mrs. Smith greeted me with a smile as I opened the front door.

"Oh, hi, Mrs. Smith." I motioned her to come into our living room.

"I'm sorry to bother you two, but I have a question." She made a bee line to the sofa and sat down.

"Cassandra is in the shower, but she'll be out in a few minutes."

I didn't know what to expect, but I was going to keep this conversation relaxed.

"Oh, I can tell you."

"What is it?" I acted surprised.

"I was wondering if you minded my recommending my nephew as a plumber for this building." she seemed slightly embarrassed; she was a good actor. "He's a good boy and a darn fine plumber, I would like to give him some more business."

"I suppose that would be fine," I answered, forcing myself not to show any emotion. "I suppose he'll work better for his aunt than a stranger would."

"Oh, thank you," she answered, carefully observing my

291

expression. "I'll call him tonight and tell him."

"We don't have any plumbing problems now, do we?" I wondered out loud.

"Oh, no," she answered, shaking her head slowly. "It's that I told him I would ask you today."

"Okay," I said.

"I read about you and Mrs. Katz in the paper the other day," she said, not getting up from the sofa.

I wondered how long was she going to sit and talk?

"You mean the insurance case we were on?"

"Yes, that's the one," she replied. "It seemed dangerous."

"It was a bit more risky than we like," I answered, not changing my expression.

It seemed to me like a dance was about to start.

"Are all your cases that dangerous?"

"No," I chuckled a little. "Most of them involve checking facts in the courthouse, and sometimes following people."

"Is it like Barnaby Jones?" she asked as her smile broadened. "I'm so sad they took it off the air."

"I hate to disappoint you, Mrs. Smith, but my life is a lot more dull than Barnaby Jones' life," I almost laughed again, partially for effect. "That insurance case was the exception, not the rule."

"What kind of cases do you usually do?"

"Well," I thought for a second. "We do a lot of background checking for corporations, we do this on high level hiring for them. We also do our fair share of divorce cases."

"What's that like?" She asked; I sensed that Cassandra was listening from our bedroom.

"We follow the cheating husband and take pictures of him with the mistress," I took in another breath. "We also check bank records, real estate records, and employment records to uncover any unreported assets."

"People do that?"

"When rich people divorce, yes, they try to hide assets from their spouses."

"Hi, Mrs. Smith." Cassandra walked in from the back hall.

"Hello Cassandra," Mrs. Smith responded as she rose from

the sofa. "You are lovely tonight."

"Thank you." Cassandra smiled back at her.

"Are you two going out tonight?" She asked.

"Yes, we're going to dinner with a nice policeman and his wife," Cassandra answered.

"Oh." She looked at the floor, then back up at me. "I must be keeping you."

"No, we have a few moments," I insisted. "I did want to talk to you anyway."

"What is it?" She didn't sound surprised.

"Cassandra and I are going to France in a few days, so, can you look after the place for us?"

"Of course," she warmly responded. "What do you want me to do?"

"We'll only be gone for two weeks, so if you could make sure everything is running smoothly in all the units, we would appreciate it."

"A friend of mine will be staying in our apartment while we're gone," Cassandra interrupted.

She didn't tell me this before, but I went along.

"Her name is Cindy, she and I were in the Political Science department at UCLA together."

"She's a sweet girl," I added something.

"Cindy is applying for a job at Georgia State, and I told her she could come out early and look the town over so she'll be here a few days with us in January until her interview is over with."

"That will be nice," Mrs. Smith sounded disappointed. "It's good to have someone to take in the mail and look after your things."

"I mailed her a copy of our key, so you can expect to see her around right about the time we leave," Cassandra said. "She's got shoulder length light brown hair, and is about five foot three, her full name is Cindy Eggleston."

"Okay," Mrs. Smith acknowledged as she trotted to the front door. "I'll keep an eye out for her. If she gets in after you leave, I'll welcome her."

"Thanks, Mrs. Smith." I closed the door behind her and stared at Cassandra.

I immediately swept the apartment for bugs, yet again that day.

"What was that all about?" Cassandra asked as I finished sweeping the last room.

"Did you hear her ask about letting her nephew be our plumber?"

"No," she sounded puzzled. "I started listening when she was asking about what kind of jobs we did."

"She asked if she could use her nephew as a plumber if we ever needed one," I said. "I suppose she wants to feel important still and I bet she's willing to ignore her KGB handler and try on her own to put a bug in our apartment."

"She already knew we were going to France for Christmas, I told her last week," Cassandra added. "I bet she would make up an excuse to have the fake plumber get into our apartment."

"Yeah," I agreed. "What has me worried is why she is so damned interested in us still."

"If we can believe those transcripts of her talking to her handler, the KGB doesn't suspect us of anything but being detectives and lovers," Cassandra said.

Us being lovers, now that's a good idea; no, there's not enough time to do it right, we have to be at the Abby for dinner in thirty minutes.

"'Maybe it's that she's bored," I speculated.

"What do you mean?"

"She probably felt very important being a spy in the White House for all those years, now all she is, is a fake working class retirees widow, where's all the glory? Where's all the fame, and where's all the rewards?"

"You mean she misses being a spy?" Cassandra asked.

"That's my guess," I surmised. "Put yourself in her handler's position, here's this seventy one year old retired low level spy who wants back into action and has latched onto a couple of private investigators claiming that we're big time US agents."

"And, all we've done since we've been back here is to work on an insurance fraud case," Cassandra observed. "Even if they looked back at what we've done for the past year, there's not that much suspicious, is there?"

"Not really," I agreed.

"Why isn't she in Russia?" Cassandra asked. "I mean, if she's a retired KGB spy, why did she stay here?"

"You read her file," I asked Cassandra. "I bet she's a native born American."

"Right, she is."

"So, she chose to stay here because she fits in here better than in Russia," I thought out loud. "Besides, the living here is a lot better than back in the old USSR."

"But, isn't her staying in the States a bigger risk for the KGB?" Cassandra wanted to know. "She could be caught a lot easier."

"I guess they assessed her as a low risk."

I had to feel sorry for the old lady, even though she potentially could make our lives miserable.

"Even if we do nothing, I think her captain will get sick of her nagging and move her out of the country to prevent problems. She is a seventy one year old woman, and this fuss she's kicking up has got to start him thinking about senility and her spilling her true story to the wrong people," I added.

"I see your point, it's kind of pathetic in a way," Cassandra said, becoming a little more grim. "I still have a problem with her being eliminated."

. . . .

"If you will wait right here, someone will be with you in a moment," The college age hostess instructed us.

We had reservations, but, for some reason, it was quite crowded tonight.

"So." Gary looked at me, then at Cassandra. "How did you two get into the detective business?" I guess he was searching for a conversation starter.

"Well, as for myself, I took it as a summer job because it sounded interesting," Cassandra started.

"You worked for him that summer?" Gary pointed to me.

"Yeah," Cassandra confirmed.

"Well," I had to interject. "We had been dating for awhile, and she seemed to be interested in my line of work, and she took a summer off and needed a job."

"Took the summer off from what?" Alice, Gary's wife, asked.

"School," Cassandra answered.

"Where were you going?" Alice asked.

"I went to Occidental College for undergraduate, and I was in UCLA grad school when I met Benjamin," Cassandra answered.

"Oh." Alice seemed to brighten. "What was your major?"

"Economics as an under grad, and Political Science in grad school."

"I went to Morehouse," Alice proudly said. "I majored in education."

"Do you teach?" Cassandra asked.

"I teach fifth grade," Alice answered with a broad smile, she seemed to be happy with her job. "I started a master's program this fall at Georgia State, so I can appreciate why you dropped out to work with Benjamin."

"She didn't drop out," I added. "She finished everything the end of last month."

"You got your masters?" Alice gave Cassandra a look of admiration.

"No," Cassandra sounded a little embarrassed. "Actually, I got my PhD."

"Wow," Gary interrupted. "I think I'll have quite a few questions during our meal about how you could juggle your detective job and school."

"Well," Cassandra replied as she slipped on a social smile. "Don't think I'm the only dinner entertainment, you haven't asked Benjamin anything yet."

"Good Point." Gary turned to me. "What's your story, how did you become a private investigator?"

"Why not take turns," I coyly answered him. "How did you become a cop?"

"Oh," Gary chuckled. "That's easy, I was an MP in the

Army, and all I ever wanted to do was be a cop."

"That's about all there is to Gary's story," Alice laughed.

"So, what about you?" Gary insisted.

"I joined the Marines at seventeen, and after I mustered out, an old marine buddy of mine set me up with an agency in Los Angeles, and I kind of liked the work."

"He liked it enough to set up his own agency within two years," Cassandra added as she patted my arm.

"Your table is ready." The hostess motioned for us to follow her to the table.

The four of us sat around the table for ten minutes before a waiter finally showed up. It didn't matter, since the conversation was quite pleasant; both Cassandra and I were happy we were making friends with another couple who were similar enough to us. I could see sadness slowly creep into Cassandra's expression; my guess was that she was thinking about the widow Smith. I had been contacted by Billy Sullivan and I knew he had another assignment for the two of us, but I hadn't had the opportunity to tell him we had a trip to France to visit Cassandra's parents so we couldn't work for the next two weeks. All I hoped was that he didn't want us to work while we were visiting France.

"You two seem sort of glum this evening," Gary Brown observed as he stared at the wine list.

"We, uh, got some strange family news today." Cassandra glanced at me.

I didn't appear that happy with her comment because I didn't want her making up some story about a relative that could easily be proven a lie. Gary Brown's a detective and I don't think he trusts us that completely yet. I know Cassandra was upset about Mrs. Brown, but, really.

"Oh." Gary set the wine list down. "I hope it wasn't bad."

"We had a pregnancy scare," I blurted out; that was the best I could come up with quickly, at least it was the truth.

"Are you pregnant?" Alice asked.

"No." Cassandra stared at me; she was both mad at me for my comment, and embarrassed at her slip.

"We have three kids," Alice spoke up, wanting to take any

edge off the conversation. "It's not that bad."

"I thought I'd hate it at first, but now I couldn't imagine a life without my three daughters," Gary added.

"Three girls?" My jaw opened a bit.

"Three girls," he said, staring at me. "That means three colleges to pay for, and three weddings to pay for."

"Wow." I glanced at Cassandra who was now smiling at me.

"I'm not good at wines." Gary looked at the list, then at me.

"Always ask for the house wine," I advised Gary. "You usually don't go wrong."

"Okay," he chuckled and looked back at the list.

"The house Chardonnay," Cassandra whispered as she leaned towards Gary.

"Thanks," Gary whispered back at Cassandra. "You're a good observer."

"It comes with the territory."

The Author

Bob Henneberger has been writing for the past decade, working mostly in Science Fiction and Mystery, He has also written short stories, plays, television scripts and articles for professional journals. He lives in Vermont, close to Lake Champlain with his wife and several cats; not that that's an indication of anything unusual.

www.ingramcontent.com/pod-product-compliance
Lightning Source LLC
Chambersburg PA
CBHW060855250626
47159CB00008B/2742